The Forever and The Now

K J

Acknowledgments

A romance novel is supposed to end in a happily ever after. It's an unspoken rule. Well, no actually, it's a spoken rule. Many authors and readers speak passionately about this rule and because of this particular rule, 'The Forever and The Now' doesn't qualify as a romance novel. It's lesbian fiction but not romance.

And yet...

And yet, 'The Forever and The Now' is a love story. It is a story about being part of a relationship that is whole and big and tiny and deep and complex; a relationship that is so very simple because it is right here. In the now.

And yet, 'The Forever and The Now' is a love story. It is a story about hope and the what-ifs and shared goals and the future and its intangibility. It's a story about a wish because while the now is here, over there is even more. In the forever.

'The Forever and The Now' is about understanding the circle of love. The now supports the potential of the forever and the belief in the forever supports the now.

It's devastating when forever's potential, its hope, is taken away. The carpet of wish, the rug of what-if, has been ripped out from under the feet of the one who is left behind.

So 'The Forever and The Now' is a love story, but it's not a romance. Because there are rules, you see.

Em Shreiber, as always, has demonstrated her genius with an exquisite cover for 'The Forever and The Now'. It is perfect for this story; the birds flying away. Birds of hope or perhaps a soul leaving? I loved it the first time I laid eyes on it, Em. Thank you so much. For your patience with my blathery DMs, my 'oops I forgot the attachment' emails, for my appendix salutations. Thank you for everything.

My betas. Cheyenne, Selena, Conny, Maggie, Laura, Sophie, Neen, M. I'm sorry for giving you just one sentence as your heads-up for this book but I wanted to know about the story's impact on your heart, about its 'stickability' after you'd read it. It was important. So thank you for trusting me. And thank you for your advice because I used every piece of it. Particularly the continuity errors! Good grief. Changing the name of a character halfway through. What was I thinking? So, thank you. You're all amazing.

Proofreading is a difficult job and one that I could never do. The need to remove yourself as a reader, become impartial to the emotion of the story. That is a skill. So, thank you Maggie. You are a genius at spotting all my ridiculous errors. There were so many. I'm sorry.

For Roanne
My forever and my now

Also by KJ

Coming Home
Goldie Awards finalist
LesFic Bard Awards finalist

Kick Back
Goldie Awards finalist

An Unexpected Gift: Christmas in Australia: Five Short Stories

Art of Magic
Goldie Awards finalist (cover design)
LesFic Bard Awards finalist (cover design)
Lesfic Bard Awards winner (romance)

Change of Plans

Ignis

A request

I sincerely hope you enjoy reading 'The Forever and The Now'. If you do, I would greatly appreciate a review on your favourite book website. Maybe a tweet. Or even a recommendation in your favourite Facebook sapphic fiction group. Reviews and recommendations are crucial for any author, and even just a line or two can make a huge difference. Thanks!

Synopsis

Bron McIntyre, forty-two, has it all together. Terrific job. Loving family. No desperate need for a girlfriend but would be interested if one came along. Bron McIntyre is Teflon.

Kate Agostino, forty-eight, is not Teflon. Yes, she has a terrific job. But a loving family? Not really. And her personal life is rapidly disintegrating and turning into dust.

When her orange smoothie explodes all over her business suit while she's on her afternoon walk, Kate simply shakes her head in resignation.

Bron, having witnessed the smoothie eruption, races to help, and suddenly her life takes an unexpected turn.

Falling in love is like watching the grandest sunset on the calmest ocean where the tiniest ripples wear silver sparkles as their hats. Kate and Bron find that sunset on that ocean with those ripples of love, but what happens when you take that love for granted? What happens when your person disappears? The answers are hard to hear and Bron chooses not to listen.

After a relationship break, a family intervention, and conversations that rip apart seams, Bron and Kate eventually find themselves, each other, and their now. And what they discover is that love is the large and the deliberate, and the simple and the small.

So when tragedy strikes, they call on its strength because, when you think about it, love can live on in the forever, particularly if it lives courageously in the now.

A beautifully poignant story about life, love and a loss so tragic that sometimes even the grandest sunset on the calmest ocean with the ripples wearing hats is too heartbreaking to bear.

We Met

January 28 in the first year of the now

T he stream near the campus wasn't overly inspiring: rocks, weeds, standard stream stuff. It was kind of like a dirt road through the cane fields on a hot day. The water was the colour of the liquid that comes out of taps when they're fed by old copper piping wrapped in verdigris, but then again it was Melbourne and the only place that showcased relatively clear water was the bay. This stream, my stream, was probably deep enough to drown in if you were so inclined.

I jerked slightly and blinked. Well, that was all a bit dark. And wet. I rolled my head, my hair swishing about my ears—*that's annoying; must get it cut soon*—and stretched out my long legs, today encased in denim and punctuated with red Chucks. The end of January was hot but I figured jeans could be worn all year round. Despite sweat because... January. The chunky men's watch on my wrist and collared polo-shirt completed the outfit. My work had very friendly rules about dress standards.

Then I levelled up on my relaxation and leaned back, arms stretched out across the top as if the wooden bench had regenerated and grown limbs.

This routine of parking my bum on the bench each afternoon at the bridge over the stream in the city centre, watching the people expressing their happiness or displeasure at the world, and dogs and ducks marching all over their grass territory happily ignoring each other, helped clear my mind.

Clearing minds was good and all but it left a beautifully empty space to be filled with random stuff, like drowning in the rocks and weeds. I rolled my eyes.

The breath I took did clear my mind, enough to stare at the bridge. The wooden sleepers, smoothed by decades of shoes and bicycles, formed a gorgeous flat surface for the iron fretwork to frame, patting it into its rectangular shape, then cradling it underneath. Eons ago, the City Council had decided that cream was the colour du jour and so the city bridge was cream and there would be no argument about the decision. Although three years ago they did pass a law—could Councils pass laws?—that heritage green entry posts should be built at each end. It had been a good decision. Pretty, yet stately. I stared at my favourite structure. Wide enough that you could lean on the railing and not annoy pram-pushers, cyclists, or people waving their arms about while they argued with someone on the other end of their airpod microphones.

Dropping my hands and reaching into the satchel leaning against my thigh, I pulled out a sketch pad and a 4B pencil. Teaching Art at the local primary school was fun and had been my goal all through uni, nineteen, no, twenty years ago, but enjoying my own creativity was, along with bench-sitting at the bridge, completely relaxing. Balancing my ankle on the knee of the other leg, I focused on the fretwork. I'd drawn it hundreds of times but there was something mesmerising about the swirls and curls. Like a metal mandala.

After twenty minutes or so, I straightened, then stretched my fairly lithe frame, enjoying the tiny pop of vertebrae, which seemed relieved to return their forty-two-year-old bones to a more sensible position. My gaze was caught by a woman, probably my height—maybe not— wandering along the concrete path that ran in front on the grassed slope. Her long, dark, almost black, hair was caught up in a ponytail, which was convenient as her head was down, eyes focused on her phone. Probably the reason she was walking so slowly. The dark grey business wear—skirt, shirt, low heels—was smart and fashionable and sexy, because, hello kryptonite. Her small handbag hung from her shoulder. The smoothie in her other hand, straw protruding through the top which covered a large clear plastic cup, was orange. Maybe orange juice? *Brilliant Sherlock.*

The woman paused and smiled at something, and I clutched at my sketch book. My brain engaged in a second of indecision about consent, then after concluding that the woman would be fine about it, I outlined all her lines, her profile, her clothes, her stance, her shape. A very yummy shape. *Oh, gees Bron. There's sketching and then there's ogling.* Suddenly, I spotted a cyclist flying down the path obviously having used the small descent that runs down to the bridge to pick up speed. He was slaloming dangerously around pedestrians announcing his presence into their ears as he rocketed past.

The next few seconds played out like a film. Almost in slow motion, three simultaneous events occurred: I frisbeed my pad and pencil onto the bench, the cyclist reached the woman's right shoulder, and with exquisite timing, yelled, "Coming through!" And the woman, jerking her body to the left, squeezed the plastic cup in fright, causing the perfectly circular shape to immediately transform into an oval. The lid burst off, and the entire contents exploded, splattering across her skirt and shoes.

I was up, quickly covering the short distance to the path.

"Arsehole!"

The woman's mouth fell open, my expletive adding to her shock. I held up both hands.

"Oh! Not you. The fuckwit on the bike," I elaborated, then winced. "Shit. Swearing. Sorry." I pointed to her shoes, my finger making a circular motion. "Crap. I'm sorry about your shoes and skirt." I indicated to the cup still clutched in her hand, the remaining contents dripping off her fingers. "And your drink." Which seemed to break the moment because the woman shook her head, and sighed.

"Just terrific."

The joints in her jaw bounced about, and casually, in a tiny part of my brain that wasn't focused on smoothies and idiot cyclists, I appreciated how lovely the woman was. Smooth voice—I knew this from just two words. Curvaceous. Aquiline nose. Dark eyes—I would have liked the opportunity to investigate the colour farther.

I gestured inarticulately. "Um. Can I help? I mean, I'm good at yelling. And swearing." Pointing to the shoes, which were being removed in frustration. "Not much good at doing anything about..." I looked up and yes, the colour of her eyes was a dark brown, the same dark brown as the rich chocolate in the kids' Derwent pencil sets.

"No. I'll—thank you for swearing at Chaos Man and also offering to help." She flicked her fingers, sending droplets of liquid onto the grass. I mashed my lips together. This moment was serious and needed serious seriousness, but Chaos Man? So adorable.

"I've got a whole packet of tissues in my satchel if you want, and a water bottle, you know, for cleaning your..." Again I gestured vaguely. I'd be bloody useless as an aircraft marshal. "I could go get them?" Indicating to the bench where my bag sagged on the seat. The woman paused, holding her shoes and my gaze.

"Thank you. I'll come to the tissues. Lead the way." She twitched her lips which could have meant 'thanks', or 'my skin feels gross' or 'I'm humouring this person'.

I grinned, then held up my hand. "Shove your shoes back on. There's duck shit everywhere." I wrinkled my brow in apology. "Shit. Swearing. Sorry."

The woman laughed as she bent down to replace her footwear, then she straightened, and glanced at her sticky fingers. "I'd normally shake your hand when introducing myself but since that's out of the question, I'm." She delivered a quick smile as she walked gingerly up the soft incline. "I'm Kate, bearer of damp clothing."

I fell into step beside her. "Bron, keeper of tissues."

Kate grinned, and because that smile was gorgeous and all-encompassing and I wanted to kneel in front of her, I couldn't help returning it with interest. We arrived at the bench and Kate threw the cup into the nearby bin, then grimaced as she gingerly eased onto the seat while I fossicked about in my satchel, pulling out pencils, art pad, wallet, phone as if I was declaring my contraband through customs. Finally, my mega pack of tissues—given space in my bag due to their excellent ability to avoid charcoal smudging on sketches—appeared.

"Here you go." I handed over the box, my gaze landing on my water bottle which I presented as well.

"Thank you. Are you?" She popped her phone into her small handbag and placed it on the ground beside her feet. Then she removed a shoe and wiped the inside with a damp tissue, pushing it deep into the toe. "An artist?"

I mentally hummed in appreciation at the timbre of Kate's voice and shuffled my gear along so I could sit on the other end of the bench. "No. Well, yes." I shook my head. Blathering. "I'm an art teacher at Melbourne City Primary School. But I do draw and sketch."

After placing the somewhat dry piece of footwear beside her on the bench, Kate moved onto the other shoe. She glanced sideways and my lips curled into a smile. So pretty.

"Teaching's such a rewarding career." Wipe. Smooth. Wipe again. Kate was asking a lot of questions which I was more than happy to answer because I figured she might have been distracting herself. "And with small children, too. Is it challenging to get them drawing well?" The shoe joined its partner and she began rescuing her skirt with a wet and dry tissue combination, which meant she didn't catch the expression on my face. Normally I answered that question with sarcasm, swearing, and a significant amount of snark, but something told me to rein it in.

I ran my hands in circles on the top of my thighs, then looked up. "It's important that the kids know that their art is good no matter how they present the finished product. So." Kate had paused in her skirt-salvaging and was focused on my face, my eyes, her hand suspended mid-clean. "I tell the kids that they always draw well because in art there are no wrong answers."

She nodded slowly. "That's lovely, Bron." *Say my name again. Please say my name.* Oh my God, I needed a girlfriend soon because I had instantly objectified then lusted after a woman I'd met all of fifteen minutes ago. Just pathetic.

"Yeah. The other teachers hate me because I don't have to do a huge amount of testing and assessment. The kids simply create folios." I laughed in self-deprecation.

Kate wadded up the tissues and flapped the hem of her skirt. "I'm sure people don't hate you, Bron. You seem like a perfectly nice person."

5

She tilted her chin at the tissues and water bottle "And kind." She passed across the now half-empty bottle across the art materials scattered on the slats.

I held the bottle by its top and tapped the end on the palm of my other hand. "What's your job if it's okay to ask?" I wanted to ask permission. This woman was refined, despite the large damp patch across the lower half of her skirt, and I felt a bit gormless and rough around the edges sitting next to her. Kate reached up to tighten her ponytail, the action pulling the white shirt tight across her breasts. Which I didn't notice. Nope.

"I'm an accountant." She smiled. "Testing, assessment, spreadsheets, and all that jazz are actually rather important. I think some days I'd rather your job though, except," she lifted an eyebrow, "I'm artistically challenged." Another smile was fired my way.

I pointed to her. "There are no wrong answers in art, remember? I'm sure you'd be great. Maybe you could create an abstract rendering of my tax return."

Kate let loose a peal of laughter, and I grinned. Then she turned and we studied each other.

"This is going to be an odd request, but would you consider sitting here a little longer? I want to dry off completely before strolling along the walkway, and I was hoping for some compa—"

"Yes." The word fell out before I'd even run it through my head, so I added sentences to cushion the intensity of my response. "I'm finished for the day and I was only doing some sketching anyway so sure, I can stay." Technically that was one sentence and complete babble, but it did the job because Kate sighed and relaxed into the back of the seat.

"Thank you." She crossed her legs, pulling the skirt taught across her thighs.

"No problem." I indicated to her gradually drying skirt to reinforce my answer.

Kate had class. Strolling along while looking like I'd had a dip in the stream was not classy.

"Would you be comfortable? With people staring at you?" She looked genuinely curious.

I rested my elbow on the back of the seat, running my fingers through the hair above my ear before leaning my cheek into my palm.

"Yeah. I'm kind of a take what you get person. If I was soaked and walking down the path and anyone said anything, I'd probably swear at them."

Kate giggled. "Yes. You seem quite the expert." Then she stared ahead. It looked like contemplation. "I wish I could stop and appreciate..." She lifted her chin at the bridge.

"Why can't you?"

She rolled her head then turned quite a serious gaze my way. Dark chocolate eyes. Beautiful classical features. I blinked and paid attention. "My job requires a lot of my time. The most I'm able to do is escape for a circuit of the stream path and that's all." She sighed.

I nearly shifted all my art gear to shuffle closer, but my brain explained how that would be particularly creepy so I stayed where I was.

"Well, I'm sorry you haven't been able to stop. She's a lovely bridge."

Kate's eyes sparkled and I really wanted to hold her hand or something else as sweet. But again, brain, logic, creepy, probably straight. "She?"

"Oh yes." I grinned. "All bridges are female. Like ships and cities."

"Really?"

"I have no idea but it sounded good."

Kate rolled her lips, then laughed, leaning on the back of the seat. "Have you drawn the bridge? It seems like it would make a good subject."

I normally don't flap my sketches about like a particularly obnoxious flag, but Kate had asked, and apparently I would do anything for her.

I plucked up the sketch book, held it to my chest. "I don't normally show people the art in these books."

She inhaled sharply. "Oh, I'm sorry. Of course, you don't need to show me. I was presumptuous." Presumptuous. In that well-modulated voice. My happy stomach butterflies fluttered.

I held her gaze for an extra second, then flipped to the page where I'd been sketching the iron work not forty minutes ago. "I like the patterns," I explained as I passed the book over the expanse of the seat, and watched with delight as Kate's lips parted as she took in the whirls and circles.

I decided to overrule my brain. Sliding my gear into the satchel in preparation to shift over at least half a seat—well, closer than I was, anyway—meant I didn't notice that Kate had flipped to the next page. I placed my bag on the ground and sort of bum-shuffled across the seat until there was only a person space between us. My breath hitched. Kate was studying the woman drawn in the centre on the page. She turned the book.

"This is quite lovely." Her lips quirked.

Caught.

"Um." Words would have been handy. A couple. One, perhaps. Not 'um'. "I, ah, well, look Kate, I probably should have asked for consent because that's necessary and polite, but I loved your lines." The appalled part of my brain smacked the talking part. "And I wanted to capture them before you walked away or got run over by Chaos Man." My eyebrows wrinkled into my forehead, hoping that Kate wouldn't stomp off in her probably very expensive, slightly damp heels.

She examined me, her head cocked to the side, then a soft smile bloomed on her face. "I'm flattered, Bron." She tapped the page up in the corner. "It's a very good likeness."

I leaned towards her shoulder—she smelled like jasmine—to study my sketch as if I'd forgotten what I'd drawn. It actually was a good likeness, which meant my hand must have taken over at the same moment my libido was running its engine.

"Huh. It's pretty close." I studied Kate's features, the strong nose, the sculpted eyebrows, the wide mouth currently curled into a smile. I was not about to study any more lines because even the idiotic part of my brain knew that that would qualify as sleazy. I returned to her gorgeous eyes. "I hope you don't mind."

"Not at all." She tapped the page again, seemingly lost in thought. Then she delivered a look that was pure business mixed with mischief. What a combination. I wanted to slide off the seat. "Would you finish the piece?"

I blinked. "Okay? I'll need to use some artistic license because you won't be there when I'm finishing it."

"Finish it now, then."

"Um." Apparently it was my favourite word.

"I'm still wet so we have time." *Oh! Just*...I breathed carefully.

8

So with a half shrug and a head bob, I plucked out my 4B pencil, and gently took the sketch pad from Kate's fingers.

"How do you want me?" *Kate!* More careful breathing.

"Just how you are. Be relaxed. Maybe look at the stream because that's the profile I was working with." My hand shimmered across the paper, and I smiled. I'd been given permission to study and draw a very beautiful woman; two of my favourite activities.

The ducks continued their discussions, the random dogs barked, bicycle bells dinged—*a much more effective alert system, Chaos Man*—and my pencil scratched on the thick cartridge paper. Noises that filled the space between me and Kate. It was lovely and I wanted to slow down simply to extend the time. But eventually there were no more lines to add.

"It's finished," I whispered. It felt like a whispering moment. Kate turned as I swivelled the page towards her and her eyes grew round.

"Bron. It's wonderful." Her gaze flicked to me and I dissolved into those dark chocolate eyes. "If I could keep it, would you sign it please?"

That was a first. "Really? It's only a—"

"I love it and as you said, there are no wrong answers in art. If I say it's wonderful, then it is. That's me on that page, so I have the final word." She raised an eyebrow, her lips arranged in a soft smirk. Bossy. Gorgeous. Sassy. If Kate suddenly announced that she wanted to step all over me, I would lay down right there on the grass in the duck shit.

"Of course you can keep it." I whipped the pad around and scribbled a signature across the bottom. "Do you want a title? Or just leave it?"

Kate stared at the stream, then shifted towards me. "I think." She gave me a long look. A focused look that held intent. "Chaos and Companionship."

My lips parted. It was a terrific title, and I wanted to say so, but suddenly there was a moment. A tiny moment where we connected. I'm positive we did. Me, dressed like a lesbian who had clearly looked up the rules to lesbian fashion in the lesbian stereotype manual of all things lesbian, and Kate, all business wear and classy gorgeousness, had a moment. Perhaps Kate wasn't straight. Perhaps she was. Perhaps I was overthinking. I wrenched my gaze from hers, wrote the title above the piece, then tore out the page.

"Here you go."

"Thank you," she whispered. Another perfect whispering moment. Then she gathered her stuff, clearly deciding that it was dry, and slipped her feet into her shoes. "I should go." We stood at the same time, and Kate lifted her bag from the ground.

"Well, um." Oh, I was having a super day with articulation.

"I think it's safe to shake your hand now." She thrust out her hand to reinforce the suggestion.

I reached forward. Her skin was warm, soft and again I wanted time to stop. "Sorry about Chaos Dude."

"Man. Chaos Man." She chuckled. "It was lovely to meet you, Bron. Thank you again for rescuing me, and for your beautiful art." She lifted the paper in acknowledgement.

"It was lovely to meet you, too, Kate. And I liked drawing you. It was my pleasure." I pointed to the path. "Watch out for the rollerbladers as well, by the way. They yell and sing in your ear at the same time. Dangerous, yet musical."

She laughed delightfully and the smile lines at the edges of her eyes complimented her humour. Then, with a wave, she made her way down the slope onto the path. And she was gone.

I stood there for a minute with a slight smile on my lips and probably a very stunned expression. That had been the nicest, sexiest, sweetest, add your own adjective, interaction that had happened to me in a long while. Finally, after tossing the tissues in the bin and checking that I had everything in the satchel, I slung it over my shoulder and made my way across the bridge.

We Flirted

February 11 to March 11 in the first year of the now

It had been two weeks since Kate. Two weeks since Kate's encounter with Chaos Man. Two weeks since I'd seen Kate smiling at me from the other end of a bench seat. Each day my brain cycled through images of dark hair, dark gorgeous eyes, aquiline nose, and curvy curves that I knew would fit beautifully into my hands. My brain was a perpetual social media algorithm; happy to fill my mental timeline with all that was Kate. Our time on the bench seat, in fact the event that had led to that time on the bench seat, felt like a Hallmark movie. Not that I'd seen one of those. They didn't televise the Hallmark channel in Australia. It was probably on pay TV—non-existent in my apartment—but I knew enough from YouTube.

I made my way to the staffroom to collect any messages from my in-box. Dismissing Hallmark movies and the associated range of very expensive greeting cards, I decided that the interlude with Kate was actually like one of the opening scenes in a lesbian romance novel. I had a reasonable collection of those, and I could see myself re-reading a few to confirm my theory.

My bridge must have felt neglected in the last fortnight, because I'd only visited two times. It needed a catch up so I slid the couple of messages from my tray and shoved them into my bag, pulling out my car keys at the same time. So many afternoon interruptions that impacted on contemplation time. Meetings of the curriculum kind which really should have been an A4 memo, visits from art supply reps who opened their Aladdin's caves of boxes, which meant I completely lost track of time as I drooled all over the new offerings. Actually, that last one was a fabulous interruption.

Then there were the inexplicable interruptions. I dredged up a conversation that I'd been roped into yesterday afternoon with Lydia, the Grade Three teacher, who was into social media like a prospector in a gold mine, and she told me—and the other four people in the conversation—about the hashtag and what its real name was because what idiot would name a symbol after a potato product. She stated with authority that a hashtag was actually called an octothorpe. Then the bell rang—the one that tells the parents to piss off from the grounds hopefully with their kid in tow—and Lydia went home, so I was left hanging, the punchline snatched away. Octo. Sure, the eight pointy bits. But the thorpe part? Of course, I didn't see Lydia at all today because that's how it works when important riddles need solving.

One of the mums, despite having duly pissed off from the grounds, clutched the top rail of the low school fence.

"Fuck," I muttered. Jocelyn Harris, mother of Harrison Harris— poor kid—was convinced that Harrison was the next Caravaggio and was hell bent on me tutoring Harrison every afternoon for an hour. Since the start of the year—four weeks ago—I'd been putting her off. Which I did now. Executing an outstanding left-hand turn, I power-walked through the Grade One and Two classrooms, popping out at another exit into the car park. Jocelyn's attention would be on the staffroom doors so I had a bit of time up my sleeve to get to my car, and roar out of the school grounds at a very slow pace because of kids and potential speeding tickets from the police who hung about on the road outside the school.

All of which happened exactly as I'd envisioned. Including not running over kids. There'd probably be a tree's worth of paperwork if that ever happened. Plus the injured kiddo situation.

I smiled thinly at the dark humour teachers and nurses and anyone in professions that care for people used throughout their daily activities.

"Probably the only way we cope some days," I muttered into my car's interior. It didn't respond, which was hardly surprising as it was concentrating on forward motion rather than conversation. Hyundai had created an excellent range of cars in 2009 and mine was living proof that if spoken to lovingly while receiving caresses on its steering wheel, it would most likely continue its excellence for another few years.

I managed to score a car park only half a kilometre away from my spot. My spot. Last year, I'd strolled up to the bridge bench and gasped. Audibly. A woman with a small child were warming the wooden slats and it took me at least a minute to remember that the bench was not mine and the location didn't have my name written on a plaque nearby. I'd had to be content with a seat farther along which gave me a limited view of my bridge, like the seats at a concert that they advertise as 'best available' but you have to crane your neck to see around the stage scaffolding.

Today, however, I felt good about the vacancy of my bench.

A feeling substantiated by proof. Not a soul.

Travelling through my breathing-arm-stretching-extraneous-thought-eradication routine resulted in one very relaxed Bron McIntyre. With my brain empty, and the path relatively free of people, a tiny grin pulled at my lips. This afternoon felt good.

Embracing the feeling, I pulled out my sketch pad and decided that ducks were today's subject. The squabbly, crabby, wonderfully partnered-for-life ducks were so accustomed to humans that they probably thought we were tall water fowl.

The page had only revealed half a drake when a voice, close to my ear, said quietly, "Do they make satisfactory models?"

"Fucking fuck!" My sketch pad flew from my hands as I leapt up, spinning around to find Kate biting her lip, her hands clutched together at her chest.

"I'm so sorry, Bron." Her eyes were wide.

I took in the ponytail in slight disarray, the business suit—this time pants—and the lips shaped into an 'O'.

"Kate." I blew out a breath.

"I saw you there and wanted to surprise you." She looked at me beseechingly.

Bending to scoop my sketch pad off the grass, I straightened and shook my head, chuckling quietly. "I think you succeeded." I tipped my head towards the seat, and Kate walked around and sat beside me.

"I'm sorry," she repeated. "I've been looking out for you each day when I go for my walk." *She has?* "Well, I missed a couple of days because of a few meetings." She was blathering. I was impressed. It meant that I wasn't the only expert blatherer in the vicinity. "Anyway, I didn't mean to fri—"

My hand moved spontaneously landing on her jacket-covered forearm and squeezing it lightly. "It's fine. Got my blood moving. Albeit faster than usual." We shared a smile. "I've been looking out for you, too." My brain instructed my hand to retreat. Fall back. But I disobeyed the command, brushing my thumb quickly over the fabric. Then I had to let go because I'd broken out in goosebumps.

Kate huffed out a breath and leaned into the back of the bench, turning her head to deliver that same business yet mischievous smile from two weeks ago. Oh. Puddle of delighted goo.

"I wanted to catch you because, well, I didn't know your last name, and I wanted to because I couldn't just ring up the school and ask to speak to Bron in case there were many Brons." I was captivated by the humour, the lights dancing in her eyes. "So I tried stalking the seat which garnered some odd looks and also the bridge became quite jealous."

I laughed, turning my body so I could lean on my elbow and cup my cheek. "Did it?"

"Oh, yes. She huffed."

"Huffed?" The banter was delightful. Was it banter? In certain circumstances it could qualify as flirting. But I knew it wasn't flirting because that would mean...that would mean that Kate was queer and there'd been no indication of that status at all. All this thinking was filling the quiet void that I'd created when I'd initially sat down.

"Mm. Huffed." Kate grinned. White teeth, full lips, lipstick, smile lines, proud nose, eyebrows sculpted into beautiful curves which mirrored the curves of her body. Swoon. She continued. "I wanted to catch you because I've had many compliments on your portrait and I thought you should know."

I blinked. "Um. Where is it that so many people are able to give it compliments?"

She turned her body to mirror mine, the trouser fabric hugging her thighs. "In the foyer of our building."

I spluttered, and stared at her in astonishment. "What?" A verbal addition to the spluttering and staring.

Kate flipped her hand slightly. "Well, the original is in my office, but I had a copy made and it's hanging above my name plate downstairs." She sent another wide smile in my direction. "Therefore, multiple compliments, envy from colleagues, and a visual reminder of a stranger's kindness."

I hummed. "Well, thanks. That's...thanks." I hummed again, letting the idea of multiple compliments softly rest in my heart, then tapped the seat between us. "Have you got time to sit for a while?"

She held my gaze. "I do, actually."

A very long second stretched between us, the ducks cheerfully filling the silence. "McIntyre."

Kate cocked her head questioningly.

"McIntyre. My last name. In case you phone the school and there are too many Brons." It felt like flirting. It sounded like flirting. It looked like flirting. But it wasn't and somehow I knew that.

"Right. Good to know." Kate quirked her lips, then looked over to the bridge. She inhaled through her nose. "Agostino," she said, then paused. "Veris. Veris Accountancy." My eyebrows rose into my hairline. Even I'd heard of Veris, which was astonishing as accountancy and I existed on different planets. My art was on the wall in the foyer of the Veris building in the city.

"Jesus Christ!" A perplexed look shimmered onto Kate's face. "Oh, shit. Swearing. Sorry." She giggled. "But wow. Veris," I said in amazement.

With a nod and a pointed finger, she lifted her chin towards me. "Also, wow. Melbourne City Primary School." Kate raised an eyebrow. I'd always wished I could do that, but I was perfectly happy when gorgeous women demonstrated that skill in my vicinity. "It's not a competition, Bron McIntyre." Bossy mischief. *Gah.* "Your job, your career is as equally valid as mine." She grinned. "So, mutual wows."

My mind absorbed that thought, while I turned back to face the bridge. I felt Kate do the same and I could have linked arms with her. Discovering Kate's delicious wit had launched the stomach butterflies again. Surely she could see how completely smitten I was. Probably not. *She's straight,* my brain informed the rest of my body, which was rioting with attraction and desire and stupid unrequited lust and what was I doing?

"How old are you?" Kate suddenly asked. I blinked. Okay, random.

"Forty-two."

"Forty-eight."

I turned my head to study her. The sentence people automatically reply with when a woman reveals her age zipped through my mind. It was irrelevant whether she looked good for forty-eight. Rude as well. I imagined she'd look amazing in any twelve month period.

"Are we competing again?"

Kate laughed and I gave myself a mental high-five.

"I was curious. You have a childlike spirit, with a wonderful appreciation for the breath of the world. The details in the small and their existence in the large."

We held eye contact. "That's...that's." *Words!* "I like that. Thank you." If ever there was a perfect moment for kissing, that was it. But it wasn't going to happen, and my common sense cheered.

We sat quietly for minutes. And some more.

Then Kate rolled her shoulders, breaking our gaze and stood, smoothing the non-existent wrinkles from her pants.

"I need to leave, Bron. I'm sorry." She looked genuinely apologetic, then picked up her handbag, flipping it onto her shoulder. Rising as well, and appreciating the height difference—Kate had to be about ten centimetres shorter than me, which would be so God damned yummy if we were kissi—*seriously?* I flipped my hand over in a sort of vague gesture.

"No worries. Thanks for the company." I smiled. "And for scaring the crap out of me. Oh! Shit. Swe—"

"Swearing. Sorry," Kate finished and giggled, then before I could move, she stepped forward and hugged me. Briefly. Like friends. In a friendly manner. Friendlike hugging. I sucked in a breath and tentatively patted her back. The statues parked on the concrete plinths along the path had nothing on me. Bron McIntyre, monument to empty desire. She pulled away first which was fitting since she'd initiated the embrace. "Thank you as well. I'll, um." *Here comes the blathering.* "I'll see you." She bobbed her head. "I'll see you soon?" The word lifted adorably at the end of her sentence, and she bit her bottom lip.

"You will. I have first class tickets for this seat." We grinned at each other, then she turned and walked down the path and disappeared from view.

~

MY BODY FELT THAT HUG FOR THE NEXT TWO WEEKS, WHICH was when we got to see each other again.

"How was work?" I asked, my legs stretched out, feet aiming towards the water, and sketch pad abandoned to my right. I blinked because that question sounded like I was Kate's girlfriend or significant other welcoming her home with a kiss and a glass of wine. The kiss sounded nice, but the rest scared the crap out of me. What the ever loving fuck was I doing?

Kate crossed her legs and angled towards me. We were sitting together again, closer than last time. Close enough to feel the heat from her body. I swallowed hard.

"Mm. It was challenging. My boss is making life a little difficult because he's old school and doesn't think that women should be in positions of responsibility."

I looked sideways at her face, her pursed lips, her annoyed eyebrows that dipped over her eyes, which were rolling at Misogynistic Mike's stupid ideas.

"Misogynistic Mike isn't old school. He simply graduated as one of the fuckwit boys who rated the girls according to which burger at *McDonald's* they liked."

Kate stared at me and a smile slowly grew on her lips. "There is so much to unpack there, Bron." Her smile broke into a laugh. "Firstly, Misogynistic Mike?" She laughed again. "If I told you his name was actually Michael, would you believe me?"

I cracked up. "Really?" My laugh fell to a smile with an associated head shake. "Well, whatever his name is, he's a—oh just before. Shit. Swearing. Sorry." Kate giggled and leaned sideways, lightly bumping my shoulder, then leaned away a little, only to return and rest there again as if that part of my body was a one-bounce trampoline.

"Bron, I'm not a shrinking violet. You can have a good old swear any time. I haven't said anything because I find the apology," she tilted her head to look up at me and my breathing shallowed, "endearing, particularly because you swear in the actual apology."

I could feel her laugh through my arm.

We talked for another forty minutes. Kate asked after my day. I chatted about the kids. I slowly, ever so slowly, rested my cheek on the top of her head, moving carefully as if Kate were a fragile ornament that I'd been entrusted to hold. She was. I didn't want to scare her. I didn't want to send out alerts about my thoughts.

We talked about life. Like wishes.

"I'd love to display my work in a gallery." She gazed at me, her eyes dark and gorgeous. "That'd be amazing."

"And complimentary and should happen." Kate's eyebrows wrinkled as if the exhibition could occur simply from the power of her thoughts. God, her lips were close. So damn close. I leaned away a little so oxygen could be reintroduced to my lungs.

"What's your dream?"

Kate pursed her lips. "I'd like to have my divorce finalised as soon as possible."

I blinked. "Well, that's..."

She nodded carefully. "Mm. A wish that'll be granted probably next month." I cocked my head. "All the paperwork is in, the court just has to finalise it, but I'd like to have it finished sooner rather than later."

I reached down and held her hand, squeezing it briefly then letting go. Kate looked so sad. A little lost.

"I'm sorry."

She tucked my hand into hers before I could move it farther away. "Don't be. My marriage was ashes and smoke at least two years ago. This process is the piece of paper that blows the smoke away."

I rolled my lips together. *Oh Kate.* I wondered about her friends. I wondered about her family. I worried that maybe her friends had drifted because of the divorce. Maybe her family had as well. I wanted to ask but Kate released my hand, then stood, which meant that we'd finished our wonderful conversation. Until next time. I hoped there was a next time.

"I'll see you soon, Bron." Yes! A next time. My heart did a little Highland dance despite the fact that I'd never been to Scotland and the amount of Scottish heritage I had could fit in to my big toe.

"Absolutely. I'll be here." *Yes, dipshit. Of course you'll be here.* I mentally rolled my eyes.

Then Kate stepped forward and hugged me. Again. Except this time my body was more prepared and I leaned in properly. Perhaps I held on a little longer. Perhaps Kate gave more of a squeeze. Like when you run your thumbs up the toothpaste tube to straighten it. That sort of squeeze.

"See you soon, Bron," she repeated in that low voice. A soft voice. It didn't have to be loud. Her sentence brushed against my neck and my skin shivered.

As she walked away, the quizzical look she gave me over her shoulder made me wonder if I'd been seen. Was it time to say something? *No!* my brain yelled. Not. A. Good. Idea.

~

FIXATION WASN'T A STRONG ENOUGH WORD. I WAS obsessed. I was that vibrating terrier hunting for its lost tennis ball. Every time I visited my bench seat, I couldn't draw, I couldn't empty my brain, I couldn't relax my body. I'd sit—perched!—on the edge of the seat, scanning the area for the tennis ball named Kate. Occasionally I'd disengage from my body, stare down at myself and shake my head. *You know you're pathetic.*

"Yes. I take full ownership of my patheticness," I mumbled. It was during one of these moments of self-flagellation that Kate appeared in my line of sight. I melted into the other Bron, the chilled, totally not watching the path, laid-back lesbian as quickly as possible.

She walked up the small slope of manicured grass, and it felt comfortable to stand and hug her. Briefly. Like a friend. None of that whispering into necks business. Nope.

"How are you?" Kate sighed as she relaxed into the back of the bench.

"Oh, you know, just hanging out." *Oh my God, you utter liar.* "Pretty good, though. You?"

Kate hummed and wiggled her hand to indicate that things were up and down. I turned properly, and tucked one leg under the other.

"What?"

"I, uh, well, my divorce came through. Earlier than expected, so yay," she said, without inflection, which was surprising because I thought her divorce was meant to be something to celebrate. She turned her head and quickly pointed to my perplexed expression. "Yep. It's inexplicable why I'm feeling like this, because I should be thrilled. But I'm...not?" Her brow wrinkled in confusion. "The divorce is good. Neil and I..." She drifted her gaze over my shoulder. "It was toxic, Bron," she said quietly, bringing her gaze back. "To be rid of that situation is healthy, but I have an odd sense of loss." Kate flipped her hand. "Not of the marriage. More like the time I spent in it as if I could have been doing something else. Something fabulous. Be someone. Be who I was meant to be." She exhaled loudly through her nose, then chuckled humorously. "Way to dive into a nice afternoon with a friend, Agostino." We held each other's gaze for a teeny tiny bit longer than was completely necessary.

"I think that was a perfect dive. Reverse pike with a double tuck straightening in to a life analysis. See? Perfect." I grinned, but the compassion in my voice was evident.

Kate's lips curled up at the edges. "I..." She giggled. "Bron, thank you. I think that's what I needed. A different perspective." Kate's eyes sparkled, and she shuffled a little so her head could rest on my shoulder.

"What perspective have you been getting?"

She hummed briefly. "My friends who focus on appearances." And that answered my question from last time.

"If it's okay to say so, those friends don't sound overly supportive."

Her small laugh vibrated my shoulder. "They're not. Not really. We've been friends since Neil and I got married. Many of them came with Neil as a sort of package, like when you buy a suitcase and they throw in a set of steak knives." I chuckled, then she breathed deeply. "I'm forty-eight so as of yesterday, we'd been married ten years." *Wow.*

"That's..."

Kate's nod shuffled her head against the fabric of my shirt. "It is. It's a great deal of time, hence my odd response to yesterday's news." She leant in farther, as if attempting to create a cheek impression in my skin. We sat in silence for a while.

"What does your family think?" I grimaced. "I'm sorry. That's really personal."

"It's fine." Her voice filled with sadness, and I wanted to lift my arm to bring her closer. The battle began; brain versus heart. After a hard-fought tussle, the heart won. Leaning away slightly, I lifted my arm and curled it around Kate's shoulders. She didn't hesitate, and tucked her body against the side of my torso, crossing her legs so that her foot swung close to my calf muscle. She exhaled a long breath at the same time I did. Hers was probably because she was thinking the thoughts of the thoughtful. Mine was because I hadn't actually taken in oxygen for two minutes and I was going to expire.

"It's just Mum. She's sixty-seven, and, well...she has opinions." Family members with opinions was like being made to eat Aunty Doreen's potato salad because it was right there and therefore expected, even though you hated the potato salad. Opinions were heavy walls to knock down.

"Many, many opinions?"

She looked up in to my face. "Oh yes. Neil was the golden boy. The catch. 'Well done, Kate. You've caught yourself a good man there. He was looking around, you know. It was just as well you found him, other-wise you weren't going to get many opportunities, were you?'" Kate grit her teeth and hissed softly. "It was like a cattle auction. He'd picked me up because I couldn't possibly have had someone else choose me, fall in love with me." *Oh my God.*

"Kate, of course someone would have fallen in love with you. You're gorgeous and...kind...and funny...and." My eyes focused on the bridge so hard that I'm sure I could have bent the metal as if I'd suddenly developed kinetic powers. No way was I looking down at Kate after that collection of compliments. "So she's not a fan of the divorce."

There was a pause and I knew Kate was still looking up at my face. Well, the side of it. "No. Even when I told her that in hindsight I knew Neil didn't really love me, my mother said I should have 'worked harder'." I spotted the finger quotes out of the corner of my eye. "I think being an only child didn't help. She was incredibly proud. She'd had me at nineteen and my father chose to walk away so my marriage was an achievement. I think she lived vicariously through the marriage, through the decade. Anyway, the divorce has sent her world slightly off kilter." Her shoulders received a soft squeeze, and we sat in silence for a long while taking in the ducks, the berserk dogs, the parade of pedestrians moving faster than the stream, and the stillness of the bridge.

"Who's in your family, Bron?" Her attention was still on the stream so I took the opportunity to subtly inhale the coconut scent in her hair.

"My Mum and Dad, my two sisters, a demented dog at my little sister's house, three kids of various genders at the sister next down in age from me. There's my little sister's partner but he's mostly in the back shed. I think that's a coping strategy. The middle sister, who's a psychologist, is married to a bloke who's a vet. There are three cats that complement their three kids but they're not colour coordinated. You'd think they coul—"

Kate had started laughing, pulling away so she could wipe her eyes.

"Oh my God." She dissolved into another fit of giggles, which was exactly the response I wanted. This was happy Kate because sad Kate broke my heart. I grinned.

"Excuse me, my family is." I narrowed my eyes as she mashed her lips together to stave off more laughter. "Just waiting for Netflix to discover how bonkers they are." Kate lost it, clutching at my forearm and breathing through her giggles.

Then as her laughter softened to a smile, we had another one of those moments like last time. Those moments that looked like flirting, sounded like flirting, felt like flirting. Oh, we were flirting. And little tingles were firing low in my stomach. Why were we flirting? It was obvious why I was, but Kate? She'd been married up until twenty-four hours ago.

I broke our eye contact, and I stared at the seat, then the sky, then the grass, finally bringing my gaze back to Kate's face, hoping she'd had time to stop looking at me like that. She had, thank goodness. But she was preparing to slide under my arm again, which helped not a bit.

"Tell me more about your family." Her voice, close to my ear, was soft and smooth. It made me nervous and when I'm nervous I babble. No breaking news there.

"Ah, well, I'm the oldest at forty-two. Then Janine is forty. She's the psychologist, married to Rick who's the vet with the non-matching pets and kids. Then there's Siobhan who's thirty-six, and still hasn't forgiven Mum and Dad for giving her an Irish first name especially since our surname is Scottish because all through school Siobhan was asked if leprechauns play bagpipes at the end of the rainbow."

Kate snorted, and slapped her hand over her mouth. "I'm sorry. I shouldn't laugh. Poor Siobhan. That must have been awful."

I shook my head, my shoulder jostling Kate slightly. "She gave as good as she got. Don't worry. Siobhan swears worse than I do. Probably because she practised on all the kids at school."

Our chat flowed around topics so light that they could have dissolved if we'd dwelt on them for too long. And topics with enough depth that we could swim about in their words. Eventually, my watch gave off invisible shouty declarations that I needed to leave because Siobhan was cooking dinner and if I was late, the aforementioned swearing would be called into action.

We stood in the half light, the air cooling, and after another longer-than-expected hug, Kate turned to leave. She'd not taken eight steps when my mouth activated.

"Wait!" I tugged my hand back from where it had grasped at air. Kate's eyebrows lifted in curiosity, waiting for me to add details to my instruction. Details like I wanted her phone number. I wanted her to stay. I wanted her to take my hug and wrap it around her shoulders for the rest of the evening. But I lost all confidence, and went with option three.

"Have a great night, Kate."

She smiled and returned the wish. Then after a long look, Kate turned and walked away and I was convinced that if I'd offered them, she would have taken options one and two as well.

We Fell

April 1 to April 24 in the first year of the now

At the core of my job was a rock solid sense of professionalism followed by an unshakeable belief in nurturing a love of art in the kids. So I was distinctly relieved that these fundamental education principles were cemented in my teaching soul because Kate could have easily shimmered across the surface of it all and rippled my equilibrium.

Kate did manage to ripple my surface three weeks after those moments that we'd sat together, when she'd leaned into me, when I'd held her around the shoulders, the moments after we'd hugged. See? Look at me not letting Kate shimmer across my calm façade.

I wasn't vibrating in hope those three weeks. Not noticeably anyway. I managed to maintain an outward countenance of Bron, leader of the Nonchalant Clan. That was until a visibly upset Kate walked into view on the path. I say walk, but her knees seemed to have ceased to function because she was robotic and stressed and I could see, even from my bench, that the guy beside her was gritting his teeth in that manner people have when they're so pissed off that they can't even raise their voice. Or they're so angry that the whispers and the quiet are more frightening than the loud. Kate stopped, her back to the stream, and flicked the quickest of glances my way. She put her hand on the guy's forearm, which he shook off, and even though his back was to me, I couldn't miss the gesticulations, underscored by very audible words.

"—listen to reason, Kate. You have no idea how embarrassing it is to have you parade around telling everyone that you're a divorcee. It's beneath you."

I straightened. *Hello, Neil, you clearly pissed off ex-husband. I didn't like you already, but you've just confirmed my opinion.* Watching the interaction like a hawk, I gently slid my satchel to the side, and scooted to the edge of the seat. Kate must have said something. Perhaps something to placate Neil. It must have been the wrong thing to say, because he darted his hand out, grabbed her arm, wrapped his fingers around her bicep and I saw her quick wince of pain.

Oh, hell no. Nope. Not having that. I was on the path in three strides, standing beside Kate and edging Neil out of the way. It forced him to release his hold.

My hands fell gently on Kate's shoulders.

"Oh my God!" I gushed loudly. "Kate Agostino! I haven't seen you in ages! Look at you!" The number of exclamation marks was frightening but it was doing the trick. Neil backed off a tiny bit, enough for me to position myself directly in front of her. "Oh my God," I exclaimed again. "Is that a Donna Karan?" I had no idea who Donna Karan was but I'd seen a billboard and I was banking on Neil having no fucking idea either. "I can't believe it! We need to catch up!" I leaned into her space, and breathed in her ear. "Work with me here."

I turned towards Neil. "Oh, you're...you're Neil, right?"

The fact that I was pretty much his height must have annoyed him immensely because he glared.

"I don't know you," he huffed.

"Oh, that's okay. I'm just an old friend of Kate's." I spun back to Kate. "Let's catch up now. Do you have a free hour or so?" I gave her a cheesy grin, which made her smile; the first since I'd spotted her.

"Y-yes. I do."

"Great!" I pretty much yelled the word. "I'm sure you won't mind, Neil. We girls need to keep up with the gossip, don't we?" I tittered, and pressed two fingertips to my lips for emphasis. This performance was not for Siobhan's ears because I'd never live it down. I linked my arm through Kate's and walked her away, tossing a, "You're such a sport," over my shoulder at her ex-husband who shoved his hands in to his pockets and stalked off.

Kate sagged in to my side. "Thank you, Bron," she murmured and I squeezed her arm. Then I snuck a look over my shoulder, and discovered that Neil had gone.

"You're welcome." I gently turned us around. "I need to pick up my satchel," I explained, and we made our way back to the bench. Flipping the strap over my shoulder, I grinned at her face. "Please never tell anyone about airhead Bron. That performance back there was for one night only. Like some sort of terrifying April Fool's joke."

Kate smiled, which grew into a short laugh. "Airhead Bron is now in the vault." Then she sighed loudly, so I tucked her arm in again.

"There's a cafe across the road. Let's head over and catch up properly. It adds authenticity to you not having seen me since the Crusades." I lifted my eyebrows. "In case Neil decides to return for another chat with airhead Bron."

Another smile drifted across her face, and she leaned into my shoulder.

The cafe was half-full so we were able to snag a table near the side windows. After ten minutes or so, Kate had perked up a little and smiled at me over the rim of her coffee cup.

"Thank you again." I shrugged in acknowledgement, then her smile dissolved. "I'm sorry you had to see that. He's...that need to save face, the anger when he thinks he's been embarrassed is very difficult to deal with." She sipped. "Was difficult to deal with."

"I'm sorry." My brain growled. It wanted me to leap up and march... somewhere, and find the prick and...do what? I didn't know, but it felt good to fantasise. *I really want to swear.* I always felt better after a decent swear.

"He...he used to grab hold whenever he was making a point so I wouldn't walk away and therefore win the argument with my absence." She blinked sadly.

"Fuck me with a chainsaw," I muttered through clenched teeth. Well, if that wasn't a decent swear, I didn't know what was. My impulsive sweary self sat in the corner, repeatedly whispering "I'm sorry".

This time Kate's blinking was more shock than sadness. "That's a new one."

"Shit. Swearing." I let her finish.

"Sorry." And for the first time that afternoon—now early evening—she laughed. Properly laughed and I grinned. Our gaze was sparkly and fun and that flirting business was front and centre. *Not the time, dipshit.* It really wasn't. Not after knobhead Neil and his manhandling of Kate.

She sipped at her coffee. "You know? He's probably right."

"Um, no. He's not."

"I do call him my ex-husband when I talk about him."

I gave her a long look. "That's because he is."

"Yes." She placed her cup down. "But I suppose it's a bit silly to call him that without elaborating farther. I really should be using his name with other people as well." She rolled her head back and I admired the very kissworthy skin on her throat. Luckily my eyeballs shifted their gaze to her face when she brought her head down. "I'm forty-eight for heaven's sake. There's bound to be a clause in a handbook somewhere which states when people should stop using generic labels." A heavy sigh punctuated the statement.

My shrug was elaborate. "I don't know. I still call women I'm dating my girlfriend even though I'm forty-two, not fifteen. That could be classed as generic." It took a moment to realise that I'd outed myself with the subtlety of a brick hurled into a pond. Kate studied me, hummed, then asked if I wanted to order anything since it was early evening and some appetisers would be lovely. She hadn't even blinked at my revelation. That was promising. I mentally rolled my eyes.

The waiter, having duly danced his fingers over his tablet confirming our order of artichoke and spinach dip with spiced pita chips, which sounded amazing, zipped off to sort it all out, and Kate gave a soft gasp.

"Oh!" She reached down and pulled her handbag onto her lap. "This afternoon's disagreement with Neil—"

"He put his hands on you, Kate." I narrowed my eyes as I recalled how angry I'd been.

"Well, yes." She bit her lip. "Okay, when Neil held on to me." I frowned again. "It made me completely forget this." She fossicked in her bag, then brought out a container, clicking open the lid and reaching inside. The something inside must have been fragile because she carefully drew it out, and cupped it delicately. I caught a flash of blue.

Then reaching across the table, she held my hand, turned it over, and electric tingles zipped through my body.

"I wanted to give you this." Kate moved the container to the side, then carefully placed a blue miniature origami paper crane on my palm. She sat back, exhaled loudly, then pressed her lips together and watched me intently. I stared at the crane. It was beautiful. Every fold and crease exact. Crisp. I looked up at Kate's hopeful expression.

She jumped in before I could say a word. "It's...um. It's a habit?" She twisted her lips in thought. "No. Not a habit. More a skill that I wanted to take away as a souvenir instead of a keyring and t-shirt. I worked in Tokyo for a couple of months about a year before I was married." She pointed to the crane that I was gently cradling, protecting it in case the fragility of the gift might see it fly away. "You probably know this already, but the crane is a symbol of hope. Of peace, love, and healing during challenging times." She laughed humourlessly. "This afternoon might qualify as a challenging time." Kate suddenly stopped talking, and gazed at me.

"Kate, this is art," I breathed.

Her body finally relaxed, slumping into the back of the chair. "No, it's not." A vague wave of her hand.

"Yes, it is." I glanced down at the crane, then up at Kate. Her beauty, those stunning classical features, took my breath away. The gift. The thought behind it—she'd thought of me—warmed my heart, and in the now muted lighting, I wanted to ease the crane on to the table, stand up, walk around and kiss Kate senseless. "It's beautiful art. Really."

Kate tilted her head in self-deprecation. "It's engineering based on mathematical principles."

"There are no mistakes in art. Engineering and maths can be problematic."

Her laugh seemed to reduce her anxiety, and it gave me the opportunity to gently place the crane next to my cup, then reach across to hold her hand. We stared at each other for a very long time.

"Thank you, Kate. It's beautiful."

Pink, detectable even in the soft lighting, brushed Kate's cheeks. It was the sort of pink—usually named something stupid like 'open umbrella'—that sits at the far end of the row of red paint chips at the hardware store. I was lost.

She slid her hand away when the food arrived, and during bites, small talk took over as if the heaviness of the prior moment needed a dose of helium.

With the crane secured in the container, and Kate waving away my promise to return the box next time we met—no question about that now—we made our way outside.

"Where are you parked?"

I pointed towards the south end of the street. "Down the end about a kilometre or so. No idea. Maths is not my thing. Too many mistakes." I grinned, and she laughed, tucking her arm into mine. It felt such a natural thing to do.

"I'll walk you to your car."

My feet froze. "Kate, where's your car?"

"It's at work. I'll get an Uber tonight and in the morning. It's fine."

"Oh. Oh, okay." Then a terrible thought struck me. "Shit." Kate pressed her lips together stifling a laugh. "Swearing. Sorry," I whispered, which forced a laugh from those gorgeous pink-painted lips. "I just had a thought. Are you going back to the house where Neil is?" I wrinkled my forehead in concern and that I'd probably overstepped my boundaries.

She squeezed my arm. "I have my own apartment, Bron. I have done so for about eight months. I'm fine and you're delightful to worry."

"Okay. Well, that's good." Our walking pace was relatively brisk despite the plethora of street lights planted along the footpath as if they'd been on special at the council depot, so our arrival at my decrepit Hyundai was sooner than I'd have liked.

"This is you?"

"Yep. Under that flaking paint and dent in the bonnet lives the power of forty horses just waiting to be unleashed onto the streets of Melbourne." I nodded seriously, and Kate giggled.

"Thank you for keeping me company, Bron." A small smile lifted her lips.

"You are completely welcome. It's been a lovely evening." My smile matched hers.

"I, um." She dug her phone out of her bag, then gazed at me. "I'd like to do it again if you li—"

"Yes." *Seriously? Can I be any more obvious?*

Kate blinked then smiled again. Wider. Fuller. "Excellent." She wiggled her phone slightly. "I should organise my ride."

I nodded, adjusted my satchel carefully so as not to disturb the crane in its box, then shoved my hands into my pockets. Kate's focus was on her screen, so I took the opportunity to slide my gaze down her body. Those curves! My upward journey was as equally delightful until I reached Kate's face where another blush was colouring her cheeks.

Caught. Again.

I pretended that I hadn't been checking her out, which was silly because clearly I had and Kate knew it. She probably thought I was some sort of predatory lesbian, ready to snatch her away to lesbian land to have my lesbian way with her.

Kate's head tilted. "My ride will be here in two minutes. Apparently there's a car just down the road."

"Right. Good. Mm." Blathery blathery.

She studied me for a moment, then stepped forward. This hug felt a little different from the others. Not as much space. In fact, hardly any space between our bodies at all. If Kate had turned her head and pressed her ear to my chest, she would have heard those forty horses galloping about in my heart.

Finally, she pulled away, then leaned up and kissed my cheek. My body froze.

"I'm glad you're my friend," she said quietly, then she gave me a quick smile. The car arrived as I responded with, "Me too," which wasn't a terrific reply but it seemed to work because as Kate slid into the back seat, she delivered a small wave and a "See you soon."

I stood at my car for a long, long time, touching my cheek where the lips of a beautiful, clever, witty woman had rested for a microsecond. God, I was a stereotype. Lesbian crushing on straight woman. A soundtrack was supposed to play at that moment. All strings and woodwinds; an orchestra of unrequited love. Lust! Not love. Lust. Yes. Much better.

Kate hadn't offered her phone number and I'd been loathe to ask for it. Maybe she was being really careful with people, trying them out, seeing if they fit. Understandable. I flicked my indicator to merge into the traffic. Maybe she figured that we'd spontaneously meet each other at the bridge and then grab coffee and appetisers. I stared at the oncoming cars, blinking in the light of the headlights. I was content with that arrangement. It felt organic, like a surprise, like I'd be even more thrilled with the unplanned nature of it all. I reckoned I would.

~

WHICH I WAS. WE MET AT THE BENCH SEAT THE NEXT DAY and the day after that, not missing any days, for an entire two weeks. We didn't exchange numbers and I was right. The idea of not knowing, not planning, warmed the air in my chest. The hope of seeing Kate walk around that bend in the path. Of her delight in knowing I was there. It was intoxicating.

We'd enjoy thirty minutes of conversation and appreciation of the stream and the bridge and each other. I would point out various artistic elements in the bridge, most of which I knew but added to after nightly trawls through the internet, and she would chat about work and facts, punctuated with a grin and eyebrow lift, that she regarded as the minutiae of accounting. The gap between us reduced until eventually our feet overlapped; her foot, courtesy of a pair of delectable crossed legs, tucked under my calf muscle. It became a habit to walk to the cafe afterwards and share appetisers and parts of our lives and, in my case, little invisible pieces of my heart.

Once in a while, probably every third day, Kate brought out her container and gifted me with another paper crane. Our gazes held and held and in my lunch breaks at work, I would sketch Kate's face because it was imprinted on my brain.

My collection of Kate's cranes began to grow, held lovingly by a large wooden bowl carved from Tasmanian Huon Pine; a birthday gift from my whole family because the expense would have been impossible for one person. The bowl had remained empty since that birthday but finally it had a treasure worth protecting.

Later, after another dinner at the cafe, Kate suggested we stroll along the path next to the stream. It was one of those nights when the stars were visible despite the light pollution in the sky. I swapped my bag to my other shoulder so we could walk side-by-side, shoulders touching.

Jasmine permeated the air, but it wasn't the plant itself. It was Kate. It was intoxicating.

It took me a moment to register when soft skin, warm and tentative, slipped into my hand. I instinctively tightened my grip and froze at the same time—an incredible feat because the squeezing section of my brain had a brief meeting with the freezing section and it was decided that breathing should cease.

Kate caught the movement, or lack of. She gently pulled us to a stop, and looked up.

"Is this okay?"

My lips curled up. Apparently the council meeting had decided that breathing could resume. I dropped my gaze to our joined hands then lifted it to meet Kate's. My smile grew.

"Very okay."

"Hmm." A nod attached itself to the sound, then she turned to look ahead because errant strollers dragging along parents were always potential hazards.

While the hand-holding, foot-touching, neck-breathing, cheek-kissing was delicious, and even if my suspicions, based on no evidence what-so-ever, of Kate showing any interest in me at all, it didn't mean that I should write a how-to manual to guide her on her journey to sexual awakening land. I'd done that once before, and the science experiment I'd unwittingly been immersed in ended with results that didn't match the hypothesis.

It didn't stop me from flirting, because, oh yes, we'd officially travelled into that territory.

Recalling our bench-siting earlier in the daylight, I murmured, "Have you been told that your hair has soft hints of blonde when the sun hits it?" My eyes took in her very dark hair, so much darker than mine, pulled into its haphazard ponytail which she assured me had been neat and professional at the beginning of the day.

One of her lovely blushes visited her cheeks. "No."

"My apologies that I've left it so long." I lifted a corner of my mouth. "It does."

What. Are. You. Doing? Apparently I *was* writing a manual for Kate. Leaving breadcrumbs, even.

On the Friday of our second week, Kate must have felt comfortable enough to reach over, take my phone, and enter a new contact.

My hand trembled a little when I stared at the phone number with Kate Agostino stamped in bold above.

I didn't make eye contact, but simply texted the number and heard Kate's handbag trill. Then I looked up.

"In case one of us can't make it."

Her gaze darted about, then she dug into her bag to pull out her own phone and created my contact. The amount of time it had taken her to trust me with that collection of digits was understandable. Kate was definitely raw from her ex-husband. Raw from friends who'd abandoned her. Raw from a mother who'd held unreasonable expectations. Kate's trust was very special.

Which is why, early the next morning, my hand shook when I flipped over the phone, dancing erratically on the coffee table. Kate had reached out to me not twenty-four hours later and my skin shivered with excitement while my heart rate stampeded about, because Kate wanted to know if I was free and could catch up. Today. Later. In the afternoon. At our regular time. *Gah.*

I felt like I was preparing to ride a rollercoaster. Perhaps I was.

It took nearly all of our bench musings and a small part of our coffee-but-let's-stay-for-dinner section for me to ignore how much the whole moment felt like a date. But Kate was a friend.

There were more people about in the early evening on a Saturday. The path was full of different breeds of pedestrians; not as many arm-waving earpiece-wearing angry folk, a similar amount of strollers, so many joggers that we had to ensure we weren't meandering lest we become an obstacle course. Because that's where we'd ended up. Strolling along the path hand in hand, enjoying the dark between each lily pad of light cast by the lamps.

An enormous weeping willow about five hundred metres from our spot—that had been a recent change in my head; our spot—draped itself over a third of the path and the branches and leaves created a secret space away from prying eyes. I led Kate behind the curtain.

"Have you seen this on your walks?"

"No." She turned slowly, untangling her fingers. "It's beautiful. The city lights are like faeries, Bron. It's magical." She eventually returned her gaze, an utterly gorgeous half smile on her mouth, her lips parted. This moment? It was a kissing moment. No doubt about it. I stepped forward into her space, into hugging distance. Hesitation ate at my confidence; one didn't get to forty-two without a partner and Olympic level blathering without vast expertise. I hesitated, but I knew this would be okay. I'd ask, of course. But somehow I knew this would be okay.

I leaned towards her, our faces so close, and paused.

"Can I kiss y—?"

"Yes." Kate's eyes were wide with...apprehension? With desire? Then her eyes hooded. Desire it was.

Her face lifted, and as she gently held my waist, I brushed my lips across hers. It wasn't really a proper kiss. Yes it was. The thousands of tiny explosions in my stomach confirmed it.

"Is this okay?"

Kate's smile conveyed the 'I'm tentative yet thrilled and oh my gosh that was amazing' memo and her eyes sparkled, filled with wonder.

"Yes," she said huskily, then swallowed.

The kiss had been brief; just enough to tell Kate that I, Bron the lesbionic lesbian, was interested in her, and kissing was certainly one way to deliver that message. Maybe I could ask for another one. We hadn't moved in the five seconds since the first kiss, which was convenient when asking for more.

It was probably disconcerting for Kate to find her identity at forty-eight years of age. Maybe. Had she found her identity? I didn't know because all I'd done was flirt with her, and give her compliments, and kiss her once. My rumination was cut short when Kate pushed up and kissed me very softly. Velvet lips stroking my skin, the warm air chasing after them. I angled my head slightly so our mouths would fit and it was glorious. Soft. Tender. And a million fireworks exploded in my head.

Kate pulled away again, but slid her arms up to drape them around my neck.

"I wondered when you'd do that."

"Do what?" I said dimly.

Kate huffed a laugh. "Kiss me." Technically she had initiated our second kiss, but I wasn't going to argue. Although I was worried.

"What are we doing?" I asked.

"I don't know. I really don't. But right now? I'm kissing a woman who I'm completely smitten with." She curled her hands around my neck.

I raised my eyebrows. "Smitten?"

"Oh, yes. Just as you are."

I blinked. "I...um"

"I saw, Bron," she whispered. "Quite early on. I didn't know what to do with it. But yes, I saw your interest because you are delightfully transparent. You do wonders for a woman's self-esteem with your," Kate rolled her lips together, "appreciation."

"Oh, gees." A touch of embarrassment.

She leaned into my collarbone. "Yes, it was unexpected." Her breath against my neck produced a full body shiver. "But when I realised, when I felt I could respond, I enjoyed it very much."

I was a puddle on the ground. See that puddle? Me. On the ground.

We Acknowledged

❦

May 23 to June 5 in the first year of the now

K ate's apartment was quaint, cozy and every time I visited I'd discover a new ornament or knick knack on the bookshelves against the wall opposite the door. A little ceramic owl. A beautiful Chinese ink-wash painting. A framed Japanese koi papercut. I felt as if I was learning about her through inanimate objects, which felt warm and intimate, so I lingered at each piece and Kate would hold my hand and tell me the reason for its existence.

A month had passed since the weeping willow moment. That first kiss. We'd enjoyed many—mostly chaste, sometimes more—kisses since then. In each other's homes. In each other's cars. In each other's doorways. My engine was revving, because I wanted to run my hand under Kate's skirt, over her shirt, find buttons that needed undoing, put my mouth on parts of her skin that weren't lip-related. I was vibrating with lust.

Kate knew it.

But pushing Kate was not an option. She was too precious. The gift of herself was too precious. I loved being able to sit together, talking, watching TV, her tucked under my arm, sharing random kisses that were sweet and delicious and hot but not heated.

I was happy to go at snail's pace, particularly as I was the lead snail waving about the shouty placard; 'I'm kissing Kate Agostino!' There may have been snail-sized beads and glitter involved. Our texts were definitely flirty and after a week, the sudden appearance of a few X's at the end of her messages filled my heart.

Last week, Siobhan, with her usual delicate tact, reckoned that Kate was a figment of my imagination and it was only because she'd looked up the Veris website that she'd believed me. That conversation had been memorable.

"You are fucking unbelievable!" I scowled across the dining table.

Mum tutted and Dad ignored all of it and cut into his lasagne.

"Well, all we've heard is 'Kate this' and 'Kate that' and you wandering around with a moony expression. I had to make sure Kate was real and not a side effect of drugs."

I threw a piece of garlic bread at her.

"Girls, act your age, please."

Siobhan cupped the side of her mouth and poked her tongue out.

So, I continued to snuggle Kate. Like tonight, with her body leaning back against mine, relaxed between my legs, watching something on TV which I couldn't concentrate on. My slight height advantage meant that I could kiss the top of her head, inhaling the fresh scent of shampoo and pressing my cheek to her dark, dark hair. She draped her hands over my arms as I enveloped her in a hug, and she always squeezed my forearms as if to reward my kisses. Snail leading the parade. Shouty placard. Possibly glitter.

"When did you realise that Neil wasn't the right person for you?" I asked quietly.

She inhaled deeply. "About the fifth year of the marriage."

"But ..."

"Yes. I know." Her nodding vibrated my chest. "It took the rest of the marriage to work up the courage to get divorced."

I leaned my cheek on her head. "Why did you stay?"

Kate didn't answer for such a long time that I thought I'd overstepped a boundary. "Because I was afraid of being alone."

"But it was toxic." My frown made my eyebrows ache. "Wouldn't it have been better to be alone?"

Kate laughed humourlessly. "Not when you've been conditioned to believe that being alone is awful and that being married is an achievement."

We sank into each other on the couch, quiet, contemplative, and perfect.

"When's your birthday?" The random question appeared in my brain and bypassed my non-existent filter.

Kate chuckled. "Trying to put me into aged care already?"

I poked her, and she giggled delightedly.

"Okay, it's July Six."

I exhaled quickly and shuffled her around so we could sit side-by-side. "Really?"

She ran her fingertips down my cheek. "I'm hardly likely to make up a random date, sweetie."

Sweetie.

I was wondering which one of us would be the first to use an endearment. I figured it would be me. See aforementioned lack of filter. But it was Kate, and I was galloping about in my paddock of happiness.

"Mine's July Twenty." Not that it was in any way newsworthy but I thought it cool that our birthdays were in the same month.

Apparently so did Kate. She raised an eyebrow. "This means there'll be a large consumption of cake in a short period of time."

I cracked up, then pointed to my chest. "Caramel mud cake from the supermarket."

Kate tipped her head. "Hmm." Then smirked. "Ricotta and custard-apple layered cheesecake with lime and ginger crumble." Another eyebrow raise. "From the artisan bakery in the city."

My expression must have been priceless, because Kate collapsed sideways onto the couch in a fit of giggles, eventually hauling herself upright and wiping her eyes.

I blinked. "No one eats those things. They're eleven hundred dollars and besides I'm positive they're made of foam and plastic."

Her giggles continued when she leaned into my shoulder and I really don't think she knew what she was doing but she shifted and ended up straddling my lap, while still wiping more tears of laughter from her eyes. I gently held her waist, and the action seemed to bring her back to the present moment. She looked down then back to my eyes.

"Oh." Her swallow was heavy. "Is this okay?"

"Very."

Our gaze held for so long that it was as if we were memorising each other's faces. I was a pro at that skill, seeing as I'd drawn her face a thousand times already. The fans of smile lines. The dips. The highlights. Her eyes. Kate slid her hands to my shoulders.

"How did I get to this point where I'm forty-eight and only discovering who I am?"

I rolled my lips, not knowing what to say. Her hands slid to the sides of my neck, her thumbs smoothing my jaw.

"I wish I could start again." She paused in her caresses to contemplate her statement.

"Start what?"

"My life. Possibly from thirty. That seems a logical number. Then I'd have known."

I leaned into Kate's right thumb. "But you wouldn't have met me."

"I might have."

"No. You wouldn't have been run over by Chaos Man and I wouldn't have rescued you. You would have been on the arm of a very dashing butch accountant who was flying to America in four hours and had asked you to accompany them."

Kate stared at me in bemusement.

"So I'm glad you found out who you are." I smiled gently. "At forty-eight."

Another long gaze, and I'm positive I spotted a glimmer of desire, or determination, or permission, or something. But whatever it was, it sent shivers of delight through my stomach. I waited, my hands on her waist, her fingers curled into the hair at the back of my neck. I waited.

Kate leaned forward and kissed my lips, then slid past my cheek to whisper in my ear. "I'd like to…"

I waited.

"I'd like to kiss you until I can't breathe."

Oh my God. Kate pulled away, just enough to see my mouth open in wonder, in desire, with lust, and she smiled shyly.

She lowered her lips, then ever so slowly parted them and touched her tongue to mine. I tightened my hold on her waist, purely in reflex. My full body shudder began at my toes, but another shudder had me pulling away.

"Oh. God, Kate. That's incre—"

She held the sides of my face and brought her lips close, hovering above mine. "I'm not finished." Bossy mischievous Kate was in the house. On my lap. *Oh God.*

$$\sim$$

THIS WENT ON EVERY TIME WE SPENT TIME TOGETHER. HER place. My place, which wasn't nearly as fancy or knick-knacky or coordinated but had a shitload of art on the walls. Most of it mine. The bowl of cranes drew a smile and long kiss, followed with a "You keep them." As if I wouldn't. But it was the drawing that Kate noticed the first time she visited.

"When did you do that one?" She wandered over to the small display easel, and studied it for a moment. She looked over her shoulder. "I don't remember you sketching me since that first time we met."

Folding her into an embrace from behind, I hummed. "That's because you didn't sit for this picture. I drew it from memory."

"Bron," she whispered, and leaned back into my chest. I gently shifted her hair, kissed her neck, and worked my way very carefully up to her jaw, overlapping the movement on her skin so that hopefully Kate would feel like somehow I'd managed to deliver thousands of continuous kisses.

I felt her swallow.

"Is this okay?"

A shallow breath. "Oh yes. Could you do that again?"

Absolutely. Never a doubt. I repeated the journey and Kate's shiver was delicious. I didn't even wait for another request, but moved to the other side of her neck. My hands roamed a little, cupping her breasts and I softly, ever so softly, brushed my thumbs over her nipples. Her soft whimper nearly blew off the top of my head.

"Do you have any idea how fucking gorgeous you are? And I'm not even apologising for that swear because it's true."

A breathy laugh. Then she turned in my arms and I fell into the darkest of brown eyes. We stood like that for at least two minutes, staring, exchanging small smiles, holding each other so close.

Then I bent my head and kissed the corner of her mouth, and I felt her smile. She brought her arms up, wrapping them around my neck.

"I...that just then...I want to, Bron. So very much. But I'm not ready. I'm too new. Newly single, newly not single, newly..." She looked at my shoulder then brought her gaze back. "Whatever I am. And somewhat nervous."

My gaze was steady as I cupped her face, lightly kissing her lips. "Sweetie, we do not have to do anything you're not comfortable with or not ready to do."

Kate reached up and brought my hands down to her chest. "I know. You're wonderfully chivalrous."

I frowned. "Kate, consent is a fundamental element for anything intimate." I frowned more forcefully. "I'd never push."

Disentangling our hands, Kate turned back to the drawing. "That's quite a novelty."

I was rooted to the spot. "Neil?"

Her chest lifted as she inhaled deeply. "Mm. Not big on consent."

That utter fucker. I needed to find him and create a Neil-shaped fence paling. Instead, I scooted around to hug Kate, pressing her head to my chest. Her body to mine.

Another long moment of synchronised breathing.

"Anyway." Kate kissed me quickly, then paused and kissed me with lips that pushed, a tongue that probed and a sigh that chased all of it, and made my bones dissolve. She grinned, turned away, then looked over her shoulder again. "That's the past. Water under the bridge so to speak, because I make my own decisions now, and my decision is that we need dinner and to curl up on the couch."

I laughed. "Now that is a plan I can get behind."

She threw me that bossy mischievous look that made me helpless. "Good. Because you're in charge of ordering." Then threw a cushion at me.

~

THE THING ABOUT BEING A SPECIALIST IN A SCHOOL, LIKE ME with my art, or Candice who corralled kids into straight lines for sport, or music teacher Justin whose ears exploded when the plastic recorders were played at various volumes, was that we didn't have a teaching partner to bounce ideas off or annoy them every five seconds with yet another photo of the woman who now held our hearts and look here's another photo and let me show you this one isn't she gorgeous?

Specialists tended to hang out together at staff meetings or drift aimlessly between cliques, like satellites whose directional radar was on the blink.

Despite getting along with everybody because everybody was great, my only true friends on staff were Lydia, Grade Three teacher extraordinaire—kids and parents and the world loved her—and Lawrence, the groundskeeper, who talked to me about art because he liked to draw flowers and about the bridge at the stream because his uncle had assisted in the lamp posts at either side. Apparently he'd been quite vocal, arguing for the affirmative about heritage value, completion of the artistic elements, and sensible things like lighting and being able to see things such as cyclists. Lawrence loved my drawings of the bridge or bits of the bridge and often asked to take a couple to show his now elderly relative. I'd framed one of my better ones last year and given it to Lawrence as a Christmas present. He'd wiped the sleeve of his green staff uniform across his eyes, muttered a "Thanks, Bron" and announced that he suddenly needed to refill the mower with petrol.

Lydia pointed to me from across the corridor on a Monday in late May.

"I want to know. Seriously, Bron. You're like a billboard advertising...you know."

The sentence editing was due to the bazillion kids swarming about, rushing to recess, so they'd be first on the playground equipment. The littlies in Grade One still needed help to even find the exits let alone the route to the climbing frames so I avoided Lydia, and Lawrence, and any one else who asked after my dreamy, moony, expression. I didn't want to gush too much about Kate. I had an irrational fear that Kate would disappear and I'd be lost.

∾

THE DELICIOUS TENSION WHEN TWO HUMAN TEST TUBES start to fizz was palpable a week later. Kate had brought her overnight bag which she'd been doing for a few weeks, even though all we did in bed, or the couch, was cuddle, and maybe touch some places—the baseball second base thing—and kiss. A lot. All of which revved my engine, and if Kate's breathy whimpers were any indication, revved hers as well. But tonight there was tension. Thick tension. Eye-contact that went on forever, but gazes that suddenly darted away, half-sentences that were understood even though most of the grammar was missing.

Dinner—a simple pasta that I'd thrown together—had been eaten with all that tension and associated eye-contact flying about. It was a wonder we'd been able to find our own mouths. Probably relied on muscle memory.

I was determined that Kate would drive our intimacy. Wherever she wanted to go, I'd go as well. Because we were going somewhere tonight. No doubt about it.

"Do you want some dessert? I've got dulce de leche ice cream which is a bit fancy but I thought you might like it." I leaned heavily against the dishwasher causing it to beep and start the two hour cycle which wasn't what I'd intended. I whipped around and frantically pressed buttons and by the time I'd reset it to something more water-saving, Kate had crossed the kitchen to stand behind me.

"No," she said softly.

I turned and swallowed. Oh good God. Aroused Kate was breathtaking. "Um?"

"No, I don't want dessert. Thank you." She carefully placed another exquisite crane—pink—on the bench beside me, then twined her arms about my neck.

"This crane is for hope."

I slid my hands around her waist. "Thank you," I whispered, and even though I knew the answer to my next question it was essential to ask it. "What are you hoping for?"

She brushed her lips over mine. "You."

"Um," I repeated. Blathery Bron was back but I gave myself permission, because...Kate.

"Could we be in another room where I'm not having dessert?" She tilted her head sideways. "That one, specifically."

Oh, wow. I melted as if I was the fancy ice cream that had been accidentally left out. Turning my hand over, holding fast to my personal promise that Kate would drive, I stared into her eyes. She gave a quick glance down, then slid her palm into mine and led me to the bedroom.

"I don't quite know what to do."

"Yes, you do." I shot her a smile. "Kiss me."

"I'm good at that." She raised that eyebrow that made me all squirmy in my stomach, but this time the feeling dropped lower and combinations of gestures like those were going to reduce me to a puddle of goo.

"Yes. You are."

So she did. Tongues dipping between lips, wrenching moans from our throats. She kissed me until I was breathless. Until both of us were breathless. I panted, a smile lifting my lips.

I held the hem of her shirt in my palms, lifted it slightly, then stopped. "May I?"

Kate. Driving.

She gave a hard swallow, then nodded. "Please."

I pulled the shirt over her head and, without breaking our gaze, laid it on the chair where I hung everything that couldn't bring itself to locate a coat hanger.

"Kate." The black bra cradling her breasts created a gorgeous cleavage line down the centre and I exhaled in wonder. This was all so excruciatingly slow and so, so sexy.

"My turn?" She cocked her head and raked her gaze up and down my body, as if deciding where to begin.

Anywhere. You can start anywhere.

"Yes, please." I stepped forward into such a very heated kiss that my clothes could have melted away. That would have saved time.

Her lips traced a line along my jaw and I couldn't help my sigh of desire. For a person who'd expressed how nervous and inexperienced she was, Kate was remarkably good at every detail of this situation. Every. Detail.

Her fingers crept under my shirt, then traced random circles over my stomach, my back, my bra. Goosebumps broke out all over my body. "Oh God, Kate." She had to have felt my nipples jutting against the fabric of my bra.

I was transfixed through my haze of lust, as she swiped her tongue over her bottom lip, as she slowly lifted her gaze, as she puffed up with pride knowing that she was responsible for my body's reactions. We grinned at each other. She was both adorable and so fucking hot.

"You're in control, sweetheart. But I'm literally dying here."

She didn't answer with words. Instead, with a focused frown, she grasped my shirt, flipped it over my head and sent it to join the pile on the chair.

Our jeans were next and probably driven by need, the gymnastics of tight fabric, socks, and shoelaces, we dealt with all of that independently. Suddenly, we were holding each other's waists, sliding our hands around to cup arse cheeks, smoothing over underwear, and pushing our pelvises together. All the while kissing and kissing, and running tongues up throats, and more kissing.

"What happens now?"

I pulled back, noted the flash of vulnerability in Kate's eyes, so I lifted my hand to caress her cheek. Then slid my thumb along her beautifully and thoroughly kissed lips. "Whatever you want to happen."

Kate leaned into my hand. "I...I want more of you."

"You have me, sweetheart." I smiled as I fell into those dark eyes. "Want to know what I'd do?"

"My imagination is running riot," she whispered.

Pulling her to my chest, I ducked my head so I could breathe into her ear. "I'd take the rest of our clothes off and get into bed, then I'd touch your skin. I'd kiss you everywhere. I'd stare into your gorgeous eyes. I ask you what you'd like. I'd like to see you come."

Her shudder was a lit match and the burn in my lower belly, in my clitoris, became an inferno. But Kate clutched me to her chest, her breasts tucked under mine. Her voice was just as quiet.

"I'm forty-eight, Bron. I'm not..." I gave her space to finish. "I'm not in the same shape as I used to be. I've got round bits and soft bits."

"Kate." I gently brought her hands between us. She looked up. "I have never lied to you or blown smoke up your arse or given you a fake compliment." I kissed her knuckles. "You are astonishingly beautiful and I can't wait to worship every part of you."

It was the right thing to say. I knew it. Kate knew it, because her confidence returned, and she released my hands to slide hers behind her back, undoing her bra, and letting it fall away to reveal soft, full, and delectable breasts.

"Ohhh." *Wow.*

"I'd like." She slid her panties down and tossed them to the side. "To worship every bit of you as well."

Well, that did it. Wide-eyed, which made Kate smile, I wrangled my bra and panties so that within a second they'd joined the ever-growing pile of garments.

We ended up on the bed, right in the centre, with the quilt stripped off. Thank goodness for central heating.

I balanced on my elbows, and leaned over Kate's body. "What do you like?"

She blinked, running her hands along my shoulders and arms and into my hair, smoothing my cheek bones as she continued the pattern.

"I...I don't know."

I twisted to the side, brushing my thigh against her clitoris, which produced a soft inhalation-squeak combination that was so ridiculously sexy that I wanted to bypass all the yum and head straight to her also yum sex. Nope. Too fast. So I meandered my fingers over her stomach and breasts, circling the nipples, which elicited gasps and whimpers, and waves of erotic fire were coalescing at my clitoris and all Kate had done to get me in that state was respond to my touch.

I kissed her neck, while my circles became smaller and smaller until I ran my thumbnail over the top of her nipples.

"Oh! That's..." Her eyes blew wide, and she stared at me like I'd found the key to the treasure box.

I smiled and kissed her lips, continuing to stroke and pinch and lightly twist.

"You like that."

"Y-yes." Kate was struggling to speak. Single words of lust.

"Now what do you need?"

Her breathing erratic, her lips shaped into an 'O', the blush on her skin blooming across her chest and up her neck.

"I need you. I...touching and kissing," she managed, her hands fluttering into my hair.

I grinned wickedly. Yes, Kate was driving but I was happy to be her GPS.

"What if I did..." I bent my head and sucked a nipple into my mouth, flicking it with my tongue. "This?"

"Oh! Ah!" I switched to the other nipple. "Yes. Yes, I need a lot of that," she said shakily. I lifted my head and held her gaze.

"I won't do anything you don't want. I hope you know that. But my greatest wish, Kate, is to make you feel so good. May I?"

Despite her lungs working overtime—mine as well—she managed to say with absolute certainty, "I trust you, Bron. I trust you with—" She swallowed, vulnerability flashing through her eyes.

That. That required a thousand kisses, a lifetime of them, but right then, I gave just one. But it carried all the care I would take of her body and her heart and what a gift she was.

I shuffled down to pay attention to her nipples again, this time working the other one with my fingers.

"Oh. Oh, Bron. Oh." Soft cries that synchronised with her fingers in my hair thrilled me.

I lightly bit on the very erect nipple in my mouth.

"Oh, God. Bron."

I was doing this. Kate was feeling so good because of me and I'm positive an aura of happiness was surrounding my heart. Leisurely working my way down Kate's stomach, kissing her skin, returning my fingers to her nipples; it was playing havoc with her breathing because she'd started to hold it, releasing it from her lungs in great gasps and tiny whimpers.

I settled between her legs, awed by the faith she had placed in me. Kate, spread out and trusting. I looked up.

Her lips, parted in ecstasy, sent out one word. "Please."

"I've got you, sweetheart." Then I bent, taking in the trimmed hair and the glistening folds, and licked, not touching her clitoris, and Kate moaned. A moan drawn from her throat to scatter into pieces across the bed.

I kept up the movement, never touching her clitoris, which was swollen and hard.

"Please, please, please, oh, oh!" Kate was unravelling, and I took that as my cue. One upwards stroke and Kate levitated off the bed. "Fuck!" I nearly stopped to laugh at the swear word. I'd remind her of it later.

I kept a steady rhythm, my tongue firm to draw out Kate's orgasm, to tease it from within, and when her cries began and her head tossed about, I held on, my hands holding her thighs, my tongue never stopping.

Suddenly, Kate went rigid, her shoulders lurching forward in pleasure as shudders wracked her body. Her hands clutched at the sheet, great handfuls of the fabric curled into her fingers.

"Bron!"

Then she fell back, her hair fanned out on the pillow, tousled from the climb to her release. Aftershocks vibrated her skin.

To feel Kate's orgasm, to watch it unfurl, to be right there with her; the emotions were too much, because tears, little needles, stung the back of my eyes but I blinked them away. This wasn't about me. Not really.

I rested my cheek against her thigh and waited. She was focussed on the ceiling. I waited because any minute now she would lift her head, tuck her chin into her neck, and stare—

Yep.

I fell into her heated gaze. Her slow smile.

"That was." She cleared her throat and licked her lips. I'd have to let her in on the essential bottle of water on the bedside table business. "That was...I've never felt anything like that."

A smile lifted my lips, and I crawled up her body, leaving raindrop kisses along the way.

"That is the best compliment you can give any woman who's just made you orgasm that hard."

She pulled me into an embrace so that my cheek tucked next to her ear. Her rapid heartbeat pulsed in her veins. "It was extraordinary." The angle of her head told me she'd gone back to looking at the ceiling.

"I will do that for you every day, Kate," I murmured into her skin.

A soft chuckle. "I think I'd expire." Our tight embrace lasted for a long time, while we lightly kissed lips when we caught each other's gaze, gently kissed nearby skin, and our breathing soon synchronised. Then she pushed on my shoulders and I snuck another kiss as I braced over my elbows. She licked her lips and frowned. "Sort of salty but sweet?"

And I realised that most likely she'd never tasted herself. Certainly Neil wouldn't have offered. Arsehole. I forced him out of my head as he had no place being here in this moment. Or any moment.

Straddling her thigh, I rocked forward and a lovely shudder whispered through her body. Then taking advantage of the skin on her neck as she arched in pleasure, I dragged my tongue from collarbone to earlobe. "You are magnificent."

She held my face. "You...you delight me." A statement of wonderment. After a long pause, her eyes narrowed, and she winked, then her lips gave a small playful twitch. "I do believe it's my turn." *Oh God.* Bossy mischievous Kate.

I swallowed, then flipped onto my back, lying spread-eagle on the sheet. "I am a blank canvas." Utter theatrics. I closed my eyes in anticipation.

There was a moment of silence and I cracked an eyelid, squinting as Kate's face came into view.

"Are you okay, sweetheart?"

"This is going to sound so stupid." She shuffled a little bit so her body was snuggled into mine. "But I'm not sure if I can give you what you just gave me. I'm not really—"

This time I didn't let her finish, rolling over and pushing up to smooth her cheek, her lips, her eyebrows.

"Kate. It's not a competition, remember? Giving someone pleasure is like creating art and there are no wrong answers in art. If kissing is where we go, then my body is a choir singing in joy. If you want to explore, I'll provide maps." I grinned. "Just think about what you like to do when you're on your own. When you pleasure yourself."

She blushed adorably. "I can do that."

And so Kate, her ears full of my gasps and moans and thoroughly unhelpful directions such as "Yes!" and "Fuck!" eventually brought her mouth to my clitoris, where she decided that sucking it would be a great idea. *Christ on a clydesdale!* I came within a second.

We lay together on the twisted, wrinkled, mess of a bedsheet, catching our breath, arms and legs draped about each other.

"I guess this means I'm no longer straight." Her words brushed against my chest.

I brought my head back to gaze into her eyes.

"It means that you're Kate Agostino."

We Discovered

⌐◦⌐

June 12 to July 20 in the first year of the now

A week later, we tested out Kate's bed. I was possibly testing its orthopaedic design, good springs that—I had no clue because she had me writhing in pleasure on the mattress. She'd worked out that inserting two fingers while sucking one of my nipples was a sure-fire way to make my head explode.

"Fuuuck!"

So, no. I had no idea whether the bed was comfy. It probably was. Didn't matter. I felt fantastic.

"Bloody hell, Kate." I was a marooned starfish.

She withdrew her fingers, contemplated them for all of two seconds, then licked her middle finger from the base to the tip. Oh my God. My eyes must have been huge, and Kate's face instantly wore a wonderfully smug expression, complete with an eyebrow lift.

"Salty, yet sweet, with a hint of something delightfully tangy." Apparently I was an appetiser on a menu, and the thought made my skin break out in delicious goosebumps.

"Where on earth did you learn that?" I wrapped my arms around her and stared into those amazing eyes, which were currently sparkling with mischief and lust. She held her thumb and two fingers together as if holding up an imaginary book. "What's that?" I smiled at her expression. Wicked. Naughty. Playful.

"That, sweetheart." She wiggled the imaginary book. "Is my visa to enter lesbian land via reputable sites on the internet where I recently spent so, so many hours researching the ways." She held back a grin.

I cracked up. "The ways?"

"Oh, yes. There are many. Want to see what else I discovered?"

I tightened my arms, flipped her over and whispered against her mouth, "First, it is imperative that I have my way with you."

She laughed, then delivered a series of short kisses against my lips. "Imperative?"

"Yes. It looks like you nee—"

Her hands found my breasts and I completely lost my train of thought.

~

OUR TEXTS BECAME FUN SELFIES WITH SWEET—SOMETIMES sexy if no one had witnessed the selfie—messages as we shared more and more of ourselves. In fact, I now knew quite a bit about Kate, and she about me. She tended to clam up about the details of her marriage but I got that. It was obviously a painful part of her history.

I didn't elaborate too much on previous girlfriends. Well, I did tell her about one in particular who had tossed my clothes that were in my closet, in my apartment to which she did not have a key, out the window of my apartment and onto the shared front lawn where she promptly set fire to them. Nice.

Texts and dinners and love-making and hanging out watching crap on TV or just spending hours talking. It was fabulous and perfect, and I just knew Kate wasn't going to be setting fire to my clothes any time soon.

Fire did feature, though. A week out from Kate's birthday, we decided, since the middle of winter was such a very sensible time, to have a bonfire on the beach and stare at the stars. Despite bonfires being illegal—Council fine—and the possibility of plagues of mosquitoes—

necessary packing of bug spray—it simply felt right to have a nighttime picnic. It felt right to sit on a rug on the sand with a woman I was slowly falling in love with. Were there rules for periods of time in which to fall in love? I'd certainly said 'I love you' in four relationships in my adult life. None of which had ended up embodying the gravity of that three-word statement. But here I was, falling and falling and falling in love with Kate, who was intelligent, and funny, and sexy, and beautiful, and kind. In six months. Surely it was too soon, so the three-word sentence stayed locked in my head, even though my heart had mounted its white steed, raised its sword, and was riding to rescue the words from their prison.

Kate picked me up after dark, getting out and tossing the keys to me, which I had to catch one-handed as my other hand gripped the picnic basket that contained enough food so if we wanted to dig into the dunes and become survivalists, we'd be fine.

"I'm driving?" I stared at the black BMW. "Again?" I shook my head sadly. "It's such a hardship, but I'll simply have to grin and bear it."

Kate poked me in the arm as she passed on her way to the other side of the car, relieving me of the basket. Then, with both of us empty-handed, we made our own little Kate-and-Bron bonfire on the footpath. Kissing is an underrated experience sometimes. Incendiary.

"Hi."

Kate smiled. "Hi back."

I still loved the fact that she had to tilt her chin just slightly to look up into my eyes. Never got old. "Are you sure you don't want to drive my car? It's fancy." I raised my eyebrows innocently.

Kate frowned as if considering the option. "Yes, I guess it is. The cracks in the dash are an exact replica of those in the ceiling plaster of the Sistine Chapel."

I blinked, then fell about laughing. "That, Agostino, will earn you a spanking."

Her eyes glittered. "Really?"

I laughed again. "Focus." She smirked. "Thank you for disparaging my vehicular masterpiece." I allowed a pained expression to cross my face, but my eyes gave away how much I enjoyed her teasing.

If we couldn't see each other for a week, we'd call and talk for hours.

Kate had never tried phone sex before so that was a fun lesson. God, she was a quick learner.

I was up to my eyeballs in mid-year reports, which meant I was attempting to cajole two-hundred children ranging in age from five to twelve years to create a folio of six months' worth of their favourite pieces. And annotate each one with a self-reflection.

"I despair for today's youth!" I whined over the phone. Kate laughed.

"You know you sound incredibly old when you say that. As if you should be standing on the front lawn and shaking your fist."

"Ha ha. No, these annotations. The self-reflections. I'm trying to get the kids to explain why they like each piece, what it means to them, blah blah blah. And from a lot of the kids, I get "I like Ms McIntyre" as their entire semester summary."

Kate laughed down the phone. "At least you have a fan-base."

Then there were the wonderful conversations that ebbed and flowed and changed direction and floated in the current.

"Do you get nervous in social situations?" I leant on my elbow and ran a finger down her arm, enjoying the goosebumps.

Kate shivered, her eyes becoming slightly hooded. "No, not really. I've been meeting people all my life and my mother drilled me in decorum and social etiquette because that's how women meet potential husbands." The eye roll was spectacular. "Being an only child meant that the type of people I interacted with were Mum's friends. But." She reached for my hand and kissed my knuckles. "I do become a little more formal when I first step into a social situation." She paused in her kisses. "I don't know. Crisp? Even when it's an informal setting."

She resumed her kisses, then looked up. "What about you? I imagine you're wonderful in large groups."

I twisted our hands so I could repay the knuckle kissing.

"Well, I was going to say I'm always socially awkward but actually I'm not really." Kate raised her eyebrows in an expression of 'I told you so'. "I tend to head in the opposite direction to you. I try to fit in so I become more flippant and irreverent until people are looking at me weirdly and therefore I've defeated my original goal. It works occasionally." Kate's smile was sympathetic but she winked as if she had confirmed an assumption.

Despite Siobhan's commentary on Kate being a figment of my imagination, I'd held off taking her around for dinner. I wanted to spend time with Kate. Have her all to myself, because I just knew that as soon as Siobhan or Janine or Mum or the kids or any of my family met Kate, they'd fall in love with her and she'd be consumed by the masses. It was a stupid thought. Completely irrational.

I decided that Kate's birthday would last for three days because that was the rule in my family and Kate thought it sounded fabulous and immediately declared the rule transferable. Which meant that Friday, Saturday and Sunday consisted of cake consumption, sex, dinners out and in, and lazing on the couch or in bed or on the rug in the lounge and sharing words and smiles.

I reached under the coffee table for the small box that I'd made from heavy cartridge paper, and floated a watercolour wash of blues and greens and white highlights across the surface of the four faces and lid.

"I really had no idea what to get you." I placed the box in her hands, then sat on my own hands, overcome with nerves. "Chocolates and flowers and the amulet of Tutankhamen seemed so passé."Kate looked up as she laughed. "So I thought 'what's something that is important?' It's a step forward in—" pulling my hands out, I flicked my finger between us —"our relationship." Kate's eyes widened, her grip tightened on the gift, and suddenly I realised that my sentence could be interpreted as a ring. Fuck. I quickly got on with the gift-giving. "Um." I was now so stupidly nervous that Kate probably assumed I was signing over everything I owned.

"Bron?" Kate titled her head and frowned. A frown that seemed to encompass a suitcase of questions and thoughts.

Deciding to just get on with it, I pointed to the box. "The box is handmade."

"I know," she said softly.

"Right. But the thing inside isn't handmade, but someone did create it." I went with a palette of open palm-shrug-hopeful-smile which seemed somewhat successful, because Kate gently removed the lid, slid aside the tissue paper, and lifted the shiny metal door key. Her head snapped up.

"Does this?" She tilted her chin at the front door, her gaze not leaving my face. She held the key as if it was made of crystal. "Open that?"

"Yeah." I leaned in, delivered a quick kiss, then pulled away because I was desperate to see—and not see—her reaction.

"Bron." Her throat worked as she swallowed, tears filling her eyes.

I panicked. "Are those good tears? Please tell me they're good tears."

"Bron." Kate pressed her palm to my cheek, her gaze shifting between my eyes and the key in her other hand. She smiled wetly. "They're very good tears. It's a perfect, beautiful present. Thank you. For this." She tipped the key back and forth. "And for this." The kiss was sweet and full and long and enough to tell me what I already knew. For this.

"But I need to give you something," Kate said, after pulling away. She placed the key back into its box, pushed it onto the coffee table, then leapt up, hurried to the bookshelf, returning with a small box tied with a green bow. She delivered it to my hands, then plonked herself back on the couch.

The opening act on my face featured the wrinkled forehead-sort of pulling down of eyebrows combination.

"Kate, is this a birthday present?" I gave her an askance look. "Because mine's not until the 20th. Besides, it's your day, so the rules state that the birthday person can't give gifts."

She grinned. "Well, rules are getting broken all over the place lately. I threw out the rule book when I met you, and I've been so happy since. Rules suck." An emphatic nod accompanied the final sentence, which was adorable and insanely sexy when uttered in Kate's well-modulated voice. She wriggled like a kid—also adorable—and kissed me. "This is only because it feels right to give it to you today. So, happy birthday," she pointed to the box, "fourteen days early."

I laughed.

Kate kissed me again. As she pulled away, a whispered, "Doesn't mean you don't get another present on your actual day" drove shivers up and down my spine. Another set joined in when she sent me a scorching, heated look. I visualised unwrapping a Kate Agostino-shaped present and my eyes must have glazed as I drifted off into that fantasy, because Kate poked my thigh and laughed.

"Open your gift, you sex maniac."

The box, basically the same size as the one I'd used, opened via one of those fancy twisty lids that formed part of the three-dimensional structure. I threw Kate an amused look.

"I couldn't help myself." She laughed. "But yours is prettier."

With the lid untwisted into a square, I fossicked about in the tissue paper and found the purple crane. I smiled to myself. I'd find out its meaning soon.

"There's something else."

I delved into the tissue paper and when my fingers felt cold metal, I gasped.

"No," I whispered. I carefully opened the paper, and tucked underneath was a bronze-coloured key, nearly an exact copy of the one I'd given Kate. I whipped my head up and stared.

She grabbed the skin on her index finger between her teeth, her forehead wrinkling in what looked like a classic case of gift anxiety. "It's...the crane...it's for...it's for love." Forty-nine-year-old Kate was a nervous, anxiety-riddled mess, who had made me a purple paper crane because I'm sure she just said she loved me and also oh my God she gave me a key to her apartment on the same day that I'd given her one to mine because we were on the same wavelength and Jesus Christ I loved this woman.

"Kate." I huffed through my smile and shook my head in disbelief. "This is a beautiful gift. Both of them. Thank you." I delivered a soft, very tender kiss, and Kate visibly relaxed, her shoulders dropping as if gravity had worked out how to function.

"I didn't want to be presumptuous."

I hummed. "Along with the other words you say during sex, please say presumptuous. I'll melt off the furniture."

Kate laughed, leaning back into the couch. "You know? If this keeps up..." Kate raised an eyebrow and flicked a finger between our identical gifts. "We'll be mind-reading in no time which makes for interesting foreplay." Then a flash of nerves whisked through her eyes. "So it's okay?"

Returning the crane and key to their box, I spun around and tackled Kate so she ended up under me, her gaze hooded. But she couldn't hide the joy.

"It's very okay. Mine?"

"Oh, yes."

"Mind-reading, hey? What am I thinking right now?"

She bit her bottom lip. Yum.

"That we should take the laptop to bed and buy a toy from that website you showed me. It should arrive by your birthday." Then she cracked up, probably at my expression, and kissed me hard.

So now, no knocking on apartment doors. Just the sound of a key, a loud "Hey sweetie, you there?" and the depositing of takeaway on the bench. It felt exceptionally, exceptionally weird at first and neither of us wanted to use the keys at all, almost as if they were made of kryptonite or some other type of dangerous substance. Artificial preservatives, perhaps.

But I came home a couple of days before my birthday and found a white crane on the bench next to a little note.

IT FLEW AWAY SO I CHASED IT. EVENTUALLY IT ARRIVED HERE which delighted me. This one is for love.

THE IMPORTANT THREE WORDS. SHE HADN'T ACTUALLY SAID them. Well, she had.

"But through the medium of crane," I said in a low flamboyant voice, and placed the origami in the wooden bowl.

I guess I was waiting for the actual spoken words. However, I couldn't explain why Kate had to be the one to say it first. No idea.

"You want to say it," I growled. "So say it!"

I was mulling over my idiocy as we drove to Mum and Dad's place for my birthday dinner. Kate had questioned why I hadn't suggested dinner with them ages ago. And then again two weeks ago. I couldn't tell her that I didn't want to share. That sounded very...controlling. Fuck. Took a while to get there, didn't it, Sherlock? Fuck.

So, here we were, driving to my parents place, after telling them that I had invited Kate for my birthday dinner, to which Mum replied, "Finally," and Siobhan, obviously hearing the news from Mum, sent me a message with a screenshot of the Veris homepage containing Kate's photo, and the text, "This Kate? Oh, be still my beating heart." Janine was more understanding.

"You can't stop people doing things, Bron. I know you're not like that and you were protecting yourself more than anything else. You were worried about us being too much and that she'd feel overwhelmed and potentially leave you."

She used her special psychologist's voice when she knew she was right.

"I'm excited to meet everyone," Kate said, quickly glancing from her concentration on the road. She'd decided that she wasn't drinking tonight as meeting my family would be intoxicating enough without alcohol thrown into the mix.

"They're excited to meet you. Believe me." I inhaled deeply, giving her thigh a soft squeeze. "I'm sure you'll win everyone over."

Kate smiled. "Thank you." This was followed by a short laugh. "I don't think my mother will know how to respond to your humour when you meet. She'll be just that little bit late to the punchline as she tries to work out whether your dry humour is a true statement or simply funny commentary."

"I'm meeting your mum?" I squeaked. Kate giggled.

"Well now, that sounds like a woman who has shown her cards. My mother is not at all scary, sweetheart. I mean, I'm petrified and so are the staff at the regional office, but other than that, she's a pussy cat. You'll be fine."

This time her thigh got an extra hard squeeze, which only served to make her laugh harder.

Deciding that just before we arrived and the crowd descended upon Kate, I should remind her of the various human and name combinations.

"I know I told you about who's who, but do you want a refresher?"

"Sure. It helps."

"Okay. So, Janine and Rick's kids. Phillipa is Pip and according to Pip, she will not be entering into any discussion regarding her name. It's Pip."

"Pip. So noted." Kate nodded seriously, a small smile on her lips.

"The twins have also edited their names because who names their twins Jackson and Jaqueline?" I sighed. "Siobhan and I reckon Rick was having a toilet break when Janine signed the birth certificates because there's no way th—"

Kate's laughter filled the car's interior. "I remember. Jack and JJ, right?"

"Yep. Jack's thrilled to be a boy and very grateful for the hormones that force him to masturbate." I took my hand off Kate's thigh to air quote the word 'force'. Kate had started giggling. "JJ's still working things out. It's all fairly fluid. Each time I visit, I check JJ's t-shirt because there is always a pin with the gender of the day. Last time I visited, the gender was coffee. I wasn't quite sure what pronoun to work with there."

A hum, just holding the giggle at bay, drifted over. "Dark roast? Blend? Latte?"

I threw her a grin. "I went with Ice Coffee, and after two seconds abbreviated it to Ice. I used it every chance I could. Eventually Ice glared at me, instructed me to piss off, then slunk off to the bedroom." I shrugged. "Twelve-year-olds are very articulate." The oncoming headlights highlighted Kate's lips squeezed together. Her composure was masterful. "They know I'm the one who really gets it and supports them without judgement, so I can get away with a bit of teasing. Janine and Rick try but slip up occasionally and JJ comes down hard. God, it's super challenging being a parent."

We drove along in silence for another kilometre.

"Did you ever want kids?" Kate asked quietly.

I didn't hesitate. "Fuck, no. Oops."

Her smile was indulgent.

"You?"

Kate breathed out through her nose. "I thought about it, but I believe people should have a one-hundred percent commitment to the idea, the action, the human. And I really didn't."

We Declared

❦

July 20 in the first year of the now

As soon as we entered the house, Siobhan was first to the foyer, having sprung up and power-walked from the lounge room. She could have qualified for the Olympic team with that demonstration. Hardly subtle. Her pink-tipped hair swished about—a walking billboard for her salon—as she came to a halt in front of Kate. It was my birthday but I'd brought the present, apparently.

"Hi, Kate. I'm Siobhan but you can call me Shiv. Or Siobhan. It's up to you. It's so nice to meet you finally." She glared at me. "Happy birthday, by the way." She returned to Kate, who wore a bemused expression.

"Siobhan, it's lovely to meet you, too."

"Bron." Apparently I existed. "Why don't you take a seat and I'll introduce Kate to everyone?" If I didn't know better, I would swear Siobhan had a tiny crush on Kate, who she'd met five seconds ago. Siobhan, who was the partner of Paul, the loveliest man in the world who could fix anything and would walk over coals for her, was crushing on my girlfriend.

"That sounds wonderful, but I know how important Bron's family is to her, so I'd love to hear her perspective. However." She gently clasped Siobhan's forearm. "It would be lovely to sit next to you at dinner if that's okay, so we can chat some more." The pure class in that response nearly unravelled me right there. I would have had to apologise to my family, bundle Kate outside, and kiss her senseless.

I duly escorted Kate into the lounge room to a chorus of 'Happy birthday'—everyone, and 'Kate!'—Mum, and—'Wonderful to meet you'—everyone, and—'That skirt is gorgeous'—also Mum, and 'You're really pretty'—Pip. Jack stared, another crush blossoming right there. Uh huh.

Mum announced that presents wouldn't happen until after dinner, and so we made our way to the table, which was covered in platters, plates, bowls, cutlery, and wine glasses, even for the kids who scored grape juice, although JJ announced with an aggrieved sigh how truly disgusting grape juice was and why couldn't they have Coke if they must drink from a glass made for grapes that had gone off.

During the introductions before dinner, JJ informed us that the gender of the day was Shimmering Galaxy. The announcement forced a sigh from Janine and Rick, made Mum and Dad look somewhat befuddled, dispatched automatic shrugs from the shoulders of Jack, Pip and Paul, and ensured that Siobhan, Kate and I desperately avoided meeting each other's gaze for at least five minutes. The pronouns for Shimmering Galaxy were they and them, apparently, "Because a galaxy is a collection of stars and therefore in that context they and them are rather suitable." Shimmering Galaxy then exhaled elaborately and disappeared in search of the stash of contraband Coke. JJ was a precious gem, an absolute unicorn, and I was determined to protect them from the world forever but far out they were a hoot.

The eleven of us were comfortably arranged around the twelve-seater table that had been in Mum's family for a generation. Paul worked his magical craftsman skills on it last year when the wood split right across the middle, giving an excellent impression of a footballer waving at the coach to take them off because they were done. Paul was the wood whisperer because when the restored piece of furniture was presented to Mum and Dad on their anniversary, it could have been the fresh recruit ready for their first game. Mum had sobbed all over Paul's shoulder, and Dad clapped him on the back with a "Thanks, mate", receiving a "No worries" in return.

The menu consisted of a range of dishes harvested from a range of continents but it always worked. Nobody cared if Pip ate naan bread with her spaghetti or if Jack decided that crumbed chicken breast should be slathered in hoisin sauce. We McIntyres did our own thing, and Kate looked thrilled. She beamed at me, then attended to her plate, pushing aside the three dumplings which were awaiting their culinary passport, and cut into the lasagne.

After the birthday toast and the "Forty-three! Oh man, you're old!" declaration from Pip, conversations split and merged and split with that flexibility that occurs when people share food during a wonderful celebration.

After I'd served myself, I'd immediately cut up all my food so that I could eat one-handed and warm Kate's thigh with the other. Resting my hand there felt right, and happiness radiated from every pore.

Janine asked one of those questions that act like house lights going down before a show. "How have you been coping since the divorce?" The hush was immediate.

I could have leant across the table and impaled her hand to the spring roll on her plate.

Kate placed her cutlery carefully and smiled. I knew her smiles. This was the tight 'I'm not comfortable answering' smile.

"It's been absolutely fine, thanks Janine." It's. Not I. It's. That's what I usually received as well. Like she was walking away from the discussion, which was fair enough because it was no one else's business. But that particular avoidance strategy seemed very well-practiced.

It still didn't stop me from stepping in, haphazardly brandishing a metaphorical sword. "J, come on. Don't go all psychology 101 on Kate. It's my birthday and I say no shop talk from anyone. Do you see me waffling on about teaching? No." I pointed at each person. "No books and catalogue stuff"—Mum—"No enginey piston thingies"—Dad—"No dead cats"—Rick—"No broken ends"—Siobhan—"No building buildery whatevers"—Paul—"And definitely no child somethings"—my finger point collected all three kids who giggled in delight. I grinned at Kate. "And no tax palaver from you either." Her eyes sparkled, and while she muttered "Okay" in mock seriousness, I knew her 'okay' was a thank you. She didn't need Neil and all of that shit brought up. Not when there was caramel mud cake from the supermarket, profiteroles and jam tarts to eat.

JJ, clearly reading the room, pinned Kate with a stare. "Aunty Bron says you can make origami cranes. Could you teach me?"

"Please," Mum and Janine instructed simultaneously, and JJ rolled their eyes.

"Please."

Kate laughed. "Of course. After dinner?" She directed the question to Mum, who gave a Mum-hum at the kids. The short, monotone version that means 'Yes' or 'Possibly if you're good' or 'If you don't clean up this mess, there won't be any treats for the next four hundred years'. I was going with 'Yes'.

"Sounds lovely. Perhaps all the kids might like to have a go. Actually, I've always wanted to try that as well. Pip, could you check in the art box in the spare room for some paper, please?" She gave a single clap of her hands. "Right. That's dinner and dessert everyone. You're all responsible for anything else after this. Now, David, Rick and Paul have decided to wash up." Rick blinked in surprise, having clearly not paid attention to any passive-aggressive statements from Mum over the last twelve years. *You'd think he'd catch on.* Dad and Paul simply nodded.

We ended up in the lounge room, adults arranged on the various pieces of non-matching furniture that Dad had collected over the years; a habit which Mum adored. We called it 'Op-Shop Transitional'.

The kids frowned in concentration as Kate very patiently took them through the process, backtracking when Pip sighed dramatically and grumbled about the difficulty of *everything*. Mum followed along from her armchair. It was cozy and I felt the smile lift the corners of my lips. So many families couldn't work, wouldn't work, or simply shouldn't. But mine did. Our pieces fit.

Kate climbed to her feet, and walked over to sit on the arm of my recliner chair. I made to stand but she gently pressed on my shoulder.

"I'm fine." Her gaze was affectionate. I knew she'd had a fun night because it was written all over her face, then something else whisked through her gaze. *Oh.* I hadn't really seen it in previous girlfriends but I didn't need photo evidence. It was there. Love. All the big, the small, the encompassing, the realisation. It was there.

I had to tell her tonight.

Not in front of my family who'd probably shout or make kissing noises or something else embarrassing.

"Do your colleagues know about Bron yet?" Dad cupped his sherry glass and tilted his head towards Kate. Paternal protection had arrived and his question contained questions inside questions. I'd been wondering the same thing but Kate needed to come out in her own time. It did sting a little that perhaps she hadn't spoken about me to anyone at all.

"Yes. That's a point," Janine added rather pointlessly.

Siobhan chimed in. "Do you reckon—"

Tension worked its way into Kate's muscles and I could feel her becoming more rigid as the questions gathered steam. Before I could wave my sword about, a soft voice issued from the couch.

"Leave her alone, you lot." Paul looked for all the world like he hadn't said a word; back curled into the furniture, his legs spread slightly. Only his head was turned to nod at Kate. Everyone paused, slightly stunned. Siobhan stared at her partner.

Paul wasn't finished. "Look, it's like me and my shed. I know." He swung his gaze to Siobhan. "That you say I'm in there hiding out but I'm not. I make stuff and fix stuff for around the house so the landlord doesn't do his block when we whinge at him. But you never hassle me and tell me to get out of there and come inside. It's like you know that I'll come out when I'm done. I'll come out and everything is hunky dory, isn't it?" He turned to Kate, flicking a finger her way. "Same with Kate. She'll come out of her shed when she's ready."

It was the largest collection of sentences Paul had strung together in years. The silence in the room was encompassing.

Then Siobhan barked out a laugh.

"I reckon Kate would rather come out of a fucking fancy closet, hon, than a shed."

The ensuing laughter, coupled with Janine's glare at Pip, JJ, and Jack as if by the power of her eyeballs, she could roll up their ears and muffle the swearing, melted the moment and everyone grinned at Kate. But I studied Siobhan whose eyes had filled with tears. She slid her hand across the stubble on Paul's cheek, and leaned forward to gently kiss his lips. I caught her "I love you so freaking much, you have no idea," and the gravelly response; "Just saying what I think, you know? And Shiv, love? I adore you."

I squeezed Kate's thigh, feeling her tension ease, then I sat forward.

"Hey! Why does sweary Siobhan always get a free pass and I don't?"

Siobhan, having snuggled into Paul's side, grinned at me.

"Well." If Mum began with 'well', it was assumed that there would be no further discussion. "Because you apologise, Bron, and Siobhan doesn't, and we've given up trying to change her."

"Well, that's bullshit."

Everyone, even the kids, turned to me and chorused, "Shit. Swearing. Sorry" and laughter filled the room.

I blushed.

"Fine." I made sure that my accompanying huff sounded suitably aggrieved. Kate giggled, leaning into my shoulder.

"Gorgeous *and* adorable."

Mum's voice cut through the hilarity. "Kate. I noticed you joining in there. Proves you're part of the family now, you know. Giving Bron shit is a McIntyre tradition."

My hands tipped over in the internationally recognised gesture of "Seriously?"

Mum chuckled. "Kate obviously doesn't let you get away with any rubbish, therefore I like her. So does David."

Dad winked at me. "I've never really taken to your other girl-friends." His shrug was apologetic but mostly matter of fact.

"That's because they've been really toxic," Janine muttered into her wine.

"I've always wanted the best for my girls and that includes love and happiness." There was a bit of a wobble in Mum's voice. "I can see that you two have something special and Bron is happy, which means I'm happy. So welcome to the McIntyre family, Kate. We're quite mad but friendly." She held up her wine glass, raised her eyebrows and collected everyone with her direct gaze, waited until drinks were at the ready, juice boxes included, and declared, "To Kate and Bron." The toast echoed around the room, and as the words quietly melted into the four walls, Mum looked at Kate. "I hope you'll be on her arm for a long time."

My eyes filled with tears and a quick glance at Kate showed that she was in the same situation. We held hands in my lap.

"Thank you, Michelle." Kate's quiet message of gratitude drifted across the currents in the room but Mum heard it because she nodded slowly as if everything in the world was in its correct place.

Later, leaning against the bench as Janine puttered about the kitchen, I commented on Mum's speech.

"That was unexpected."

Janine shoved the cheeses onto the top shelf in the fridge, then came to join me, both of us leaning over our elbows and staring into the lounge room.

"What was?"

"Mum's congratulations speech. The toast."

"Mm. I think a lot of that is Kate's doing, you know, rather than yours."

"Nice."

"You know what I mean. She's delightful."

I sighed. "I know. She's incredible."

"Mm," she repeated and I angled my head.

"Mm? That's a psychologist 'Mm'."

Janine tsked. "It's not. It's the 'Mm' of a middle sister who sees things." She shifted to face me. "Don't stuff this up, Bron."

I frowned. "Gees, J. I won't." My hiss carried the words.

"I'm just commenting. You tend to become a little laissez faire about paying attention to people. Taking them for granted a bit. That sort of thing."

I glared. "J, I'd never stop paying attention to Kate. I couldn't. She's amazing."

Janine held her hands up in surrender. "Okay. Just an observation."

"No more observing."

She smiled. "A final one. Kate's lovely."

I chuckled. "Good observation."

"You two are sweet together."

My pause was longer than the normal space between the to-ing and fro-ing in a sisterly conversation and Janine looked at me quizzically. I didn't meet her eyes.

"I love her."

"Does she know that?"

"Not yet." I stared at the bench top.

"Then I'm going to pretend I didn't hear that sentence because I'm not the first person you should say it to." Janine watched me draw circles in the bench. "When are you telling her?"

"Tonight." I looked up and found myself captured in my sister's smile.

"Good." She flung an arm over my shoulders. "You're happy."

I straightened and turned the shoulder hug into a proper embrace. "I am."

"Then don't fuck it up."

~

"YOUR FAMILY IS WONDERFUL. I LIKED THEM A LOT." An enormous smile seemed to light up the interior of the car. I grinned in return and fiddled with the heating. Winter and nighttime driving meant fluctuations between cold and colder.

"Well, they *loved* you," I said.

"I had the best time, Bron. The kids—" She tapped the steering wheel. "JJ is fabulous. I was never that confident or self-aware at twelve. And Siobhan! Oh my goodness, what a force."

I laughed. "Siobhan is a foul-mouthed firecracker, but she would defend her family, people she loves, anyone who needed defending, to the death. She has the biggest heart but hides it behind profanity."

"The balance that she and Paul have is lovely." Kate turned into my street because she'd promised a sleepover as one of my birthday presents and my stomach tingled in anticipation.

The tingles shot through my body when, in the elevator, Kate took three very slow, slinky steps towards me, and wrapped her fingers around the railing on either side of my body. Her eyes, dark with desire, had me licking my bottom lip as all the moisture left my mouth.

"Do you know what I want to do?" she purred.

My inhalation was very measured. "No, but I'm so looking forward to it."

The elevator pinged and the doors opened. *Damn.* Or maybe not because Kate and dark eyes and long hair and slinky seductiveness and— I grabbed her hand, and she giggled at my eagerness as I led her down the corridor and into my apartment.

"Do you want to go down to the car and collect your presents?" She closed my front door and turned, only to discover that I'd stepped into her space. My hands found her waist.

"No. I'll leave them down there. We could have another drink or—" I lifted my chin towards the bedroom, and raised my eyebrows.

Kate laughed. "Hold on. I have something to give you before I give you...me."

Gah. Puddle of goo.

She twisted out of my embrace and made her way to the wooden bowl, three-quarters full of her cranes. She plucked out the most recent. The white one. Then returned to meet my gaze. Her expressive eyes flared with affection and happiness, and the emotion I'd seen at dinner.

"This is my other gift." She placed it in my palm.

"But..." I blinked. "You've already given me this."

"No, I haven't. That crane," she glanced at it, "is for love." She stared into my face. "I gave the crane to you, Bron, because I love your humour." She stepped closer. "I love your beauty. Your dedication. There is so much about you to love. So the crane?" She placed her arms around my neck. "I gave it to you because I'm giving you my heart." I swallowed. "I love you, Bron. So very, very much. The *you*."

Then she kissed me and it was the sweetest, strongest, softest kiss ever. My tears had begun while holding the crane, so I placed it on the hall table, and gazed at Kate.

"Thank you for loving me." I flicked away my tears. "You're such a gift and you're," my breath hitched, "giving me your heart." I held her face and smoothed my thumbs across her cheek bones. "For a while, I've been determined to say something and tonight seemed perfect and it's not because you said it. It's because I want to." I kissed her lightly. "I love you, Kate, with everything I am." My voice trembled. "I love you."

Our kisses held our hearts and later when we made love, it wasn't the sweaty, sheet-destroying version I'd envisaged. That night, we made love to share our hearts some more. And it was perfect.

We Celebrated

December 3 to December 25 in the first year of the now

Being in love was like watching the grandest sunset on the calmest ocean where the tiniest ripples wore silver sparkles as their hats.

We floated on that beautiful ocean for months, spending nights and nights at each other's apartments, spending days and days messaging and talking, sitting so close that after a while lying down became a more comfortable option, which led to other interesting activities.

At work I was clearly wearing the Badge of the Besotted because one Tuesday lunch time in early December, Lydia sat heavily on the bench seat across from me, flipped her blonde braid over her shoulder and leaned her elbows on the table.

"Nice day today." That was true. The temperatures had been creeping up in the day and the hum of air conditioners vibrated the air in the city.

I paused in my sandwich consumption. "It is." Her gaze didn't waver.

Then she pointed emphatically at my face. "Right, so weather report done. I've left you alone for days, weeks, veritable eons because clearly you've been in no fit state to speak coherently. I've sent you the odd wave, the briefest hello, a smile from across four thousand metres of grass on the oval, but!" She glared. "As a friend and colleague, I would like to know her name, her birthdate, her star sign and all sorts of measurements except the ones that make me stick my fingers in my ears and go 'la la la'."

My smile grew slowly.

"That!" she exclaimed. "That is why I've left you alone because who needs people all up in their business when your face does that. When your face tells people you've got a crush, or a friend with so, so many benefits, or when you're in love."

My smile grew.

"Oh, Jesus Christ, McIntyre. You've gone and done it. Finally!" She raised her hands in a dramatic gesture worthy of one of Siobhan's.

"Want to see a photo?" I plucked out my phone.

"Does the Pope shit?"

I squinted at her, then bent my head, scrolling through the bazzillion photos of Kate, me with Kate, Kate with trees behind her, Kate with flowers, Kate in her car, next to her car, on the lounge, looking over her shoulder. Finding the one I wanted—Kate, all windblown hair and sexy eyes and her beauty pouring out of the rectangle—I swivelled the phone around.

Lydia peered at the screen, then snatched the phone from my hand. "Fuck me. She's gorgeous." She looked up then back to the photo. "What's her name?"

"Kate." I couldn't hide the grin.

Lydia returned the phone and cupped her chin in her palm. Her other hand rolled over itself as if to indicate that she required the rest of the story. So I filled her in. Chaos man, damp clothing—her eyebrows rose—meetings at the bridge, coffee dates, soft kisses—"You were gone on her by then, weren't you?"—dates at each other's homes, in restaurants—"Nope. *That's* when you were gone"—and cranes and keys and birthday dinners.

I left out the 'I love you' moment.

"Oh my God. This is a romance novel. The lesbian version which I wouldn't know anything about but it can't be too much of a leap from the bodice rippers with buff bods and heaving bosoms."

"Well, no, actually, there is a huge diff—"

"You've told her you love her, haven't you."

"How the fuck do you know that?"

"Your expression," she circled her finger at my face, "says 'I finally told my girlfriend that I love her and I'm so excited that I need Lydia to sit with me at lunch so I can babble about how wonderful my girlfriend is because I know Lydia won't mind that I took fucking months to let people know'."

I laughed. "You're right, actually. I've been so nervous about our relationship that I didn't want anything to jinx it."

Lydia huffed. "As if. You're Bron McIntyre. Life is super smooth for you, and I don't think you even realise it. I mean, you even have parents slip-sliding on your Teflon."

"Well, Teflon aside, I wanted to take small steps with Kate. Small steps with telling people. I didn't invite her to meet my family until July."

"July?" A bark of laughter followed. "I bet that went down well." Last year we'd decided to hold my birthday party at a local Vietnamese restaurant and I'd invited Lydia. She and Siobhan had got on like a house on fire. I figured Lydia was visualising Siobhan's and other family member's faces at the delay.

"I think I'm meeting her mum at Christmas." I grimaced, and Lydia squinted at my expression.

"Kate's mum is..."

"Olivia Agostino, the general manager of all of the Harris Supermarkets in Melbourne. She's a force at sixty-eight and probably not retiring until she's a hundred and not pleased that Kate decided to divorce her dickhead husband. She's suggesting strongly that dickhead ex-husband might still be a catch." I exhaled loudly.

"That's an opinion." Lydia rested her elbows on the table again. "Does she know about you and Kate?"

I closed my eyes for a moment, then found Lydia studying me. "No."

"Because..?"

"Because Kate hasn't come out to her mum yet and is vacillating about the idea." I grit my teeth in frustration, and Lydia lifted her index finger, pointed, then dropped it down.

"Teflon, Bron. What are you now? Forty-three? You told me that you came out to your parents when you were twenty and all they did was announce how pretty a rainbow flag would look in the lounge room as it matched the furniture." She tipped her head. "Kate's coming out might take a while. Perhaps that particular flag doesn't coordinate with her mum's soft furnishings."

I pushed my fingers against my eyelids. "You're right."

"That's what my kiddos say."

"They're eight-year-olds."

"And wise beyond their years."

SCHOOL FINISHED FOR THE YEAR AND I STARTED THE Christmas-through-to-end-of-January holidays which never failed to irritate the rest of the workforce. What people didn't realise is that I spent most of the time planning next year's curriculum for six grade levels, finding and developing resources, sorting and archiving children's work with the hope that those kids who'd moved up a grade level would take the extraneous work home in February. Hardly a holiday where I was lying on the beach each day.

The concept of coming out came up again the following week when I asked Kate if she'd thought more about it and would it be a possibility and when did she think she'd do it? Unbelievable. I had no filter. I really needed to stop comparing my coming out experience to Kate's. I really needed to stop taking my experience for granted. I really needed to shut my mouth. No wonder Kate was becoming irritated.

"I'm still not sure." Kate sat up from where she'd been lying on the couch, her eyes closed in bliss, directly across from the wall-mounted air-conditioning system. She turned to me square on and shrugged.

I sighed at her indecision and the shrug. "Just take the leap, Kate. What's the worst that can happen?" My hand flip was probably the last straw because she stood up and marched into the kitchen for a glass of wine.

"The worst that can happen, Bron?" Her voice travelled on waves of frustration from the glass cabinet. "I'd be ostracised by my straight friends, even if they are vacuous and self-absorbed. They're still my friends, I guess. My work colleagues might find the idea distracting. And!" She came back to the couch. "I'll most likely alienate my mother, who, even though she drives me to distraction, is still my mother and I'd rather not experience that consequence." Her voice was clipped.

After a large gulp, she plonked the glass on the coffee table, and sat heavily. "Then she will tell everyone she knows even though she'd be mortified by my news. The need to gossip would outweigh the mortification, particularly as she'd receive sympathy about her wayward daughter who not only divorced a lovely man but decided to become one of those lesbians." She growled, plucked up her wine, took another large swallow, and set it back on the table. After a moment, she turned to me and sighed.

"Shall I tell her I'm a lesbian?"

"Are you?"

"I don't know! Where's the catalogue with all the options?"

I laughed. "Oh, Kate."

"What?" Her frown was Oscar-worthy.

"You're whoever you want to be."

Her frown was still in place but now its message was one of helplessness. "What should I tell my mother?"

My smile was mischievous. "That you've been abducted by a lesbian who injected you with mind-altering chemicals and turned you into a sapphic Goddess."

Kate leaned over and poked my shoulder. "Be serious."

I laughed, then stroked her arm. "Okay. I'm sorry your mum is going to be a hard nut to crack."

"I don't know if I should even bother."

I tried not to feel the little sting of hurt. I'd had a girlfriend ages ago who'd been in the closet and I understood it. Really I did. But to be constantly reduced to 'this is my flatmate', 'this is my friend', 'this is my good buddy', 'this is my pet dog' totally sucked.

"I don't want to talk about this any more." Kate hoisted her glass. "Let's decorate the tree. It's only nine days until Christmas." Then she realised that I hadn't been offered wine. "Oh, sweetheart. Sorry. Let me get you a glass."

Our tree, which we'd decided to put up in Kate's living room as there was more space, was one of those plastic versions—a real tree in an Australian summer was plain stupid—with the fairy lights already installed. I was incredibly grateful for that feature because I'd always been the one in my family who'd been volunteered to string them and the amount of "Shit. Swearing. Sorry"s I'd muttered was ridiculous.

Another glass of wine followed, then another—in celebration for each decoration—and eventually the placement of various baubles and garlands of tinsel became more haphazard. Our tree took on a distinct list to starboard.

Kate found some Christmas music from somewhere and we slow-danced to 'White Christmas' which we found hysterical and eventually we ended up in the bedroom, kissing, making love, and falling asleep.

CHRISTMAS DAY BEGAN THE SAME WAY, ALBEIT AT MY PLACE, with slow lazy sex, teasing the orgasms from our bodies by trailing fingers and sliding tongues and dropping kisses onto skin that heated the sheet beneath us. We dashed out of the bedroom at the same time, which made us giggle, to retrieve the gifts we'd organised for each other. Kate gave me a crane, the underside of the wings filled with tiny writing explaining all the reasons why she loved me. My tears were instantaneous. My gift was a watercolour painting of a sunflower—her favourite flower—which I'd spent ages on to make it perfect because watercolours weren't really my best medium. I'd used Yellow Gum as the wood for the frame to match the hues of the piece and Kate must have loved it based on her reaction—adorable squeals and kisses.

Then we joined the mania of the McIntyre Christmas hosted by Janine and Rick this year as it was their turn. JJ met us at the door and informed us that the day's gender was Rough Riding Reindeer. I caught Siobhan's eye and glared, reinforced by pointing. Images of rough riding were a literal thought cloud above her head, but despite the smirk, I knew she wouldn't say anything. Her level of respect for JJ's genders and pronouns was pretty much on par with mine. However, I was absolutely positive that while JJ had worked out the collection of genders she'd like to wrap herself inside, she'd kept up the practise so she could announce the most extreme, nonsensical genders simply to stupefy her parents. Her evil grin when she explained that she/them were the day's pronouns seemed to make Rick's face ache.

Christmas lunch was, as per normal, a pot luck of meat cold cuts, two cooked chooks, four different types of bread, multiple salads, two pavlovas and various sweets with ice cream. It was chaotic and wonderful. All the adults participated in Secret Santa, which had been organised two weeks prior—I ended up with a set of Palomino Pearl pencils which was over the set budget and I wondered who my Secret Santa was to gift me such fabulous art gear—and the kids each received a big present that we'd all chipped in for. The air conditioner blasted across the living room and Paul and Dad fell asleep in their armchairs, both wearing purple party hats and necklaces made of tinsel. It was perfect.

Then it was on to Olivia's for dinner.

Halfway along the highway, I opened my mouth again because obviously I hadn't made my stupid point clear enough.

"I was serious the other day. You could, you know." I glanced at her as she sat in the passenger seat all loose and relaxed and gorgeous.

"What?" she murmured languidly.

"Come out to your mum."

Kate stiffened, then shuffled backwards to sit upright. "You're pushing me, Bron." Her voice flattened.

"I'm not." My teeth filtered the sigh. "I just want to be recognised. I'm too old to be the flatmate, Kate. I can't do that any more."

I caught the movement of her fists clenching. "I'm not going to be guilted into something I need time to come to terms with myself."

"You've had a year to do that." *Excellent, brain. Well done.*

"There's a time limit for coming out?" She pivoted in her seat. "Will a buzzer go off telling me time's up?"

"Don't be snarky."

Acres of silence crammed into the car.

"Bron. My mother expected me to bring Neil tonight." Her voice contained great handfuls of sadness.

I whipped my head sideways to stare at her for longer than the driver's manual recommended. Kate continued to peer out of the windscreen, but she smoothed her hand across my thigh.

"What? But..." My irritation at Kate redirected itself towards Olivia and her meddling.

"I know. She still holds on to the hope that we'll reconnect."

I blinked. "You're divorced."

"Yes." It was an emphatic 'yes'.

But I had to check. "And unlikely you'll get back together?"

"Completely unlikely." The thigh smoothing paused as I felt her studying my face.

"What did she say?"

Kate laughed humourlessly. "Katherine, sweetheart. You've had your moment of frivolity. I think it's time you apologised, settled down with Neil and worked on your relationship."

"Wow." *Katherine? That's like when I get Bronwyn because I know I'm in deep shit.*

The thigh smoothing restarted. "Please don't push. I know how important coming out is, and I promise I'm not denying you. Just give me time. That's all I need." She squeezed my leg. "Love me for me, sweetheart, not for how far I can fling the door open. Please." There were tears in her voice and I felt like such an arsehole. There I was; twenty-three years out of a closet; a closet so far behind me that it was road kill. I took it for granted that coming out was easy for everyone.

So, we arrived at dinner, and I was completely aware that I'd be the flatmate, although because Kate was Kate, I'd probably be the best friend who she lunched with, and then we went shopping together at the fancy stores on Graham Street.

Olivia met us at the door.

"Katherine! Merry Christmas!" She kissed Kate's cheeks and smiled somewhat curiously at me. A small worry niggled that perhaps Kate hadn't even mentioned me arriving for Christmas at all. I quickly banished it.

Olivia sailed ahead into the rather formal sitting room—it was definitely not a lounge room—leaving Kate to close the door. Her hand gestured vaguely for us to take a seat.

"Is this the friend you've mentioned?" The question was clearly for Kate but she smiled at me. I breathed out. I had been spoken about which was reassuring. I wouldn't be an anonymous person off the street that Kate had felt sorry for. I hurled my snark back into the corner.

"Hello dear, it's delightful that Katherine has found a new friend. She seems to have cast aside her others so it's no wonder she's been rather depressed of late." Olivia turned her gaze to Kate. "I've noticed how distracted you've been." The distraction was definitely me, us, sex, and being in love. That was enough to distract anyone from their mother's meddling.

It wasn't a jolly pre-dinner experience. Kind of like new sheets which you forget to prewash so you end up lying on stiff cardboard. That sort of not-jolly. Kate gave her mum a crystal figurine and after scanning the room and not finding any sign of other crystal figurines, I reckoned the gift was one of those that you buy someone when you don't know what to give. Poor Kate. That sucked.

Dinner was strange. It was the antithesis of the boisterous and relaxed version at Janine's. This one was awkward, and the distance between us, our spines parallel with the backs of the chairs, was canyon-sized, even though we were sitting at the same table.

The meal was catered, which pleased me immensely, because I hoped we could control our portion sizes. Lunch had been so enormous that the concept of more food led to thoughts of undoing the button on my pants. *Hmm. Not a good idea.* We didn't claim ownership of our food allowance but it turned out to be fine. We ate tiny servings of tiny food on tiny plates and my stomach exhaled in gratitude. Tiny seemed to be the theme of the night. The chat was tiny, although the silences yawned between us. The amount of Champagne in the elegant flutes was tiny. Everything. Tiny.

Then the moment arrived when the tiny talk capsized and suddenly we were wading into the depths.

"I was hoping that you would have invited Neil tonight." Olivia replaced her cutlery, smiled at Kate, who promptly froze, her fork halfway to her mouth.

"Mum." She slowly laid her fork on her plate as if trying to stretch time so she had the opportunity to gather her thoughts. "Please stop."

I focused on my tiny food and pretended to be invisible, then reminded myself that I was forty-three, not seven, and could support my girlfriend. I knew it wasn't my place to step in or open my mouth or do anything that might be mistaken as two cents worth of opinion, but I could be there. Not being tiny.

"Oh, Katherine. You've had enough time for frivolity and to carry on with some nonsense. It's time to settle again." *What's wrong with frivolity?*

Kate inhaled, and I wanted to embrace her shoulders, or scrape all the tiny morsels of food onto one plate, smoosh it all together, and announce that the pile right there was Kate's feelings towards Neil. Olivia might not get the analogy.

"Mum, stop it. You're so angry that you can't even see that I'm happy. I'm happy!" Kate brought her hand down, and just before it smacked onto the white tablecloth, her hand slowed so her palm pressed lightly next to her plate. Tiny. "I wasn't happy for 10 years."

Olivia exhaled in contrast to Kate's inhalation. Both of equal strength. "But of course you were happy. You and Neil are delightful together."

I noted the use of present tense. Olivia really, *really* hadn't let go; her need to live vicariously through Kate's marriage was deeply ingrained.

"No, I'm happy now. I live, Mum, truly live more than I ever have before because I own my decisions. My marriage was basically your decision." Olivia stiffened. "I really didn't have decision-making power in my marriage."

The straight line of Olivia's lips slashed across her face. "Katherine." It was almost, not quite, but almost a hiss; the type people do when someone is eavesdropping. Tiny hiss. "You're embarrassing me with my friends and you're behaving like a teenager. People ask after you and I have to tell them that you're divorced. You're nearly fifty, for heaven's sake."

God, this woman was a throwback to the 1960s. Imagine if Kate came out to her as well. It'd send her dashing for the smelling salts, a cup of tea, Bex, then she'd need a good lie down on the couch. I saw what Kate meant about picking her coming out moment, and I felt like a right arsehole for pushing.

"Yes, I am nearly fifty, which means I'm perfectly capable of making my own decisions. I choose my direction." I wanted to squeeze her thigh.

"You simply need a husband. A husband like Neil. He can give you love and understanding." Olivia shook her head and began to collect plates and cutlery, and my mouth decided to join in the discussion. Because of course it did.

"She has it," I said quietly, gazing at Olivia and ignoring Kate's very tiny whisper.

"Bron." The word rippled softly.

Olivia stood, her hands clutching the small pile of crockery. "Pardon?"

"She has love and understanding." I stood as well, lacing my fingers through the stems of the wine glasses. I felt, rather than saw, Kate push her chair away and suddenly the three of us stood frozen as if replicating a scene from a Wild West stand-off.

"Who from?"

"Me." I walked in to the kitchen to settle the glasses on the counter. Walking was good. Excellent.

Olivia laughed as she followed me, arranged the plates in the dish-washer, then patted my arm. "It's lovely that you're her friend and I appreciate the love of a friend. Why, I have many friends that I love but a woman needs a man on her arm." She nodded wisely, then beamed. "Do you have someone special, Bron?"

There was a strangled cough from the dining room, and I wanted to turn and mouth, "It's okay." It would be incredibly unfair if I answered Olivia's question with the whole truth. I might have done some questionable things in my life, but outing someone without their consent was not one of them.

"Yes. Yes, I do." *And that's all I'm going to say.*

Olivia turned her smile to Kate, who, now that I looked properly, wore the stark features of a cartoon character; large eyes filled with apprehension and a white-as-milk face. It looked like she was about to pass out.

"See? There you are, Katherine. Your friend has a special man." Her face wore the confidence of someone who was convinced they were right. "You'll have saved Neil's telephone number, of course, so why not ring him tonight and wish him a Merry Christmas. It's polite and a step forward in reestablishing your marriage."

Kate slid her gaze to me; holding it for a long moment.

The conversation for the next hour reverted to tiny so it wasn't diffi-cult to carry it, deflecting Olivia with blather about school and curriculum and the state of today's youth while Kate hummed at appropriate moments and breathed.

~

THE DRIVE HOME, TO MINE, WAS QUIET, FILLING THE CAR with expanses of silence which were comfortable, yet not. My fingers curled tightly on the steering wheel.

"I'm sorry." My murmur floated across the space between us where the gear stick and hand brake squatted, right into Kate's lap. "I'm sorry for being a shit and pushing and not believing you when you said it would be next to impossible to come out at the moment."

I released the wheel and laid my hand, palm up, on her thigh. I didn't dare turn my head. It was Kate's decision so I focused on the blue and white cat's eye markers dotted along the line in the centre of the road.

"You were being difficult, Bron. Impatient," Kate said, her words chased by a heavy sigh which drifted aimlessly, making me feel like it carried more than frustration at me. It was a sigh that held Kate's sadness at her mother's inability to accept the truth, at Neil's seemingly constant presence in her life.

Then her hand slipped into mine and she squeezed my fingers. "Thank you for apologising."

I gave a singular nod. "It was necessary. The apology."

"Mm. It was."

We held hands until I had to flick the indicator and other important car-related actions. If I'd been able to lean over and operate the various functions one-handed, I would have. I would have probably killed us.

"You know? Those friends Mum was talking about. They're the sort who are dismissive of gay people, yet have a curiosity that borders..." She squeezed my fingers again. "It's like a warped fascination. So if I come out, they'll crawl back to find out the juicy details. To peer at me as if I'm an oddity in a circus."

"Really? That's so—"

"Outdated?"

"Yeah. Don't they have gay friends?"

"Oh, yes. Gay male friends who they view as camp and harmless, ready to be called upon for fashion advice or a fun shopping trip. They're seen as accessories, rather than real people. Real people who have a sexuality. Real people who are whole and flawed and unique. The gay men in my friend's lives, in many of my social and collegial circle, are viewed as sexless and harmless."

I shook my head. "I've seen that." Taking my hand quickly off the steering wheel, I pointed. "Bet their reaction to lesbianism is so, so different."

"Uh huh. Lesbians are predatory animals who will make a move on any woman in the vicinity and therefore should be vilified because otherwise no-one is safe."

"Far out." I turned into the street. "They've got tickets on themselves. As if every queer woman wants to get into their pants. I mean, I've seen it before. That," I wiggled my hand, "weird dichotomy with gay men viewed as safe and sexless and lesbians viewed as hunters who are going to leap on any straight woman and have their way with them."

Kate snorted. "I certainly don't want to." Then she hummed. "Your family literally threw a parade for you when you came out. At 20, right?" She didn't wait for confirmation. "It's been easy for you, Bron. I don't think you appreciate it. I'm coming out at forty-nine after ten years of marriage to a man, and when I do, I expect a huge backlash, not only because of my age, but because of my supposed place in society and the firm." She exhaled through her nose. "The firm."

Yanking the handbrake up as I put the car into park, I turned to her, the streetlight casting shadows across Kate's features. I was right; she did look unbearably sad. Yet thoughtful. Yet determined. Like she'd made a monumental decision

She swept up my hand, holding it at her chest. "I know I've been all over the place with this. The coming out."

I smiled internally. It sounded like Kate had laid some serious capitalisation at the start of those words.

Kate looked out of the windscreen, then back to me. "Will you come with me to the Veris New Year's Eve party?"

I blinked for a moment, then shrugged. "Absolutely. How fancy do I need to be?"

"Black tie."

I dropped my head back on to the headrest. "Oh, gees."

There was not a single laugh at my theatrics, so I rolled my head sideways.

"I'm..." Kate trailed off and I sat up, a frown taking up residence on my forehead. "I'd..." It was as if she couldn't get her car off the starting grid. "I think I might say something."

"A speech?" It was odd to have stuttered sentences for something as innocuous as addressing her colleagues at a work do. I assumed Kate gave speeches all the time as part of the position she held.

Kate, still clutching my hand, pressed it to her chest. Hard, as if gathering strength. "More like a statement," she whispered.

I blinked again. "Um, okay. I'll definitely be there for the free drinks, food, and your co—" The realisation was thunderous in my head. "Really?" My eyes were huge. Gee, I could be obtuse sometimes.

"Mm." A deep breath. "As you said, I'm old enough and I've had a year to think about it."

I winced. "I'm sorry for saying that."

"Well, it was certainly blunt, but I did take it on board, then ummed and ahh-ed about it all." The determined glint in her eyes flashed again.

"Kate..."

"So." She inhaled all of the oxygen in the car. "I think this will be easier than coming out to my mother. But let's see how brave I am on the night. I'm all talk now but I could fall in a heap."

"I'll catch you," I whispered.

Kate, leaning over the angled handbrake, started the kiss softly, but she ran her tongue along my bottom lip and I groaned, opening my mouth for her to slip inside. My hands fluttered next to her cheeks, but Kate wasn't so shy; grasping my head, sliding one hand around the back of my neck and kissing me senseless.

We broke apart, breathing heavily. "I know you will." Kate wriggled, pointing down to the handbrake. "Ow."

I chuckled. "Also." I pointed to the fogged-up windows.

"Well, now I don't feel forty-nine." She reached over and collected her bag. "Perhaps sixteen?"

"Ah, those were the days." That earned me a quick kiss on the cheek.

"Come on. There are presents to bring upstairs, and maybe a repeat performance of that kiss."

We Announced

~

December 31 to January 3 in the first and second years of the now

I imagined that any Veris party could never be anything but black tie, as everyone in the gala room looked entirely comfortable in their tuxes, and gowns, and skyscraper heels. I'd hauled out my black tux complete with mandarin collar, buttons in burgundy and the pants sporting a thin pinstripe down the outside seam. I adored the minimalist style of the collar because it appealed to my inner artist, but I also knew that a mandarin collar wasn't supposed to be worn to a black tie event. So I was breaking the tuxedo rules; tuxedo time-out for me. I couldn't have cared less. From the way Kate was lasciviously eyeing me up at her place, she didn't care about black tie rules either.

Meanwhile, I was too busy staring, dumbstruck, as Kate, dressed in a black velvet dress with long sleeves and an asymmetrical neckline that exposed so much skin at her neck and shoulders, sauntered out from the bedroom accessorised by a clutch purse, a raised eyebrow, and a smirk.

"Oh, Jesus. Fuck me." I raked my eyes down her body, taking in the hair twisted into a showy-yet-not style, to all that skin, to her breasts and curves and legs and her shoes which were black stilettos with thin, barely there, straps that tied about her ankles. I'd never seen anyone, *anyone*, look so amazing, so fucking sexy, and because I was wearing men's shoes, we were the same height and the instructions for how to breathe fell out of my head.

"I would gladly, sweetheart, because you look edible and there are all sorts of images running through my mind right now." She leaned in and kissed my mouth, pulling away to run her thumb along my bottom lip, whisking away the smudge of lipstick. "But we should get this show on the road." A flash of anxiety zipped across her face.

"You know." I reached for her hand. "You don't have to do this. Yes, I've been a pain about coming out. Yes, I take my experience for granted. But if this is not the right time, then don't."

She wiggled our joined hands. "I figured that I spend the majority of my day with these people, therefore I spend the majority of my day lying and hiding and denying and it's exhausting, so telling them means I can get on with my work, get on with the business of being me."

I kissed her knuckles. "I will be with you the entire night. Right there. Being Kate's person."

She smiled, her eyes twinkling, then indicated with her chin towards the hall table where two red cranes sat. "Hope, because tonight is floating a little on that abstract noun." Kate let out an unsteady breath. "And healing during challenging times, because if this isn't a challenging time, I don't know what is. I hope I'm not in pieces after tonight."

I couldn't reassure her or dismiss her fears, because I didn't know how her coming out experience would pan out. *Crystal ball, anyone?* But I'd be there.

My bridge knew about my commitment because I'd said so as I stared at it for about twenty minutes yesterday. With my arms stretched out on the back of the bench, feet stretched out in front of me, my brain emptied like it always did, leaving all the important thoughts such as Kate and Christmas and love and commitment. And Kate. So much beautiful, regal, gorgeous Kate. Visiting my bridge always shone a spotlight on the awesome, allowing the awful to disappear for a bit.

The open double doors to the gala room on the fifteenth floor of the Veris building welcomed one and all and I was eternally grateful I'd chosen the tux and not my dinner suit. I'd attended a few flash evening events during my career; Teacher of the Year award, Education Department Gala, that sort of thing, but this was another level. As befitting a high-flying accountancy firm, the people in the room advertised their wealth through their clothing, their accessories, their mere presence, and as I'd discovered over the year I'd known Kate accountancy didn't mean tax returns. Not at Veris. At Veris, there was always a person who oversaw a team, such as the team who looked after risk management accountants and profitability analysis accountants and the auditing consultants who disappeared from Veris for a week to tidy up a business that was imploding on itself. That person was Kate.

It was a lot, and I'd felt very insignificant as if my career lacked importance in comparison. That feeling only lasted for a little while after I gave myself a severe talking to about the art of teaching and educating the minds and creativity of small children and—Kate had been furious when she'd heard my ridiculous self-doubts, reminding me of the time ages ago when we sat on the bench at the bridge and she'd told me that our jobs were not a competition. So I entered the fancy-schmancy Veris New Year's Eve party with my head held high.

"Kate! So thrilled you're here!" The woman wrapped her hand around Kate's forearm and air-kissed each cheek. "I was just telling Henry that I simply must find you tonight." I looked askance at the woman. *People who state that they simply must find someone are either bail bond agents or stalkers.*

"Oh? Well, you've found me." Kate sounded done with the conversation already. The woman, decked out in red including her hair, laughed lightly.

"I wanted to pass on my..." her forehead wrinkled as she attempted to finish the sentence, "thoughts for your divorce. I mean, you've been in my thoughts." Kate's eyes looked ready to roll and I was happy to join her.

"Thank you, Francesca. It was for the best." The tight, please-leave-me-alone, smile fell onto Kate's lips.

Then Francesca registered my presence. She stuck out her hand, limp as if a dead fish had attached itself to the end of her arm. "And you're here with Kate?" It was one of those questions where the person is supposed to supply the actual answer, then introduce themselves, then compliment the dress.

During my brief handshake, which was like testing whether pasta was al dente, my responses followed protocol. "I am, Francesca. My name is Bron, and that's a lovely dress." She beamed.

"Thank you. And how do you know Kate?"

The sixty-four thousand dollar question. I turned to Kate. Her answer would create my road map for the remainder of the evening.

"Bron is my friend."

Right. Okay. Well, baby steps. Friend was very close to girlfriend so we were getting there.

Shaking off Francesca and her weird condolences-but-not-really commentary, we made our way farther into the room, Kate clutching a supportive Champagne. I could tell she was itching to hold my hand or touch my forearm but she was hyper-aware and this impacted on her ability to maintain normal conversation. Not that anyone really noticed. I was introduced as Kate's friend, people hummed and nodded and smiled and strung together a few sentences about fiscal funds or something. On a few occasions, I was able to discuss teaching and education as a social construct which was pleasing, but generally I listened to Kate drift in the currents of her particular pool of expertise. It was all very sexy and I worked hard on reining in my admiration and lust.

Then she directed us towards six people, each with a glass filled to various levels, and we were absorbed into the group.

"Bron, this is Justin, Leo, Kia, and Rita." She tipped her glass during each introduction, then caught my eye. "They're the senior team leaders in my division." The team leaders shook my hand, Leo and Rita introduced their partners who smiled, then gestured that they were off to the bar and would anyone like more drinks and that they'd leave us to chat about work. Sounded like an escape plan to me and I grinned to myself.

"Lovely to meet you in person."

Kate had mentioned her team very briefly but I was a visual person so this was much more effective. "This is quite the party, isn't it? I've never been to such an elaborate do," I said, catching Rita's eye, smiling into her open face. In fact, all four of them, with their open faces and genuine smiles, closed about us, like witches casting circles of protective energy, and squared their shoulders as if they would be rather irritated if someone else wandered into our space. They came across as a nice, friendly team who would back Kate in any new idea or decision she'd share at—

Oh.

I held my breath. If there was ever a more perfect time or group of people to announce...her announcement, then it was now.

"Bron, how do you fit into our mighty leader's picture?" Justin chuckled, and I swallowed a mouthful of champagne, coughing slightly as the bubbles hit the back of my throat. Then I parted my lips in readiness to...what? Say what?

With a very tiny shift towards my shoulder, Kate breathed deeply, and I watched her make eye contact with each team member. "Bron is my partner."

A small moment of silence. And blinking. Then everyone gave a version of the upside-down 'U' and a nod combination. The physical version of 'okay, cool'.

It was Leo who pointed at me, and grinned. "Got yourself a catch there, Bron. She's a super manager and," he beamed at Kate, "a terrific person."

Kate's exhalation was so long that she could have filled the room with enough carbon dioxide for the plants dotted about the alcoves to thrive for two-hundred years.

Kia rubbed Kate's arm. "Good for you," she said quietly.

With our eyelids working overtime to dash away mascara-destroying tears, we made more small talk, Kate's team choosing deliberately to avoid the 'when-did-you-know?' or 'how-did-you-meet?' questions, and I had to restrain myself from embracing them in a group hug in gratitude for their tact. The entire process had been smooth and—well, no. It hadn't been smooth. Mine had. Kate's heart was probably tachycardic, so I leaned into her shoulder and brushed my little finger against hers; my gesture a wave of support from the sidelines. Subtle pompoms. *I'm here if you need me.*

Kate slipped her palm into mine, and I beamed.

Eventually, after receiving promises from Justin, Leo, Kia, and Rita to catch up later in the night, we found ourselves in a small alcove next to a robust ficus who was still happily absorbing the gift from Kate's lungs.

Kate's eyes were huge. "Oh my God."

"Sweetheart." I held her hands.

"Oh God, that was amazing and awful and spectacularly frightening and my heart feels like it's trying to catch up with my brain. But." She disentangled her hands and clutched my shoulders. "They didn't care. They. Did. Not. Care." She pressed her fingers to her lips. "Actually, they did care. They cared for me. Oh my God."

"I know." My smile grew. "I'm so proud of you. Not that you need me to say that but—"

She clutched my shoulders again. "Yes, I do. I acknowledged you just then, so it's important, because you and I? We're a we, Bron."

I wanted to cry—again—but my tears instantly disappeared when, over Kate's shoulder, I spotted the imminent arrival of a Veris employee who worked on the floor above Kate. Neil, his strides short and quick, was definitely not coming over to congratulate Kate on her announcement. "You've got this," I murmured quickly in to Kate's ear, and we turned as one to confront a very pissed off ex-husband.

"I cannot believe you!" he hissed, looking around for potential eavesdroppers in our small secluded alcove that couldn't possibly hide another person. He bared his teeth. "Not only have you paraded about as a divorcee, besmirching my name." *Besmirching?* No wonder he and Olivia were best buddies. "Now you've decided to become a lesbian." His furious gaze flicked to me, then back to Kate.

"I didn't just decide—"

He spoke over the top of her. "You. Are. Embarrassing. Me."

I could feel Kate shaking. Confrontation like this was her Achilles heel. I'd asked her during the year how she could easily deal with tension when creating contractual agreements or when the boss of a random business cracked it when they were told that their financials sucked, yet she fell to pieces and walked away when she had to deal with Neil or her mum. *Even me, sometimes. But that isn't important.*

She explained that she could disconnect at work, but when it was about her, the personal Kate, she couldn't deal with the tension. Couldn't think of the words to use. She'd never been able to because it was instilled in her from when she was young. No standing up for herself in that house. Nope. So she became flustered and the only solution was to walk away from the tension and the absence of all the words.

Confusion must have been written all over my face if Kate's frustrated sigh was any indication. "You're not solving the problem, though," I said.

She'd studied me. "Actually I am."

So, I knew she was preparing to walk, probably run, from this entire situation and my role here was to be the supportive girlfriend. Demonstrate how much I loved her. How much she needed me to stay so she could close this chapter with Neil. I channeled my best Emma Thompson, because we were guests at a fancy gala, and people expected class.

"Well, this is awkward."

He whipped his head around at my snark and launched his hissing-bared-teeth combo.

"You're that...that woman who interrupted us that day."

"You have an excellent memory, Neil."

"You're a...lesbian?" *You're toilet paper, Bron?*

I smiled winningly. "Yes, Neil, I am." Then clasped Kate's shaking hand in mine. Neil's enraged eyes followed the movement.

"Well, that explains a lot." He twitched as if his entire mission in life was to clamp his fingers around Kate's arm.

She flinched, but blew out through her nose, as if gathering resolve.

"What does?" Kate asked, the strength in her voice moving from fragile to determined in two words.

"Why you left. It explains everything."

"No it doesn't. Bron's my girlfriend. She didn't turn me into a lesbian and you can't catch it like a virus, Neil. Don't be ridiculous." She shook her head.

"You know what's ridiculous? Policies that protect people like you." He jabbed his finger at me, then glared at Kate. "And you. Otherwise I'd be making your life uncomfortable because all you've done is make life uncomfortable for me." Was this guy for real? A homophobic 1960s throwback. Unbelievable. I didn't think people like Neil existed anymore.

However, his unstable anger was laced with a vindictiveness that concerned me. Unstable. *Yes, that's the word.* I needed to step in.

I was still channeling Emma Thompson. "Neil, you are deeply unpleasant, and I truly hope you'll fuck off preferably to the end of a very short pier and therefore into the ocean." Out of the corner of my eye, I caught Kate's lips rolling in to hold down the smile. Good. An unexpected and positive side effect of my classy smackdown.

His face reddened, which actually enhanced the interesting starkness in his colour palette with his black hair and blue suit. Ever the art teacher. I continued while I had an opening.

"It was Kate's decision to leave, Neil."

We had a tiny audience now, because with his shoulders thrust back, his chest puffed, and his voice raised unconsciously—rather interesting how fury sat at either end of the pointy line; disturbingly quiet or Shouty McShouty—Neil was on his way to broadcasting his personal beliefs to a few of the Veris staff, and embarrassing the heck out of himself.

"I don't give a flying fuck about Kate's decision."

Oh. Okay. The fucks were flying. Goodbye Emma. Time to channel Siobhan. "Mate, I can—"

"I'm not your mate. Ever." He stepped forward with his puffy chest to make his point. At eye level. I bet that chaffed his balls. "But how Kate talks about the reasons for our divorce and then parades you around like some sort of prize means that I'm tarred with this—" he lowered his voice, "sick perversion as well."

The accidental laugh fell out of my mouth, and Kate squeezed my hand. "Jesus, Neil! 'Sick perversion' went out years ago. Get with it, man." I gestured; a sort of flipped over hand as if to indicate his lack of 'cool'. "It's 'homosexual happiness' now. Try that one on. Kate's happy with me as I am with her."

Kate nodded. "I am. I'm happy now."

"We share a love, Neil, and you can enjoy all the flying fucks that you like." I pulled my hand away and stepped into his space. "Kate can talk about whoever, however, whenever, whatever, and all the other 'W's she likes because guess what?" I growled. "It's not about you, so stop with the Kate embarrasses you shit." The small group of people, standing about pretending not to listen, sipping their drinks, nodding and gesturing silently like extras on a TV set, murmured in agreement.

Neil flicked a glance over his shoulder, then turned, his finger raised as if to make another point. But I was great at having the last word. Growing up with two sisters will teach you that. I stepped even closer and his aftershave, *eau de unpleasant*, filled my nostrils. My tone dropped to soft and scary just for Neil's benefit.

"You're not going to touch her again, Neil, because I will fucking cut off your arm and use it as a new pole for the rainbow flag outside city hall."

~

THE PHONE CALL TWO DAYS LATER FROM OLIVIA WAS JUST AS much fun although this time I didn't step in and threaten to cut off her arm.

"Mum, Neil didn't make me happy. Bron does. I'm incredibly happy with her." Kate glared at the coffee table as she cradled the phone, the speaker icon illuminated. She'd wanted support for this interaction and I tried not to wince with each barb and jab and Neil-clone commentary as it fell into the room.

"So, all of a sudden you're a...*lesbian.*"

"No! I'm Kate, your daughter." Her voice cracked. "Your daughter who's fallen in love with Bron who happens to be a woman. It doesn't—"

"But you're not a lesbian, Katherine. That's impossible. You've never shown any signs of it before."

Like hives or kidney disease.

"Maybe I'm not a lesbian, Mum, but I'm certainly not heterosexual." There was spluttering down the line. "I don't know what label I am, but all I know is that I'm in love. Maybe that's my label." Kate took a deep breath and looked me dead in the eye. "You need to accept that, Mum."

"Of course I don't. It's enough that you're divorced. Now you're homosexual. Can you imagine what my friends will say?"

Kate's shoulders slumped, and her gaze fell to the carpet. "I'm sorry." *Uh oh.* The apologies had started. Olivia was going to force Kate to run, so I waved my hands theatrically, bending to make eye contact and mouthed, "You can do this." I accessorised my words with elaborate eyebrow raising.

Kate blinked slowly, then held my gaze. "Mum, actually I'm not sorry. If your friends are concerned about who I love, then they should have been concerned with who I didn't love, and that was Neil."

Olivia huffed. "I don't see how—"

Kate interrupted. *Yes!* "You do see, Mum, but you choose to *not* see.

Please accept me for me. I'm still the same person that I was before this phone call. That's all you need to know."

The silence was deafening.

"I have heard all I need to know. Goodbye, Katherine."

Kate slumped into the back of the couch, the phone clutched in her hand with the black screen a void of disappointment, and she swallowed and swallowed, her eyes filling with tears. It took two steps to round the coffee table and bring her to my chest. I rubbed soft circles in her back.

"So this is the awful side of coming out that people talk about," she mumbled into my shirt.

I wouldn't know. My parents had never erased me as a person.

We Asked

March 1 to June 30 in the second year of the now

"I didn't realise I had to have a coming out story," Kate said two months after the New Year's Eve announcement. She sighed, leaning farther into my shoulder as we paid no attention to whatever was on the TV.

"You don't."

She pushed off and turned to me square-on. "You know those friends that I said would boomerang back to stare and point at the oddity that is Kate Agostino?" I nodded. "So, apparently I need a coming out story for when that happens."

"Um."

"Mm. Like a 'where did you meet' story, or a 'how did you know' story, or a 'what are you' story or a 'how did you break all your bones' story." She widened her eyes in frustration. "I wasn't aware."

"Oh, Kate." I lifted my arm and she snuggled into my side.

"Yesterday," she mumbled into my jumper, "Nadine, in Leo's team, stopped me in the corridor and said, "So you're definitely not into men at all then?" to which I replied, "I'm into Bron. Please stop asking" then promptly searched for Leo to suggest that a staff seminar on tact and diplomacy might be in order."

I snorted. "I'm sorry."

Since Kate had been married to a man, Olivia and some of Kate's staff, like Nosy Nadine, were bound to maintain a predisposed image of her that was seemingly straight. But Kate's heterosexual relationship, The Marriage To Neil—it was capitalised in my head—was in the past, and that didn't define who she could love in the future. Like me. She loved me. I squeezed her shoulders and she burrowed in farther.

The concept of a coming out story became the topic of conversation for the next month. It came up at the oddest times.

The dishes were being rammed into their slots in the dishwasher and I winced at each bang, my shoulder hugging the door frame. Kate was on a rant, and I was determined not to stand in the way of that particular steamroller.

"I am growing painfully aware that I have to come out over"—another plate was wedged into its allocated space—"and over"—that was a glass— "again. I've now felt the freedom that comes from speaking my truth." She whirled around, jammed her fists on her hips and stared at me in frustration, so I wrinkled my forehead apologetically. "But I grapple with the fact that in order to maintain this feeling, I have to *come out,*" she threw her fingers up and air-quoted the words, "for the rest of my life."

She narrowed her eyes at the irritation of the lifelong process.

"That's...well, it's true. That's what happens, unfortunately. I feel like I'm constantly coming out, even twenty-three years later. To parents, even though it's none of their business, new staff. That sort of thing. I give a potted version of my coming out story if people ask." I chuckled, "You could mention me in passing if you want to slide more easily into your story." My gaze had wandered about the kitchen in the middle of my response, so I wasn't paying attention to Kate's expression. The silence brought my focus back, and I found Kate studying me, her mouth set in a line.

"I don't need to use your story as a catalyst to tell my own," she said evenly, which made me rock back on my heels.

"I...know, Kate. I was just..." *Oh boy. Words. Gone. Shit.* I took a deep breath. "Kate, it's empowering to stand proudly in your truth." I pushed off from the door frame. "I also know that a person does *not* need to *come out* for their identity to be valid. Coming out is ever evolving." I flicked my hands as if to say, 'it's fine', or 'this is how it is', or 'I'm blathering and you're gorgeous'.

However, Kate seemed to interpret my gesture as 'Gees, Kate, just deal with it'. "I didn't *need* to come out? Bron, you were so insistent that I should come out. You pushed, and so I did even though I'm pretty sure I wasn't ready."

"But you made the decision!" I shook my head in frustration, and shoved my hands into my hair.

Kate moved to step around me. "Yes, I did, but how much of that decision was based on your need for me to do it?" She paused, then her gaze took in my face but didn't make contact with my eyes. "We're not arguing about this. I'm going for a walk."

"Do you—" No, apparently Kate didn't want me to join her on a walk. I swallowed heavily. Going for a walk literally. Going for a walk figuratively. Walking away from tension. *Kate, please don't do that.*

Nadine wasn't the only staff member who'd decided to run live commentary on Kate's life. Neil was being generally unpleasant, finding ways to cross paths with Kate to mutter completely awful remarks so that she became jumpy as hell at work. Her team noticed, and had a word to a manager who mentioned it to another manager who played golf with another manager and Neil's unpleasant behaviour came around to bite him on the arse, because the rather important manager on the end of the number four driving iron then had a word with Neil. Kate was again able to walk the corridors unmolested.

I still got some very bad vibes—proper police-ish word there—from Neil and so I kept an eye on Kate to see if she was getting any shit from him again.

We didn't discuss the coming out argument again and things settled down. But I overheard a conversation a few days later between Siobhan and Kate in the dining room as I made my way down the hall from the bathroom. I froze and held my breath.

"Did you score a radar?" Siobhan's voice was filled with gleeful curiosity.

"The gay radar that people talk about?"

"Yup. Did the gay Gods send one down via a little rainbow balloon so that you can carry it around in your handbag and aim it at babes to see if they are?"

Kate's laugh was full, and I knew she'd be wiping away tears. "I think it only works on Bron."

"Figures." There was a pause. "You good, though?"

Another pause. "Yes. Bron and I had a...disagreement a while ago about the coming out experience." I heard Kate's sigh. "Shiv, I am so grateful for my second chance, and in hindsight I don't have any regrets about coming out when I did, because I wouldn't have been strong enough to deal with it all before then." I blinked. That wasn't what she'd—didn't matter. Kate's story. Kate's truth.

"I became exhausted pretending to be someone I wasn't." Kate still sounded exhausted. The constant coming out could do that to a person.

"Did Bron push?" Siobhan sounded tentative.

"Yes."

"Yeah. I figured." *Nice, Shiv. Way to toss me under a bus.*

"Really?"

"Mmhmm. She tends to plonk her good fortune or whatever—her easy ride—onto others, with the hope that they'll have the same slippery-slide journey as her. But it doesn't work that way. I get it, you know. If life's that comfortable, and it has been for her—it always is—then you lose track of how much you have to be thankful for. I don't think Bron does it intentionally, you know? The ungrateful thing. I really think she needs it to be pointed out to her, which sucks because she's forty-four freaking years old." Siobhan's volume increased in the last sentence.

"Not quite forty-four yet."

"Ha. Well, in three months." There was another pause. "She's a good person, you know?"

Kate's smile must have been wide and powerful because it made it up the hallway. "Yes. Yes, she is."

"You two are so perfect together. All hearts circling your head shit."

Kate laughed. "I utterly adore her."

"I know."

"I want us to move in together." I nearly face planted the carpet. *What?*

"About fucking time! Oh. Shit. Um, you know. About time."

"That was almost an apology, Shiv." I could imagine her eyes twinkling.

"Fuck, can't be having that."

~

I kept Kate's admission to Siobhan about moving in together secret, firstly because it wasn't my place to say anything as technically I'd been eavesdropping, and secondly, I think I wanted it to be Kate's suggestion because it hadn't even occurred to me to merge our lives like that. But when given exciting, astounding and completely unexpected information, rolling it around in your head for a week does wonders for clarity.

Apparently, tortellini is a great meal to eat when dropping life-changing bombshells on to the dining table.

Kate placed her cutlery on her plate. "Bron?"

I stilled my hand, halfway to my mouth. "Sweetheart?"

"I was asked another one of those 'but how are you gay when you were married?' questions today."

I growled. "Jesus! They won't let up, for fuck's sake." I winced. "Shit. Swearing..."

"Sorry," Kate said quietly, and I saw what Siobhan meant about the hearts floating around our heads. "Mm. They asked why I'd not only got divorced but become gay particularly because Neil and I owned a house together."

"That's illogical." I laid my fork on the plate, the tortellini still attached to the end. "Why would having a house together be the reason to *be* together?"

"You don't think two people who are in a committed relationship should move in together?" She stared at me intently.

"Sometimes, sure." I shrugged.

"What about if those two people were to purchase a small place because they're in a committed relationship?" she said very carefully.

For a close-to-middle-aged woman, I can be the biggest, most clueless idiot in the entire world, because suddenly I caught on. My eyes roamed across Kate's face, which was broadcasting hope, love, anticipation, and anxiety. It was a lot. My week of washing machine thoughts about this very moment had finally wrung out one conclusion; I wanted to be wherever Kate was. Apparently, she wanted to be with me. And to do that, we needed to be in the same location. In a house, a purchased house according to Kate, which scared me slightly, because even though I had pretty good savings, it wasn't enough for a real adult property, that's for sure. I must have spent too long having all those spin cycle thinkings because Kate's face fell and she looked down at her plate.

"Are we those two people, sweetheart?"

Her head shot up, and all of the emotions reunited. She swallowed. "Yes." She swallowed again. "If you want to be."

I reached across the table. "I want to be." Out of nowhere—that's a big lie—tears ran down my cheeks. "Yes, please." I squeezed her hand. "I don't have a lot of money but if I go for the deputy principal position at work then I'll be on better pay and—"

"You don't need to have a lot, Bron. I insisted on an equal split with Neil for our property and other things so a small two-bedroom cottage or similar is very doable." That must have been a hell of a moment with Neil. Ick. It was probably only the presence of her lawyer that halted the sorry-but-I'm-walking-away-from-this-tense-and-very-personal-encounter.

I imagined I was just as blurry as she was, based on the amount of tears we were shedding. I'd already assumed that Kate would pay more for the house or whatever it was that we were buying, seeing as she was on a much higher salary than any teacher could ever earn, but it was a relief to hear my assumption confirmed. I winced to myself. Assumptions like that had got me into trouble before. I would need to check in with her along the way during this purchase, otherwise I knew—as did everyone else it seemed—that I'd become all a bit blasé about the house and the moving in and the merging and Kate would wonder what the hell had happened to Bron, the love of her life, and replaced her with Bron, the ungrateful shit.

I knew Kate was a highly focused machine when given a task to complete or a problem to solve because I'd seen her in action during our eighteen months, like when she'd run me through the intricacies of a successful contract that her team had scored last year. It was enlightening and scary and such a turn-on.

So when, for the thirtieth time, she flipped her iPad around, beamed over the top of it, and curled her arm around to point at the screen, I really wasn't surprised.

"This one?" The question wasn't 'Do you think this might be a good investment and should we ask for an inspection on the property?' Nope. The question that Kate asked was 'This one is perfect and I'm in love with it already and please say yes because I want to buy it now. Can we?'. Her eyes peering over the top of the screen were like the liquid dark chocolate of Labrador puppies, pleading to be picked up and cuddled. I laughed, took the screen from her hands, and she scooted closer.

I was a sucker for Kate's eyes, which was hardly newsworthy, because they were adorable, and said such a lot and when she was aroused, those eye—house, iPad, focus.

"Now, this one? This one is great!" I flipped through the photos, which showcased each room, the small backyard, the patio, the single garage, which I imagined, if we bought the house, would be where Kate parked her car because mine enjoyed the elements. Then I caught a glimpse of the asking amount and paused my swiping. "Bloody hell!" That was a significant jump in price from the one we'd talked about. I stared down at her hopeful expression.

"But it's doable." Her voice and expression synchronised.

"Gees, Kate. It's at least forty-thousand over. I don't have enough to be anywhere near the fifty-fifty split for this." I gestured to the rather beautiful little blue and cream cottage on the screen which was perfect and I could already see us living in it and come on, heart, that was really unfair of you to fall completely in love with the house in five seconds.

"I have enough."

I flicked a glance at her. "Mm. This is where it gets sticky, Kate. I don't want to feel beholden to you."

She shoved off my shoulder. "You will not be *beholden* to me. We are a couple." She lightly smacked my arm. "And we make decisions based on what's best for *both* of us." Another soft smack. "So I say we look at the house and make an offer that's under the asking price but not so low that it offends people."

It turned out that another skill to add to Kate's repertoire of awesomeness was property negotiation, which was hardly surprising given her job. But to watch her work her magic on the hapless real estate agent was fabulous, and when the paperwork was all done and the owners agreed to a quick settlement, we were moving into our new home by the end of May. It was fast, and utterly breathtaking.

∾

KATE'S FOOTSTEPS CLICKED ACROSS THE WOODEN FLOOR and I looked up from my coffee. Her business suit, low elegant ponytail, heels, subtle makeup and her eyes that carried the bedroom, stood in the doorway of our little old-fashioned blue and white kitchen. My puddle of goo gave an encore performance.

"God, you look amazing." I pushed my chair back, rose slowly without breaking eye contact, and slunk around the table, a smirk growing on my lips.

Kate pointed. "No." But she couldn't suppress the smile. "Sweetheart, I have the world's most boring meeting to attend this morning, and despite a desperate desire to skip it, I can't, so—"

"We could create lasting memories for you to reflect upon during said boring meeting."

Kate burst out laughing. "Is that my coffee?" She pointed at the travel mug on the bench, and I nodded. "Thank you." Kate looked me up and down. "I so wish I could wear..." She gestured to my jeans, rugby shirt, sneakers, and shoulder-length hair which was engaged in an interpretive dance that would have made Siobhan shudder.

"I'm not sure the Veris Gods would be thrilled."

She snorted, picked up her coffee mug, leaned in to kiss me, and kissed me again as I snaked my arm around her waist. Then my kiss in return was totally hot, which was completely in retaliation for how gorgeous she looked.

After a careful breath, Kate shifted back. "Right, well, that'll keep me going during this morning's meeting." A quick grin. "I'll see you tonight. I love you."

"Love you, too."

I had some time so I wandered about the house again. Our lives had merged at the end of May and here we were at the end of June, still discovering more about our quirky cottage. Like the one floorboard near the ensuite that squeaked and the cream walls which changed to a lighter tint at the lounge room because the previous owner had obviously run out of paint and they couldn't match it at the paint shop.

I trailed my finger across the seam at the top of the leather couch. The furniture was mostly Kate's because it was nearly new, classy, comfortable, and actually resembled furniture. We'd retained some of mine even though it generally looked like it had arrived in my old apartment after hauling itself off the footpath. The few pieces I kept were sentimental. Like the hall table. I'd sanded it back to its original wood, then stained and varnished it, arranging it at my front door. The table had puffed up with pride that day.

Sentimental, like the bowl, nearly full with Kate's cranes. Looking into the opening of the bowl was like looking into the lens of a kaleidoscope. I never asked Kate where she bought her special paper. I didn't want to know. The cranes simply appeared, wearing their technicolour dreamcoats; each one bearing its individual message. Although, when I thought about it, I hadn't received a crane for ages, but that wasn't surprising, I guess, as we'd both been so busy.

Finally, I checked my watch, realised that I needed to get a move on, and shouldered my backpack. Larry, our neighbour, who lived in a heritage red version of our cottage, waved at me from his armchair on his front porch. When we'd moved in, Kate had noticed Larry peering over the railing observing our to-ing and fro-ing, so we paused in our box transference, leaving most of it to Paul, his mate, and Rick, and wandered over the grass strip separating our two homes. Kate tilted her head up, and smiled, probably blinding Larry in the process. "Hi, I'm Kate and this is my partner, Bron." Her eyes sparkled.

Larry blinked at both of us. "Well then, my name's Larry." Then he pushed off the railing, held up a finger as if he needed a minute, then made his way carefully down the four steps at the front of the porch. We walked around to meet him, and he stuck out his hand; the back of it wrinkled, skin translucent, with the soft brown marks of age rising above the veins. Brief afternoon and morning chats and longer weekend conversations quickly established a neighbourly friendship, where we learned that Larry was eighty-two and lived by himself.

"My wife died. Heart attack. One minute she's baking a loaf of banana bread and the next she was gone." He'd stared unseeingly over the top of the railing as we sat drinking tea on his porch two weeks after we'd moved in. "I never told her I didn't like banana bread." He breathed out loudly. "Helen was the love of my life, you know? I always told her that. That I loved her. She was my best friend." Another deep breath. "That's what's important, isn't it? To tell your person that you love them. That you're grateful that they're in your life." He leaned his elbows on the small table that we were sitting around and contemplated us.

I held back my tears. "Yeah. Yeah, it is." My voice was rough.

"You two like that?"

Kate answered. "Yes, we are."

Larry nodded. "Good. Not many folks get a love of their lives."

Tears threatened a bit more and a quick glance at Kate showed her in a similar predicament. Then Larry gestured at Kate. "Do you bake?"

Kate blinked. "Um, not really?"

"What can you cook?"

"I can make a pretty good vegetarian lasagne," Kate eventually supplied. The look on her face was priceless, then Larry turned his head and frowned at me.

"Do you like Kate's lasagne?"

Deer. Headlights. "I do, actually."

Larry harrumphed. "Good. If she ever gets it into her head to bake banana bread and you don't like it, tell her. You might not get the chance one day."

So, as many afternoons as I was able to, I sat with Larry on his porch and we'd talk about politics, and social change, and how to fix a tap washer, and what in God's green earth was a meme? I still visited my bridge, just to check in and say hi, but it wasn't often. I figured she didn't mind.

We bought a small lawn mower so I could cut the grass in our backyard—Kate would leer at me from the back door as I trundled past in my tank top and threadbare shorts, which did wonders for my libido—then Larry's backyard, even though he told me not to and that I was a meddling woman, then the shared strip of grass in between our homes. He'd shout instructions and I'd mow in wiggly lines on purpose, leaving a tiny patch of dandelions for the bees, which usually got him worked up. Then he'd laugh and we'd share a beer on his porch.

I waved back at Larry as I clambered into my derelict car and reversed out our driveway. Our driveway of our house. I still couldn't believe it.

∽

ON JUNE THIRTY, KATE THRUST A WINTER JACKET AT ME after dinner.

"We're going outside to look at the stars."

I squinted at her. "Honey, it's cold and some of the stars aren't visible because of the light pollution and—" I cut myself off because Kate was bouncing on the balls of her feet, which was incredibly adorable for a nearly fifty-year-old.

"Just...just put that on and follow me outside." Her beseeching smile and wrinkled forehead won me over. So, shrugging on the parka, entirely grateful that I'd left my boots on, I trailed after Kate onto our back porch. We leaned our backs against the railing, freshly painted last week in the brightest white available at the hardware store, and peered into the sky. I was right. There were about six stars visible, but that seemed to be an adequate amount for Kate because she snuggled into my side and sighed.

"Are we looking for—"

"Sshh."

I duly sshh-cd.

After five minutes or so of staring in silence, during which I'd actually spotted another four stars, Kate's breath warmed my neck, resulting in a delicious shiver that travelled across my skin.

"If you see a certain star one night, you can make a wish on it." Her voice was soft in the dark grey of the night, in the stillness of the air, in the quiet as if all the traffic had decided to pull over and idle for a few minutes. Her voice slid into our breathy puffs of air; tiny clouds which hovered for a moment only to be whisked away by invisible strings.

"Yeah. I used to do that."

"I do, too." She tilted her head to lean her cheek on my shoulder.

"Do you think that if you wish on a star and ask for a second chance, you'd be granted that wish?"

I hummed. "I guess." I hadn't actively thought about wishes and stars and staring at the night sky and as I stood there, with my girlfriend huddled into my side, I realised what a wonderful experience I'd been missing out on. We needed to do this more often.

"Bron?"

"Kate?"

"I wished on a star the day the divorce was settled. Want to know what I wished for?"

I knew that rule. "Aren't you supposed to keep the wish a secret?"

"Not if the wish-asker—" I chuckled. "It's a word," she said and I felt her smile. "Not if the wish-asker wants to share it." She hugged me. "I love you."

I hugged her right back. "What did you wish for?"

"I wished for a second chance. I wanted that wish to be my best wish ever. I wished that I could get another chance at the forever and the now. I wished for another go around with a marriage."

My greatest wish right then was that Kate wasn't leaning on me so she wouldn't feel how utterly frozen I was. Not frozen from the temperature but from the sudden realisation that I'd guessed what she was talking about. I held a very cold breath.

"Bron?"

"Kate?" I croaked.

"I'd like to have another chance, a forever chance, with you. Would you marry me? Please?"

The breath I was holding whooshed out, like horses pulling a carriage of words.

"Oh my God, Kate." I leaned away and caught her gaze. Her smile was tentative, so I gently held her face, and infused every ounce of love I carried for her into my response. "I would love to be your second chance. My answer is yes, please. Thank you for asking me, for trusting me to be your forever and the now." Then I kissed her, our lips sliding together until Kate broke away, tears streaming down her face. She pressed her hand to her chest, creating the crinkly sound that parkas make when the material is shuffled about. Then grimaced.

"Sorry. Cold lips."

I laughed at her expression. "It was your crazy idea to propose out here. What if I couldn't answer because I'd turned into an icicle?"

She winked. "I would have warmed you up."

I laughed again. "Get inside, my crazy fiancé." Then I pressed my lips to her cheeks, catching each tear. "I love you so much."

We Promised

〜

July 1 to August 1 in the second year of the now

Because we didn't need a great deal of time to organise the wedding, seeing as it was to be in our backyard, we decided that August One was perfect. Janine, who'd popped around to drop off a bag of lemons from the tree in her backyard, pronounced it an auspicious date.

"An auspicious date?" I blinked, plonking the bag on the drainer next to the sink. Janine slid on to a stool and leaned her elbows on the counter.

"Yes. August the first represents soul, prosperity and is ruled by the sun."

I stared. "J, you do know that you're a psychologist, right? Holding a degree that you achieved after studying for years about how logic can play a role in the way people think?"

"Yes. I'm aware. But I've discovered that numerology and other alternative methods of understanding the world are valid and can assist patients to unravel issues blocking their forward movement."

"Right."

Kate's birthday, five days after the proposal, was pushed back a week, simply because Things. Were. Happening. And. Everyone. Was. Flat. Out. We all wanted her birthday party to be special, seeing as it was her fiftieth.

"I don't need anything special," Kate mumbled through a mouthful of toothpaste.

"Too bad. You don't turn fifty every day."

"Thank God." She spat out the toothpaste and rinsed her mouth. "I don't want flash for our wedding, as well, please." She straightened and spoke to my reflection in the mirror. "My wedding to Neil was organised mostly by my mother and there were guests among the hundred who attended that I wouldn't have known if I fell over them."

I hummed in acquiescence, then, from my position at the doorway, admired her calf muscles, taught and toned from her long walks every second evening. I'd said, maybe the second time I met her at the bridge, that Kate would look great in any set of twelve months and the set currently containing the number fifty was extraordinary. God, I loved her so much.

Kate went to replace her toothbrush in the holder but missed, her hand swishing past the plastic container. She tsked, and tried again.

And missed a second time.

"Kate?" I stepped forward, then paused as her third attempt was successful.

She gave a dismissive hand wave as she turned from the basin. "God, I must be tired lately. That's the second time I've misjudged something. Pam banned me from making my own coffee last week, deciding that it was now part of her PA portfolio of responsibilities, because of the mess I've been making on the counter." She laughed in a sort of resigned manner, and leaned up to kiss me. "I've got to go, sweetie. I'll be home early tonight so we can continue this discussion about the lack of flash occurring a week from now."

Setting Kate's odd clumsiness aside, I continued with the preparations for her not-a-big-deal party. I'd promised not-a-big deal. But it would have *some* flash. In fact, the only birthday party that wouldn't have flash at all was mine. Forty-four years of age was nothing important and I'd be happy with another caramel mud cake from the supermarket.

THE BOOMERANG FRIENDS WITH THEIR PENCHANT FOR peering at Kate as if she was the latest zoo exhibit were not invited, despite Kate stating that they were still friends, technically, because they all went to lunch once a month.

"*That's* the criteria for friendship?"

My expression must have relayed my confusion, and frustration because Kate rolled her eyes.

"It's not a great foundation, I know, but I'm loathe to completely toss them aside. Besides, our conversation is superficial and it means that I keep my toe in the water, particularly as two of them are colleagues, albeit in different departments." She opened her hands in a pleading gesture. "It's necessary."

I could understand. There were some staff members who, despite being able to maintain superficial conversations and socialise with, I actively avoided due to the said superficial conversations. So Kate was right; sometimes they were necessary.

But Larry was invited, who was chuffed and embarrassed and excited to receive the invitation. He delivered a brief shoulder shuffle, then excused himself to disappear inside so he could begin the hunt through his wardrobe for something warm that also qualified as 'good gear'.

Lawrence, singularly, and my family, variety of plurals, turned up en masse and suddenly the backyard was filled with noise and bonhomie and after ten minutes, I rescued Lawrence as he'd been dragged almost instantly into a conversation with Rick about snakes and how many Lawrence had encountered in his role as groundsman for the school.

It was a cold day but no-one minded. The blue, cloudless, skies compensated for the goosebumps and it meant that Kate's cake and the food wouldn't sag in resignation like it did in summer. The Veris team who'd embraced Kate's coming out arrived in fifteen minute intervals; Leo and his partner Julia, Justin, Kia, and Rita, whose partner had been Mitchell at the New Year's Gala, but was now replaced with Ben. My colleague invitations included Rescued-From-Snake-Interrogation Lawrence, who was now happily chatting with Dad, seemingly about engines based on their hand gestures.

And Lydia, who arrived, embraced Kate, wished her happy birthday, then, like a guided missile, found Siobhan, and hugged her in a little side-to-side jig. Paul took one look at both of them, shook his head and wandered off in search of beer.

Even though it was impossible, I wanted to bottle the atmosphere in the backyard. Kate didn't want flash or extra special, but it turned out to be both because there were wonderful people spread out in groups and pairs, holding plates of food and drink in recycled plastic, and the conversations softly undulated like when you're sitting in a canoe and a boat has motored past on the other side of the lake so all you feel are the delayed ripples in the water. Comforting. And extra special. Kate's mum may have tossed her aside, and Neil was...Neil, but actually, Kate's family was right there, standing on our patchy grass, eating fancy cake from that shop in the city.

My fiancé caught my gaze, and I was struck again by how beautiful she was. The side profile that I was constantly itching to sketch. Her strong nose. Her walnut-coloured hair that she refused to put into a bun because it "looked old". Those astonishing brown eyes which held every expression inside sparkles and stars.

She matched my grin, mouthed a "thank you," then winked at me, and suddenly I was a puddle of goo on the deck of the back patio. You'd think I'd be used to it by now.

Our rendition of the Happy Birthday song was fairly appalling but heartfelt. The adults sang to their own rhythm until we synchronised by the time we arrived at 'Kaaaaaaaaate'. The kids demonstrated much more expertise and led the 'hooray' bit because, based on Pip's eye-roll, we needed guidance.

I was thrilled with the instant togetherness of the group, because they'd all been invited to the wedding, and tension at that upcoming event was banned. As was glitter. That stuff was a pox on the earth.

∼

KATE BRUSHED AWAY HER STUMBLE AS SHE MADE HER WAY across the backyard towards our little garden shed three weeks later. I quickly flicked down the tarpaulin before she arrived. Deciding that employing my artistic talent to create a wedding gift for Kate was a stroke of genius or just working with something readily available. Straight after her birthday, I began painting a mural on the side of the shed of two women walking hand in hand along a track, like the one in 'Lord of the Rings' where the trees arched over the top of the path to create secrets and solitude. The women's horizon of opportunities and the now and the forever lay ahead. I wanted to complete it before the wedding; not too early, but enough to allow the paint to harden. All of which meant that I had limited time to finish so I worked on it as much as I could.

My gaze, focused on blending Kelly green and emerald for the arch of trees, caught the quick movement of Kate's misstep so my head whipped up, and I dropped my paintbrush in to the enamel paint pot. That'd be a degreasing job later.

"Sweetheart!" I was up and supporting her elbow in a single motion.

Kate patted my hand. "It's nothing. Didn't even fall. The grass must have leapt up and grabbed my foot." She chuckled, and pointed to the shed wearing its blue plastic curtain. "What are you up to?" There was a soft tremor in her arm and I cocked my head in concern.

"I can't tell you. It's top secret and if I blab, then a crowd of female agents will descend upon our house and march through the door demanding explanations and cups of tea." I frowned into her face, which caused a burst of laughter to bubble from her mouth.

"Will they be wearing suits?"

I smirked. "Lech."

Kate liked putting things in order and making sure everything was just so, which meant that, not only had she organised a simple and decidedly lovely birthday for me, she took over the wedding planning as well. I left her to decide on the cake. I really didn't mind what she chose because I figured that it would be a fabulous selection and therefore it was another component of the planning. She did huff at me when I'd said all of that but it was probably in acknowledgement of my hands off approach.

Janine and the kids—gender of the day was Wedding Wonder to which I rolled my eyes and JJ grinned evilly—arrived one Saturday in July to help with twisting artificial vines together to insert into the spaces in the metal archway that Kate had decided we'd say our vows under. I went looking for Kate and found her hunting for scissors in the kitchen.

She wriggled into my torso, exhaling a deep breath, as I hugged her from behind. I knew she was smiling, as that particular hug was one of her favourites. Then words fell out of my mouth, which I wished I'd collected and flung to the side.

"You could invite your mum, you know. It would be a show of—"

Kate twisted out of my embrace and glared. "No." She waved the closed scissors in the air.

After a surreptitious backwards step, I let my shoulders sag. "I know she said all of that at Christmas, but maybe—this is your wedding, Kate." I splayed my fingers, flicking my hands out. "We're getting married. Perhaps she'd like to be here."

The glare intensified. "No. My mother has chosen to *not* be a part of my life and I'm not backing down on this, Bron. It feels just like the coming out situation. I feel pressured."

I pulled my head back into my neck. "I'm not pressuring you!"

"You are. I don't want to talk about this." She slammed the scissors down on the counter and stomped off. I shook my head. *Great.*

"It's most likely pre-wedding jitters." Janine leaned against the door frame, her head resting on the wood.

"Maybe."

"Bron, don't push. If she doesn't want to invite her mum, then she doesn't. Not everyone has a supportive family. You're lucky." She fixed me with a contemplative gaze. "I'm not sure you realise that."

So I knocked on the door of the bedroom and after the quiet "it's okay," I walked into the room. Kate was sitting in the armchair we'd managed to squeeze into the corner beside the bed which she'd insisted wouldn't fit but I'd insisted it would. Kate was the one who sat in it the most, which made me smile.

"I'm sorry."

"I know, but you're trying to mend a bridge which has packed its bags and moved to places unknown." She looked up from her carpet contemplation. We gazed at each other for a moment. Then she flipped her hand as if the gesture brought an end to the argument. "Do you think, once we're married, that the kids will call me Aunty Kate?"

I shrugged and grinned. "Don't know. Why don't you ask them?"

She hummed. "I've never been an aunt." Another hum. "Or a sister. Just a daughter and a wife." Her voice was filled with melancholy, her lips pressed together. "And I really didn't enjoy the wife label, and the daughter label is not great at the moment. It'd be nice to be an aunt. I'd do a good job."

My eyes filled with tears, and she pushed off from the chair, and folded her arms about my waist. "I'm sorry I walked away from our... argument before. I'm trying not to do that as much."

Tightening my embrace, then letting go to sweep up her hand, I breathed deeply. "Come on. Let's see if the kids can handle *another* relative in their lives."

It turned out that Aunty Kate was 'epic' and 'awesome' and JJ outran Pip to deliver an exuberant hug that rocked Kate back on her heels, her laughter filling the room. Jack shyly nodded, then grinned, then darted his eyes about the room, then nodded again, then pronounced the whole idea excellent with a "yeah." I knew his crush was still going strong and that he was embarrassed by the age difference, but his bedroom walls displayed posters of Sandra Bullock and Halle Berry, both around fifty, so he clearly liked older women. I completely understood.

~

THE CLOUDS THREATENED RAIN ON THE MORNING OF OUR big day, but Kate stood on the front porch, rolled her hands onto her hips and glared at the sky. She brought out her bossiest boss voice. "Don't even think about it," she yelled, and I caught Larry laughing silently from his porch.

Clouds are very obedient when yelled at by a hot fifty-year-old woman in a white dressing gown and slippers, so they didn't "even dare think about it" and duly dissolved into the blue.

I checked the mural an hour later and found that the paint had hardened to the same strength as the steel underneath, so I led Kate, now in jogging pants and a hoodie, across the grass and placed her just so in front of the blue tarpaulin. She gave me a quizzical look.

"Bron?" She narrowed her eyes over a tiny smile.

Suddenly I was nervous. I'd thrown paint all over a shared part of the property. What if she didn't like it? What if she decided that the wedding was off because my mural would look stupid in the photos?

"Um. I, um..." *Words. Now.* I gestured at the shed. "I wanted to give you something for our wedding. It's to represent us, where we are and where we're going." I held her hands. "I love you so much and this gift," I tipped my head towards the tarpaulin, "well, I wanted to show you that you're my forever and also my now." I kissed her, then reached up and removed the row of bricks, holding down the tarp, from the roof of the shed. It fell away, after an extra tug from me, and the mural was revealed.

Kate gasped, her eyes roving over the entire piece. She covered her mouth with a trembling hand and tears fell freely.

"Bron," she breathed through her fingers, her gaze pausing at various parts of the painting. "Bron." Finally her gaze landed on me. Me, standing there in my baggy shorts and rugby shirt and sneakers and my bottom lip caught between my teeth. "Bron," she repeated.

"Do you like it?" I wanted to shove my hands in my pockets and rock back and forth. So I did.

Kate stepped forward, lifted her hands to caress my cheeks and leaned in to deliver the sweetest, gentlest kiss ever. "I love it. Thank you. This," she removed a hand to wave at the shed, "is breathtaking and beautiful and perfect. I love you." Kate's eyes sparkled. "I think you've taken artistic licence there. My bum's not shaped that delightfully, I'm sure."

I grinned. "Believe me, woman. It so is."

It turned out that Kate had created a gift for me, too. I held the four cranes, attached so that they hung together, one under each other. It was clever and gorgeous and the cranes embraced the ethereal nature of the marbled paper.

"The four meanings." She tucked her hand into my elbow and pointed to each bird with her other hand. "Hope because I know that our marriage will be loaded with it. It's such a wonderful emotion. Peace because I found it with you. You gave me peace, sweetheart. Love." She squeezed my arm. "We have that everywhere and in everything, and," her finger hovered at the bottom crane, "healing during challenging times." Kate took a deep breath and looked up into my face. "You gave me the space to heal. I was able to step into those challenging times, knowing that you were there. And if you bore a damaged heart, I hope our love has mended it."

I didn't know what to say. I mean, I did. "Thank you, sweetheart. This is beautiful." They really were. The cranes were wonderful.

"So you like it?" The question was an echo of mine.

I curled my hand under the hair at the back of her neck and brought our lips together. I kissed her, and kissed her, pouring every ounce of hope, and peace, and love, and healing into her lips. Then I brought my mouth to her ear. "How are you so perfect?"

Kate giggled softly. "That's biased." Her sultry voice sent shivers through my body, then she licked my jawline. "Come on. We need to get changed. Everyone will be here in three hours."

Mum and Dad were the first to arrive, two hours early. Mum hugged me, caressed my cheek, beamed into my face, said, "Congratulations, love," then the 'Mum Look' appeared.

Um.

"Traditionally, I'm supposed to help out the bride but there are two of you, so I'm going to be with Kate and I know you understand, honey." She delivered her singular no-argument nod but with tears threatening which reduced its effectiveness a little, so I embraced her and murmured a "Thanks Mum".

She fossicked about in her bag, thrust a mini packet of tissues at me, then promptly disappeared into the main bedroom with the express instructions not to enter.

Right.

Just as well I had my wedding clothes in the spare room. Dad bustled outside to see to the tables and the arch and that the mowing company had trimmed the lawn edges crisply.

Lydia, resplendent in chiffon and silk that flowed elegantly about her larger body, arrived very soon after with trays of food which she magically fitted into our already full fridge.

"I cannot believe this, McIntyre." She grinned at my smile which grew by the second. "Forty-four and getting married. Finally. How long have I known you?" She answered her own question. "Six years, and this is the first time." Lydia wrenched open the little bar fridge at the end of the kitchen and pulled out a bottle of cider. "I've seen you properly in love. What's-her-face six years ago doesn't even come close to Kate. Not even in the same galaxy."

I laughed. "Hyperbole, much?"

She punched my shoulder as she went past. "Nope."

Because Kate was still cloistered in the bedroom with Mum, I gave Rick the job of carrying the certificate table, while I greeted the celebrant Alison, and directed her to the arch to set up and organise our spots to stand. Kate and I had decided to use one little slice of tradition. I was going to wait at the arch, Kate would descend the stairs and make her way through the guests to my side.

Realising I was running out of time, I hustled into the spare room, unzipped the suit bag and withdrew the dark blue mandarin collar jacket and the black dress pants. I'd fallen in love with the outfit when I'd wandered past the store on the way to chat with my bridge a month ago. I placed the two pieces on top of each other on the bed.

Siobhan barged into the room, followed by Pip and JJ. Then Rick, the last to barrel in, shut the door, frowned at the bed, and hummed, which confused the hell out of me.

"Hair. Now." Siobhan grabbed me by the shoulders and spun me around, while JJ shoved a chair against the back of my knees, which resembled, frighteningly, a well-practiced interrogation technique. Pip lifted my jacket and reverently laid it farther up the bed. Then she pulled out a mini sewing kit from her pocket, and handed it to her father.

"Good on you, Pip. Let's see to those buttons."

What?

"Don't move," growled Siobhan, and I snapped my head back to the front. "Rick's gonna check that your buttons, all fifty fucking billion of them—"

"Swearing, Shiv, please." Rick sounded pained.

"Well, she will go wearing a jacket that takes a team to stick on her body, like she's the bloody emperor with an entourage." Scissors and a comb were flashing about so I let the comment roll over me.

"Rick," I said to Siobhan's chest. "Why?"

"Why me? Because I'm the only one with enough speed and skill to get this done. The button situation just occurred to me this morning and I was worried that one would pop off and you'd be lopsided for the photos."

Aw. "But speed? Skill?"

He was muttering. "Cut here, Pip. That's it. I'll need the midnight blue thread now." He raised his voice. "I figured that securing your buttons wasn't much different than when I'm suturing the rescue cats after their spaying. Cut here, Pip, please."

"Um." I stared at Siobhan's comb. "Well, thanks Rick. That's really thoughtful."

JJ's soft laugh laced with wickedness came from behind and I actually felt it drape across my back. Such a sassy thirteen-year-old.

Finally, after a 'Good luck' and 'You got this' and 'Fuck, I did a good job' and 'Shiv, really?' they all departed and I set about making myself look good enough for Kate. After the twentieth conversation with the mirror, I exited the room and found Dad nursing a beer while sitting on the couch.

"Hey, Dad." I parked myself on the seat next to his. He leant down and plucked an open beer from the tiny cooler bag at his feet. I grinned —trust Dad to bring his own stash—and accepted the drink, then we tapped the rims together.

"How are you doing, love?"

"Bit nervous." I took a sip.

"Yeah. I remember that feeling."

We sat in companionable silence for a beat.

"It's always lovely to see two people getting married who are also each other's best friends."

I nodded at the carpet. "Yeah. She is my best friend." Then I angled my head and raised my eyebrows. "I also fancy the pants off her."

"Helpful if sex is involved."

I spat out my mouthful. "Dad!"

His smile was part mischief, part 'I won', and part tenderness. "What? Nakedness, at least in the lower half, is generally required. Although there are some things a father doesn't need to know."

"Oh my God," I whispered.

"I may not say much, love." Dad spoke to his beer. "But I see an awful lot. Honey, your love, you and Kate, oh my goodness, it's wonderful. And you're good for each other." He paused for a long moment. "She's scared."

I frowned, the bottle halfway to my lips. "About what?"

Dad rested his elbows on his knees and tilted his head to catch my eye. "You don't know? Bron, love, she's scared that she's going to lose you."

"But I'm not going anywhere." Dad clearly had the wrong end of the stick.

"She knows that. What I think is she's scared that *she'll* go." He patted my knee.

Now I was even more confused. "What? Walk away?"

"No, love. Just disappear into the marriage. Sort of dissolve."

"Dad..." I had no idea how he'd come to that conclusion but my eyes welled up anyway. "I'd never let that happen. She's..."

"She's your forever person?"

"Forever and for now."

Dad inhaled. "Good. Then hold on to her. See that she stays, doesn't dissolve, or doesn't run away because I reckon you've found your one."

After that deep, meaningful and entirely strange conversation, I found myself standing at the arch, shifting my weight between each foot, absorbing the smiles and thumbs up from the small group spread out on the grass. The mural, to the left of the arch, had received an abundance of compliments and now when I took in the entire moment, the setting couldn't be more perfect.

Then my breath stopped as Kate stepped out onto the back deck and made her way down the steps, with Mum following behind, pretending to be invisible. I couldn't take my eyes off Kate. She was sublime.

Her hair was down, curled slightly into soft waves and she glowed with happiness. It was as if she'd captured the sun under her skin. I grinned as 'oh my God' rippled through my head like a wave machine. My heart felt bigger than the sky as she made her way carefully through the group, which parted to give her space.

The ivory dress was fitted and showcased every single luscious curve of her body. She wore sandals that made me swoon and carried a single sunflower in her hands. How the hell Janine had found a sunflower in winter I don't know.

Then, just before Kate reached me, I blinked. I knew that dress. I'd seen photos of it in a velvet-covered photo album on Mum and Dad's bookcase. Sure, the dress was modified with less lace to create a sleeker look, and the hem taken up in deference to Kate's height difference and the walking over grass situation, but otherwise, I knew that dress. I whipped my head around, searching quickly for Mum, then stared into her face. Tears pricked at my eyes. Christ, I was doing a whole lot of crying lately. Mum pressed her hand to her chest, bobbing her head from side to side just once, as if to say "Of course I offered." Then she lifted her chin towards Kate, drawing my attention back to the woman in a beautiful, modified, well-loved and significant dress a couple of metres away. A woman who I was about to marry.

Janine had asked me last week what I was saying in my vows, and I confessed that I'd only half written them.

"Really? What on earth are you struggling with? It's Kate, for God's sakes." Janine plonked cutlery on the bench, pointed to JJ and Jack, then the table. The unspoken language of parenting.

"I want to say everything, but not send people to sleep."

"Just say that she's awesome, and funny, and you love her, and she's got great boobs." JJ's voice travelled from the dining room, followed by a strangled cough, a "Shit, JJ. That's—" and the sound of feet stomping up the stairs to Jack's bedroom.

I didn't add the line about great boobs, although I wholeheartedly agreed, but I did finish the vows and so after Kate's beautiful messages of love and commitment, then my promise to grow my love and our love, our eyes had an intimate conversation while the celebrant said all the necessary legal parts.

And just like that we were married. We were thrilled to kiss upon request, then I shook my head at Siobhan's and Lydia's wolf whistles, while Kate bit her bottom lip at their antics. I squeezed her hands, and we looked down at our ring fingers adorned with a simple band.

"You're beautiful," I whispered and her smile was worth every letter in the alphabet.

Alison cut gently into our space. "If you could come to the table, we'll finish with the paperwork."

A marriage certificate is fairly boring considering the importance of the occasion it represents. Even still, mundane or otherwise, it was metaphorical gold, because it conveyed permission from the government and protection from society's prejudice. It was also a declaration of our love, although we didn't need a piece of paper to demonstrate that. People got the picture fairly quickly.

For the decades since I'd been allowed to sign paperwork, my signature had never looked the same each time, which was probably illegal, but I couldn't help it. So I stared at my scrawl in resignation, then shrugged, and passed the pen to Kate, her thigh pressed tightly to mine. I snuck a quick glance at our friends and family, and smiled at Larry's thumbs up. He'd decided that a three-piece tweed suit was both warm and qualified as 'good gear', which was gorgeous. My attention was brought back by Kate's soft tsk of annoyance. The pen was shaking and she'd grabbed her hand with the other in an attempt to still the tremor. It was probably left-over nerves; I had them as well, or perhaps coming down from the adrenaline rush. Whatever it was, it seemed to abate, and she took a deep breath and placed her signature—fancier than mine—at the bottom of the paper.

Another quick scan of our audience, and my attention was taken by Mum's intense gaze directed at Kate. She had her head tilted in that 'Mum' gesture of 'I don't know what I just saw but I'm going to find out'.

I widened my eyes at her when she slid her gaze to me. If she was going on a detective mission to investigate Kate's tremor or whatever it was, she'd come up with nothing.

Kate's hand on my back returned me to our certificate-signing task and I smiled at her touch. "Larry and David need to witness," she said quietly.

We stood while Larry and Dad signed under our names, then Alison shook our hands, gestured to the guests who paused as one before Paul, of all people, declared loudly, "Goodo. Where's the beer?"

 We Grew

October 29 to February 18 in the second and third years of the now

Kate came home later than normal one night at the end of October. She dropped her handbag on the hall table next to the bowl of cranes, peeled her suit jacket off and hung it on the one spare coat hook, then turned to find me watching her from the arm chair in the lounge, a smile growing on my lips.

She strode over, kissed me, then straightened, one hand on her hip, the other clutching a magazine.

"I'm officially old." The magazine was tossed on to the coffee table, then she sat heavily on the couch, and bent to remove her heels.

That was a loaded statement but I was a brave woman. "Why?"

Kate huffed, crossed one gorgeous leg over the other, and reached behind her head to remove the barrettes to let her hair tumble onto her shoulders. "Well, I took your advice." She narrowed her eyes at my smirk. "Ha ha. Your advice to see someone about these ridiculous headaches I've been having. Anyway, I went to the optometrist and it turns out that I do need glasses."

"That's why you're old?"

Kate waved her index finger at me. "No. No, no. The need for glasses is fine. I accept that. No, I'm officially old because." She pointed the finger at the magazine as if it was an offensive item. "While I was waiting for my appointment, I happened to flick through that and found an article declaring that women over a certain age." She poked her chest. "Shouldn't be seen with long hair, or wearing any of the three primary colours." I snorted. "And!" The finger stabbed towards the ceiling. "Loose fitting clothes are necessary to hide parts that have sagged."

I couldn't help it and cracked up at her long-suffering expression. "Sweetheart, you're not old, and you have beautiful hair, and you should choose all the colours, and please keep wearing your fitted clothes." I pointed my own finger. "However, I'm a bit worried at the sudden onset of kleptomania. Stealing magazines from an optometrist's waiting room is a serious offence."

Kate was smiling before I'd started the final sentence. We stared at each other, then burst out laughing, and she sagged into the back of the couch. I hauled myself out of the arm chair and settled at her side, tucking her in close, then I rubbed at the wedding band on her finger.

"Have you had dinner?" I asked quietly.

Kate rested her cheek on my shoulder. "No. I was too upset at being labelled a woman of a certain age." I chuckled, so she poked my thigh and I felt her smile. "What did you end up eating?"

"I didn't. I waited for you." Then my stomach growled to back up my statement.

∼

DINNER ON OCTOBER TWENTY-EIGHT *WAS* ACTUALLY organised.

"What's the occasion?" Kate's seductive voice came from the doorway, and after a quick transformation from my instant puddle of goo, I pulled myself together, then beamed across the sunflower in the vase, the table cloth, and the wine glasses that I'd only just finished fussing with.

"It's our anniversary." I spun her gently and removed her jacket, hanging it on the back of a chair. "Do you want to have a shower first and get changed? Or have dinner now?"

Kate turned back around and curled her arms around my neck. "It's not our wedding anniversary, sweetheart. Dinner now, by the way, thank you. So it's the anniversary of what?"

My hands found her waist and I tugged her closer. "It's our twenty-one month anniversary." Then I backed out of her arms, moved into the centre of the kitchen—all of three steps—and pretended to unfurl a scroll. "It is written in the great book of anniversaries and other important dates that many people forget at their peril." Kate slapped a hand over her mouth. "That the twenty-first anniversary is an auspicious event." I channelled Janine for a moment.

"An auspicious event? I can't think of anything that should be celebrated in the twenty-first month."

I pointed my finger. "Well, you haven't been reading the proper ancient scrolls." She giggled, and I pointed again. "So listen, and all will be revealed."

Kate's eyes sparkled as she pretended to zip her lips with her thumb and forefinger, then leaned her shoulder against the door frame. I cleared my throat importantly.

"Twenty-one months ago, in a land far, far away, at the bridge in the centre of town, a dashing almost middle-aged art teacher was minding her own business by surreptitiously sketching a beautiful woman completely without her consent. That woman was backlit and a choir of angels was singing." Kate snorted and slapped her hand over her mouth again. "The art teacher couldn't think of an excuse to approach the beautiful woman without embodying that personage known as creepy unexpected stalker." Kate was gradually giving in to her laughter. "Until!" I pointed to the ceiling, then took a step towards her. "Until the sudden arrival of a saviour, riding gallantly through the crowd, heralding his arrival to one and all with the fine words, 'coming through'." I stepped closer. "This saviour was dubbed Chaos Man and I will be forever grateful for his appearance because twenty-one months ago, you threw a smoothie all over yourself and I found a reason to meet the most gorgeous woman in the world." My next step brought me right into her space. "Happy anniversary, sweetheart."

Her response was instantaneous. Laughter bubbled up from her chest and she slipped her arms about my neck, and I felt every shimmer of her happiness in my heart.

"I must find Chaos Man one day and thank him for creating such a perfect moment." Kate's eyes were still sparkling but I could tell that the sparkles were laughter and tears and love and everything that sparkles can be. She pressed her lips to mine, then we grinned at each other.

"Red or white wine for dinner?" I stared into her beautiful face, then I kissed her again because how could I not?

～

In late November, the incoming text alert pinged on my phone as I stared forlornly at the pile of vegetables and other related produce on the bench, hoping desperately that it would somehow turn itself into a meal. I figured that wielding a sharp implement would inspire me, so I hauled out the largest knife we had and stood in front of the uninspiring hill. It certainly wasn't a hill I'd die on. There were better hills to defend such as the pineapple on pizza hill.

I dropped the knife on the wooden chopping board, and plucked up my phone.

A smile grew on my lips and I slapped the phone against my chest like a giddy teenager.

"I love you, Kate Agostino."

The text, bracketed by a couple of kiss emojis, informed me that a bag of Thai takeaway was currently in Kate's car—I imagined it tucked up beside her briefcase—and it was only five minutes away from home so could I grab some plates, please?

I love Thai food, so it gave me a warm fuzzy that she'd bought that particular cuisine. But my heart did an extra bounce on the 'I love my wife' trampoline because Kate really wasn't a fan of Thai at all, yet there she was bringing home my favourite dinner. Just for me. Just because.

I threw the pile of you're-not-Thai-food-so-too-bad-suckers back into the fridge.

～

Suddenly Christmas was upon us.

"When?" Kate dunked the teabag up and down in my cup, then

squeezed the bag into the sink, and transferred the cup into my waiting hands.

"When what?" I blew across the top of the tea. "Thanks for this." Kate nodded and indicated with her chin that she was going outside to sit on the porch. I followed her, appreciating the way the linen shorts shaped her delicious arse, then I glanced at the carefully decorated Christmas tree in the corner of the lounge and a wonderful feeling of this-is-home filled my heart.

We sat together on the top step and Kate exhaled heavily. "When did it suddenly become December? Why are we suddenly two weeks from Christmas?"

I'd been thinking the same thing, but I had the answer. "We all attended a seminar three years ago about kids and their perceptions of the world." I puffed at the surface of the cup. "Apparently, when we're young, each second of actual time is packed with mental images, so a kid's mind is able to capture thousands of images per second, and that's why time appears to pass more slowly. For them, anyway. They're processing at a million miles an hour but their brains reckon time's going slowly. It's the whole 'Are we there yet?' syndrome." I took a sip of the cooling tea. It was slightly ludicrous to drink a hot beverage on a particularly hot and humid Saturday in December, but there was a breeze hanging about, attempting to bring comfort and joy, which seemed appropriate this close to Christmas.

"So as we get older, we capture less images per second?" Kate, her tea held carefully with both hands, twisted her body, shuffling a little so she could face me properly. I mirrored her movement, and we both ended up leaning against the porch uprights.

"Yep. Basically. The seminar presenter said that over time, the rate at which we process visual information slows down, and this is what makes real time speed up as we grow older." I shrugged. "Still haven't quite got my head around it." I stared over Kate's shoulder then brought my gaze back. She was smiling over the top of her cup. *Yum.* "The theory about the kids makes sense. It's not that their experiences are deeper or more meaningful than ours, it's just that they are being processed in such a rapid way. We're just slower because our brains don't get as much bang for their buck." Kate grinned, and I widened my eyes at her in mock frustration. "Paraphrasing, Ms Agostino." I returned her smile. "Kids process so quickly that time slows down. Like a yin yang thing. Our processing is crap so there's real, proper time between each actual image because we're slow, which means our time speeds up." I rolled my head back, clunking it lightly on the wood behind me. "It sounds good, anyway."

"It sounds very logical."

"It sounds like I've forgotten professional development content." I grinned. "Thereby proving my point." I pointed to my head. "Crap brains."

~

CHRISTMAS LANDED WITH A TSUNAMI OF GOOD CHEER, goodwill to all men—"Genders!" yelled JJ across the dining table at the McIntyre Christmas lunch, this year at Siobhan and Paul's—and a whole lot of food, air-conditioning and contemplation.

That morning in bed, Kate kissed me, began to turn away, and I tackled her, both of us laughing and rolling around under the sheet. It was the perfect start to what we knew would be an enormously busy day. Once we were showered and dressed, I walked Kate out to our tree, bent to retrieve a small box, then placed it in her hands.

"Merry Christmas, sweetheart."

Kate chewed at her lip, and blinked away the tears that had gathered. "Thank you, darling." She held the box for so long that I wondered if she'd either been struck by an enormous wave of emotion or paralysed in awe of my gift-wrapping skills. Probably the former. Then she caught my quizzical look, smiled, and undid the bow.

I shuffled about on the balls of my feet because my gift was hand-made just like last year. Created specifically for Kate just like last year. And demonstrated my love. Just like last year.

I'd made a model of our backyard shed and recreated the mural on the side of it. Each week, putting in an extra hour or two after dismissal, until I was kicked out from the art room by Lucas, the lovely cleaner with the extra wide grin, the suction barrel strapped to his back as if he'd walked off the set of Ghostbusters, who would frown, shake his vacuum nozzle as if to say "Bugger off home, Bron,", ensured that I'd finished the model in time. My first attempts had resembled dilapidated buildings that should have had tumbleweeds rolling through them, but eventually one shaped itself into perfection and it sat there in Kate's palm.

"Do you like it?" I asked tentatively because Kate hadn't said a word throughout the entire unwrapping process. "I wanted you to be able to see the mural every day instead of having to traipse outside and stand on the grass with the ants."

Her tears fell. "Bron, this is beautiful. I-I don't know what to say." She placed the model lovingly on the hall table, turned and literally threw herself into my arms. "You are a gift," she mumbled into my shirt.

I embraced her body, her vulnerability, her love, her tears. I embraced my Kate.

She took a very deep breath, then pulled away and slid open the small drawer in the centre of the hall table and carefully withdrew a crane. I smiled. Handmade gifts were extra special.

"It's." Her eyes filled with tears again. Perhaps they hadn't left. "It's...this one is for love and I think every crane I've ever given you has been." Kate blinked and a few of the tears escaped, rolling down her cheeks. She lifted trembling hands, fingertips smoothing the skin.

It was an orange crane, with writing across the wings, and underneath when I turned it over. All messages of love. Just like last year. Yet, as I kissed her, I couldn't help feeling a little prick of hurt. Kate had always, *always*, prided herself on the meticulousness of her origami folding. The exactness in the corner to corner lines so that it was impossible to see the second corner under the the the first. The cranes were perfect. But not this one. It wasn't as crisp, and it wasn't meticulous, and even from thirty centimetres away, I could see the overlapped corners.

Why?

"Thank you, sweetheart". I kissed her again, then placed the crane next to the model of the shed, and took a moment to take in both gifts.

"I'm sorry." The words were dripping with pain.

I turned quickly. "Why? What?" Her hands were clasped at her abdomen, fingers twitching together, so I undid the knot of tension created by knuckles and nails to hold her hands in mine.

Kate's expression was difficult to decipher. Sadness, frustration, irritation, but mostly sadness, yet smothered in love, which lived in her eyes, and overrode the fluidity of emotions across her face.

"I'm sorry," she repeated, her voice even softer than before so I tugged her towards me, drew her arms about my waist and she leaned into my shoulder.

"Sweetheart, what's wrong?"

"You have no idea how many cranes I made before that one, but I." Her whole body seemed to lose all structure, and I tightened my arms. "I couldn't get them exactly right. My fingers weren't working properly and the corners kept slipping." She took a shuddery breath. "But I so wanted to give you something handmade. A crane. But then suddenly it was Christmas and I'd run out of time, so I chose the very best one and I wrote my messages. So, even though the crane isn't perfect, please know the words are." *Oh, Kate.*

"Honey, I love it." I did. She'd made me a crane, and I hadn't received one for so long.

"I'm glad." She sighed. "I've been working too hard, lately."

"I know you have."

JJ HAD DECIDED TO RETIRE THE GENDER OF THE DAY WHICH must have relieved the hell out of Janine and Rick. However, after flinging open the front door even though it was Siobhan and Paul's house, JJ wished us a "Merry Christmas", delivered hugs, and informed us that many Christians believed gift-giving was "A three wise men deal, but you know? Gift giving was totally before those Christian dudes 'coz it has its roots in Saturnalia 'coz the pagans originally gave offerings to the Gods."

Then, with a grin full of mischief, she bounced back into the living room, stealing a chocolate-coated shortbread biscuit off the dining table on the way. Kate and I made eye contact and cracked up. Janine and Rick had another six years of JJ's teenage years. I needed to buy buckets and buckets of popcorn for that show.

Jack had decided to become a vegan in late October, so Janine spent a month trawling through the internet searching for recipes that could be classified as Christmas fair.

We'd gone around for dinner two weeks ago and Janine dropped her forehead to the dining table and moaned, then whipped her head up.

"Kate, do you have any idea how hard it is to find vegan *anything* for

Christmas? For a thirteen-year-old teenager? For *anyone*?" Besides frustrated, Janine seemed truly baffled.

She looked at me, and I held up my hands as if she was threatening to steal my jewels, money, and first born. "I don't know. I'm the original carnivore. Stick me in the Neolithic exhibit at the museum and you wouldn't know the difference."

Kate giggled and squeezed my thigh.

"What about vegan mince stuffed meat loaf?" Kate suggested.

Janine and I blinked.

"That sounds...edible." Janine leapt up, ripped a sheet of paper from the shopping list on the fridge, scooped up a pen, slid into her seat, and scrawled Kate's suggestion across the top. She leaned forward. "What else?"

"Egg-free pavlova?"

I stared at my wife. "Um."

Kate winked at me. "Even though the break-up was necessary, my second boyfriend was religiously vegan and creating romantic dinners was an adventure."

So Christmas lunch, the table covered in the traditional McIntyre eclectic fare now with the addition of Jack's vegan dishes which everyone seemed to enjoy—"This is actually good!" announced Rick in surprise, shovelling in another mouthful with great gusto, and receiving a withering glare from Janine—was its normal riotous occasion. Siobhan and Paul stretched the celebration into the early evening and we lapsed into food comas after dessert and leftovers.

"I know what you're doing, Shiv," I muttered to Siobhan as we scooped leftovers into containers to shove into the fridge.

"What?" She smirked and hauled out all the boxes I'd already placed inside so she could play fridge Tetris.

"Spinning out Christmas Day so Kate doesn't have to think about missing dinner at her mum's." I passed her a square Tupperware container crammed with potato salad.

"Really? Is that what I did?" She somehow shoehorned the container into the void. "I just figured people shouldn't drive with that much food in them. They'd never reach the fucking steering wheel."

I'd told Kate last year that Siobhan was the kindest person in the world but hid it behind profanity so I watched with sisterly love as

Siobhan tucked her heart away behind exploding clothing and dangerous driving.

New Year's Eve was the next event on our social calendar, but we decided to spend the night at home, ready to ring in the moment with take away, ice cream and dark chocolate. Probably sex judging by the yummy tension in the air. With half an hour remaining in the year, Kate grabbed my hand, and led me down the outside steps to the tiny path that ran to the shed. We were basically in the middle of the backyard.

"Are we looking at stars again?" I murmured into her hair as I wrapped my arms about her torso, her back against my breasts.

Kate curled her fingers over my wrists and sighed. "We could, but I thought I'd add to the occasion." She disentangled herself, then tossing a pleased look over her shoulder, marched across to the outside socket, and flicked the switch. The backyard was instantly filled with tiny dots of colour.

"Oh my God," I breathed, turning slowly so I could take it all in. Somehow, without me knowing, Kate had strung fairy lights along all the fences, over the clothes line, and the A-frame of the shed. I arrived back in my original position to find Kate standing close, so very close.

I leant in and brushed my lips over hers, fingertips landing softly on her cheeks, smoothing the skin. "I love you."

Kate smiled against my mouth. "I love you, too." Her gaze held mine, her eyes reflecting all the colours and all the love, then she reached in to her back pocket, and pulled out her phone. "Two minutes." She placed the phone, screen side up, on the grass and draped her arms over my shoulders, curling her hands into my hair. I shivered.

"This year has been monumental and amazing and I'm very, very, happy you're here." I had more words to add to those, but they were pushing and shoving like frantic train commuters and I couldn't organise any more sentences. I hoped that Kate could read them on my face.

"This year has been a revelation and perfect and I'm so glad that we are the forever and the—"

The first firework launched from, of all places, the Veris tower in the city and lit up the sky. We grinned at each other.

"And the now," we said together, and our kiss was soft, building and building in passion until I wanted to rip Kate's clothes off, kneel on the concrete and make her scream into the night. We broke off, panting, our eyes dark with coloured desire.

"Oh! Wow." God, the woman could kiss.

"Will you dance with me? I've always wanted to dance on New Year's with my person in the backyard of our house under the washing line," Kate said, deadpan.

I cracked up, and Kate grinned. She leaned down and tapped on her phone, then Taylor Swift's *Lover* drifted from the speaker. It was perfect.

Our dancing was small in deference to the limited solid ground available, but everything else about the moment was big.

Later that night—morning—on our crisp white sheets specially chosen to begin the new year, Kate gently pushed me down and carefully, slowly, delicately unravelled me with her tongue and her fingers and her intense gaze which she held until my eyes slammed shut when I came with a shout, her name spilling from my throat.

She didn't want me to reciprocate.

"Just hold me, Bron."

So we curled in to each other, under our white sheet, which fluttered in a breeze that somehow knew to drift tenderly over us through the little holes in the fly screen.

~

IN THE MIDDLE OF JANUARY, SIOBHAN AND PAUL ASKED ME and Kate to dinner. I was immediately suspicious.

"Why?" Kate screwed up her face allowing the tiny wrinkles around her eyes to take charge of the skin.

I hauled wet clothes from the washing machine and dumped them into the laundry basket. "Firstly, Siobhan *phoned* me. She never phones me. She texts." I hefted the basket, balancing it on my hip. "Secondly." Kate opened the back door, then followed me over to the clothes line. We grabbed a shirt each, shook them out and pegged them to the interior line. "She's cooking our favourite meal. Not yours. Not mine. Ours, which means she's researched this information from Janine because Siobhan wouldn't have known that independently. And!" I waved a pair of soggy undies at her. "She hasn't invited anyone else."

Kate laughed and hung up another shirt. "I think you're reading way too much into the invitation. Perhaps she's genuinely inviting us to dinner because she's genuinely inviting us to dinner."

I harrumphed and rearranged Kate's sock-hanging so that the pairs were pegged side by side.

It turned out, just as I'd suspected, that Siobhan and Paul needed a favour.

"You didn't have to lure us here with steak, scalloped potatoes, and roasted carrots."

Siobhan glared. "I didn't *lure* you, for fuck's sake." She turned to Kate. "Were you lured?"

Kate rolled her lips together. "I feel completely unlured. This is a lovely dinner, by the way, Shiv." Then she laughed at my look of outrage.

Paul's lips curled into a smile. "Well, all luring aside, we'd love it if you could look after Fruitloop for two weeks while we go to Sydney to see my folks."

Fruitloop, their black miniature poodle, immediately leapt off the couch, barked while spinning in such tight circles that he created a mini air whirlpool, then sprung back onto the couch and promptly fell asleep.

Kate grinned and I sighed dramatically. Generally speaking, I'm not a dog person, so the thought of looking after Fruitloop for two weeks didn't thrill me.

Siobhan's face fell. "Bron, I know he's a demented dog. You know that's how he earned his name, but you also know he's sweet and harmless and—"

"Chews stuff."

"Well, yes. But we're working with Rick on getting him out of that habit."

"Rick chews stuff?"

Kate's peal of laughter and the sparkle in Siobhan's eyes appeared simultaneously.

"Come on, Bron. Kate's on board." She raised her eyebrows hopefully at Kate, who nodded, and turned to me, raising her own eyebrows. It was as if we were playing Hot Potato with facial gestures. Siobhan continued her pitch. "You're the only ones who can."

That earned another grumpy stare. "So we're the last resort." It was ridiculous to now act offended by the idea that we'd not been considered first right after being offended that we'd actually been considered at all. I was an idiot.

"Well, Janine and Rick can't because of the cats. Mum and Dad can't because Fruitloop won't get a proper walk because Mum will be so busy chatting to all the neighbours that Fruitloop will have a snooze between driveways. Besides, you've got a fenced backyard with actual grass."

That was a selling point. Fruitloop would be happy all day by himself and we wouldn't be cleaning up dog shit off the carpet when we arrived home.

Then Siobhan smiled through gritted teeth, eyebrows raised apologetically. "Just don't hang your towels too low on the washing line. He likes to do a run up, grab hold of one—probably your best—and go for a bit of a swing as the line spins around. Teeth marks in your bath mats and all that."

We stared at Siobhan and Paul, who nodded in resignation.

"What...what does he do when he finishes his...turn?" Kate seemed genuinely, although tentatively, curious.

Paul circled his finger in the air, then flicked his thumb. "Off into space. Seems to land on his feet every time, usually a couple of metres away."

It was impossible not to laugh as we visualised a black miniature poodle auditioning for Cirque du Soleil.

So, at the beginning of February, we became parents to a gregarious, absurd, curly-haired pooch, whose genetic structure placed more emphasis on creating fur than common sense.

It turned out that I was dog-person-adjacent, and not completely averse to throwing a soggy, nearly bald tennis ball about the backyard for Fruitloop when I came home from work. I'd catch Kate, who always arrived home an hour later, leaning on the railing of the back porch, a glass of wine in each hand, and a smirk that contained an entire paragraph along the lines of "I told you so," and "You're ridiculous," and "I'm telling Siobhan and Paul."

"Shut up," I muttered, then smiled at her laughter, and washed my hands so I could drink wine in the sunset with a small dog curled up on my lap. Kate knew better than to mention that development.

Three days before Siobhan and Paul returned from Sydney, Kate stared at the curly-haired cushion sleeping on the couch between us; the latest development in a never-ending tide of Fruitloop-inspired developments.

"We should think about getting our own dog after we give him back." Kate seemed surprised at her suggestion as if she hadn't meant to say it out loud. She met my incredulous gaze.

"Um." I blinked. "Really? But we've barely coped for just two weeks."

Kate laughed. "Barely coped...please. That dog loves you and even though you pretend that you can't stand him, you're all bluff. Look, I know that you've avoided looking after him—"

"I've looked after him!" I spluttered.

Kate's expression was a mixture of disbelief, a smidgeon of indulgence, and a good dose of annoyance. "Actually, you haven't, sweetheart. For two weeks, I've walked him, fed him, cleaned up after him, and you've pretty much patted and played with him."

I considered her words. Kate had been excited to look after Fruitloop. She'd wanted to take on the responsibility. Hadn't she? Had I even checked?

"Oh."

Kate nodded sadly. "I know I blurted out that idea just then, and it sounds wonderful, but we'd both have to be on board." Her hand slid into Fruitloop's fur at the same time as mine, and we tangled our fingers together.

"I'm sorry." I truly was.

Kate hummed, wriggled her fingers away and stroked her hand along the seashell curl of Fruitloop's body.

"I get to play fetch tomorrow," she said, winking at me.

"Well, I'm not great at tennis balls but I'm a champion at fetching sticks. I'll bring them back every time. Promise. Just don't throw them too far. I'm old, you know." Kate giggled, and I smiled. "I really am sorry," I repeated. Not realising that Kate had done everything for two weeks was mind-blowing. When had I become so oblivious?

The next day, due to a longer than usual staff meeting, I arrived home after Kate, parked behind her car, and stared out of the windscreen. The storm had started as soon as I'd left work and the light and sound show in the sky was spectacular. Huge raindrops began to splash onto the glass, so I grabbed my bag and keys, threw myself out of the car, kicked the door closed and galloped up the front steps. The door was slightly ajar which I was incredibly grateful for—thank you, Kate—because it meant I could barrel into the little foyer and shake my hair about just like Fruitloop.

"Hey sweetheart. You here?"

"Bron!" Kate's voice was thready with anxiety.

I dumped my bag and raced into the kitchen to find her staring at Fruitloop's little food bowl.

"What's up?"

"He was here and then I went to the pantry to get his food and when I came back, he was gone and he doesn't leave when there's food, does he?" Kate was shaking.

"Sweetie." I stepped in to hug her. "He'll be around. Perhaps the storm spooked him. I'm sure he's under the bed or somewhere, because it's not like he can get out. All the doors are cl—"

But they weren't. The front door had been ajar when I came home, and I don't remember closing it after me. Kate's eyes grew round.

"Oh God, no."

We Lost

February 18 to October 10 in the third year of the now

We dashed outside, pausing briefly so that Kate could kick off her heels and shove her feet into a pair of sneakers that were kept inside the front door. The rain was still at that will-it?-won't-it? stage with enormous drops falling as if all the little ones had decided to take the plunge together.

"Fruitloop!" Our cries battled with the waves of thunder that surfed across the twilight sky. Kate raced down the driveway so I veered right to bellow for the little dog under Larry's house, which resulted in Larry bursting out of his front door.

"What on earth? What are you doing out in the storm?"

"Fruitloop is missing." Saying it out loud made it real and I gulped down a sob. Larry nodded, turned quickly, grabbed the rain jacket from the hook outside his door, and bustled down the stairs at a speed at which an eighty-three-year-old really shouldn't be moving.

"Here. Put this on." He shoved the jacket at me. "Go help Kate. I'll try the neighbours on the other side." He'd hustled off before I could protest about jackets, and rain, and wet grass, and broken hips in the elderly.

I found Kate halfway down the street, her cries now hysterical, so I raced in front, and brought her to a stop. Making sure she held my gaze, I tugged the jacket over her body and zipped it up.

"We'll find him. Let's try the bushland at the end of the street."

Kate seemed to think my idea was genius because she swerved past me and took off, her soaked business pants glued to her legs. The bushland, all eucalyptus trees, banksia shrubs, and grasses the height of a small poodle, loomed in front of us. Kate, defying her fifty years, leapt over the low log railing, yelling for Fruitloop at regular intervals. I slotted my calls in between hers. The trees created shadows that loomed across the well-trodden trail so I whipped out my phone, and swung it about, even though the light from the torch pulled the shadows along like a ghostly forest.

Suddenly Kate stopped and spun around, her long hair plastered to her face. She dragged it away in frustration. "This isn't working. We need to split up, because he could be anywhere. He's such a tiny thing." She shoved her fist against her mouth and bit into her bent index finger as her chest hitched with her sobs.

Splitting up was an idea born from panic, so I shook my head. "No. Come on. Let's go a bit farther."

Then, before we took our next step, a small whimper, which would have been inaudible if smothered by thunder, came from somewhere off the path. I opened my mouth to call but Kate held up her hand. The whimper, this time a little higher in pitch, came again. Kate crouched down in the dirt, and held out her hand, soft, relaxed, offering safety and comfort. "Fruitloop?"

I stood frozen. Was I supposed to crouch as well? If I did, would my movement spook the dog? Should I say his name?

"Fruitloop, sweetie." Kate's voice was calm yet shaking with fear. "I can hear you, sweetie. It's okay. The storm's going now, okay? Why don't we take you home? Okay, sweetie? You can come out now, Fruitloop." The nonsensical sentences seemed to work, because a little nose appeared, followed by a pair of eyes that were the size of dinner plates; no mean feat on a dog the size of an overly indulged cat. Fruitloop whined and Kate inched her hand forward, pausing to allow him to come to her. Eventually he emerged from under the bush, trembling, bedraggled, sopping wet, and covered in enough nature that he could be a floral display. He glanced up at me—Bron the plaything—then crept over to Kate—the provider of food. That made sense.

With Fruitloop tucked inside Kate's jacket, we slowly made our way back to the house. We were soaked anyway, so it didn't matter what speed we travelled.

Larry was waiting for us at the end of his driveway. "You didn't find him?" His mouth turned down in worry.

Kate pointed to the tuft of curly hair sticking out above the zipper. "He was in the bushland down the road." Gravity pulled on Larry's shoulders, and he smiled, his face wrinkling in relief.

"Oh, thank God. He's such a wee fellow, and black, too. Wouldn't have seen him. Who knows when he would've been found?"

"We'll get your jacket back to you tomorrow," I said, suddenly tired as the adrenaline began to leave my veins, but Larry flapped his hand.

"No hurry, Bron, love. I'm not going out in too many storms for a while. Nearly went arse over tit going up the Harrison's driveway." My mind filled with ambulances and more elderly hip replacements. Christ.

"Thanks for your help, Larry. You head off and we'll get Fruitloop inside."

Kate continued to cradle Fruitloop all the way into the kitchen, while I triple-checked the front door. I found her on her knees as Fruitloop shook himself, creating an arc of water, leaves and twigs, then she plucked out as many of the remaining bits and began to rub him dry with a towel. I squatted down beside her.

"Let me take over while you have a shower."

"No, it's okay. I can do it."

"Kate." I recognised her compulsion to care, to coddle, to comfort because she probably felt guilty for leaving the door open. Kate paused, her hands around Fruitloop's body, and she nodded slowly.

"Okay." She passed the towel. "When he's dry, give him some food, and we'll make a bed for him in our room, because I think it's better if he doesn't sleep in his cra—"

"I know what to do. I'm not a child, okay?" Apparently, adrenaline was still galloping about inside both of us. Kate with her obsessive need to create order out of chaos. Me with my teenage snark as I attempted to release the vibrating energy in my bones.

With the humans duly showered, and Fuitloop asleep on the couch, we stood in the lounge room, our gaze shifting from each other to the dog and back.

"God, we can't tell Siobhan and Paul about this." I shoved my hands in my pockets and gave a small laugh at the end of my sentence.

Kate's mouth dropped open. "You're kidding, right?"

"What?"

"That's what you care about, Bron? Your sister and her partner's reaction?"

"No, of course not."

"This was a traumatic experience, and you don't care."

I sucked in a sharp breath. "What?"

"Actually you probably do care but only about the front door being left open."

"What?" I repeated. That was unfair. Oh boy, we really had a truck-load of surplus adrenaline to work through.

"Bron, for all you care, Fruitloop may as well be a mobile cushion." Her eyes flashed.

"I do care, for fuck's sake!" I caught myself. When had I given up apologising for swearing? Right then? I folded my arms across my chest. "Of course I—".

"You don't show it. Not to him and certainly not tonight. He's an entertaining toy that gets in the way when he needs feeding or brushing or someone to collect his shit." She tossed her hands in the air. "I don't want to argue about this anymore."

I grit my teeth. "God, stop doing that."

"What?" She'd already begun to turn away.

"That." I uncrossed my arms and flicked a hand at her. "Decide that we've finished our discussion and leave."

Kate took another step farther. "But we have finished."

"No. We haven't." I opened my hands in frustration. "You have."

Kate looked at me over her shoulder, her lips thin. "I'm not arguing with you. I'm simply choosing not to participate." She stalked away.

"Yep," I said softly.

I DON'T KNOW WHEN IT BEGAN. A LITTLE WHILE AFTER THE Fruitloop incident, perhaps? All I know is that Kate and I took a step back in our relationship. Just a step. Nothing serious. But enough for us to eventually notice, and then, of course, it became the elephant in the room.

Maybe it was around JJ and Jack's fourteenth birthday in March.

"Fourteen! That's, like, really old, dude," I sassed at Jack as we walked into the Mexican restaurant. He rolled his eyes.

"You sound like you're forty-four, Aunty Bron."

"Ooh, burn," Siobhan and JJ said at the same time, and they grinned at each other, then laughed at my attempt at epic side-eye. Kate chuckled.

"Even I know better than to attempt conversation in the native language of teenagers. Ethnography is not your thing, sweetie."

I rolled my eyes and pulled the twins into a hug. "There you go. That's your present. Physical representation of undying love and affection."

"And these," Kate said, handing a gift bag to each as they disentangled themselves. Then she took the remaining steps to the tables which had been shoved together to create enough space for our chaotic family and I blinked. *That's a new development.* We always arrived anywhere together. It was that 'we' thing rather than 'I'. *Apparently not.*

I caught Siobhan's narrow-eyed look, studying me then sliding her gaze to Kate, who'd settled onto a seat next to Dad. Kate looked up, smiled, beckoned me over, and patted the back of the empty chair to her left. I exhaled quietly. See? We were fine, and I was going to put that weirdness down to work stress or just plain old weirdness from the planet Weird.

At the same time, a promotion to deputy principal was waved about in the staff meeting at work and without me even submitting an application, Paula, our principal, wandered into the art classroom, stepping carefully over the raindrops of clay that littered the floor, and offered me the job.

I blinked at her.

"But I didn't apply," I said in utter confusion.

"Hmm. I know." She checked for substances then leaned against the nearest table. Paula's business suits and substances didn't cross in the Venn diagram of life. "But you're the most qualified as far as administration of teams, your work on policy, and you're very capable of organising the minutiae of the school administration that sits between Ty and myself."

Ty, the school's incredibly competent office manager, who seemed to possess eight arms to accomplish the infinite number of tasks he dealt with each day, probably didn't need a deputy principal, but since the departure of Charlotte, and the Education department's insistence that schools actually possess a deputy principal, apparently Paula had decided that I was a suitable replacement.

"Um." *Goodbye, words.*

"Are you interested?" she asked, which was a pointless question considering she seemed to have glued my name to the office door.

"Well, I had been considering it." I flipped my hand in admission, and Paula beamed.

"Excellent. Pop your application in by three so we can meet the department's human resources requirements and we'll get you organised." She stood and tugged on the hem of her jacket.

"Paula, I need details. We're only a month into the school year." I waved my arm about the art room. "What about my classes? What about...everything? I'm not sure if I can—"

"Of course you can. You'll still teach two days a week." She pointed. "Your choice of days, and Michael can teach the remainder."

Michael was the casual teacher who covered for any staff who were absent, including me, during the year. He was excellent, and I nodded in agreement.

"Okay, well, yes, he's a good choice." And the idea that I'd still teach kiddos in my creative space filled my heart. *All right, then. Why not?*

Therefore, after a week of sorting out the details, Paula informed the staff at our Friday afternoon meeting—Lydia gave me a long look, then mouthed, "Teflon"—and I discovered a cardboard rectangle bearing my name inserted into the metal holder on the office door next to Paula's.

It turned out that Kate and I had both accepted promotions that week; my deputy role and Kate to senior manager. I didn't even know she'd applied.

"Of course I told you," Kate said briskly that Friday night. She tossed the tea towel, soggy from when she'd dried the dishes, into the laundry attached to the kitchen, where it landed in a wet heap on the floor. Then she leaned her hip against the bench.

"I have absolutely no recollection." I flicked through the mail on the counter, found nothing of importance, then looked up at Kate.

"Bit like the recollection I have of you applying to become deputy principal." She raised her eyebrows and gave me a half smile. "Congratulations by the way, sweetheart. That's wonderful."

"Thanks. Same for you. So, what do you do as senior manager?"

Kate pressed her fingertips together and her eyes gleamed. "So much more, which is exciting, but one aspect I'm looking forward to is approving monthly indirect cost recovery calculation and revenue recognition." Then she reached around and tugged on her ponytail, pulling the band away.

I grinned. "Busy." And incomprehensible, but I loved how smart Kate was, and how sexy that word salad had sounded.

Kate shook out her hair, straightened her shoulders, gave me an affectionate smile, and kissed me on the cheek.

Then walked out of the kitchen.

I waited, staring at the rectangle of space in the wall wondering if Kate would return, but she didn't, and it got late, and we went to bed, pecked each other on the lips, then went to sleep so I didn't get to tell her about my new job that I'd begun the same day as hers.

And she never asked.

Something I knew without a shadow of a doubt was how fortunate I was to have found Kate. To love her. But even that knowledge didn't stop me missing the little teeny tiny signs of our love becoming brittle; transparent with indifference.

If I thought hard enough, I probably could have pinpointed when that knowledge of my love and fortune might have sent me a giant letter informing me of the fragility. But I didn't get that message. I was so busy at work. She was so busy at work. And we started not to see each other at all.

I recalled the strange conversation between Dad and I on my wedding day. Where he'd declared that Kate was scared of losing me. That she was scared she'd lose herself; sort of dissolve into the marriage.

I remember I'd said that I'd never let that happen because she was my forever person.

She was my forever.

I was losing her because I assumed she'd always be found.

The brittle moments were teeny tiny, like when I was driving to work one morning in June, and I remembered I'd told myself to fill the car with petrol two days ago otherwise I'd stop in the middle of the M1 and I'd be a car-size version of a traffic cone.

"Fuck!" I glanced at the petrol indicator on the dash and frowned in confusion, flicked my gaze to the road because road rules and all that, then glanced back at the gauge. The red needle pointed to full. How?

Then I remembered—all this remembering—that Kate had borrowed my car last night to pop down to the shops for more milk. She must have filled up the car as well.

A smile grew on my lips. Yep, I was the luckiest woman in the world.

But I forgot—all this forgetting—to send a quick text to say thanks. I forgot to send that GIF of the dancing petrol bowser with the purple hearts around it. I forgot the act of kindness because when I got home, it had left my brain entirely.

Complacency.

The brittle moments were teeny tiny, like the night in July when I came home late from a mind-numbing policy meeting with the deputy principals and principals of the four schools in our network. A casserole pot sat on a wooden breadboard in the middle of the counter, and a quick check under the lid revealed an amazing beef concoction that was one of Kate's favourite recipes. I ladled a good helping into a bowl, shoved it into the microwave, and watched vacantly as it spun around. Fabulous aromas filled the kitchen after I'd taken off the cling film and I inhaled deeply. The first bite was even more fabulous.

I felt Kate's presence before she'd even said a word. Then, "Hi, sweet. How was your day? What was on for such a late night?" And I looked up as she wandered past, touching my shoulder, on her way to a cup of tea that she'd only just made judging by the steam.

"Good. Um, admin meeting. You're not eating?" I assumed not, given the going-to-bed-hot-drink ritual that was clearly underway. I shovelled in another mouthful. Asking why I was late felt weird. She knew, didn't she?

Kate smiled tightly. "I've already eaten." Then flicked her gaze at the clock. *Nine o'clock? Really?*

"Oh."

Turning towards the door, she paused and pointed towards my bowl. "You're welcome, by the way."

I delivered a doubtful frown towards the food, then aimed it at Kate, who sipped at her tea, one foot either side of the line where the darker floorboards transitioned into their lighter cousins. "Maybe your mind is full of work lately." I chuckled. "I did say thanks."

Her sigh seemed sad. "No, you didn't." And she walked away.

Complacency.

The brittle moments were teeny, tiny like when we were in bed one night in August and I recounted a funny moment with one of the kids in the art lesson that day.

"Kate?"

"Mm?" She blinked and brought her gaze back from where it had been directed at the ceiling. Then shuffled so she lay on her side. Her body still turned me into a puddle of goo so I took a moment to appreciate the swell of her breasts and the way the doona flowed over her curves. Then I was the one to return my gaze.

"I was telling you about my day, but you're really not interested."

"Yes, I am."

I scratched my forehead. "What did I say, then?"

She lightly flipped her hand on the bottom sheet. "One of your kids tried to get paint out of a bottle and it didn't come out so they tapped it and it came out and made a mess."

That wasn't what happened at all. The only accurate part was the upside-down bottle. "I thought so," I said quietly. "You're not listening."

She huffed. "Okay. I'm sorry. Tell me again what happened."

"I shouldn't have to." *Uh oh.* The petulance in my reply was cringeworthy and I wished I could suck the tone back into my mouth with the power of Lucas's jet-fighter vacuum cleaner.

Kate glared and hitched the doona higher up her body. Goodnight beautiful breasts. "For fuck's sake, Bron. You asked for my attention!" *Swearing? When had that started?*

"Um. Well, it doesn't matter. I'm going to sleep, sweetie." And I rolled over, feeling the fabric shift as Kate did the same. I heard the whispered words even though I'm sure I wasn't supposed to.

"I guess some things don't matter." Then another shuffle. "Goodnight, sweetheart."

The brittle moments were teeny tiny, like in September I realised with startling insight that my deputy principal job wasn't that difficult. Busy but not difficult. I'd got into a pattern with some of the tasks and found myself completing those on autopilot. And the spontaneous events—"Things that crop up, Bron," according to Paula— simply happened. That's all. They happened. I'd become so complacent in my role that I began to not notice or not care about the results of my work. I took the pay rise, rolled on, and continued to miss my art room.

All of the teeny tiny brittle moments didn't connect as if they were part of a wonky Lego set, because all the big, like birthdays—Kate's fifty-first and my forty-fifth—and our anniversary and other people's birthdays and fun, festive occasions managed to outweigh all that small.

But we—the now—were wrong and some of it? all of it? was my fault and I didn't know how to fix it.

Janine certainly had opinions in early October.

"You don't see her anymore." She pointed a peeled cucumber at me then violently chopped it into uneven pieces.

"Yes, I do," I argued from where I sat on the other side of the bench. I needed space between me and Janine's knife merrily dismembering the produce.

"No, you don't." This time it was the knife aimed my way. "Kate really believes that you take it for granted that you'll *always* see her. And therefore you don't."

"You two have been talking?" I mentally slapped my brain. I was a genius at focusing on the part of a conversation that wasn't the most important. Not. Important.

"Bron, those friends of hers are so far up themselves, they're stumbling around in the dark, plus they've got an opinion about everything and most of those opinions are toxic." The knife was frighteningly close. "Her team are...well, they're her team and they're hardly people she can confide in when she's their boss. And her mum's still a bit iffy."

"How do you know all of that?"

"Because she told me!" Janine yelled, her voice hot with anger, as she slapped the knife on the bench, the metal clanging on the marble.

A silence fell between us.

"Jesus, Bron. Sometimes I think I know more about your wife than you do."

I breathed heavily. Once. Then swallowed.

"And yes, Kate really believes that you are becoming complacent in your relationship. I fucking told you not to fuck it up and you've taken the first step towards doing exactly that." This time she pointed a carrot. "Sort stuff out or so help me, I will kick your arse so hard. Kate's fabulous and you know it but you've forgotten."

Yet, I continued to show complacency—every now and then—and Kate continued to walk away—every now and then—and I began to wonder if one day she'd keep going.

I felt sick in the stomach.

ON THE EVENING OF OCTOBER TEN, I FOUND KATE LEANING against the railing on the front porch, cradling a glass of wine. I rested on my elbows, careful with my own glass, and brushed her shoulder with mine.

"Mind some company?"

Kate tilted her head, her smile full of affection. "I never mind, sweetheart. What have you been up to?"

"Filling in the paperwork so that Paula knows I'm serious about resigning from the role as deputy principal."

She widened her eyes. "You're really going to do it?"

"Yep. It's just not me. I mean." I swirled the wine in my glass. "It is a job I can do, but so is art teaching and I know which one I'd rather be doing full time."

"Good decision, darling." She stared out over the front lawn, and sipped her wine. Suddenly she blinked furiously, then shook her head.

"Damn," she murmured.

"What?" I moved so I could see her face, which wore a look of total frustration as if the emotion was all the clothes you had to wear on board the plane because your suitcase was over the weight limit.

"Just some blurry vision. I don't think the prescription is right yet in these glasses because occasionally things are blurry and I've even had a sort of double vision as if the glasses are multifocals." Kate hummed in annoyance, but seemed to dismiss it, even though I wasn't sure she should, then she straightened.

I sighed. "You heading inside?" I pushed off the railing to follow her.

But she hadn't moved from her spot, except to turn to me, her expression soft. There was something shifting underneath the soft and it worried me that I couldn't read the message.

"Bron."

"Kate?" I lifted the end of her name.

"I'd like us to go to marriage counselling."

We Drifted

October 10 to January 31 in the third and fourth year of the now

"What?" I closed the front door, probably with too much force but this was a situation that called for some theatrics. "Of course we don't. People do that when there's no turning back." I followed her footsteps into the kitchen, reluctant to relinquish my wine.

Kate, her hands also occupied with alcohol, tilted her head and sighed. "Yes, but if they're sensible, they do it at the point when they're disconnecting."

I glared. "We're not disconnecting!" *Liar, liar, pants on fire.*

"Yes we are." Kate placed her glass on the bench top. "I know it's two different situations because I really didn't love him with my whole self, but maybe I should have suggested counselling with Neil early on."

"I am not fucking Neil!" I said through gritted teeth, slamming my glass on the dining table so the wine sloshed about.

"I know that! I'm sorry. That was...that wasn't what I meant. What I'm trying to tell you is that." She tossed her hands. "I'm brave enough

147

to say it in this marriage because...well, I adore you and that makes me brave." The hands turned into fists of determination, and she tucked them into her stomach. "But, we are disconnecting, sweetheart, and this marriage. This!" Kate ping-ponged her hand between us. "Is incredibly important! Much too important to throw away. And I hope you feel the same."

I clenched my jaw because the adoring and the loving was mutual and I was on a boat caught in an unexpected storm. "Of course I feel the same, Kate! I utterly adore you as well, so we don't need some shrink to tell us how to be married. I get enough shrinkage from my sister."

"Bron..."

I inhaled shakily. "I...I just feel like we'd be a failure. People go to counselling because they're failing."

Kate shook her head. "Counselling is a tune up and we're not a failure. At all. I want to grow with you and walk through life together. But we do have things to work out." She took a step towards me but I wasn't ready to hug because all my pieces were fracturing and I wasn't sure if Kate could put them back together yet.

"We could do that ourselves," I pleaded. Kate's very long look spoke silent words, and my breath hitched. "I don't understand." I did actually, but my brain had shut down the logical adult sections and it was functioning purely on the sections labelled 'no' and 'why?'

"Yes, you do, sweetheart. I want us to be the forever couple that we are, not the forever couple that we might not get to be." She took another step. Oh boy, she was not playing fair. She'd smile that smile and crinkle the skin around her gorgeous eyes and lift that eyebrow and my heart would explode like it always did. Like it had always done. And I'd be a puddle of goo in no time.

"I..." This felt insane. We'd been married all of a year and a bit and now we were off to counselling. I was on the verge of tears.

"Can we at least try?" Kate whispered, so close. So close.

"But I love you." My voice cracked and the tears lost their grip on the verge and tumbled down my cheeks. "I love you, Kate." Squeaky, fractured, husky voice. "You're my forever and you're my now."

She stepped into my space and all the other space, the inside space, filled with love like it always had.

"I love you, too, sweetheart, and it's because I love you and you love me that we need to do this. I can't conceive of a life without you. I don't ever want to lose *you*," she pointed, "and sometimes counselling shows us that. So let's make sure we are always our forever and our now," she said, as if it was the most logical conclusion in the world.

It was all very sensible, all very true, and so very Kate, and even though my heart kept splintering and repairing, only to splinter again, I agreed.

~

"I'M ALL FOR IT," JANINE ANNOUNCED THE NEXT AFTERNOON when I'd called her to get a psychologist's opinion, not the opinion of a scary knife-chucking sister.

"But it's too soon for us to be like this, J," I said incredulously, leaning against the driver's window inside my car. I stared at the cracks in the dash.

"Is there a time in a relationship when you're supposed to be like this? A milestone?" It sounded like she was on her laptop.

"You know what I mean."

"No, I don't"

After that perceptive conversation with Janine, who was clearly distracted, I bit the bullet and phoned Siobhan, who was at work because *Wham* was blaring in the background and someone was asking her where the supplies of modifying foam were.

"I'm at work, Bron."

"I know. I...I..." Great. I'd started with stuttery-no-proper-words-Bron right off the bat.

There was a pause, then a whispered, "Take over here, Michel. I'm just popping out the back." Then the music and chat and instructions faded and Siobhan continued. "Janine told me."

"Oh, for fuck's sake." I lightly thumped the steering wheel.

"What? Like we're all foreign agents and can't talk to each other?"

"Okay. So, yes. Kate and I are going to marriage counselling, therapy, whatever."

"Wow. Who's the teenager today?" I heard cardboard tearing, which was probably Siobhan in search of the modifying foam.

"Shut up."

"You rang me."

I sighed.

"Are you splitting up?"

I ripped the phone away from my ear and glared at the screen. "No!"

"You glared at your phone. Stop it."

My response was to growl and Siobhan gave a laugh-grunt noise.

Then she paused again. It was definitely a contemplative pause.

"Am I your favourite person in the world?"

"Shiv..."

"Answer the question."

I shrugged even though she couldn't see it. "Well, you're family so I have to love you."

"Of course. But am I your favourite person?"

I stared at the sun visor. "No."

"Janine?"

"No."

"Mum?"

The lump in my throat grew and tears pricked at my eyes. "No," I whispered.

"Dad?"

I grit my teeth as the weird nose tingle right before the onset of tears began.

"No."

"Yourself?"

"Definitely not." I almost laughed.

"Then who is it?"

Quick breaths and nose tingles and throat lumps all ganged up on me and forced the tears from my eyes. I held my sobs at bay, pressing my palm to my mouth.

"Bron, hon. Who is your favourite person in the world?"

"Kate."

"Then tell her, and meanwhile go to counselling, because maybe you'll find the magic words to bring her back."

It never ceased to amaze me how insightful my annoying, Sweary McSweary little sister could be.

∼

THE COUNSELLOR WE FOUND—BERNADETTE—LOOKED about twelve, but was apparently thirty-eight, and I was doubtful about her limited life experience to deal with counselling of any description, let alone marriage, particularly when I discovered her complete lack of marriages.

During the preliminary phone call, we agreed to her eleven-week package, which seemed like a strange number for a package of anything because usually a package was five or ten. Janine would know the meaning of eleven. It was probably a number that represented honesty and compassion or something.

Bernadette told us that there would be nine sessions, one per week, before Christmas and then two as follow up towards the middle of January after the Christmas holidays. It all seemed very reasonable and business-like and so damn weird.

"Can I just say that it's too surreal for words?" I stared at my wife across the dining table.

"Yes. You can definitely say that because I see the surreal nature as well, believe me," Kate laughed, staring at me with that beautiful look of love and connection and what the hell were we doing if those two nouns were sitting happily in our lives? Kate's expression sobered. "We need it, though, sweetheart."

"Yes. No. Yes." I frowned in confusion. "Sweetheart, it..."

Kate raised that amazing, gravity-defying eyebrow.

I dropped my head in surrender. "It's important and necessary." Then I looked up through my eyelashes. "Do you know we haven't had sex for three months?"

Kate coughed through a mouthful of roast lamb. "I'm not answering that."

Yep. We needed to work on the walking away from conversations situation.

Our first session felt like a doctor's appointment.

Bernadette, legs crossed and looking thoroughly relaxed, sat in an arm chair opposite Kate and me, where we perched, not at all thoroughly relaxed, on the couch. I figured by session five we'd be in lounge-by-the-pool mode. Sure.

"So what brought you to me?"

"A car." *Rein it in, McIntyre.*

Kate sighed. "We have a wonderful marriage but there are a few cracks starting and I—we. We want to ensure those cracks don't become so irreparable that we discover we're on different sides of the canyon."

I'd always loved the way Kate thought about things visually and I could see us on those opposite sides shouting across the ravine. I needed these counselling sessions just to erase that image. Revelation number one.

Bernadette explained that couples didn't have to be in crisis or have fallen out of love to attend counselling.

"That's good to know, Bernadette, because we do love each other." If my jaw was any tighter, I'd crack something.

Kate looked at me with affection and sadness, which was an awful combination and ripped at my heart. "Yes, we do love each other very much," she said. I held her gaze for a long time, then turned to Bernadette.

"So, that's enough, right?"

"No."

"Why not?"

Thirty-eight-year-old Bernadette, who looked twelve, steepled her fingers, elbows on the arms of the chair. "Because simply loving someone is not enough. It makes the love static, where one might become complacent," she flicked a finger at me, "and the other might walk away." Kate received the second finger point. "Without watering the seed—"

"Okay. Yep. Got the analogy." I was being rude but this still felt so wrong. Bernadette didn't bat an eyelid. She was probably used to extreme emotions in her pastel office and my bratty behaviour was nothing in comparison. "Sorry," I mumbled.

Bernadette studied me with a look of understanding, which made me uncomfortable.

"Bron, you told me that you haven't ever had a need for therapy of any description because you have your family."

"Exactly." My face wore that lovely teenage expression of 'duh'. Jack and JJ had nothing on me. *That's because the twins are much more polite and respectful, you shit.*

I glanced sideways at Kate who was rigid with stress, which my behaviour was doing nothing to alleviate. Tears were cathartic, apparently. Maybe if I cried the entire river that was dammed behind my eyes, I'd feel better.

"Do you see what happened just then?" I returned my gaze to our counsellor.

"What? Pardon?"

"Did you hear your reply? Your family is your counselling team and you completely expect them to be."

Siobhan and Janine and Mum and Dad and, maybe Paul and Rick at a pinch, were always around to lend an ear. "That's what families do."

Bernadette delivered a small smile. "Have you ever thought that expecting them to always be available is a form of complacency? That if they weren't there, you'd have to look for other people to be your counselling team."

Well, this sucked. It was all 'Bron, you're selfish', and 'Bron, you take people for granted'. What really sucked was that Bernadette was right and I knew it. I called on the power of every God and Goddess and all the Avengers to force back my tears behind the dam, even back into their cage.

She wasn't finished. "Or you would come to a professional. Bron, this is not about your family counselling team versus Kate's lack of one. It's about seeing each other through an objective lens. Me."

I turned to Kate who hadn't called on any powers because she had tears coursing down her cheeks and I realised that we were having counselling because both of us needed to, not just Kate. Revelation number two.

We filled the car with silence, that teeny tiny, brittle silence, on the way home, and found ourselves starring in a movie where one person looks over at the other just as they are turning their head away. I didn't know people actually did that. Who knew?

"Did anything good come out of session number one?" Kate eventually asked.

Despite epiphanies and revelations, brattiness takes a while to leave your system. Much like weed.

I sucked my lip under my teeth. "She's got nice pot plants in the foyer." Yep. Counselling was coming along swimmingly.

At the next session, it was Kate's turn to date Bernadette's spotlight. It was uncomfortable watching her fall apart but I abided by

Bernadette's strict instructions, via a palm-up-hand-stop gesture, not to swoop in.

"Tears are cathartic, Bron." I knew that. I'd willed myself not to experience anything cathartic last session. Bernadette focussed on Kate's face.

"Kate, you can't keep living in the quagmire of your relationship with Neil. It was easier to walk away because the arguments were toxic, weren't they?"

Kate nodded, blinking away tears and more tears and all the tears. She delved into her pocket for a tissue and I desperately wanted to hold her.

"Perhaps spend time reflecting on who you are rather than who you were."

Kate swallowed. "I need to work on engaging sensibly and positively with conflict." Bernadette beamed, and wrote notes in her clipboard.

"Are your tense moments with Bron toxic?"

Kate sucked in air. "Not at all." She looked at me, her eyes filled with sadness. "Not at all," she repeated.

"Then your answer makes sense."

Which was a big lie because we had a fabulously toxic argument two days after that session.

"Really not sure this is working, you know," I said, muting the TV. I was a dog with a bone. *Let it go!*

"Are you working on the hewor-homewi-ho—" Kate shook her head in frustration. "Christ, words lately. Ugh. So frustrating." She delivered an exasperated look at the wall as if it was responsible for her faltering speech, which was a new, and entirely random behaviour for a normally articulate person. "Working on the homework Bernadette set us?"

"Not really," I admitted. "I'll probably get detention."

"Bron, will you please take this seriously!" Kate sprang from the seat and stalked around the couch. I stood slowly, annoyed with myself, annoyed with Kate. Just annoyed.

"Walking away doesn't help, Kate. I wonder if this is how Neil felt." As soon as I said it, I wanted to vacuum the air and bring the words back into my mouth. Kate turned. Her face had lost all colour and suddenly I couldn't breathe. "Oh God, Kate. I'm so sorry. That was an awful thing to say." We stared at each other for a moment, then she turned and walked slowly towards the bedroom. "Kate, I'm so sorry. Please don't walk away."

The quiet snick of the door catch was more devastating than if she'd slammed it into the wooden frame.

I rocked back and forth as if I was about to start the run up for first place in the high jump, and twisted my fingers together at my chest. "Oh God. Oh God." I was the worst person in the world. Forget the teeny tiny, brittle moments. That was a fucking boulder into a pond. What the hell had possessed me to think that, let alone say it out loud to my person? I was appalled, and needed to apologise immediately.

I crept to the door as if the carpet was dotted with land mines, and stood outside vacillating between knocking, staring at the wood for eight hours until I collapsed with exhaustion or whispering Kate's name.

I decided on the knocking-with-whispering combination. But I wasn't able to implement it because right then Kate's voice issued softly through the door.

"Not tonight, please."

I didn't analyse how she knew that I was right outside the door. My answer would probably be along the lines of 'Kate could probably hear my churning thoughts' and 'we know each other so well' and 'we've forgotten how to know each other so well' and 'we're going to counselling so the knowing returns to being an action and not a thought." Revelation number three. What a fucking awful moment for a revelation.

I didn't push past Kate's request, so I slept on the couch that night. It wasn't a great option, not because the couch was the most uncomfortable piece of furniture in the world; pretty, yes. Uncomfortable, also yes. It was the wrong option because I should have gone to Kate and slept in our bed, holding her, mending a heart that would be sore from my sandpaper words.

The next morning, after peeling my store mannequin of a body off the couch, I discovered that Kate had left early for work. The bedroom and walk in robe gave me that information, so I threw on my own formal business wear—knee-length shorts, collared shirt, Chucks—and wandered into the kitchen to toss some lunch into a cooler bag.

I opened the fridge, expecting uninspired produce squinting at me, and grumbling a, "Yeah?" What I found was a little red cooler bag nestled on the middle shelf next to Kate's special Gouda cheese, and a note.

BRON,
    Your lunch is inside. Have a good day, sweetheart. I'll see you tonight.
I love you.
    Kate. X

THERE'S A CRITICAL MOMENT WHEN HOUSE PAINT IS NEARLY dry but not quite and if it rains, the paint runs, flowing together like two rivers merging at the delta, and creating lines in the building's facade. Kate's kindness, her understanding, was the rain on my not-quite-strong-enough paint and I collapsed onto a dining chair, staring into the kitchen through a film of sad.

Each session followed a similar format. Bernadette would ask us stabby, pointed questions, we'd answer with our gazes aimed at the ceiling, the floor, our hands, Bernadette, or each other. The last gazes were the hardest because we saw the layers and barriers and yet they were the easiest because we knew each other so well. And slowly, despite our argument, I started to see a little sliver of light in the whole exercise, particularly after session five when Bernadette leaned forward and smiled.

"Your eyes, Bron ." She paused and I wasn't sure how to answer or even if I had to because it wasn't a question.

"They're...on my face?"

Kate snorted and I grinned. *Yes.* We were back. Well, not at all, but humour was good, right?

"You said your eyes light up when you talk about Kate to others." Bernadette's intense gaze collected mine, but I broke it and turned to Kate. That was a gaze I loved, and I fell into the dark brown of her eyes.

"Of course they light up," I whispered.

"Do your eyes light up when you talk *to* Kate?" Silence, then I looked down at my hands. Fuck Bernadette and her fucking stabby, pointed questions that pierced at my heart.

"I...not always," I whispered, as if I couldn't move past that volume.

Bernadette hummed a very counsellor-y hum. "Bron, you can't light up for Kate if you keep the matches hidden." Oh, for God's sake. We must have signed a multiple analogy waiver divesting our right to fold our ears into themselves.

Then she tilted her head at Kate. "I think that goes both ways."

Bernadette asked more stabby, pointed questions in the sessions leading up to Christmas.

"Bron, what have you noticed that's changed in your relationship?"

I chewed my lip because it was a shitty question. My shoulders bunched. "You don't give me cranes anymore," I said quietly to Kate, to my hands which sat limply in my lap, to the thick carpet under my shoes. I began to cry. No super powers today. Just tears.

The breath hitching beside me meant that I wasn't alone in my misery.

"You don't give me sketches anymore." No super powers today. Just tears.

We went into Christmas armed with nine weeks of enlightenment, and it wasn't awful. In fact, it was as if we'd come up for air after much too long under water. Lunch was at our house, which meant that we hardly saw each other because of the food preparation and the arrivals and the presents and the movement of noise that travelled from room to room as if it was undertaking a house inspection. But we sat together and touched; hands on forearms, arms about shoulders. Briefly, but enough to know that we did look at each other, which wasn't the same as seeing at all.

Then suddenly, in our second last session in the middle of January, everything clicked into place. My brain fell silent, poured itself a cup of tea, crossed its legs, and said, "Well, now. At last." I knew what it was that Kate and I were doing. I knew what it was that Kate and I needed.

Which was why our final session blindsided me.

"This may seem like an odd suggestion but I'm a firm advocate for it as the strategy clears the air and creates space to really see each other." My brain, now upright, and spilling tea all over the carpet, transmitted alarmed messages throughout my body because Bernadette was serious and formal and pleasant and nice and she was going to tell us about firm advocacy and air-clearing and I knew that whatever it was would be dreadful.

"I'd like to suggest a relationship break."

"What?" My voice rose to match my body, which had leapt from the chair as if ejected from a cockpit. Bernadette blinked and after a moment I realised what an utter cliche I was, what with the leaping and the shouting and the fingers splaying, so I slowly sank into my seat. "What?" I said, much more calmly, but no less horrified. "You want us to break up?" The horrified was then replaced by petrified because what if this was Kate's plan all along? Out of the corner of my eye, I saw Kate's expression, and she looked just as appalled as I did. Okay. Not her plan.

"But..." Kate whispered.

Bernadette patted the air. "Let me explain." *Yes, please do. Absolutely. What the ever-loving fuck?*

"For starters, a break is not the same as a breakup. Rather, a break is solo time away from each other for the purpose of gaining clarity about what isn't working. For you." She pointed, waving her finger in a line to collect both of us. "A break can be helpful to sort out how you feel about yourself. To reflect." I was positive she'd memorised this. There were probably couples all over Melbourne on breaks, working on themselves, gaining clarity, having solo time. In my experience, solo time meant some decent masturbation.

"—that it's not because you don't love each other." I tuned in. "But you need this space to work on yourself. Do it with love and assure each other that you love each other. Completely. I'm suggesting that perspective is necessary when the lens isn't clear." I wanted to rip open her filing cabinet and find that waiver.

Bernadette wasn't finished. It was like sitting through an agonising TED talk.

"So, we'll work together now to set the amount of time that suits both of you. It needs to be enough time to give you space so you are able to accept and repair negative behaviours. When you're always together, you're not able to have that space to think."

"So the last ten weeks were what? The run up to the worst long jump pit in the world?" My hands were fists.

She ignored my outburst, which wasn't very professional, surely.

"Bron, Kate." Bernadette gazed at each of us as she said our names, and flipped a page in her notepad. Then she insisted we set ground rules. I blinked at that. Ground rules? We loved each other. Done.

But Bernadette had us deciding that we'd still be monogamous. The idea that we'd cheat made me feel so violently ill that I nearly rushed over to her ficus plant to throw up. Then we had to sort out the length of time for our enforced separation of agony—our break. Three months, apparently.

And all of a sudden, with both of us still reeling from the very idea, we were shaking hands and thanking Bernadette—*why?*—for her insight and assistance, and we were on our way home.

The road narrowed as my thoughts churned. So many questions ranging from 'What the actual fuck?' through to 'Who will move out?' through to 'What goes in a suitcase for three months?' through to a statement. 'I didn't want a break. Ever.'

"I don't understand, sweetheart. You're my forever person."

"And you are mine," Kate responded as we sat on my side of the bed and stared out of the window into the inky night sky. "We've lost our GPS, Bron."

"Or we're using different apps."

Kate huffed a laugh. "That sounds like Bernadette."

"Oh good," I said to the window. "You noticed that as well. It drove me bonkers."

We turned at the same time and grinned at each other.

"I love that cheeky, beautiful smile. I'd give anything to see more of it," Kate said.

"You will."

Our smiles slid away because they belonged to that moment, and other moments were waiting their turn.

We resumed staring at the sky.

"It'll be good."

"I know," I agreed even though I didn't, but my GPS was broken and I was so lost.

Then she turned her head again and gave me a long, considered look. "We'll do it." She sounded definite. Resolute. Strong. And so incredibly brave.

I didn't feel brave. I felt the ice shift and crack and I knew I couldn't get to the edge in time. Normally ice didn't crack for me at all. I simply skated. But Kate was brave. And strong on her thin ice. "Are you sure?"

Her face shifted as her resolution backed off. "No." Okay, maybe not so brave and strong. But I'd come to realise—revelations galore—that not only did Kate need this break, I did as well. And it wasn't because we didn't love. We did. It wasn't because we didn't trust. We did. It was because we didn't see and, as Bernadette had said, space and time might help to open our eyes. I wasn't going to lose this woman. My Kate.

"Well, I'm sure." I swept up her hand. "I'm sure." The ice under my feet cracked a teeny tiny bit—so brittle—but I felt brave enough to stay out there and not run to the edge.

Kate rolled her lips together, her eyes wide. "Okay. Then I'm sure as well." She squeezed my hand. "It doesn't mean I don't love you, because I love you endlessly. But we need to do this."

I sighed. A huge, proper, contemplative sigh. "I know." And with those two words the break was signed and sealed.

~

A WEEK BEFORE SCHOOL BEGAN AND HORDES OF CHILDREN descended upon the campus laden with new backpacks, new lunch boxes, new uniforms, and new sentences about the awesomeness of their holidays, we participated in our third curriculum day in preparation for all that new.

Despite my gregarious nature, I wasn't interested in socialising with anyone. The contemplative bath of ick had claimed me and I was wallowing. So, I took my lunch and my bath of ick, wandered out to the staffroom courtyard, and slid onto the bench seat at the wooden table.

Lydia plonked herself onto the opposite bench and leaned on her elbows.

"So, a break, hey?

I almost regretted telling her about it last night but I'd needed someone to talk to and for the first time I didn't want that someone to be one of my family.

"Mm."

"Like I said last night, it sounds sensible."

"And like *I* said last night, Lydia, it sounds horrible."

She rolled her head back and stared at the sky. "Think about it."

"I have. I am. It's horrible."

She dropped her head forward. "You love Kate."

I widened my eyes. "Yes. That's not up for—"

"She loves you."

"Yes. Where are you go—"

"Let each other go for a while to heal yourselves. To fix yourselves." I absorbed her thoughtful look and glowered.

"What? If you love someone, set them free?"

Lydia growled. Actually growled. "McIntyre. Fuck, you can be such a shit," she snapped.

My gaze darted over the surface of the table. "I'm sorry."

"Yeah." I caught her shrug out of the corner of my eye. Lydia was bombproof.

"I move out at the end of this month," I said to the grooves in the wood.

"Look at me, Bron." I did, because she'd used her teacher-in-the-classroom-everybody-freeze voice. She pointed. "Here we go. Art is impossible without empathy."

Random. "Um...I know."

"Do you?" Lydia fixed me with a penetrating gaze.

I scoffed. "Lydia, I create art every day. I know how to empathise, for God's sake."

"So tell me." The penetrating look was laser-like. I pitied any kid who was on the end of that glare after they'd hurled an eraser across the room.

"The artist has empathy for the subject because to create beauty, the subject needs to be cherished and seen." I flicked my hands over as if the answer was obvious.

Lydia sat back, hands flat on the table, and braced her body. "So, isn't your marriage to Kate a work of art?"

"You sound like our counsellor." Lydia closed her eyes at my response. "But you're right. It is a work of art."

"And you two created it?"

"Yeah."

"Then you must have empathy for each other to create that art."

" You know I know this, right?"

"Could have fooled me."

It was my turn to close my eyes. "Kate wants to work on her flaws." I shook my head. "But she doesn't have any. She's perfect."

Lydia barked a laugh. "No, she's not. Beautiful, hot, gorgeous, clever, funny. But flawed."

I blinked

Lydia pointed again. "And so are you."

"What? Hot and gorgeous?" I grinned.

Lydia's gaze travelled from my face down to where the tabletop cut off the rest of her appraisal, then she flicked her eyes back to mine. "Yes, actually. And flawed, hon. So step back from your art because your art will still be there and for a long time. I've seen you two together and you make me sick. But you need to do this by yourself. Fix your flaws." Lydia could challenge Bernadette to a counselling contest and win based on all that analysis.

"Why are you so wise?"

"I'm not." She smirked. "It's because the fumes from all that craft glue have melted neurons in your brain."

We sat through a long and friendly pause, then Brodie's yell from the sliding door to the staffroom resounded throughout the courtyard.

"We're starting again, you two. *Workplace Health and Safety* procedures, so you need to hurry if you want the best seats." His sarcasm leaked all over the concrete pavers.

I ignored him and gazed at Lydia. "We're having this break to work on our stumbling blocks."

"The flaws as alluded to previously. The ones you need to fix." She rolled her hands in the air which meant "Yeah, got it. Move on."

"But I'm not fixing mine and neither is Kate."

"Right...because?"

"Because they're part of me. Part of her. What we have to do is see them and accept them and." I flipped my hands in response then tapped my fingers on the wood. "Make them work into who we are as Kate and Bron."

A smile grew on Lydia's face.

"What?"

"You said Kate's name first." Her smile slid easily into a smirk.

I stopped moving my fingers. "I...It rolls better."

"Hmm. Or it's because Kate's the most important name for others to hear?"

"No." My face scrunched. "It's because Kate's the most important to me."

"Hmm. Okay." She pointed again. Her finger was getting a work-out. "Flaws. Go."

I breathed out. "Not seeing or appreciating what's in front of me and showing complacency." I laughed. "You know what she said? That it's not her job to jump up and down waving pom poms so that's she's so obvious that I'll see her, and then she said that she wouldn't make the cheerleading team anyway because she's 51."

Lydia snorted. "See? Funny."

I grinned. "Yeah. She is."

She tilted her head. "So, complacency, huh? Well, hi, Teflon chick. Bit of complacency there, right? It'll be good for you to finally see what we all see." We held each others gaze. "Hers?"

"I told her that it's not my responsibility to find the solution for her...for her walking away thing."

"Walking away?"

"Yeah. She walks away from conflict every single time."

"Oh!" Lydia brought her hands together in a prayer gesture and pressed her index fingers to her mouth. "Oh boy. You need to learn fast."

"Why?" I started to bundle up my lunch scraps and rubbish.

"Can't you see?" She stilled my hand with hers. "If you two don't agree on something, she walks away and you don't care. Do that for long enough and, bang, you're done."

Bernadette, you're fired. There's a Grade Three teacher at Melbourne Primary School who is shit-hot at getting right to the absolute point in a single lunch break.

My heart was strewn with debris but eventually I'd need to grab hold of a broom and start cleaning, because at the end of January, I moved out of our little cottage.

We Detached

❧

February 1 to April 21 in the fourth year of the now

T he generic serviced apartment, located on the tenth floor of the generic building in the generic street, was owned by Veris and usually housed visiting consultants hired by various departments of Kate's firm. Now it housed a lost Art teacher.

The furnishings were also generic, probably bought at the same warehouse that supplied doctor's waiting rooms.

"I bet Bernadette shops there," I muttered, wheeling my suitcase over to the couch. I scrubbed at my face, trying to erase the worst Sunday ever. The very act of me packing a suitcase sent Kate into such an epic case of ugh-tension-I'm-walking-away that she actually left the house and marched up the street. I knew she'd returned because I heard the sound of the jug in the kitchen, then five minutes later Kate leant against the door frame of the bedroom.

"I made tea if you fancy one."

I turned, clutching four pairs of socks, several undies, and a shirt that worked for school and weekends, and tossed the lot into the open suitcase.

"Bron..." Kate passed the cup.

"Sweetheart, you know what I was thinking last night? That this is like one of those yoga-type retreats where you're supposed to commune with the freckles on your skin or something, except ours is a really important, life-changing, love-of-our-lives-finding, digging-into-our-hearts version." I gave her a wobbly smile. "Without the yoga and the freckles contemplation."

Kate sipped her tea, the surface trembling so that she held the cup with two hands. "That's...you've got to stop sounding like Bernadette."

I must have looked appalled, because she giggled. "I'll have you know that my analogies are more creative and inspire much better imagery."

Her eyes sparkled, and again that little voice in my mind wondered why on earth we were doing this break at all. Not when we had jokes, and giggling, and smiles, and sparkling eyes. But I knew. Those jokes and sparkles were in such limited supply that eventually we'd use them up and be back to where we were.

Our kiss was sweet and so full of love we could have created rainbows on the front porch, then I was in my car, and driving towards three months of no contact with Kate—Bernadette's suggestion—but knowing I'd return as a wife who knew the damage of ingratitude. Hell of a task considering I'd worked on that particular personality trait for forty-five years. So three months? I frowned and grit my teeth. Christ, I was up for that challenge.

Meanwhile, I had an apartment to consider. Such as the lack of smell as if it had been forensically cleaned, which made me slightly concerned about what I'd find in the closet. I made my way into the kitchen, and discovered gleaming counters and cupboards, and it took all my willpower not to bend down, and look along the top of the counters just to gauge how spotless they were.

At least I had cutlery and other essential items, which I found after opening and closing every cupboard and drawer simply to keep myself occupied. Closets and bedside cabinets were next, and the emptiness inside each piece of furniture was loud and when I stood still, the silence echoed through every carpet fibre and from all the ceiling lights.

The apartment contained superfluous doors, and I decided to leave them closed. I wouldn't be entering and exiting those spaces especially if

I wasn't going anywhere for a while. I wanted to sit. Just sit. I'd given up requesting the same from my mind. It was much too busy flinging thoughts into filing cabinets, which kept opening sporadically and spewing those thoughts all over my brain.

I stood at the entrance to the bedroom. "Looks comfortable," I said, nodding at the bed, but I knew in the three months that the mattress would become uneven because the shape of Kate wasn't there to balance the rectangle. Sprawling all over it felt somewhat like cheating which was so utterly ridiculous I laughed out loud. "Difficult to cheat on someone with a piece of furniture," I muttered, and continued to put my belongings on my side of the bed.

YOU GOOD?
Yeah.
Okay.

JJ's TEXT WAS SURPRISING, VERY WELCOME, AND hilariously brief, but the idea that she'd—JJ had settled on that pronoun for now—bothered to use data to check up on her aunt made me feel all warm and fuzzy.

I didn't text Kate that night, although the desire was overwhelming, but I knew I'd damage our agreement. Our break wasn't about our cracking connection. Our break was to find out how unbreakable we were.

So I didn't text, but I figured Kate, based on absolutely no evidence except hope and wishful thinking, would be itching to text me as well. I stared at the wall, the cheese on the take-away pizza settling comfortably into a cold, congealed existence. Of course I had no idea if Kate wanted to text.

I sipped at my wine.

In three months, I wanted to meet Kate as brand new, lips spontaneously pulling into a smile, as if on a date but not really because we knew each other so well.

But not yet.

I drank more wine.

Then a bit more.

A slice of pizza somehow made it into my palm and I stared at it in confusion. It looked like one of those rubbery play foods that little kids expect their very patient parents to eat at highly organised tea parties. I tossed it back into the box.

I missed Kate.

"What category of missing, McIntyre? The 'I need you because I'm not complete without you' type of missing? Or the 'I'm not good at being alone' type of missing? Or the 'there's a hole in my life' kind of missing?"

The tune to 'There's a Hole in My Bucket, Dear Liza" slithered into my brain and glued itself to way too many neurons so that I couldn't shake it, like that infernal 'Baby Shark' song. After I'd warbled the second verse—"Well, fix it dear Bro-on, dear Bro-on", I plonked the glass on the table. "Aaaaand...you're done. Bedtime."

~

SCHOOL WAS A SAVING GRACE, BECAUSE DESPITE PRIDING myself on professionalism and integrity in my work, paradoxically I was able to use those traits to tune out certain thoughts then invite them back in as I dropped into autopilot.

However, I did begin to make efforts to pull my head out of my arse. Such as the morning of the second week when I bothered to find Paula and thank her for suggesting and then approving my application for the deputy role last year. I'd realised in January that I hadn't actually thanked her properly for the compliments about my experience and my expertise and while it felt a little like completing the steps in an addiction program, it needed to be said. Authentically.

"You're welcome, Bron! Having you on board for that period of time was a saving grace particularly with proofreading six-hundred report cards!" She beamed across her desk.

"That was an experience, for sure, being on the other end of those report cards." I grimaced, and she laughed. Then she tilted her head.

"Are you okay?"

How to answer that? My wife and I are having a break and I need to learn how to see? Yep. Nope. Not sharing that with my principal.

"Yeah. Just start of year stress."

Paula nodded in understanding. "It's always the green light at the end of the red light gantry during the formula one, isn't it?"

With the astonishing information that my boss was a walking encyclopaedia about single-seat, open-cockpit, open-wheel, front and rear winged, formula one racing cars, I nearly ruined it all later that week when I drove out of the school driveway, indicated to turn left, and realised that instead I should have flicked the lever down because my apartment was in the city.

After a kilometre, I pulled over to the side of the road, fossicked in my satchel and found my phone.

"What's wrong, McIntyre?"

"Nothing. Do I need a reason to phone my friend?"

Lydia's eyebrow lifting was audible. "Yes. Normally you do."

I leaned my forehead on the steering wheel. "Just wanted to say hi."

Silence trickled out of the speaker.

"Well, hi. Even though you only saw me two hours ago."

"Oh. Well, you know…"

"You're lonely, aren't you?" Lydia sounded…she sounded like she'd won a bet with herself.

"A little."

Another silence. "I'm not your Kate substitute, Bron."

I filled the car's interior with my sigh. "I know that."

"Do you? Because I'm not prepared to be option two just because you can't talk to Kate. That's not valuing me and it's certainly not valuing her."

My forehead deserved the bruise it would have tomorrow as I thumped it on the steering wheel. "Oh God. I'm so sorry."

"I know, babe, but I'm glad you're on this break, because even though it's about you and Kate, it's gonna be good for you individually because seriously, woman, you need some gravel under your arse. No more Teflon Bron, right?"

Intel on Kate was delivered via Janine at the end of February. Technically I should have shoved my fingers in my ears and sung 'La La La' in an annoyingly loud voice. But I didn't because I was desperate for news even if it was simply what Kate had for dinner last night.

"What time are you coming over for lunch today?" Janine sounded frazzled which was hardly surprising for a Saturday as the kids took up her time with various sports, activities, and lessons while Rick was at the clinic all morning.

"Twelve-thirty if it's still okay. What can I bring?" I asked distractedly, not really paying attention to my words. I was busy enjoying a kid's cartoon programme and if anyone ever asked, I'd tell them it was for research.

There was a pause on the end, which gave me a chance to hear Jack eloquently tell JJ that she was a bloody twit who needed to get over herself.

"Bron?"

"Yeah?"

"You're always welcome to come for lunch." The noise from her forehead wrinkling resounded through the phone.

"Oh. Yeah, right." I snapped off the TV.

"Just turn up like normal. You don't have to check with me if it's okay, you know."

"Yeah." My vocabulary was astonishing lately. "Yeah, J. I do. I really shouldn't just rock up and expect that you'll be there ready to serve lunch and entertain me or listen to my latest story or whatever."

"I'm..."

"You okay, Mum?" Pip's voice was tinny as if she'd asked from the other end of the room.

"I'm fine, sweetie. Aunty Bron is arriving at twelve-thirty and bringing cheesecake."

"Cheesecake. Gotcha." I smiled. "Thanks, J."

I'd checked in. I'd made sure that my arrival at lunch was still fine. Despite being 'welcome any time', it felt like the right thing to do: to check.

Huh.

I stared over the top of the TV on the wall.

Cheesecake duly consumed, I nestled into one of Janine's comfy chairs in the lounge.

"I can tell you're busting out of your skin to know."

"Know what?" I raised my eyebrows innocently.

"You're kidding, right? You know that Kate talks to me. I'm the non-judgemental, good-at-listening, making-eye-contact, relative-and-friend that she's always needed."

"Hmm," I agreed. Janine was and it was lovely.

"Well, I'll paraphrase a little because keeping details in my head is important, but I'm also ensuring you don't vibrate out of my house in a state of tension."

I grinned. "Yes, please."

"She went around to Olivia's place, sat her down and explained that even though Olivia had hurt her deeply, she still loved her and that wouldn't change. She said that Olivia missing the wedding was devastating, but admitted that not sending an invitation was childish. She told Olivia that it had been your suggestion to invite her but she'd been the one to say no." Janine stared at me. "Did you really suggest that?"

I nodded. "I did. It...I thought it might mend...I don't know...a bridge?"

"Hmm. There's hope for you yet, my wayward sister."

"Shut up. Actually don't because I want more information." I made 'gimme' hands.

"Well, Kate told me that there was crying and tension." Janine sat forward and grinned. "But!" She slapped her knee. "The biggest point is that Kate stayed, parked right there in her mum's fancy, formal lounge and did not move. She stayed exactly where she was until they'd hashed out everything."

"Oh wow!" My mouth opened and smiled at the same time. And the gesture filled my face.

"Yep. I mean, she said that even though she's back in 'the fold'." Janine flicked her fingers up to air-quote the words. "It's still not great, because apparently her mum likes to use Kate's lesbianism as some sort of social leverage. Lesbianism is the latest talking point at lunch."

"Oh, for fuck's sake. Kate's not even using labels, really."

"That's what I said. But the main thing is she stood up for herself, Bron. She didn't run away." Janine smiled wryly. "Kate said she'd spent four hours gearing herself up for the confrontation, but she did it."

I cheered inside my veins. "I'm so pleased for her. This is..." I curled my fingers into fists and gave a sort of stationary gallop on each thigh. "Massive." Then I delivered an extra hard thump on my right thigh. "She might not have done that with me in the picture."

Janine gave me a long look, then threw in a slight head tilt as if waiting for the penny to drop.

"I'd step in, wouldn't I? Save her. Fix it, so that the running away would only be solidified farther."

"Hey there, Sherlock. You got it."

I closed my eyes and sighed.

～

MELBOURNE IS A CITY OF FIVE MILLION PEOPLE BUT sometimes it feels like a small town. I pulled open the door of *The Sacred Elf*, exited into a sea of probably a million of those citizens, and paused to swap the paper bag which contained JJ's birthday present for next week—a white gold and silver Wiccan nathair amulet—to my other hand so I could shove my phone into my back pocket. Jack's present had been much easier to source: a gift card for some sort of video game he wanted, where accumulation of resources and destruction of people seemed to be the objective.

"I hear you and Kate are married." The sneer cut through the crowd, landed in front of me and I jerked my head up to find Neil, in business wear despite being a Saturday, glaring as if I had no right to occupy space on the footpath. I blinked. See? Small town. I wanted to spin around and hide amongst the opium incense cones in the store.

"Yes. Yes, we are." I forced a polite smile onto my face. It probably looked like I was in pain.

"Well, congratulations," he ground out. "You won."

"What? It's not a competition, Neil." My expression must have been priceless.

"Yes, it is. Everyone knows she never loved me." His jaw bunched. "I failed."

I waved the hand not holding the bag in frustration. "Jesus, Neil. There's no trophy, for fuck's sake. Kate's not a prize. That's an appalling thought process. Kate's an astonishing, beautiful, kind person! A person who is not a prize." I could feel my anger rising and my shouty voice was creeping into attack mode.

"She was mine."

"And also, for those playing at home, Neil, a person has free will and cannot be owned." I apologised mentally to those people in the world where that free will and lack of ownership was a myth. "You didn't own her."

Neil and I had begun an epic verbal tennis match and people were noticing. We'd be selling tickets any minute now.

"10 years wasted," he spat.

I tossed that same hand, although I really should have whacked him with the bag. The amulet was heavy enough to knock some common sense into him. "Really? Really? That's how you see it? That's..."

"It's unfair," he whined petulantly.

"Oh, for fuck's sake. This is why I became a lesbian!"

He pulled his head back into his neck. "Really?"

"No, you idiot!" I glared. "Didn't you hear what I said? Kate's not a possession."

"She never loved me." And with that statement it seemed as if the sugar of his petulance dissolved into a cup of hot resignation. "She loves you and said she won't walk away from you like she did from me." His bottom lip nearly popped out but I think he remembered that he was an adult and probably should be adulting.

"Well, that's good to know." It was excellent to know. "I'm glad you saw that at the New Year's Eve party."

He shook his head quickly. "No. She told me that last Thursday."

"She did?" I blinked. The moment dragged as people flowed past, and I fizzed with happiness and Neil resembled a deflated balloon.

"Yes," he sighed. "She reminded me that our ten years together weren't wasted because it had been a learning exercise for both of us." He barked out a laugh, and stared over my shoulder. "A learning exercise." He shook his head, perhaps wondering why he didn't hold a degree for that ten-year experience. "Anyway," he brought his gaze back and pointed, "you're her person. Kate loves you and she said I need to accept that."

I was thrilled that Kate had spoken to Neil, and it didn't escape my attention that she hadn't mentioned our break, because Neil would have led with that tasty piece of ammunition.

"Yeah, you do, Neil. Accept it and move on, ma—" I caught the word in time, remembering that Neil had gone ballistic last time when I'd used the word 'mate'.

He breathed deeply, delivered a powerless glare, then shook his head again. The head shaking was clearly disbelief or maybe it was to settle the jigsaw of his worldview back into place. His capitulation to Kate's stance, to our relationship, to our wedding, to our love, suggested that all his fight had packed up for the day and gone home.

"I don't like you." Well, okay. Maybe not all of his fight had left. One little archer still remained and aimlessly fired their last arrow, hoping to connect with something solid. I watched the arrow land in the dirt between us.

"Neil." I tilted my head. "I'm not overly fond of you either, but I'm really glad we had this spontaneous discussion." I delivered the same pained smile I'd led with at the beginning because I was done with him, with holding up humanity on a Saturday morning, and I wanted to snuggle into the warm blanket that was Kate and her wonderful Velcro feet that were gripping the earth. "I need to get going," I said, pointing vaguely up the street. "You have a good day, okay?" I wanted to be the first to leave, but had only taken four steps when I looked back. Neil was staring into the display window of *The Sacred Elf*, but I doubted he was contemplating purchasing oracle cards. Or maybe he was. He looked like he needed some direction in life now that Kate had fought off another of her dragons.

~

THIS YEAR, JACK AND JJ'S BIRTHDAY EVENTS WERE HELD IN seperate locations, which seemed logical and healthy considering that they were turning fifteen and had settled on the idea that maintaining distance was a rational and sane decision. Despite having to split their human resources, Janine and Rick were thrilled with this recent development.

Jack's party consisted of sitting in front of the enormous television in Janine and Rick's rumpus room with six of his mates all wearing headsets and clutching controllers, while consuming their body weight in preservatives. Jack looked to be the captain of the army of zombie people on the screen because the game paused, and he came over to accept his gift.

"Thanks, Aunty Bron. This is awesome."

"Well, even though I'm old and decrepit, I still know that a gift card is gold." I gestured vaguely at the screen. "Even if you want to spend it on land mines or something."

He snorted. "That's definitely sounds old and decrepit."

I smacked his shoulder which, at fifteen, was now at the same level as mine and I wasn't a short person. *What are they feeding kids these days?*

Wishing him and his friends a great night, I made my way upstairs, pausing when I heard one of them announce loudly, "She's hot!"

Jack's response was immediate. "She's my aunt, bro. Some fucking respect, yeah?"

I grinned. One hot aunt who was exceptionally proud of her very awesome nephew.

Compared to Jack's, JJ's party was as if I'd stepped through a portal into an alternative universe. JJ's understanding of friendship was if the person was kind and had a modicum of humour and wit about themselves, then they were excellent. The planet of JJ was surrounded by orbiting, wonderful satellites who all fit with each other—or didn't— and they respected the parts that sometimes didn't connect. The final step in the staircase leading to the mezzanine space in the local independent bookshop creaked loudly, and all eyes turned. JJ beamed and sort of power-walked over to me, adding a tiny skip halfway along. I was hugged exuberantly.

"You should totally stay," she exclaimed after I'd told her I wasn't going to. "There's a reading and then Saffron is doing a live charcoal sketch. The owner has let us have the space for an extra hour so Troy, One, and K can experiment while we help them with ideas." I looked over to the three people, presumably Troy, One and K, who were clutching a keyboard, violin and djembe. Interesting combination of chamber music instruments. I delivered a friendly wave.

About twenty fabulously eclectic people were in attendance, and I considered staying just to chat with every one of them. Their thoughts would be fascinating. But I was not crashing a fifteen-year-old's party just because I couldn't turn off teacher-mode for a night.

JJ squeaked when she opened the gift and I received another exuberant hug.

"Okay, well, you have a great night. Who's picking you up?"

"Mum. She's dropping Pip and Dad home first, because they've taken Pip to dinner." I loved the trust that Janine and Rick placed in the twins. Despite years of challenges, mainly from JJ, Janine and Rick knew that their kids were trustworthy, authentic and would always, always call if they needed help. So taking Pip out for dinner instead of chaperoning two teenage parties was delightful. JJ raised her eyebrows innocently. "I hope she comes a bit earlier because she really needs to meet K. They want to be a psychologist." She smirked knowing perfectly well that Janine would try her best but...I narrowed my eyes, and she cracked up.

"Right, I'm going. Have a great night, JJ"

I'd reached the bottom step, waved quickly to the owner, and was about to exit, when JJ's voice halted my movement.

"Aunty Bron!" She rushed over.

"Yeah? Is something wrong?" My aunt-alert fired.

She shook her hand, bracelets jangling. "No. I just wanted to check if you're doing okay. That's all."

Reminded of JJ's text a month and half ago, I drove my instant tears to a vacant parking lot and smiled. "I'm good, thanks. You should get back to your party." I lifted my chin towards the staircase.

She grabbed my hand, dragged me over to the velvet-upholstered wingback chair then sat opposite me on an ottoman. Clearly the location for weekly book clubs or lesbian first dates.

"I don't believe you."

I glared. "I reckon I'd know if I was good or not."

"Most people don't."

"JJ, don't give me that attitude, please." I sighed.

She leaned forward. "Why not? You're giving it to yourself. I'm just joining in."

My jaw dropped. "You're a shit. A little adult-like shit," I enunciated, which she clearly took as a compliment, because she sat back, crossed her legs, glittery stockings catching the light, and nodded.

"Aunty Bron, I'm a little adult shit because I have to be. I'm going to get crap from people because of how I look, how I am, pronouns I want to experiment with or not and I don't give a f—." I pointed at her. "Damn if they give me that crap. But I've had to start now, you know, working out how I'm going to cope with that crap. I'm fifteen, which means I get to think a lot and I Google a lot and I watch people carefully to see if I'm setting myself up for crap. But the point is I watch people and I've worked out that having an attitude and wearing an adult cape that says "Yeah, I'm the shit. What's your problem?' works wonders."

"Oh, JJ." I leaned across and held her hand.

"Yeah. So I'm allowed to give you attitude because I'm good at it and I hate." Her bottom lip wobbled. "I hate that you and Kate aren't together anymore because she's my favourite absorbed-into-the-family person who's ever been a girlfriend of yours." She squeezed my hand. "Wife."

I swallowed thickly. "Absorbed makes us sound like a giant sponge."

"We are. Kate's been sucked into the McIntyre sponge and." Her mouth was a straight line. "We can't let her go down the drain."

"JJ, Kate and I are just having a break. That's all, okay? Simply to work on parts of ourselves that will help us be together forever."

The drift between pseudo-adult to real-life teenager in the space of a few minutes was probably frustrating and I imagined that our break resembled a divorce from various angles in JJ's perspective.

"Don't just say words to her, Aunty Bron." JJ looked me dead in the eye. "People do that and, yeah, okay, words are nice and everything, but they only reach, like, the seventy percent point of what you want to say."

I tipped my head in curiosity. God, I loved this kid.

"Seventy percent, Aunty Bron, isn't enough 'cause you don't get to say what you need to say."

My hand squeeze prompted more thoughts.

"It's why straight guys get it, like, really wrong. They think words dropping in at seventy percent and then a bunch of roses for the other thirty is enough because it says to the woman, 'here's my whole message', but it's not, is it?"

I shook my head. The kid was so wise. *Why can't adults be this wise?*

"It's like listening to a song that hasn't reached the last verse," I added, and it was her turn to tip her head.

"Fu—Gees, we're, like, a combined Yoda or something."

I let go of her hand and lightly punched her shoulder and JJ's laughter filled the bookshelves, shuffling the pages with her insight and joy. We grinned at each other.

"Fine. I won't just say words when I see Kate again. By the way, you've left your hosting duties to embody Yoda, and why are you so sassy to me?"

Another laugh, this time combined with raised eyebrows. "Because I'm your favourite."

I hauled her out of her seat, and pulled her into a hug that said everything. A hundred percent everything. And only then did I add words. "I love you, JJ. You're an amazing human, and it's my privilege to be your aunt."

Her eyes filled with tears. "Thanks," she replied huskily.

"Enjoy your party. Don't let the djembe guy dominate. Those percussion blokes are serious spotlight thieves."

~

I TOOK A CLEANSING BREATH WHICH, REALLY WASN'T THAT cleansing considering the marshy banks and the duck shit fertilizing the grass. Still, I figured that as long as I was breathing, deeply or otherwise, then that was a bonus.

I apologised to my bridge for neglecting her and tried to ignore the fact that my brain was brimming with wishful thinking for, yet the fear of, Kate strolling past on her afternoon walk, then glancing up at the bench and spotting me propped not-at-all casually on the wooden slats.

"This is a mistake," I muttered. *Why, yes, you dumb arse. It is.*

In retaliation for that insightful thought, my brain rebelled, informed my hands to drag out the sketch book and watercolour pencils from my bag, then stare contemplatively at the bridge.

I pulled my jacket closer about my shoulders and balanced the sketch book on my knee. And smiled. JJ had sent me a text that morning detailing the presents Kate had delivered the day after the twin's birthday. Apparently she'd apologised for the simplicity; both receiving gift cards, but had explained that as an adopted aunt, she had to work her way up to highly individualised offerings that wouldn't offend or cause the kids to roll their eyes so violently that they'd sprain something. I'd snorted at those words. So Kate.

The glow in my heart was an enduring flame of love.

The sketch developed under my hand, almost automatically, then my imagination frolicked, adding details completely from memory. The weeping willow grew on the paper, and finally I sat back and blinked.

It was beautiful, and I wasn't saying that to top up my tank of self-esteem. It actually was beautiful and probably the best colour-work I'd done in a long time.

"That's lovely, dear."

Inhaling too quickly, I closed my mouth, which was crowded with swear words, and turned to find an elderly woman, probably Larry's age, who'd appeared out of nowhere and was leaning into my space from where she sat at the other end of the bench. I smiled.

"Thanks. It's...it's...I like to draw this bridge. It's special."

"Always helps when the subject is one you love."

After a moment of staring which was probably impolite, suddenly I wanted to leap up, race down to the path, grab the mum walking past with the kid hanging off one arm, haul her back to my bench and ask her if she could see the old woman, because this moment felt like one of those weird dream sequences in movies where a dead person appears to offer the lost character some advice. Instead, I nodded.

"Mm. It is." More nodding. Then I carefully closed the book, slid everything back into the bag, and uncrossed my legs. My knees protested at the movement, and I gave a wry smile, wondering if Kate was feeling the same lately. We could be making heat packs for each other.

I froze, my hand clutching the strap, my body braced to stand. That was it. I'd forgotten to make heat packs. *Oh Kate. I've forgotten to notice. I've forgotten to see if you needed. I've forgotten to pay attention even when you don't ask.* The metaphor was revelatory.

"I've forgotten to make heat packs," I said, staring vacantly.

"That's okay, dear. I leave the iron on all the time."

I smiled in solidarity at my bench companion, then stood, wished her a pleasant afternoon, and drove back to school, picked up what I needed, and went back to the apartment. I knew what I was going to do with the sketch.

The spare frame flattered the colours in the piece and as I crept away, like Tom Cruise in *Mission Impossible*, from the front door of our cottage, I hoped that Kate thought so, too. My brain had played on the seesaw in the playground, tossing up whether to write a message or not. Eventually, I didn't. The drawing seemed enough.

The attendant in the foyer of the apartment building waved me over when I strolled through after my nighttime adventure.

"Bron McIntyre, right?"

"That's me."

He drifted his hand sideways along his counter, lifted an opaque Tupperware container, and thrust it in my direction.

"Package came for you tonight."

I shrugged. "Cheers."

I pressed the button for the tenth floor and stared at my warped reflection on the inside of the lift's silver doors and that odd curious-but-not-really-curious sensation sat with me for nine floors. Then it dawned on me. A bubble of emotion rose from my chest and sat on the surface tension of my throat. It had to be menopause. Or peri-menopause. Or something. All of these emotions pretending to be fire-works were too big, simply because Kate and I were on a break. But it wasn't that. Tupperware. The limited number of people who knew where I was staying. Tupperware. I unlocked my door and dropped my bag. The container was now made of spun glass and I gently unclicked the lid.

The crane was exquisite. Perfect. White with tiny speckles of colour scattered randomly over the paper's surface. I'd never received one with that design. She must have found a new paper shop.

For two minutes, maybe three—I wasn't counting—I stood just inside the door, and held the crane in my shaking palm.

There was no way that Kate knew I'd carefully leaned the drawing against the cottage door. Just like I had no idea that she'd leave me a crane.

I huffed a laugh in disbelief. Surely, Bernadette wouldn't insist that we repeat our break or sit through another nine weeks of analogies because there was no way ESP could count as communication.

We Counselled

April 21 to April 30 in the fourth year of the now

Hundreds of years from now, historians will write about the Great McIntyre Intervention. Many will label it an inquisition while others will explain that it was simply a friendly familial chat. Whatever those historians decide, I had no warning that I was due to play a starring role in this significant, history-making event.

The weekend before the break was due to end, I was invited to lunch at Janine's house. Clutching a salad and three bags of chips mainly for Paul and Rick's consumption, I let myself in to discover Mum seated comfortably on the green armchair—the latest Op Shop purchase—while Siobhan had claimed the entire couch.

Hey, Mum, Shiv." I dumped the chip packets and the salad on the dining table and delivered hugs. I could hear Janine in the kitchen, so with hugs duly delivered in that room as well, I wandered into the lounge to sag into the other armchair opposite Mum.

"Where is everyone?"

"Rick's taken all the kids to a movie." Siobhan laughed. "That was like watching international trade negotiations."

"Dad? Paul?"

"Car show," Mum replied.

"Shed," Siobhan answered at the same time.

A warning tingle fizzed at the bottom of my spine. We'd only ever had a couple of proper send-the-men-to-Mars interventions, such as the one when Siobhan, at seventeen, had wanted to hitchhike to Byron Bay and set up a market stall where she would offer her services as a dope connoisseur.

"Like a wine taster, but for dope so that growers know exactly how their product is developing and if it'll be received well by the public," she'd explained seriously.

The first Great McIntyre Intervention.

My coccyx tingles were sending out messages that the second GMI was about to get underway.

Janine called us for lunch, and in amongst the salads, the shrimp patties, and the spicy chickpea wraps, was light conversation and smiles and laughter. All perfectly normal. Except it wasn't.

Siobhan and I cleared the table, and without making eye contact, loaded the dishwasher. Oh boy.

Janine and Mum were still seated at the table, so the only logical thing to do was to return to my chair.

Then, with eyebrows raised and holding my breath, I caught each woman's gaze.

"So, I'll need a drink for this." I made to stand.

"Oh no. We are doing this alarmingly sober." Mum's tone of do-not-try-me echoed about the table.

"Fine. I'll get a soft drink," I retorted defensively, and stalked into the kitchen, yanked open the fridge, yanked out a can, yanked on the ring pull, and a rainbow of fizzy drink splattered over the floor.

"Fuck!"

My jaw muscles performed a stationary tango while I squelched across the spray of sugared water, grabbed the damp mop from the laundry, and cleaned up the mess, then kicked off my sneakers. I'd deal with them later. Gripping the now much lighter can, I breathed deeply, briefly closed my eyes, and walked calmly into the dining room.

"Okay. What is it we are doing alarmingly sober?"

Mum stared at me. "It's an unspoken rule in our family that we help each other in times of duress." It was as if she was reciting the Book of Ages. "An unspoken rule that certain events require the four women to come together to share guidance."

"An unspoken rule…" I blinked at Mum, aware that Siobhan was also studying me from across the table. Thank God Janine was seated to my left otherwise I'd be caught in her glare as well. I imagined her eyes were narrowed. "Since when?"

"Since Siobhan…" Mum inhaled deeply. "Well, since Siobhan." Which encompassed every escapade that Siobhan had ever embarked upon. "Then since Janine took it into her head to cycle the Great Ocean Road despite not having any training so she could impress that young man who was…" Mum's opinion of Dale was not high. "And," she pointed at me, "since you are the biggest idiot from Planet Idiot to ever land on earth."

I gulped down the single mouthful left in the can. "Mum, I'm forty-five years old."

"Exactly," Janine chimed in. "So, why are you like this?"

"Like what?" I knew what. Bernadette's words rolled around in my head. I expected my sisters and my mother to be there as a shoulder to lean on, but when they needed to tell me to pull my head out of my arse, I wasn't game enough to listen. I took the first for granted, and dismissed the second. So yes, I knew what.

"You! Having to be on a break. Having to fix things."

Suddenly, as one, it was as if we realised that standing during this discussion was necessary. Or at least moving about. Janine dragged a stool around the kitchen counter and sat heavily, folding her arms, like the barrier of laminate and chipboard could deflect the room's energy.

Mum stayed where she was which was unsurprising as her command of a room was so effective that she could sit on the floor and everyone would still shut up.

Siobhan couldn't settle. She stomped, then stopped, then stomped, actively avoiding my path because I'd decided on a similar pattern of movement.

"Look, I know it's all my fault." I wrapped my arms about my stomach and Siobhan stopped, then whirled around.

"Nope. You don't get to win gold in the martyr Olympics," she growled, gripping the back of a dining chair.

"Paul spent months restoring those, love. Remember that, please, before you throw one at Bron," Mum muttered.

"It *is* my fault!" I flung my arms out.

"So, Kate's completely blameless?" Janine had joined the fray.

"No." I cut a glance into the kitchen.

"Then." The word returned my gaze to Siobhan's stormy eyes. "Shut the fuck up with the 'it's my fault' crap."

"Fine!" I paced some more. Then stopped. "You know what? This sucks. Yes, I know I'm complacent about stuff. I get that. Fine! Put a tick against that trait on the list of how shit Bron is. But I know about it! It's not like it's news!" I was breathing heavily, eyes flashing as they connected with Mum's whose were parked on her face underneath raised eyebrows. As they connected with Janine's whose were comically wide. As they connected with Siobhan's whose flashed in response, an almost visible arc of energy between us.

"I know I'm flawed, particularly when it comes to relationships, either familial or romantic. I. Know. This." I waved my arms randomly. "But you know what? We all are. So you can't invite me over to yell at me like I'm an idiot when I know exactly what the fuck I have to do!" I gripped the back of another dining chair and Mum narrowed her eyes. "I know how to ask Kate to love me. To keep on loving me. I—" I clapped a hand over my mouth, swallowed quickly, then yelled at myself in a similar volume to pull it together. "I know what to do and you don't need to tell me what to do to make that happen. I have that knowledge, okay? And it's my responsibility to action that knowledge. I know what to do."

The silence was monumental. It always was in McIntyre arguments. But this felt huge, and the weight of it pressed on the bubble of my courage and it burst, leaving behind the sadness, the realisation, the understanding.

Janine nodded slowly and delivered a low hum, instantly echoed by Mum's version. Siobhan was fixed in the same position; clutching the chair across from mine. We were a still life of seething siblings.

"I've lost her," I whispered.

"Gah! Stop being so fucking dramatic. You haven't lost her. You're finding her. You're finding yourself for once in your fucking life. And it's because of Kate. She's the strong one." Siobhan could have powered Melbourne with the sparks radiating from her body. Sparks that I was replicating. I hoped Janine and Rick's insurance was up to date because we were likely to incinerate the house. "But so are you."

My head drew back into my neck and I stared at her. "What?"

"You're just as strong as Kate. Look at all that stuff that just came out of your mouth. Did you hear how strong that was? Did you hear how much responsibility you're finally taking for your own crap?"

"That's bullshit! I've always taken responsibility for crap."

Clearly, Mum and Janine had decided to leave Siobhan to captain the entire intervention, which should have been easier for me to deal with because she was only one person, but it was Siobhan and she was Joan of Arc.

"Bron, you haven't needed to take responsibility for crap, because you've never had any to deal with!" Cracks had begun to appear in her armour and she blinked back tears. And again our actions were reflections when I felt tears prick against my own eyes.

"You've got to realise, Bron, that complacency isn't just fucking off mentally, it's about being scared. If you choose not to see anything, then you don't have to be vulnerable. How much are you hating this intervention right now?"

She stared, daring me to answer. I felt both Janine and Mum lean forward in anticipation.

"It's fucking awful." I gripped the wooden top railing of the chair until my knuckles turned white.

"Exactly." Siobhan pushed away from the furniture and cast her arms out. "You know why?"

"Because you're swearing at me?"

Janine's sigh filled the kitchen.

Siobhan growled. "Stop it. See? Deflection. Complacent. Scared. You've done this." She gestured vaguely at my body. "With other girl-friends."

I ran through a quick highlights reel. Siobhan was right. Annoyingly. I had probably been the reason the majority of them left. They'd been ignored.

"But this—" I flapped my hands about. "This intervention is not about fixing me. I don't need fixing. I need accepting. I need to accept me. This is about helping, giving advice, it's ab—"

"Do you even want advice?" Janine's calm voice issued over the counter and fell at my feet.

"Of course I d—"

"Because you're not great at taking it. You're not great at appreciating it."

I was hating this so much. I began to shake, little shakes like the ones that shiver in knees and fingers, because I was fighting with my desire to dismiss whatever their advice was going to be, or stay and appreciate that my family was going to help with maps and instructions but I had to get gravel rash while I worked hard.

Janine obviously took my silence to mean that I'd decided to ignore her, so she hopped off the stool, stormed over to the pantry and tossed packets of flour, chocolate chips, and sugar onto the bench, and then added milk, butter, and eggs from the fridge. Janine coped with stress by cooking.

"You know, for an art teacher, you suck at being a wife." She banged a mixing bowl onto the counter.

"What?" *What?* "Those two nouns are not even related."

"Yes, they are." The harsh clang of the muffin tray ricocheted off the cupboards. "Bron, what's one of the key features of painting or drawing or anything arty?" She poured flour into the bowl, not measuring the amount, simply basing her judgement on years of experience. I peeled each finger off the back of the chair and made my way tentatively over to the kitchen bench. I was wary of Siobhan, who looked like thunder but had obviously subbed out for Janine.

Janine glared at me, cracking the eggs one-handed. "Answer the question."

"Art is what you feel," I said eventually.

"Sure. But what else?" She aimed a wooden spoon in my direction.

"Well, you look for the details."

"Hmm." Chocolate chips were added to the mix. "You haven't been looking at the details."

That was it. "Oh, for fucks sake, J. Don't go all psych on me. What is it with therapists and fucking analogies?" I glared at the ceiling.

Janine smacked the spatula onto the counter, the noise pulling my attention, then she turned, ready to let me have it.

"Fuck you! I'm telling you this because you can be such a blind idiot, wandering through life. Everything's always come so easy for you. You and your perfect life."

"Hardly perfect," I said belligerently and Janine looked at me as if I'd appeared through the floor. "Not everything has come easily!" I folded my arms, protectively curling them across my chest.

"Bullshit. Like, when you knew what you wanted to do as a career, so you did it. Easily. Everything has been easy. Your road has no potholes, Bron. You *expect* things to be smooth which means you take everything for fucking granted."

I gaped at my sister.

Who wasn't finished.

"We can't all be like you. Do you think I take this house for granted?" She opened her arms as if to embrace the four walls. "Not with a fucking great mortgage and a job that could disappear up the arse of Aladdin's genie at any moment." She returned to beating the mixture, which was on track to becoming the lightest, fluffiest muffins ever. "Fuck you, Bron. And! You're kicking up a stink because Kate suggested therapy, then the therapist suggested this break and you, of course, saw it as some sort of failure. Which means that it's a bump in your smooth road. What about what Kate wants? What she needs?"

"But I don't think that anymore," I said, my forehead wrinkling.

"You don't?"

"No. I don't see it is a failure now."

"Could have fooled me." Siobhan followed her remark into the kitchen and Janine, focused on her muffin tray, must have realised that the invisible coach—probably Mum—had called for another substitution. Siobhan was on the field.

"Why?"

She didn't answer my question, instead choosing to lean against the counter and shake her head. "You know why Paul and I work?"

That was easy. "You're opposites and opposites attract." I shrugged.

"Yes and no. I'm a sweary extrovert with pink-tipped hair and a severe case of attitude. He's a beautiful, caring introvert who accepts everyone for who they are." She rolled her fingers into fists. "And. I. Tell.

Him. That." She hissed. "I love him and I get so petrified that I'll love him so far into his shed he'll never return. So I *don't* take any of that for granted." Her breath hitched. "And I hate that you do. Bron and her brilliant, easy, smooth as a baby's bum life. Bron and her easy marriage that'll be just fine because everything is fine but you're going to 'just fine' away the one person who's ever, *ever*, been the best thing that's happened to you."

She smacked the counter and it's a wonder she didn't break any bones. I couldn't look away.

"Tell me something you would say about me at my funeral."

"Oh Jesus Christ, Shiv. That's morbid."

"Do it!"

"Okay." I looked about the room, at the cupboards, at Janine bent over and shoving trays, filled with muffin batter, into the oven, and then gazed at Siobhan. "You have the biggest heart in the world and would give the shirt off your back to anyone who needs it and yes, you say Paul accepts everyone for who they are, but you are really the world's most non-judgemental person and even though you swear a lot, it's all because you care so damn much."

Siobhan's eyes were glassy with tears, and I heard Mum blow her nose. "Are you grateful for that? About me?" she asked softly.

"Of course."

It was like a volcano erupting. "Then why in the ever-loving fuck haven't you ever told me *all* of that?" she yelled, the force of her words rocking me back on my heels. "And that's why you haven't lost Kate, you idiot, because you've told her just enough to keep her on the radar. So now you are finding her. Tell her *why* you love her. I know you did in your vows and probably when you were getting together, but tell her. Show her! See her!" She choked on a sob. "And why the fuck am I telling my big sister all this shit when you should know it. You say you do, but you don't and it's taken some therapist to suggest three months apart so both of you can get your GPS out and find each other. Fucking hell, you two belong together. I've never seen a more perfect, forever, death do us part couple. Find her." Her hand over her mouth, holding all the sobs at bay, meant that mine could fall freely, and I hiccupped through each one. "Say something."

I blinked frantically. "I'm sorry."

"Good start. But wrong answer."

"Thanks?"

"Keep going."

The words spilled out. "I'm grateful for you and J and Mum because you see me and I need to appreciate that the scrutiny is based on love, not judgement. I'm grateful for the day that I met Kate when she dropped her drink on her skirt and that our love developed slowly and gently and that she's the sweetest, sexiest, loveliest person in the world. I'm grateful that she chose me. That she continues to choose me."

Siobhan's outline, in fact the entire kitchen and dining room— Mum had disappeared into the furniture—dissolved as a waterfall of tears hampered my sight.

"And *that's* the right answer." Siobhan thumped her fist on the bench. "Have you ever said all of that to her? *All* of that? And more, because there should be more. And not just words." I wondered if she and JJ had been chatting.

I shook my head. "Bits and pieces."

Siobhan scoffed. "Find some of that fucking awful craft glue and stick those pieces together. And again...why am I, the youngest sister, telling you this?"

"Because I'm a clueless idiot." Murmurs of "Yep" and "Yes, love" came from opposite ends of the space as Mum and Janine bookended the intervention.

"Exactly." Siobhan pushed off the counter and walked over to the cupboard containing the eclectic assortment of mugs. Her route took her past my spot, and I put my hand out, but she twitched away.

"Don't touch me. I'm so mad at you."

"Okay," I whispered, withdrawing. Then I made eye contact with Mum and Janine. "Why don't I boil the jug and make everyone a cup of tea?" I knew our intervention was drawing to a close. We'd all said what we needed to say. We'd all heard what we needed to hear. And I was so grateful for all of it, no matter how uncomfortable it had been.

"Yes, thanks," Janine replied, checking on her anxiety muffins through the oven's glass door. Mum nodded and smiled that Mum-smile as if cups of tea were the laying down of arms.

I tilted my head to catch Siobhan's eye. "Tea?"

"Yes," she said abruptly, staring at the cups. "I hate you."

"I hate you, too."

I opened my arms and moved forward at exactly the same time that Siobhan spun and threw herself at me. Our embrace was tight and full of so much love that no other emotion could have wedged itself between us.

After a moment, Janine joined in, then Mum, and we held on, each of us at various stages of tear-leakage.

"Thank you," I said, which seemed to be the cue for disentanglement.

"I don't want another one of these for a while, you hear? From any of you," Mum announced, then grinned at our aggrieved expressions.

Siobhan held my hands. "I'm sorry for being extra, extra sweary with you."

My mouth dropped open. "You...just apologised for swearing, Shiv." I shook my head in wonder. "Well, fuck me."

Siobhan squeezed my fingers. "Kate's got that bit covered, I think."

～

A DIVINING ROD. I STUDIED MY PHONE. DEFINITELY A divining rod, the way I was waving it about in frustration, in the hope that I'd find something, maybe see a sign. I paced around the lounge of the apartment, nearly tripping over my suitcase, which I'd packed last night in the excitement of returning to Kate.

And here I was, Sunday morning, suddenly nervous and creating then deleting texts as if I was an author writing their first draft.

WHEN WOULD YOU LIKE ME THERE?

GAH. THAT SOUNDED LIKE A PEST CONTROLLER ASKING when they should arrive to spray the roof cavity.

Delete.

IS IT STILL OKAY TO COME OVER?

. . .

Oh, look. I was a fourteen-year-old with the self-esteem of an artist with imposter syndrome.

Delete.

"Just turn up, McIntyre, for God's sake," I informed the blank screen.

Then the phone vibrated in my hand, and a text magicked itself into the middle of the black.

I'll see you soon? At the house?

My heart flipped over. Kate had said 'the house', not 'her house'. But then why would she? But she could have. *It's been her home for three months.* Maybe in her mind it was now all hers and I didn't belong th—

The follow-up text saved me from my brain.

I'll see you soon? At home?

The words were perfect. And I cried. Again.

I stood outside the front door of our home, the late afternoon sun casting shadows across the deck and rocked my feet in and out in indecision. For a dreadful moment, I wondered if Kate even wanted me back at all. My eyes closed in resignation.

Should I knock? That seemed a little silly. *Send a text? Something like,* "I'm here."

Oh my God.

I glared at the lead-light glass in the door, gearing myself up to give my brain an intervention all on its own.

"The door's open, Bron. Stop standing there thinking things."

Well.

I crossed the threshold, deciding that my suitcase could be left to the elements on the porch, and gently closed the door behind me. Kate was standing not five steps away, but I didn't take those five steps. Those five steps were necessary space simply to say;

"Hi."

"Hi back." The smile, slight and warm and tentative and relieved and so much more, grew on her lips.

"How've you been?" The ridiculous question skipped away from my mouth but I left it to fall pointlessly to the floor because I felt dizzy and I couldn't see anything in the world except Kate's beautiful, dark-brown eyes.

"Missing you."

We Built

May 1 to July 31 of the fourth year of the now

Our first night together after the break was an odd combination of shyness and familiarity. I knew the house, the bedroom, the walk-in robe—all the clothes from my suitcase reclaimed the spaces they'd left behind. But I felt uncomfortable in my skin as if I hadn't quite worked out how to wear it while moving about in the familiarity. I think Kate felt the same. So that night, after touching faces and sharing smiles of relief and disbelief and tenderness at the known and delight in the new, we slept like sea otters, holding hands, loathe to drift apart.

By morning our bodies had relaxed into their Bron and Kate shapes so the design for our forever drew its first lines on the drafting board.

It was just as well we'd both taken a day off work because we needed time to reacquaint, to reconnect, although our breakfast consisted more of superficial catching up rather than eating. I think I ate cereal? Who knew? It was more important to hear Kate retell her last three months at work, her weekly coffee catch ups with Janine—we grinned at that; both of us knew we'd been eavesdropping on each other—and her incredibly fragile relationship with her mum that still needed access to a metaphorical sewing machine and the medicinal threads of contact and communication.

We companionably completed the necessary, such as hanging out the washing, and split some tasks, like the grocery shopping, when one —Kate—needed the space to breathe.

The gentle kissing wasn't awkward like I'd feared, although our first kiss started with our lips forgetting their shapes, but finished with such unity that our smiles lit up each other's faces.

"Hi," I said very quietly.

"Hi back."

We prepared dinner together—a chicken and vegetable stirfry—and when I wielded the large knife, Janine's utensil-laden tongue-lashings sprang to mind. I attacked the ends of the snow peas, and recounted my interactions with Janine, her dangerous kitchenware, the enlightening conversations with JJ, the Great Intervention, and Siobhan's expletive-packed, pointy-sharp diatribe.

Kates eyes were wide. "Siobhan actually said that?"

"Yep."

"Wow." Kate slid the peeler across the skin of the carrot. "Your family interventions are brutal."

I laughed, laying the knife on the wooden chopping board. "They are. At least you had your *intervention*." I flicked my fingers in the air and air-quoted. "With a couple of McIntryes at a nice cafe, indulging in Devonshire tea on coordinated crockery."

Kate giggled. "I hardly call morning tea with Janine, and occasionally Michelle, an intervention."

Sidling across, I bumped her shoulder. "I'm proud of us."

She leaned in. "Me too, sweetheart."

I smiled at the chopping board, then picked it up and tipped the vegetables into the preparation bowl. "Long way to go, I guess."

Kate snuck her arm about my shoulders. "I want a long way to go. It means I get to go there with you."

"Sap."

Kate snorted. "Yes and proud of it, thanks very much." We shared a brand new grin that fitted like very old jeans.

I dug about in the pots and pans drawer and fished out the large wok. "So many people are cheering us on," I said contemplatively, plonking the wok on the gas burner, and swirling cooking oil into the base. "Pretty much everyone, even Neil."

"Neil?"

"Oh! I didn't tell you." I waved the oil bottle about, and Kate took it from my hands, twisted the cap back on, then leaned into the bench to listen, smiling gently, with her dark eyes twinkling, and her hair loose about her face. I nearly lost my train of thought. God, she was perfect. "I ran into Neil and we had a bit of an argument about you, and then some more arguing...also about you, then a bit more arguing about... you." Kate rolled her lips in. "Then he kind of, but not quite, said congratulations on our wedding which seemed to be the catalyst for him just," I shrugged, "deflating, sort of like he'd lost a prize."

Kate hummed. "Yes, he'd see it that way. Women are trophies according to Neil, but at least he wished us well, sort of." She pushed off the bench, turned on the stove, and heated the wok.

"I think he felt compelled to. You'd given him new instructions for life only days before I gave him a bollocking in the middle of the footpath on Graham Street."

Dinner was lovely. Not just the food, but the conversation. It ebbed and flowed and eddied when we fixed on a topic that swirled and whirled then tossed us away to a new discussion point.

"I love you." The words fell out of my mouth mid-eddy, mid-ebb, mid-flow and Kate paused, her mouth open to add to our chat, chopsticks halted mid-air so that the food fell off.

"I love you, too," she said, placing the empty chopsticks across her bowl.

I mirrored her movement. "How did you know I'd come back?"

"You promised." Her gaze was intense.

I held it, then breathed out carefully. "I'd like to try something."

Kate cocked her head.

I waved my hand. "It's not weird or anything. It's a strategy, a technique that Janine spoke about ages ago that she uses with clients. I don't know the name of it, but essentially we sit opposite each other for five minutes and look at each other's eyes, and nowhere else. Just sit, be, and focus. Thinking stuff about that person, thinking about yourself, thinking about each other together. Thinking whatever you like. But you can't speak and you can't break eye contact." I gave a self-deprecating smile. "Blinking is fine, obviously."

Kate frowned, then took a deep breath. "Can we hold hands?"

"Absolutely."

Another deep breath, and it occurred to me that perhaps Kate knew about this strategy and was freaking out.

"Are you?—We don't have to do this, sweetheart. It was just an idea," I said.

"No, no. I want to. Let's move our chairs over." She stood, grabbed her chair and set it in the middle of the kitchen, so I followed suit, then we faced each other. Kate looked as petrified as I felt. What a raw and intimate journey to embark on right after chicken stirfry. Right after a three month break. But I was determined to try this. It had landed at the front of my memory bank when my brain was going through a spot of interior decorating.

"If you want to stop." I reached for her hands, holding them lightly at our knees which touched as if kissing. "Then just say the word."

Her lips twitched. "Like a safe word?"

I rolled my eyes. "Kate."

"Sorry. Okay."

Placing my phone on the floor beside my chair, I set the timer for five minutes.

"Ready?" I squeezed her hands.

She nodded, so I leaned down and tapped start.

At first, probably the first twenty seconds, I fought against the urge to look away. Staring into someone's eyes is confronting. I knew if I tried it with any of my family members, I'd never last a minute. The vibrations of energy, the unspoken words of decades, the layers of sibling sensibilities would impact on the efficacy of the exercise. Staring into Kate's eyes wasn't confronting but it was challenging. I wanted to look away to gather my thoughts. I wanted to look away so my gaze could travel across her face.

But I didn't because the brown, all the darks and lights and the circles of walnut and caramel and flecks of gold and the love and the colours and the affection and...and...a treasure chest opened and the oddest thing happened. Our blinking synchronised. I knew this because Kate wasn't blinking while I held her gaze. We were closing our eyes at the same time.

The weighted silence that had settled on my shoulders, pricking at my awareness of the house creaking, the fridge humming, the lorikeets in the trees, was brushed aside by a silence that was tender and delicate and very faint tears in those eyes that held mine lost their balance and slipped over the edge. Then Kate invited me in to wander inside her gallery.

I love you, Kate.

I see you.

You are my person.

I'm so sorry I took our love for granted.

I'm sorry I hurt you.

Your smile is sunshine.

I love the way your chin lifts when you're determined to prove a point.

I love the way—

The colours in Kate's eyes coursed together and through the prisms in my tears those colours became rays of light.

Then I simply breathed. And cried. And breathed. And gradually, as if my brain knew what was required, I withdrew until my hands felt hers again, the fridge hummed, the house creaked, and the timer went off. And I breathed.

Kate sat back and scrubbed the heels of her hands into her eyes. I wiped at my tears with quick finger flicks. Then we stared at each other.

"Kate."

She reached up and held my face, smoothing her thumbs over my cheeks. "Sweetheart, I saw you just then and it was glorious. You. You are glorious. And do you know what else I saw? I saw you seeing me." Her smile wobbled.

Ah, more tears. I swallowed heavily. "That's all I've ever wanted to do and I nearly ruined it."

"You weren't entirely to blame. It's difficult to see someone who keeps running away." Kate's head tilted a little to reinforce her statement.

"When I looked at you just now, I saw the you I met when that orange slushy splattered your skirt. I saw the you who made me—makes me—origami cranes." I twisted my fingers into hers. "I saw the you who I want to walk through life with, and all the reasons why I want to do that. We've got years and years, Kate, and I want to see you every day of every month of all of those years. I choose to see you."

"Oh, Bron," Kate whispered. The timer may have stopped but our gazes were still locked.

"You've always been braver than me," I said, giving a slight nod.

The features on Kate's face knotted in incomprehension. "You're exceptionally brave."

"No. Well, maybe. But not really. I was—I am—petrified of losing you. I hate that phrase 'feel the fear but do it anyway'." I made an indistinct noise in my throat. "It's stupid. I felt my fear, but didn't do it anyway because that lacks true motivation. It lacks reason. I felt my fear and did what I needed, because it wasn't about fear, really. It was about love. It is about love, because you were right about us. You were right about me. You were right about..." I gestured to the door knowing that she'd understand the vague nature of it, that it encompassed the contemplation, the comprehension. "You were right about all of that."

Kate leaned forward and brushed her lips to mine. "So were you. You were right to do what we did. It takes strength, and we've got that strength. Honey, I'm not perfect or that strong if I'm honest. I simply needed. But mostly I wanted. You." She kissed me again. "I want you."

I slid forward on my chair, so my knees intertwined with Kate's, bringing our lips and faces and smiles closer. More accessible. Soft.

"It's called the mutual gaze." Kate drew back and rested her hands on my thighs.

"This?" I pointed vaguely at our eyes. "How did—?"

"I think in about our sixth year of marriage, Neil insisted we try it to connect properly so our sex life would intensify or at least function effectively—his words. It was completely unsuccessful, of course, because the mutual gaze only works with someone who I can be totally vulnerable with, someone I trust unequivocally, and frankly, someone I'd want to experience it with in the first place."

"I'm sorry. I shouldn't have—"

"Bron, you didn't know and, like I said, the mutual gaze only ever works when all the reasons I just listed are present." She pushed forward again, and kissed me firmly. "Which is why it worked tonight." I leaned against her forehead. "We can do this, Bron."

I sighed in relief. "We are doing this, sweetheart. You're my forever person."

～

FOR THE NEXT MONTHS, OUR LOVE DEVELOPED MORE LAYERS as if we were a tree and all our rings were on display. We built more rooms in our heart houses, choosing to use the tiny pieces of life Lego, because we knew that to build with the tiny: the tiny gestures, the tiny moments, the tiny touches; all of those tiny pieces—with the occasional large piece which was grand and spectacular and usually a ridiculous colour like purple—would create the Kate and Bron.

Tiny pieces like; "You're beautiful, Kate," I called after her as she walked towards the bedroom one morning. She paused, turned around, then leaned her palm on the doorframe, looking too sexy for words in her suit and heels and I was close to dissolving into that puddle of goo.

"You mean that." Kate quirked an eyebrow at her lack of question mark.

"Yes. I do." I stepped forward. "I promised you at our wedding that everything I ever say to you would always be truthful. So yes, you're beautiful."

Kate reached for my hand, tugging me closer. "Thank you."

"You're also—"

Her finger shushed my mouth. "Uh huh. Take it easy. You don't want to use up all the compliments in one go."

I grinned against her finger, then kissed it, and drew back. "Point taken. I'll finish the rest of the compliment tomorrow." Then I frowned. "Although split praise is uncomfortable and the first part could be forgotten by—"

"Bron."

"Right." I smiled cheekily, which made her eyes sparkle. Then I kissed her nose. "I love you."

～

TINY PIECES LIKE; OUR MORNINGS, WHICH WERE HAZY AND soft and although we needed to get moving for work, we made sure to cuddle and kiss softly, just to say 'hi' and 'I love you' knowing the other words would stroll along later. I enjoyed the way curves in the skin around her mouth always threatened a laugh, except when the headaches wrinkled her forehead and a hiss of pain darted through her teeth.

"That's two in three weeks, sweetheart. What's going on?"

Kate pressed her temples, then inexplicably the top of her head. "No idea but it's a simple headache. Nothing a couple of Panadol and a coffee won't fix."

On the days when the headaches punched needles into her brain, I slid my fingers through her hair, or massaged her feet; both of which produced a rather erotic purr of contentment, so Kate received the same attention on non-headache days as well. Just so I could hear the purr. I always stole a kiss or four, particularly on top of her head where the pain seemed worse.

~

TINY PIECES LIKE; "NICE PICK, SWEETHEART." I TOOK IN THE dining area of *Fred's*, the restaurant of choice for tonight's date. It advertised Australian cuisine, therefore it was an assorted menu that rivalled a McIntyre Christmas lunch.

We'd been on two dates—both dinners—and it actually felt as if we were dating again. Not the brand new, new, new dating where eyes can't settle or do settle and freak out the other person. This was dating where we'd known each other before, knew each other now, but the forever was unknown. It was powerful and intimate, yet contained the associated thrill, and yes, the new, and the excitement, and the anticipation, as we rediscovered each other and ourselves in a way that made me feel like I was falling in love all over again. Which had been Bernadette's point. *I must send her a gift basket or a really expensive bottle of wine.* I was so incredibly grateful to have been given a second chance. Maybe I'd wished upon my star without meaning to. It was probably one of the stars that the Grade One kiddos made where they smothered the cardboard shape in glue then dumped a tub of silver glitter over it so that the cleaners didn't speak to me for a week.

But it was more than new. We laughed together, not separately, and the lines at the corners of her eyes would deepen with her joy. We played together. We slow danced in the lounge, watching the TV attached to the iPad, and trying to copy the more gentle performances from *Strictly Come Dancing*.

Our attempts were awful and we'd fall about giggling. One night, Kate stumbled and I laughed at the fun of it, then I caught the haunted look in her eyes, even though she quickly joined my giggles.

"Are you okay?" I whispered in her ear as we threw our arms about each other.

Kate laughed shakily. "Just a misstep." Then she poked at YouTube on the iPad. "Let's try a different one."

Fred's waiters were an attentive bunch, and we were able to order with speed and efficiency. Kate decided that she wasn't that hungry, and so deemed a soup sufficient. I, on the other hand, called on my McIntyre upbringing and chose a Vietnamese crispy beef coconut pancake and Greek fashoulakia.

"Do you want some?"

"No thanks, sweetheart. This is perfect," Kate said, indicating her barely touched minestrone. I decided not to fuss—nagging was such a turn-off—but I was going to ask about the not-eating situation later in the week.

"It started during our break." Kate shrugged, the movement shifting the seatbelt on her chest as we wound our way through traffic to the grocery store two days later. "I just don't feel hungry sometimes. I didn't think you'd notice, because I'm not even aware of it myself."

I had noticed and I intended to continue noticing.

Tiny pieces like; random hugs and bum pats and soft touches and fingers that brushed on the way past in the hallway. Acknowledging each other. Recognising the now.

I needed to feel her skin. The intimacy of her naked body next to mine without the desperation of arousal and want and desire; a situation Kate preferred.

"I'm not ready."

So I held Kate close and dropped kisses on her cheeks.

~

TINY PIECES LIKE; SENDING TEXTS THROUGHOUT THE DAY full of emoji strings or words or both, discoveries of cranes on the bed or the kitchen counter or the bathroom. My wooden bowl was nearly full. I sketched landscapes and bridges and portraits on sticky notes and hid them in her briefcase.

~

TINY PIECES LIKE; CROUCHING TO FOSSICK UNDER THE couch for the remote control, blindly patting the carpet and eventually pinching the end with my fingers. I stood and my left knee gave an almighty crack, which really should have created a searing bolt of pain for that volume of noise. I blinked in astonishment.

Kate looked up from the iPad. "What was that?"

I rubbed my left knee. "My kneecap. There it is, ricocheting around the lounge." I moved my eyes as if following its journey about the room. "It'll be back on Monday."

Kate giggled, flipped the cover over on the device, then patted the seat beside her. "Come here."

I needed no further instruction, and scooted under her arm. "What's on for tomorrow? Anything take your fancy for a Saturday?"

I felt her hum.

"We could go to that new...that new..." She grunted in frustration. "That...God...what's it called where there are stalls and lots of—market! The new farmer's market. Let's try that tomorrow." She squeezed my shoulders.

I took a moment to respond. "Are you okay, sweetheart?"

Kate sighed, then gave a soft laugh. "Yes. I couldn't remember the name, that's all. Some words escape me." She laughed again. The kind where you don't take yourself seriously at all. "Must be getting old. You know me...always forgetting the names of things."

I sat up and took her hand in mine. "I do know you, sweetheart, and you *never* forget the names of things."

Kate decided that she was simply tired and it wasn't important. But I added it to my list of 'Weird Things That Kate Was Doing Lately'. It was a short list, and I was hoping it wouldn't lengthen.

~

THE TINY PIECES OF LIFE LEGO WERE INTERSPERSED BY THE large and spectacular.

We'd decided to combine our birthdays and so at the end of July, a chaotic bunch of people descended on the local child-friendly pub, where we monopolised an entire section of the dining area as far away as possible from the live band who weren't awful but could have done with some rehearsal time.

Invitations had been scattered about in a careful and selective manner and so Kate's colleagues, Lydia, all my mad lot, Larry, who could only stay for an hour so Paul bought him a beer quite early on, filled the space. I'd invited Lawrence but he couldn't attend as it was his night to chair the monthly meeting of the Woodturner's Association, which was an excellent excuse. I appreciated a beautifully turned bowl, particularly when it was filled to the brim with cranes.

I also invited Paula, my principal who'd become a friend over the course of the new year. When Paula walked into the pub, Lydia's eyebrows shot up and she whipped her head around.

"Our boss is here, McIntyre. Why? Why do you do these things?" Her eyes threw mischievous daggers. "Now I can't get shit-faced and say inappropriate things."

"What are you talking about? You don't need alcohol to say inappropriate things." I returned her grin and I heard Kate chuckle beside me, so I rubbed her thigh under the table. Sitting next to Kate surrounded by people we loved was the best gift ever and since we'd insisted on a no gift policy, this gift was perfect. I shifted closer to my wife to enjoy more of the warmth from her body.

Everyone sang happy birthday, including the blokes at the bar who added an interesting baritone to the shambolic rendition. Again, by the end, the kids saved the entire package of mismatched notes, tone, and pitch. With a full heart, my hand effortlessly found Kate's under the table in our booth, where we automatically interlaced our fingers, and shared a smile, our gaze holding for a long moment, dropping to glance at lips, then back to eyes.

"It's not fair, you know." Lydia's whine cut through, and I looked across the table. Siobhan's smile grew as she caught the teasing note in our friend's voice.

"What isn't?" Kate asked, lifting our joined hands and slowly kissing each of my knuckles. My brain misfired, but I was aware enough of Kate tossing a devilish look at Lydia. *Oh God, Kate.* Puddle of goo. Right there on the sticky floor of the *Golden Arms* pub.

Lydia waggled her hand in our direction. "You two. All loved up and gorgeous and totally not passing around the bottle." Siobhan snorted and slapped a hand over her mouth, her shoulders vibrating.

Kate bit my knuckles lightly, one at a time. *Gah.* "I'm not sure what you're on about, Lydia." Innocence was written all over her face. I couldn't add to the teasing, because Kate's mouth was making my body heat and I knew that her need, her want, her desire to fuck me senseless had awoken and I wasn't sure I'd be alive tomorrow.

Lydia stared at Kate, who'd paused our hands halfway to her lips. Siobhan finally gave in and her laughter filled the table.

She pointed at Kate. "Jesus!" she said. "Forget passing around the fucking bottle of love." Lydia joined the laughter. "Bron's dying over there and seriously, you need to head off before she bloody combusts at the table."

I glared. "Really? Mind, much? It's like you think I can't deal with a bit of flirting from my own wife."

All the puff in my argument evaporated when Kate leaned in and kissed my ear. "I want you" she breathed, and my eyes went round. This time, Lydia and Siobhan's laughter was loud and raucous and most of the group turned to grin at the sound.

"Yeah, sure. You're totally dealing," Lydia said.

Siobhan's eyes held amusement, but I saw all the other layers; the affection, the happiness, the relief, and as she lifted her chin towards the door, I saw the sisterly love.

Simply to prove a point, and simply because I wanted to, I kissed Kate, then again, and that exquisite swoop low in my belly awoke—it had never been asleep, really—as I gazed at Kate's long hair held away from her face by a small silver clip, her curves on show in a fitted green jumper, her smile bracketed by lines that advertised life, and love, and joy. And her eyes. Kate's eyes were dark as heated longing took center-stage. But in the background, tenderness and devotion and all the glittery lights guided the way forward.

We Cherished

July 31 to March 10 of the fourth and fifth years of the now

We hardly made it into the house.

"God, I want you so much," Kate growled into the side of my neck as I backed her up against the wall just inside the door. She scrabbled at the hem of my jumper, wrenching it over my head, then her hands found my breasts, and she thumbed my nipples through the fabric of my bra.

"Jesus!" I hissed, my fingers faltering as I undid Kate's jeans. All the while, our kisses were deep, sometimes messy as we were driven by lust, but mostly they were fast and furious and finally, when we'd kicked away our clothes, I grabbed Kate's wrists, held them together above her head and pressed my naked skin against hers.

And rolled my pelvis.

Kate gasped.

I slipped my thigh between hers and pushed into her, coating my skin with her wetness and heat.

Kate moaned.

I dragged my teeth up the side of her neck and softly bit her earlobe. Her body trembled.

"Bron." She drew my name out on a low groan, and I pulled my head back to stare into her eyes.

"God," I growled. "You are the. Sexiest. Woman. In. The. World." My thigh thrust at her centre with each word, and Kate keened with longing.

I kissed her deeply, our tongues sliding together, then I released her hands, sliding mine down her torso, tweaking her nipples along the way, and whispered against her mouth. "Don't move."

Dropping to my knees, I held her gaze; dark and sparkling and hooded and not and delicately touched the tip of my tongue to her clitoris. Her mouth fell open and her hands twitched, attempting to grip the wall; she was clearly aching to clutch at my hair.

"Please," she hissed, staring into the dark room, then down at my face.

My tongue touched again, and she jerked, chasing the exquisite stab of pleasure.

"Bron."

Her moans and sighs and gasps surrounded me.

"Don't move."

And I dove into her sex, enjoying the taste of the woman who'd said yes for the now with a promise for the forever.

Kate's legs trembled and every needy sound she made, louder and louder and more and more, echoed about the room. I lapped at her clitoris, then wrapped my lips around the swollen bud and gently sucked, flicking my tongue across the tip.

"Bron! Oh God. Oh God. Yes." I pulled back and fell into Kate's desperate gaze.

"Now." My quiet instruction brought an immediate response.

Her fingers peeled themselves off the wall, fell into my hair, tugged at the strands, and I moaned.

Kate's body, bowed, strung tight, froze for a moment as I sucked, then with a cry, her nails scraping across my scalp, she shuddered and shuddered, soaking my chin, as I pushed my tongue hard against the sensitive bundle of nerves, guiding her through the orgasm. I held her thighs as her hands slapped against the wall, then back to my head, then the wall, as if unsure what surface to cling to during her release. Finally her hands fell, fingers smoothing my hair as her breathing slowed and I sat back on my heels, wiping my chin, and stared at my beautiful wife, panting, sated, and slumped against the wall.

Kate's gaze stretched up to the ceiling then dropped to catch mine. She wore a look of wonder.

"Oh my God."

We woke early the next morning, which was surprising considering the two orgasms we'd shared not long after the first.

"We need to christen every room in this house," Kate announced by way of a morning greeting.

I laughed, disentangling myself from her embrace, and disappeared into the bathroom. The smile on my face felt like it would never leave.

I waited for her in bed. "I missed you so much during our..." My gaze skated about the room as if that explained everything.

"This?" She waved her hand languidly down the length of her body then trailed it back up. I grinned.

"Yes. But..." I frowned, which produced an identical expression on Kate's face.

"But?"

"But I missed her the most." I kissed the small freckle at the top of her left breast and Kate giggled, falling back, so I pounced, tackling her, and rolling us so I ended up underneath. My attention drifted down to Kate's breasts, which were resting on mine as she pushed up onto her elbows.

"Did you know that morning sex can boost your immunity?" Kate shifted to expose more of my body, and while her voice sounded like she was reading aloud from a photocopier manual, her fingers trailed in random patterns up and over my nipples. Her dark brown eyes held mine.

I shook my head, just barely. "No," I answered shakily. My stomach clenched. Christ, Kate could reduce me to a trembling mess with only a few soft touches.

"Mm. Morning sex can also count as a workout." She raised an eyebrow and circled my nipple, drawing tighter and tighter circles until she pinched it, twisting it lightly and I gasped.

"Can it?" I managed, the words almost lost in my hard swallow.

Kate toyed with the other nipple, then delivered a gaze so scorching that it travelled across my skin, through my veins, and straight to my clitoris. The moan pushed its way from my throat.

"Kate," I breathed.

"Yes, sweetheart?" Her voice was quiet, focused.

"More."

Kate dragged her fingers to my sex, applying the same tight circular motion to my clitoris.

"Oh, Jesus!" *Yep, instant trembling mess.*

"Touch me as well," Kate demanded, straddling my thigh and lifting so I could slide my fingers in. Bossy Kate, one of my favourite versions, stared at me, ravenous, wanting, starving. *Oh, fuck me.*

Our rhythm synchronised and it wasn't long before Kate's jaw clenched and we panted and gasped and held our breaths as we came, the pieces of the Kate and Bron jigsaw sliding and merging once again.

~

WE ATTACHED MORE LARGE AND SPECTACULAR PIECES OF life Lego while rebuilding our heart houses like our anniversary and Christmas and New Year; each an interesting experience in its own right. Our anniversary was low key. Just us and take-away Chinese and words and not-words. It was perfect.

Christmas, however, was not low key. Siobhan and Paul hosted, and Fruitloop thought it a marvellous situation; so many humans with hands attached!

As per usual, we chipped in for the kids' Christmas presents. Jack was over the moon—which translated as a brief smile, and a "Thanks everyone," and a nod of genuine gratitude directed at Janine and Rick—with his audio sunglasses, and immediately went about testing the blue-tooth capabilities of the inbuilt headphones in the frames.

JJ, in her typically eclectic fashion, asked for a pair of fuzzy slippers, a hardcover of 'The Girl Who Smiled Beads' by Clemantine Wamariya, and a gorgeous vegan leather black duffel bag; the sight of which made her squeal in delight.

Pip, rolling her eyes at her older siblings, unwrapped a new tablet and promptly squealed as well, earning her a poke in the shoulder from JJ as if to say, "Who's the squealer now, kiddo?"

One of the surprises of the day was the presence of Olivia Agostino. My hackles were raised. Actually, they probably hadn't been lowered since Kate suggested that inviting her mum might be one of the threads of contact and communication that could stitch their relationship together.

Surprisingly, Olivia had agreed, and my two sisters, their partners, Mum, and Dad, all had identical reactions at the news of the additional guest.

"Really?" Siobhan's voice reached a new octave at the end of the word.

"Mm," I said.

"I didn't ask you first, Shiv, and I feel dreadfully rude. I'm sorry." Kate spoke up so her words travelled over to the phone from the other end of the table. "I managed to catch Mum at a moment when she was talking about the loneliness of Christmas, etcetera, and I suggested Christmas with Bron's family and she accepted then and there."

"That's fine, Kate," Siobhan projected, her voice loud through the speaker. "The more, the merrier. Have you sent her the preparative memo regarding a McIntyre Christmas?"

Kate and I fell about laughing. "I don't think anything prepares someone for our Christmas, Shiv."

So, there was Olivia Agostino wearing a Picasso-esque face of expressions ranging from deer-in-headlights, to incredulity, to a decent splash of condescension which raised those hackles again, and to involuntary fascination depending on which McIntyre wandered into her personal space.

"I'm sorry," Kate whispered into my ear as we shared a cuddle on the couch.

I shrugged. "It's okay. Everyone here can hold their own, and besides, now that your mum has poked her toe through the gap into your life, she'll discover just how much we look after each other, Ms Agostino." Kate smiled, then nestled into my neck, kissing the skin and humming along to the Christmas carols.

"I love you," she murmured and hugged me tight. I was alight with joy.

Olivia decided early on, after being introduced to one and all, that Rick, the successful vet, was deemed worthy of conversation. Rick looked incredibly uncomfortable with his involuntary nomination but was obviously coping well with the superficial, high-brow, elitist chat that Olivia engaged in at her country club because she hadn't left him alone for at least fifteen minutes. Perhaps he had clients cut from the same cloth, or maybe he was treating her like a recalcitrant, highly-strung Pomeranian who needed pacifying before he rammed a thermometer up its bum.

It amazed me that Olivia was only two years older than my parents. She seemed so many more, as if she'd sucked on life through a straw instead of taking great gulps of it like Mum and Dad. It made me sad for Kate.

Then I watched in horror as, from across the room, JJ fixed her gaze on Olivia and Rick and narrowed her eyes. "Oh, shit," Kate and I said at the same time. A wicked smile slowly pulled at JJ's lips as she lifted herself from the floor, where she'd been sitting cross-legged reading her new book, and casually made her way towards the pair. Oh dear God. I so wanted to be a fly on the wall for that interaction.

However, the interaction that I did overhear was the one between Olivia and Kate, who were standing near the dining table later on. There is a little corner wall in Siobhan and Paul's house that hides a supporting beam and I stopped behind it, not wanting to interrupt. I was becoming an expert eavesdropper these last few years.

"You're swaying, Katherine. I didn't realise you drank so heavily now."

I frowned. Kate hadn't touched a drop of alcohol today.

"I haven't—"

"Look, you're clutching at the table. It's rather embarrassing. So," Olivia stated, that topic firmly closed. "Neil sends his regards and was wondering if you'd like to meet for dinner."

"Mum, I know Neil didn't say anything of the sort and besides he and I are—"

"Oh, I know. Neil's gone by the wayside. A mother can only hope. However, there is a lovely fellow in middle management at the executive office who I could introduce you to."

"Mum!" Kate sounded utterly appalled. Unsurprising.

Olivia huffed. "Yes, yes. You're already married, Katherine, and moved on, but you've had one divorce so another one won't matter."

My mouth dropped.

Oh. That...she didn't...oh my God.

Ready to conduct open warfare, I made a move but paused mid-step when I heard the steel in Kate's voice.

"That's it, Mum. Out of all the hurtful things you've said about my divorce, about my relationship with Bron, my love for Bron, and our marriage, that is by far the worst—No. Don't *even*," Kate snapped.

I imagined that Olivia had tried to respond, defend or somehow justify herself.

"No apology will ever be enough. Oh, and let's add in today's judgement, Mum. Your judgement of this incredibly kind family. Judging their differences, then judging their acceptance of those differences. Can't you see how happy I am here? I love you, Mum, but I won't allow you to behave so reprehensibly towards people I love as well. The McIntyres are my family, just as much as you are. But the McIntyres see me as Kate. Just Kate. Not Kate, Bron's wife. Not Kate, the divorcee. Not Katherine, wayward daughter. Just *Kate*. I thought inviting you would be an opportunity for us to reconnect, for you to see another aspect of my life, but no. So, stay if you want to, but I get the feeling that you won't."

There was a silence while my heart broke for Kate.

"Well...well," Olivia stuttered. "Well, it's getting late so I best make a move." I wondered if she'd ask Kate to say goodbye on her behalf, but I didn't think so. Olivia Agostino's manners were flawless, even if her opinions wallowed in the sewerage underneath the footpath.

As Olivia sailed past, smiling tightly at those around her and making a beeline for Mum, I sidled around the corner and put my hand in the small of Kate's back. She was shaking from the awfulness of it. A thought, not really fully formed, tickled at the back of my mind as I took in Olivia's rapid journey across the carpet. I snuck a look at Kate. She wasn't swaying at all. What on earth had Olivia been talking about? I added it to the list of 'Weird Things That Kate Was Doing Lately' and my mouth turned down at the thought that possibly the list had lengthened.

Kate's mum didn't thank Siobhan despite Siobhan and Paul hosting the lunch. I'd watched her instantly dismiss my wonderful sister when she'd laid eyes on the pink-tipped hair.

Olivia left and Mum made eye contact with me as I held my fractured wife, then, ensuring I saw it from across the room, she held her hands over her chest, and nodded quietly in understanding.

~

WE CONTINUED TO CREATE THE KATE AND BRON HEART houses, knowing full well that our tiny pieces of life Lego were supported by a motley crew of cheerleaders, each with their own unique way of telling us how much they were encouraging our forever.

"Sorry to turn up unannounced," Siobhan stated, sliding onto the dining chair and crossing her legs.

"No, you're not," I responded, continuing to unload the dishwasher.

"Okay, fine. I'm not." She held her hands up in surrender.

"Why are you here?" The two wineglasses swung upside-down from my fingers, and I slid them into their runners under the cupboard.

"Can't a little sister visit her big sister?"

Alarm bells rang and I narrowed my gaze at her guiltless look; the innocent type with the big eyes. "You never say things like that unless you want something or to tell me things I don't want to hear."

"Today you get a two for one deal."

I looked at the ceiling. "Jesus Christ, Shiv." I spun around, picked up the kettle, filled it with water and set it on its stand. "Tea or coffee?" I sighed. Caffeine, soft or hard, was going to be required for this.

Siobhan whipped her phone from her pocket, glanced at the screen, nodded, then slid the phone away. "Bourbon."

"Oh God."

After turning off the switch to the kettle, I pulled out the half-full bottle of bourbon from the top cupboard, cracked some ice into two tumblers, poured the liquid, and sat opposite Siobhan at the table.

Our cheers was silent, then after a sip, we stared at each other, and I felt very much like I'd been unwittingly inserted into the chess world championships.

"So how's it all going?" Siobhan's question tested the metaphorical chess board, sending forth her king's pawn.

"Fine? You saw me two weeks ago, Shiv." I moved a mental chess piece anywhere. Siobhan was a master at the back and forth of questions and answers and I could feel the loss coming.

"Uh huh. Just checking, you know, on my big sister in a checking up kind of way since checking up on my big sister now that she's returned to her senses is important, you know, in a checking up kind of way."

I squinted at her. "Uh huh."

Siobhan sipped at her bourbon, while I held her gaze in case she snuck in with her queen piece and killed me.

"How's your person?" Siobhan said eventually.

I swallowed my mouthful, noticing that our glasses were nearly empty. "I don't own Kate."

Siobhan loosely waved her hand. "Psh. You know what I mean."

"Kate's fine." I drained the rest of my drink. "This is weird, Shiv. Why are you being weird?"

"Have you kissed her every single morning?" She swallowed the remainder of her drink as well. "Cooked her dinner? It's in the manual of—"

I glared. "Shiv, I swear to God—"

"I've brought Thai, so dinner is covered, Shiv. The manual is saved." Kate breezed into the kitchen, placed a bag of deliciousness in the centre of the table, hugged Siobhan around her shoulders, then turned to me. I'd stood up in the meantime and we smiled softly at each other.

"Hi."

"Hi back," she said, and held my face as she kissed me.

"Right-o." Siobhan shoved back her chair and grabbed her glass and mine, ran them under the water at the sink, turned them upside-down on the drainer and leaned against the counter nearest the dining table. "I'm off to join the wallpaper section at the hardware store. You two share the coconut rice properly. World War Two started because of that very issue."

Kate broke away and giggled. "Do you want to stay for dinner?"

"No, thanks. Paul's had a day off and been in the shed the whole time which means he's been restoring something or building a sex swing. I'm hoping for the latter. Bye!"

I coughed violently and Kate cracked up, bundling Siobhan into her arms and squeezing her tightly. "It was lovely to see you, even if briefly."

Siobhan grinned. "Same." She flicked a wicked look my way. "I weirded out your wife."

"I'm sure she appreciates it." Kate's look was mischievous.

I shook my head at their antics, and snuck a look in the bag. My heart expanded. There was an extra side of tao hu tod, the deep fried tofu snack—my favourite—and extra satay sauce. There was never enough in the little plastic pots.

"You remembered," I said, making eye contact with Kate, and Siobhan could have travelled to the hardware store and transformed into bland wall paint from the amount of attention she was receiving.

Kate smiled quietly. "I never forgot." Another little Lego piece clicked into place.

The silence in the room was rich and thick.

"Right! Now I really have to go."

"Wait!" I swivelled and held out my hand. "You wanted something."

Siobhan gave a tender smile. "I got it."

OCCASIONALLY WE HAD TO DISMANTLE PARTS OF OUR HEART houses because we'd connected the pieces incorrectly. That was to be expected. It was never going to be perfect. Whose marriage is perfect, anyway? So we removed pieces, studied the pile, then rebuilt.

The rebuild was always fun.

I replaced the bottle of milk in the fridge, closed the door, and froze as Kate waltzed in, tightening her ponytail, tilting her head slightly to assist in the action, which exposed the line of her throat, then she swiped her tongue across her bottom lip; the whole time completely unaware that she was reducing me to a puddle of goo.

All of that in heels and a business suit. *Jesus.*

My silent appraisal mustn't have gone unnoticed, because Kate raised an eyebrow and smirked.

"You're good for my ego," she murmured, pausing at the kettle, ready to fill her travel mug with tea.

I studied her.

"What?" Kate's smirk morphed into a frown.

"Gosh, Kate. That's a pretty serious case of hives you've got there."

She gasped, whacking her mug on the bench, and patted at her face, bending to peer at her reflection in the glass of the microwave door. She whipped around. "Where?"

My lips curled up at the edges. "Why don't you call in sick? It looks like you're allergic to work. I've called in sick as well, because I'm suffering from the same affliction." I smirked, and she inhaled, probably in relief at not being covered in itchy, raised welts.

"I could kill you," she growled, then bit her lip, and narrowed her eyes. "You're asking me to play hooky from...school?"

I took a step forward and her eyes darkened. "Yep."

"Bron, I'm fifty-two years—"

"Never too old to have a yes day." I took another step.

"A yes day?"

"Yup. Whatever we suggest, the other person has to say yes to it." I gave her a provocative look, dragging my gaze up and down her body. "Wanna play?"

Kate seemed to consider the idea for a moment, then her lips curled in to a smile. She pulled out her phone, then pressed a single button— her PA was on speed dial, which was efficient—all without breaking eye contact. So fucking sexy.

"Good morning, Pam. How are you? I won't be coming into the office today. I'm not well."

"Hives," I mouthed, and she widened her eyes in a mock glare.

"Could you send my apologies and reschedule my meetings until tomorrow? Oh yes, I'm sure it's only a twenty-four hour thing. Yes, one of my headaches again. Okay. Thanks so much. See you tomorrow." She tucked the phone away and I took another step right into her space.

"You'll get caught for lying," I murmured.

"I'll tell on you as well." She tugged on the hem of my shirt, so that our bodies touched. "Well, what are we doing?"

"You need to change clothes because you in a sexy suit is delicious but completely inappropriate for what we're doing today."

"Really?" Kate tugged at my shirt again, bringing my lips to hers. "What." Kiss. "Are." Kiss. "We." Kiss. "Doing." Kiss. "Today?" I felt her smile against my mouth.

"I don't know. You make my brain mushy when you kiss me."

Kate laughed then pulled away and I grinned into her joy. Then I was struck by a brilliant idea.

"Ever had sex while there was a risk of someone catching you?

Kate's eyes glittered. "Yes."

I choked. "Really?" I said incredulously. "W-When?"

Kate ran a single finger across my bottom lip. "Today."

～

PROBABLY THE MOST RIDICULOUSLY SPECTACULAR LIFE LEGO piece was the combined birthday party extravaganza for Pip and the twins in the middle of March. On a Sunday evening.

Clearly, combined celebrations were all the rage but smooshing together a fourteen-year-old's birthday with that of two teenagers turning sixteen was insane.

However, there was method to Rick and Janine's madness as they'd hired an amusement centre which housed multiple spaces to accomodate the most eclectic of tastes. Jack and his friends were thrilled to discover a zone filled with dark lighting and neon flashing things, doof-doof music, carpet of an indiscriminate colour, and games in which the objectives were to kill people or drive erratically in vehicles. Sometimes in the same game.

JJ encouraged all her friends to hang out in a sort of chill out area which had enough soundproofing to block the discordant music, the animated characters screaming as they lost animated blood after being caught in the doors of animated space modules, and the yells of delight from the younger children leaping about on trampolines.

The delighted yelling was mainly Pip's, who was in her element with all the running, jumping, cartwheeling space and associated apparatus. Rick's facial gestures resembled a live broadcast. I didn't need to see Pip to know what she was up to; Rick had it covered with every tic, grimace, and twitch as his youngest attempted anything remotely dangerous. All he needed was the commentary.

"And here comes Pip with a forward-tuck-roll-and-a-half-pike-star-jump-with-a-final-leap-into-the-foam-pit! The crowd goes wild!" I murmured, then swivelled my head and grinned. Yep, foam pit.

Janine marshalled everyone an hour and a half into the night ostensibly to direct them to the food kiosk, but I'm sure it was mainly to conduct a head count in case one of the kids was stuck under a trampoline.

Jack and his buddies joined the group, ambling in with the strut-slouch that teenage boys seem to perfect for about eighteen months. The walls of the amusement centre were dotted with posters from various films, and all four boys stutter-stepped as they passed one poster in particular. Jack seemed to have moved on from his Kate Agostino crush to a wide-eyed, flushed face, heavy swallowing fascination with Kate Winslet. Entirely understandable. The two Kates were smoking hot.

Both Jack and JJ were walking hormones at sixteen, but with Janine and Rick's open communication and their insistence on consent and respect, the twins were the epitome of permission in intimacy. I figured, anyway. JJ hadn't come to me with questions, answers, or observations yet. I doubted Jack would, but I hadn't closed that door.

I'd witnessed one interesting parental moment between JJ and Janine last week when I'd dropped by after work.

"I'm inviting Essee to the party next week, Mum, just in case you'd forgotten."

Janine passed a pile of folded washing to JJ. "S-E?"

"E, double s, double e." JJ lifted the clothes to punctuate the spelling. "Essee."

"And Essee is..?" Everything about Janine—shoulders, eyebrows, hands, cheeks, the ending of her sentence—lifted in confusion. She paused in her towel folding.

JJ rolled her lips in and a glint of mischief sparkled in her eyes. "A bisexual non-binary lesbian male."

Gravity took over Janine's body, and she sank onto the couch, her mouth open, her forehead wrinkled in confusion. JJ held the silence for another moment before falling about laughing. "Oh, Mum. That was so good."

"Well, I don't know anymore!" Janine actually sounded quite distressed and JJ, suddenly looking contrite, plonked down and wrapped an arm about her mum's shoulders.

"Mum, I'm sorry. That wasn't a great joke at all. I'm sorry." She

217

leaned into Janine. "Essee is a boy at school. He's in my graphic design class and we've been hanging out a lot. A lot. I'd like to invite him for dinner this weekend before the party and—" an unusually shy expression crossed her face and she looked over at me, so I pointed to the kitchen.

"Should I go?" I mouthed.

JJ shook her head, then looked Janine dead in the eye. "I'm hoping that Essee and I can be...something. You'll like Essee, Mum. Dad will, too. He's a genuine, kind, friendly person. With good manners." She paused. "So should Essee and I have sex here or over at his place?"

I was reminded of the interaction as JJ and Essee strolled past on their way back to their chill-out zone, so I turned to Kate, and leaned close to her ear so I could win the competition between my retelling of JJ and Janine's moment and the buzzing, dinging, yelling, and inarticulate noises from the animated zombies.

Kate's laughter was delightful when I finally got to JJ's question, and I grinned, holding her hand while happiness fizzed inside.

Suddenly, Kate's fingers dug into my skin. "I'm going to the bathroom." Something in her voice made me turn quickly, but she'd already crossed the carpeted area, her movements tense and wooden. It wasn't even a decision. I took off after her and pushed through the door, scanning the multi-stall space.

One stall was closed.

"Kate?"

I knocked tentatively on the door.

"Kate?"

The fast breathing of someone in distress echoed onto the tiles.

"Kate! Sweetheart, what's wrong?"

The silence was much too long, so I dropped to my knees and peered under the door. Kate's shoes filled my view, then she stood up, flushed the toilet and I scrambled to my feet as she opened the door.

The panic in Kate's eyes was all-encompassing.

White had never looked so stark on a person's face.

She pushed past me and flicked on the faucet, cupping her hands then splashing water over her face. I was beside her in an instant.

"Honey, what happened?"

Kate held herself very carefully. "One of those headaches just came on so suddenly and the pain, Bron. The pain was so awful that I knew I was going to throw up." She washed her hands, rubbing them together very gingerly as if the action would set off another bout of vomiting. I ducked my hands under the tap, quickly swiping at soap along the way.

Now was not the time to advise making a doctor's appointment.

Now was not the time to add another item to the list of 'Weird Things That Kate Was Doing Lately'.

Now was the time to—

"Can we go home?" she asked faintly.

"Absolutely."

"I'm sure it's just the lighting in the centre."

I didn't believe a word in that last sentence. I knew she didn't either. We exited the bathroom and made our way across to Janine, who took one look at Kate and instantly went on full alert.

"J, I'm taking Kate home. She's not feeling well."

Janine ping-ponged her gaze between the two of us, then nodded. "Let me know if I can do anything."

I squeezed her forearm. "Thanks."

On the journey back to our little house with its front porch, and wooden floorboards, and tiny kitchen, and back shed with the mural on one side, and hall table holding a bowl full of cranes, I clutched Kate's hand as despair and foreboding galloped about in my heart.

We Knew

March 11 to May 31 in the fifth year of the now

Waking up the next morning and announcing that she felt much better, Kate promised to phone the doctor from work. I wasn't thrilled that she'd be delaying the call, let alone going into her office.

"Last night, you were throwing up in a toilet, Kate. That says something. Please don't go to work. Rest!" I pleaded, all but tying her to a chair, which would have been really kinky and awesome under different circumstances.

But she went to work, phoned, and informed me that an appointment wasn't available for ten days.

This was hardly surprising as Geraldine Wilson was such a popular and well-respected general practitioner that securing any type of appointment with her was like getting your hands on the Holy Grail.

We'd discovered Dr Wilson after chatting to Larry about needing a local GP. According to Larry, Geraldine was a 'good sort' who 'didn't make up stuff' or 'write things on your chart that were wrong' and she 'listened properly when you wanted to tell her about real problems'. We'd filled in the new patient forms the next day.

"I'm going to be wasting her time you know. It's simply a bit of a headache, although last night's was rather extreme. Anyway, I don't mind waiting to see her, Bron. I've had the headaches for a while so waiting ten days is nothing, really."

I lifted my eyebrows from across the dining table. It sounded like she was trying to reassure herself more than me.

Ten days is not nothing, really. Kate was hit by three volcanic nighttime headaches during the wait.

I hated seeing her in such pain; her face so pale, eyes dull, and her fingers trembling. Each time, she took the next day off. Each time, she swallowed pain medication, which seemed to have no effect at all. And each time, I grabbed a soft cushion, laid it on my lap, and gave a little pat, gesturing with my chin for her to rest her head. I'd stroke her hair, she'd smile that beautiful smile, her eyes would flutter close, and she'd sleep. And the lines on her face would relax. It was as if every worry disappeared or at least went on an extended lunch break.

~

FRUSTRATION FIZZED IN MY STOMACH WHEN KATE recounted her conversation with Geraldine the night after the appointment.

"Why didn't you tell her about the other symptoms?"

"They're not symptoms, Bron." Kate hung up her jacket and stepped out of her heels, while I perched on the armchair, the one that we'd squeezed into the space in the bedroom.

"Alright, then the...other stuff. The forgetting words thing." I pulled up my mental list. "The stumbling."

Kate sighed. "All of which are not connected, so I only talked about the headaches because that's what I'm dealing with at the moment. It's what worries me the most." She shimmied out of her skirt, draping it at the end of the bed, then twisted the buttons on her shirt, and slid it off her shoulders. Standing there in her underwear, her fingers delicately holding a white business shirt by its collar, would have normally reduced me to a wide-eyed incoherent puddle, but I was much too concerned about the headaches to pay that sort of attention to the Goddess in front of me.

"Bron, Geraldine thinks it might be a collection of rolling migraines, which worried her a bit. She wanted to know how long they'd been going on. I said a month or so."

"*Liar!*" my brain screamed. Because, right then, with that answer, I knew that Kate was more worried than she let on.

"Besides, you've been looking after me with aspirin, and hot water bottles, and cold packs, and." She smiled affectionately, and dropped her shirt into the clothes hamper. "Those delightful massages."

Kate's phone rang, and she frowned into the screen.

"Hi, Geraldine. Did I forget something?"

I glanced at the clock on the wall. Seven-thirty. Late for a GP to be ringing a patient who'd been in her clinic only three hours prior.

"No, no. Bron and I are just talking about the appointment this afternoon. Yes, migraines does sound—an MRI? Really? That seems a bit much. Well, yes, I agree. Being thorough is a good idea. What are you looking for?"

There was a pause, then Kate's free hand flew to her chest, and she inhaled quickly, pressing her lips together as if to lock the air inside her lungs.

"Out of the ordinary? You mean..."

Kate blinked quickly and she made eye contact with me. *What the hell? An MRI?* I stood and guided Kate to the chair, catching Geraldine's voice, made tinny by the phone, as Kate sat heavily.

"...a mass of cells or similar..."

My throat closed. *Oh God.* I stayed close, holding Kate's hand, now clammy and trembling.

"Cancer?" Kate whispered.

Geraldine's answer was quiet, but in the stillness of the room, it felt as if the world could hear.

"...not get ahead of ourselves...on the twenty-sixth...email the referral to the neurological centre..."

"Oh...oh. Okay. Well, that's definitely being thorough. Right." Kate had begun blathering, so I squeezed her hand. "Right. Right. I'll make sure my PA sorts out my schedule. Thanks for ringing, Geraldine."

Kate hung up and stared at the carpet, breathing and breathing, and holding my hand, and the phone dropped to the floor.

"Bron..."

I knelt in front of her. "Honey, Geraldine's being thorough just like you said, and I bet it'll end up completely unnecessary. The test will only confirm that you're fine and we can go back to migraine management."

She nodded, reaching for my other hand. I kissed one knee, then the other, and she gave me a wobbly smile.

"Will you come with me when I have the MRI?"

"Of course I will. There was never any doubt. I'll give the Grade One kids the keys to the art supplies cupboard because we're going to this appointment together."

Kate giggled softly at the idea of six-year-olds with free rein to paint and glue, then swallowed.

"I need a shower and something to eat. Cheese toasted-sandwich?"

"On it."

~

THE NEUROLOGICAL CENTRE IN THE HOSPITAL WAS SEDATE and calm and the carpet was more lush than I expected, but the furniture was the same as what was in Bernadette's office so I figured that Michael Opperheim bought his chairs from the same warehouse. I don't know what I'd been expecting; framed prints of Rorschach test results on the wall perhaps.

Michael Opperheim was a lampost-shaped man topped with a halo of hair, and as he folded himself into the armchair opposite our couch, I caught the empathy, the sincerity, and the focus in his eyes, which were all excellent qualities for a surgeon whose speciality was cutting into people's brains.

"Kate, Dr Wilson referred you to me for an MRI and discussion of the results."

Both of us were silent. There really wasn't anything to say in response to a statement like that. Our fingers twined together, and I felt marooned on a couch-shaped island as we watched an approaching storm.

"As you know, with the information you gave us about your symptoms over the last year." I'd insisted that she verbalise my list of 'Weird Things That Kate Was Doing Lately' to the clinician before the MRI, who'd blinked then written very quickly and at great length on Kate's chart. "We were then able to focus the MRI so we could create a more detailed analysis."

We started nodding. The kind you do when you're listening, but don't want to. For a heart-stopping moment, I imagined that Michael would tell Kate to stop nodding, otherwise she'd shift about whatever they'd found and they'd need to do another MRI.

Because I knew they'd found something.

The empathy in his eyes sparked to life and Kate gripped my fingers.

"Your list of symptoms and the results from the MRI have given a strong indication towards a glioblastoma multiforme."

"You're kidding," I blurted, a default two-word statement for when I couldn't deal with the information I'd just heard.

He looked at me. "I wish I were." The empathy was on high beam.

"That's cancer, isn't it?" Kate asked softly, and I swivelled towards her so quickly that I could have been auditioning for the Melbourne Ballet Company.

"Kate..." *Oh God*.

"Yes, it is." Michael's words were quiet but spoken too loudly for my ears. Awful words that we couldn't unhear. "We don't know for sure, so we'll run another round of tests just to confirm."

Shallow breathing beside me brought my attention back and I watched in despair as Kate covered her eyes, then her mouth, then her eyes, as if she wasn't sure which part to save from the news. Then she ran her shaking hand through her hair, jerking it away as if whatever was inside her head might magnetise her fingers to her scalp. She stared blindly, then, without looking, reached over so that both her hands clutched at my arm.

"What do you know for sure, Michael?" I asked, hoping that Kate didn't mind that I was stepping in.

He gave me a thoughtful look.

"If it is a glioblastoma, then headache medication will not have any effect on the pain. That's first and foremost."

"I've...I've been massaging Kate's head and using hot or cold packs,"

I said desperately, as if my small therapies would create magic. I couldn't remember when I'd felt so useless.

"All of which are excellent, Bron. Keep doing so, even if we find that the headaches and associated symptoms indicate something else entirely than what we think right now."

I descended into silence, while Kate, still clutching my arm, stared at her lap. Then she inhaled deeply.

"I have questions, Michael, about glioblastoma," Kate said, and straightened, leaving her hand locked with mine. "I'd like to know more."

"Of course." He crossed his legs and absurdly I thought that his relaxed demeanour was because of the insignificance of the diagnosis, rather than his experience delivering this type of news.

"I'd like some numbers for this." She fluttered her hand at her head.

"We don't know for sure if—"

"Yes, you do," Kate said sadly. "The next test is simply to find out the location of the cancer's centre and how large it is."

I was watching a tennis match. Kate and Michael with their questions and answers, and all the while my mind was screaming.

"Yes. You're right, Kate," Michael acknowledged.

"Numbers, please. I work very well with numbers," Kate repeated.

Michael hummed. "Glioblastomas are rare. They occur in only five percent of the population. They are aggressive because they grow not as a single mass but a series of tentacles." I stared at him utterly appalled, imagining an angry octopus-like growth inhabiting Kate's brain.

"Oh!" Kate said. "Oh. Right."

Michael wasn't finished crushing our hearts. "The arms, for want of a better word." *Come on, Michael. Please use a better word.* "Makes surgery difficult, because they aren't a solid mass."

"So?" I said, adding extra 'o's to the word, because his sentence hadn't finished.

"So, if the next MRI indicates glioblastoma without a doubt and we find the centre and the range, then we'll try chemotherapy first."

That's a word I never thought I'd hear.

"What's...what's the cure rate?" Kate gripped my hand, almost cutting off the circulation.

"Based on your list of symptoms, and how long you've been experiencing them, combined with the results of the MRI, it looks like the glioblastoma has been present for about eighteen months."

We both leaned forward because that sentence did not answer Kate's question. I held my breath.

"Cure rates for a glioblastoma that has been developing for that long." He paused and I internally screamed. He was like a presenter at the Academy Awards delaying the announcement of the winner. "Are twenty percent."

I was too shocked to say anything. *Twenty percent.*

Kate dealt with her numbers. "That's a fifth of the patients, Michael. That's a reasonable statistic," she said impassively.

I stared at Kate. She was much too calm. I could sense her building mental walls, ready to run away, and if she did, I'd join her.

Michael raised his hand from his knee. "That's an average, of course. A statistic like that can't predict what will happen for you, Kate. Your age and overall health play a role."

"K-Kate might be one of those people who beats it." Life vest in turbulent seas.

"Yes." Michael's eyebrows lifted. "Medicine and disease, particularly cancer, are renowned for their unpredictability."

MRIs ARE CLEVER LITTLE THINGS. IT TURNED OUT THAT Kate's cancer *was* a glioblastoma and it was shaped like a star, which was pretty on the imaging printout but made me sob later that afternoon while hiding in the bathroom at home because I didn't want Kate to see me fall apart. We'd already done that in front of each other after Michael's first round of devastation.

The glioblastoma was a scene-stealing diva.

Michael whipped the plastic model brain from his desk, and plonked it on the coffee table in his office, then he poked at the top and bottom sections at the front.

"The centre is located here, and the tentacles reach here, here and here." He could have been pointing out the exit doors on a plane.

Kate was trembling.

"The MRI has confirmed my suspicions about the glioblastoma's placement. Its location." He pointed to the plastic brain. "Is sometimes initially determined by your symptoms, such as occasional loss of motor control." I yanked out my mental list of 'Weird Things That Kate Was Doing Lately' and placed a tick next to the first dot point. "It can affect speech, such as remembering words and speaking fluently." Tick number two. "It affects coordination." Tick number three. "There may be issues with vision." Tick, tick, fucking tick.

"What happens now?" we asked at the same time, then reached for each other's hand at the same time, and probably inhaled that ratchet-like gasp at the same time, but I wouldn't know about that because my head was screaming. Still.

Michael moved his medical kindergarten toy and leaned over his knees. "I think we should do a once-a-day thirty day schedule of chemo-therapy."

"Oh."

"Okay."

"Oh," Kate repeated.

Michael filled our heads with numbers, which Kate appreciated, and schedules, and dates, and times, and the what-ifs, and the what-nows, and let's-worry-about-that-if-we-get-to-that.

I didn't like the idea of a 'that'.

"If this schedule doesn't produce some significant results, then we'd need to look at surgery."

Ah. That was the 'that'.

"Can I go to work?"

I spun on my section of couch fabric. "What?"

"Sweetheart, if I don't have work to occupy myself with this next month, then I'm going to go crazy, because all I'll be doing is rumi-nating on what's happening inside my brain and while work can be bland, it will make a nice change from," she swallowed, "everything else."

"Yes, you can," Michael replied. "Although, you'll need at least two hours each day for travel, set up, the infusion itself, recovery, travel, rest." He peered at Kate. "Are you in a position to—"

"Absolutely," Kate confirmed.

∼

THAT NIGHT, I SAT ON THE EDGE OF THE BED, AND anxiously bounced my leg. "Do you want to tell people?"

Kate finished smoothing cream onto her skin. "Yes." She wiped her fingers on a tissue, and leaned on the door frame of the bathroom. "It's important for everyone to know." She smiled wryly. "I'm not sure that people will *want* to know, but I want to tell them."

I nodded. That made sense. A problem shared is...still a fucking enormous problem that was growing in Kate's head and she was having chemo from tomorrow and oh God this wasn't about me but I couldn't barricade the dark thoughts and I didn't know—

"Sweetheart..."

I stared at Kate.

"Bron, it will all be okay. You're thinking things again."

My smile was tiny. How could I not think things? I'd googled brain cancer the other day until my laptop surrendered under the weight of the dozens and dozens of tabs I had open.

"How do you want to tell people? Individually? Or in groups?"

Kate crossed her arms and stared over my head in thought. "I think I'd like to talk to Michelle and David first." She dropped her gaze to mine. "Yes. I want to tell them first."

"Okay." I was paralysed with heartache.

Later, when we hadn't gone to sleep because we were thinking things, I stroked Kate's forearm.

"Are you going to tell your mum?"

Kate tucked her head under my neck. "Yes, but it's going to be difficult. Not the type of difficult like when I tell every one else. That's going to be..." She trailed off, probably imagining our family's reaction. "This will be difficult because my mother makes my failures about her. They all reflect on her, and she thinks that friends and colleagues will judge her based on these failures."

"Your disease is not a failure," I growled.

Kate pulled me towards her, and quickly tapped her temple. "This will be viewed as a failure. I shouldn't have allowed the disease into my head, let alone gain traction, you see. Mum will be *disappointed* in me." I felt Kate's huff of sadness against my skin. "She's been top of her class in blame and disappointment for fifty-two years." Kate sagged. "But, yes, I'll tell her."

228

Kate was absolutely correct. Olivia did express disappointment. To her credit, she also expressed concern but leading with a rhetorical question—"Why did this happen?"—followed by an accusation—"Why did you leave it so long?"—reduced the empathy of "What treatment are you having?"

Kate was crushed.

~

FOR THE NEXT MONTH, I SPENT EVERY DAY, EVERY HOUR TO be honest, bouncing on and off the mini-trampolines of caring for Kate, trying to come to grips with the everything and the all, thought-projecting and what-iffing, housework, and going to work even though I didn't want to.

Janine was the one who insisted that I show up at my job.

"You're hovering over Kate."

I looked at her askance. "I'm not...hovering."

"Yes, you are. You're the worst version of a helicopter parent."

So I went to work, taking Kate to her treatments once a week, then leaving so quickly at the end of each day that the Grade Six kids, who normally sprinted to the gates or pole-vaulted the fence, became used to seeing the back of my car.

All the McIntyres and Lydia and Larry and members of Kate's work team shared, either individually or in pairs at most, the role of ferrying Kate to hospital, then hanging out at the house for a few hours afterwards.

Lawrence called on Kate once, balancing shyly on his chair and sipping his tea. Kate's eyes sparkled as she recounted the visit, which was peppered with Lawrence's "Right you are" and "That's the spirit" which made Kate smile and when she hugged him at the door as he was leaving, apparently his blush was as bright as the halogen globes in our downlights. I wanted to dash to Lawrence's house, barrel inside and hug him as well. He'd put a smile on my wife's face and it was the best gift I could have received.

Kate lasted two weeks running her office while dealing with daily chemo. Working at home was easier mainly because she became so tired from the treatment. And although the chemo was reducing their occurrence, the headaches kept returning like a well-trained homing pigeon. Once a week was one time too many.

Eventually, with one week left in the schedule, I was given my marching orders.

"I've only got about ten days of leave left," I said, my face screwed up in confusion.

"No, you haven't." Paula inhaled deeply, and moved a pen from one side of her blotter to the other. "I can add as many days as I like. Call it a perk of my job." Her mouth turned down. "Hardly a perk in this situation, but the leave is indefinite so take as much as you need."

I chewed the inside of my cheek, which Paula seemed to interpret as 'stubborn and frustrated'.

"I *need* you to take as much as you require, Bron. Please. While everyone cares and sympathises, the kids are noticing your anger and sadness." She held up her hand. "Understandable, of course, but you're appearing desperate."

I glared, not at my principal, but at my friend. "I'm not appearing desperate, Paula. I *am* desperate." A wave of fatigue crashed over me.

We stared at each other.

"What am I supposed to do?"

It was rhetorical and overflowing with despair and rage at my inability to do something, anything, to make Kate better. To make her fixed.

"You do what you need to do," Paula said, and put me on leave.

During that week, I visited *OfficeMax* to create t-shirts with tiny twenty percent patterns scattered all over them, because Kate was that twenty percent. We'd wear them to her treatments and the nurses would smile.

Kate decided to throw herself into a frenzy of crane-making.

"They're all cranes for hope and love," she explained, her head bent over her busy fingers. I stilled her hands.

"Sweetheart."

"I need to, Bron. I need to while I still can." Her reply was tinged with so much sadness.

230

"Sweetheart, you're the outlier according to Michael. You're the twenty percent or even more, so this flock covering the table doesn't need any more siblings."

She giggled softly.

～

KATE'S CHEMOTHERAPY RAN ITS COURSE, THEN MICHAEL'S secretary called.

"Dr Opperheim would like you to make an appointment, please. Are you able to come in tomorrow afternoon?" she asked, her tone brisk but not really, impersonal but not really. I think she was used to people reeling from news of a brain octopus and pretending that they were fine, but knowing that seeing Michael was an important thing to do, yes, we were able to come in the following afternoon.

"The chemotherapy has not been as effective as I'd hoped," he began without preamble which was rather abrupt but, like Brussel sprouts, probably important to deal with first.

"That sucks," I responded and Kate nodded at my succinct assessment of the situation.

"It means that our next option is surgery."

Kate sucked the oxygen from the room. "That's a...lot."

I held her hand.

"Yes, it is, but your glioblastoma." *Brain octopus.* "Is very aggressive." *Angry brain octopus.*

"It's necessary, isn't it?" Kate asked. I could tell that she'd asked the question simply to use up words because there were too many crowding into her mouth.

"Yes, and there are side effects." Michael's expression became serious, his tall frame resembling a bent lamp post.

"Okay." Kate's trembling rippled through her body which was pressed tightly to mine.

"Surgery can stimulate any cells left behind to grow up to seventy-five percent faster than before." *Angry turned on brain octopus.*

"I'm the twenty percent," Kate whispered.

"Yes, you are," I said fiercely. "Bugger the seventy-five percent. You're going to accountant-boss-lady all over that number, sweetheart."

She grunted a laugh.

The surgery was scheduled for the end of May, and I hoped when Michael peeked inside Kate's head he'd see the astounding kindness, the generosity, the wit, the playfulness, the bravery, the soul of Kate. I hoped he'd see her.

We Worried

May 31 to October 14 in the fifth year of the now

Michael looked like he'd called forth the spirit of Fred Astaire. He danced, in a sedate-and-serious-bringer-of-good-news-surgeon-like manner, into Kate's room on the fourth and final day of her recovery.

"We've reduced the mass at the centre by sixty percent," he stated after he'd checked data and printouts and charts and Kate's folder. He beamed. "You seem to be the outlier."

Kate loved the numbers, of course, whereas I'd had trouble printing twenty percent on fabric because I couldn't remember which direction to aim the percent symbol.

"I love you, Ms Twenty-percent," I murmured in her ear, and she glanced my way, a smile slowly growing on her lips, then she winked. *Oh. Puddle of goo.*

Michael, in between his joyful yet contained tap dancing, informed Kate that sixty percent was as good as it got. The end. He wasn't able to undertake another operation because Kate's brain would get very angry and release the Kraken.

"What's next, then?"

"More chemotherapy for a month, then medication for a month, then more chemotherapy, then medication, then more chemotherapy, then medication. The treatment is generally scheduled in groups of three."

"The primary colours," I said, and Kate chuckled, then closed her eyes.

"Will it work?" she asked, her eyes still shut.

"I hope so. We doctors believe in hope just as much as we believe in our skills, because why not? Hope can bring unexpected results. Hope combined with your numbers, Kate, point us in a very positive direction."

THE DISHWASHER HAD BEEN STACKED BY A TODDLER OR BY me. Probably me. Kate was home, handling her chemo as if she was the entire Avengers team, smashing at the brain octopus and shouting "Bring it on!" to the treatment like a freaking boss, all the while looking much hotter than Black Widow.

Meanwhile, I couldn't stack a dishwasher. Sighing, I whipped the plates out and started again, and thought about the concept of hope. Hope was a crane and technically a crane could fly. I nodded. That made sense. Hope was future orientated, and we focused on the horizon when we called it forth, willing ourselves to reach it, as we held hope close so we could huddle about its warmth.

Hope kept Kate sustained all through June's chemotherapy, although she was more fatigued during this round.

I prowled the house at night, checking out the contents of the fridge, practising my dishwasher-stacking skills, and circling back to the bowl of cranes with its gravitational hold on my heart.

One night, mug of tea in hand, and having shrugged on a jacket, I rested my elbows on the top bar of the railing around our porch. Dark purple, a plum of sadness, blanketed the evening sky and I gazed at the final threads of the sunset at the bottom of the world. I was sure I could see the dark bleeding into the light. My attention returned when footfalls sounded on the steps leading to our porch. I smiled at Larry in his collared shirt and ironed pants and sensible shoes and wrinkles of friendship.

"Hi, Larry." I lifted my mug. "Cup of tea?"

He shook his head and joined me at the railing. "No thanks, young Bron." We rested in companionable silence. "You can hear the cicadas tonight."

"You can," I confirmed.

"How's Kate today?" The answer to that was the reason he'd come over, and I loved him for it. Ever since we'd asked him to witness our marriage certificate, he'd adopted us as found family and would often pop over for a 'chin wag' and a 'cuppa'.

"She's...um...well, she's okay. Tired, but that's to be expected."

"Mm."

I sipped at my tea. "Thanks for coming by the other day."

"No worries, love. I had to return your Tupperware anyway, so I thought I'd stay for a chat. Siobhan was around for a visit, too. She's a cracker, that one."

I laughed. "That's one way to put it." We dropped into silence again as the dark ate the light and I took in a lungful of air hoping that it would shove the sadness aside.

I sighed, which was a wasted opportunity.

Larry turned to me, standing upright because he didn't lean sideways on things as it "hurts my hips".

"She's a strong lady, your Kate. With you by her side, she'll pull through."

"Mm." The sound pulled my lips in.

"Kate lights up the room as soon as she walks in, doesn't she?"

I gave a brief nod.

"My Helen could do that. Maybe no one else saw that light, because they weren't Helen's person, but I saw it." He contemplated me with my mug of tea and canvas jacket and jeans and must have liked what he saw because he smiled.

"Kate's the light in your room, you know."

I wrinkled my forehead. "Which room?"

Larry lifted his hand and pointed to my chest. "That room."

HOPE KEPT KATE SUSTAINED ALL THROUGH JULY'S NOT-chemotherapy-tablets, as we celebrated our birthdays. She insisted, her hands planted on her hips, standing in the kitchen in her white dressing gown and slippers, that she didn't want a single bit of fanciness or palaver when all she was doing was turning fifty-three.

"I'm turning forty-seven and I like palaver, thanks very much," I said cheekily.

She smirked. "Really?"

"I might...occasionally...never."

Kate giggled.

We ended up having a combined birthday—again!—at our house but we held it at lunchtime because a party of any size would be impacted if one of the birthday-havers was asleep in an armchair.

It wasn't anything flash; just family, who drifted in and out of the kitchen, picking at the pot luck platters that everyone had brought which was perfect because it was a McIntyre celebration after all. JJ appointed herself a type of conductor with additional duties as a Grenadier guard as she marshalled her family into pairs and, on the rare occasion, threes, and filtered them— probably with a hand-held security detection scanner—through to Kate so that she wasn't overwhelmed by noise and movement. I hugged her on my way to the kitchen to investigate the sausage rolls.

"You're awesome, kiddo," I murmured.

"I'm calling on my experience from when I was a library monitor in Grade Three." She shook her head. "So many kids trying to sneak out without scanning the barcode. Should be a criminal offence."

I cracked up, and Kate, who'd overheard JJ's comment, grinned, and I fell in love with my wife all over again.

HOPE KEPT KATE SUSTAINED ALL THROUGH AUGUST'S chemotherapy. Yet, despite the headaches abating, other symptoms took to the stage. Kate stumbled a lot, clutching at furniture, towel rails and memories.

A shuffling noise, as if something was scuffing the wood, woke me one night. I flicked the side lamp on, and immediately checked to see if Kate was in bed. Because that's what I did. Checked on Kate. The Kate-shaped space was vacant and tension took hold of my heart. Wrapping a dressing gown about my body, I followed the noise to the kitchen where I found my beautiful wife staring into the fridge.

"Hey sweetheart. It's late. Do you want to come back to bed?"

She pulled her head back and smiled into my face. "Hello, sweetheart. I'm hungry, which is unusual yet delightful. I thought we had some eggplant dip but I must have been mistaken."

I tried to rein in my shaky breath. I leaned around her, and brought out the tub of eggplant dip from the shelf. Right in her line of sight.

"Here it is." I huffed a laugh. "Sometimes I can't see things when they're in front of me either." My next laugh, short and singular, jarred the silence in the room, and Kate studied me, reached for the container, then nodded.

"You don't really, Bron. But thank you for covering for me. It must be difficult." She smiled sadly.

"You're never difficult. Ever. We're going to fight this, Kate, and you'll be well in no time."

"Exactly. I'm not running away from this one." Her gaze became contemplative and she resumed staring into the fridge. "I'm sure I put that dip somewhere."

I coaxed her back to bed, and she snuggled into me, our skin touching gently, our lips kissing as if they'd been taught by butterflies.

"I'm so tired, sweetheart." Her breathing deepened, slowed.

"Can I stroke your hair until you fall asleep?"

Kate exhaled. "It's my favourite thing."

My gift for Kate on our anniversary was her favourite thing. I stroked her hair, massaged her feet, and she sighed and purred, then cracked an eyelid and smirked.

"You're a tease," I said.

"You are only finding this out now?" Her smirk slid into a grin. "Goodness. I'll have to give more obvious hints."

∼

Hope kept Kate sustained all through September's not-chemotherapy tablets although it was most likely the spontaneous craft lesson Kate led. I was the only student.

Kate marched into the dining room with a large box, and I immediately leapt up, banging my knee on the table leg, and relieved her of the load.

"Ow. Shit." I grimaced, placing the box on the table, and rubbing my knee. "What's in there?"

Having sat during my theatrics, Kate tilted the box and pulled out a handful of square paper. Beautiful square paper with swirls and dots and marbling and gold highlights. My mouth instantly became an 'O' and I breathed out slowly. It was the paper for the cranes. Paper soon to be hope, and love, and peace, and healing in challenging times.

Kate flapped her hand, gesturing for me to sit.

"You haven't seen me make your cranes before. They've just appeared as a piece of my heart so I'd like to make one from the beginning."

"I'd love that." I scooted my chair around so I sat beside her left elbow. Kate was beautiful in any situation, but right then, she was radiant as she demonstrated her skill, her love, her heart, and I forgot to watch her fingers because the tip of her tongue was poking out so I was another puddle of goo.

"You're not watching," Kate said.

"I am!"

"You, Bron McIntyre, are a terrible liar." She laughed. "Here." She passed a crane with three folded edges. "I can't get the creases sharp. Could you do it?"

I dropped my gaze to the little not-yet-crane. I could see where the corners were supposed to line up but they were slightly off, so I surreptitiously manipulated the corners to align them, then I ran my thumbnail along the edges.

"Thank you. For the crease and for..." I looked up and fell into Kate's wonderful dark brown eyes. She was right; I was a terrible liar.

She worked on the crane, probably slower than normal, and after each fold she passed it to me and I creased the edge. Our crane arrived at the final twist of its wings, and I blinked back tears.

"This one..." Kate paused, then smiled. "This one is yours."

"Then this crane represents forever."

~

But hope couldn't sustain Kate when she collapsed in the first week of October. For whatever reason, September's not-chemotherapy tablets had created problems and Kate would often vomit or shake or suffer from an unexpected, though smaller, headache. Side effects we'd not seen before.

So I was hoping that the next round of chemo, due to start in a few days, would solve the problem. And it did. Kate's vomiting, shaking, headaches instantly stopped and she had seven super days, joking with Siobhan, and laughing with JJ, and talking quietly with Mum, and flirting with me.

Kate's cry woke me. I flailed around under the covers, attempting to untangle myself, then flicked on the side lamp, and discovered her curled into a ball, her body violently shaking. Kate's hands clutched at her head. *Fuck.* This one was enormous.

"Okay. Sweetheart. Okay. We're calling an ambulance. Okay."

Kate's open-mouth wail ripped me apart.

I held her and rocked her and sent white noise of hush into her ears as we waited for the ambulance to arrive.

Kate was rushed to hospital, and transferred to the neurological unit where they stabilised her with magic.

The next day, as my eyeballs grew thorns and my throat held barbed wire, Kate woke, looked around the room in confusion, and informed me that I was making a fuss about nothing.

"Kate." I swallowed around the coil of rust. "Do you remember what happened last night?"

She gave me a quizzical look. "No. I'm in hospital so something must have happened that was serious enough for me to end up here."

I was thankful she had no memory of last night, because last night was horrifying and my heart hadn't stopped beating out of my chest until a minute ago when she'd opened her eyes.

"You had a bad headache and we came to the hospital to get it checked out," I summarised, and Kate inhaled slowly.

"And again, Bron sweetheart, you are a dreadful liar."

A knock at the door interrupted the apology that had formed on my lips. Michael Opperheim walked in and stood at the end of Kate's bed.

"You gave us all a scare last night, Kate," he began, and Kate turned her head and glared at me.

"Bad headache, my arse," she muttered. I couldn't help smiling at her comment.

"Your side effects from this schedule of chemotherapy were certainly extreme so what I'd like to do is continue the chemotherapy, but." My stomach twisted. "Combine the treatment with the tablets you've been taking in the alternate months." I reached forward and held Kate's hand. It felt tiny which was odd because I'd held that hand not five minutes ago. I studied her. She looked so tired, and somehow smaller. A reduced facsimile of Kate.

"Therefore, we'll keep you in for nine days. Today is." He looked at his phone, which was strange because surely doctors wrote the date a million times a day. Maybe they flicked that job off to the nurses. "Saturday, so we'll see how you've responded by next Sunday. I have every confidence in you, Kate. You've defied quite a few odds."

Michael sailed out of the room and our silence spoke volumes.

"Well..." Kate said eventually, running her thumb across my knuckles.

Everyone asked to visit during the next nine days and I took over JJ's role as conductor and guard. Kate drifted in and out of sleep, so generally the visits were for my benefit because I wouldn't move from Kate's side, even sleeping in the Bernadette's warehouse armchair pushed against the wall.

On Thursday, Michael bounced, as much as a lamppost can truly bounce, into the room and beamed.

"Combining the medication has certainly made a difference. Your side effects have disappeared and even the chemotherapy is working more efficiently."

After more happy exclamations, which bolstered our confidence and spirits, Michael departed.

"That's amazing, sweetheart."

"It is, isn't it?" she replied, a faraway look in her eyes and I wondered where she'd gone.

On Friday, Kate asked to make another crane so I brought in a blue square, and we began the crane together but didn't get very far because Kate succumbed to exhaustion. I took the half-finished crane home. It seemed wrong to complete it without Kate, so I left it for another visit.

On Saturday, we were entertained by another Michael Opperheim Broadway number, and although prefacing his report with 'maybe' and 'could do' and 'might not', he seemed relatively happy with how Kate was faring. However, he decided to keep Kate in a further two days citing concerns about percentages and control levels.

Later, we held hands. "Michael says that you're on the mend," I said, grinning widely while smoothing Kate's skin.

Her expression softened. "I think so, sweetheart."

"You don't think you are?" I hunted around in my head for something that would put a smile on her face. JJ's sex moment? *No, done that.* Fruitloop? *God, no.*

Kate gave a slow nod. "But you know? Funnily enough, I do think I'm on the mend. I was a bit more myself yesterday and today I feel almost healthy so the treatment is clearly working." Kate frowned as if annoyed at her negativity.

"See? There you go. You'll be back home in no time." I breathed a sigh of relief. No need to trot out Fruitloop or other McIntyre moments. "You're that twenty percent, sweetheart, and I love you."

Kate's eyes, filled with love and hope and stars that sparked, held mine and she smiled. "I am and I love you." Then she winked slowly and in that white hospital gown, under that white sheet, in that white room, her face the palest of the pale, I cherished her with every atom of my soul.

"You really are gorgeous, Kate Agostino."

"Back atcha, Bron McIntyre."

On Sunday, I held her hand. We always held hands.

"Everything's going to be okay," Kate said quietly.

"It will be. I know it." I bent to kiss her knuckles. "You heard Michael. There's improvement." I kissed her knuckles again. "There's improvement." If I repeated the phrase, it would be set in stone because that's what happens. I *could* see the improvement. Well, not really. But Michael said he could, although he wasn't as excited today, but that was to be expected, right? I needed one of Kate's wishing stars.

"Bron?"

I lifted my head. I hadn't realised it had dropped.

"I know everything will be okay," Kate said, then smiled. "Twenty percent is actually quite a lot."

We Mourned

The Forever

K ate died on Tuesday afternoon.

IT WAS AN UNASSUMING MOMENT. VERY KATE, NOW THAT I think about it. I would have missed it if I hadn't been gazing at her shape, her face, her eyes. Because it was her eyes that opened, finding mine and there it was. All of our now and decades and decades of our meant to be.

Grief didn't visit me then. It arrived later and forever. But at that particular moment, I was with Kate, and I smiled softly like I always did when she was adorable and sweet and perfect.

I discovered how busy grief is. No-one prepares a person for the paperwork. They should. *Here's a manual. Study it. There'll be a seminar, an assessment, followed by a lesson on the colours of noisy silence. It* would have been helpful. A guide to the forms that satisfy the government regulations, and the hospital protocols, and the legal records; all those faceless people, all notified that my wife had died.

Kate would have laughed. *Welcome to my world, sweetheart.*

I spoke to people. So many people. Meanwhile my heart grew numb. Paralysis radiated like those tie-dyed shirts, blooming into my torso, my arms, my legs, until I couldn't speak, and my fingers wouldn't grasp the pen.

Olivia Agostino, a small figure but such a large presence, interrupted my journey along the footpath away from the hospital where Kate was but not really. I felt Mum's hand in the small of my back because I must have swayed like in a car when you brake abruptly. My family, a little army of scaffolding for my dissolving frame, smiled politely at Kate's mum because that's what you do when someone you love dies, but you dislike their relative.

"I'm sorry, Bron."

It was a common start to the inevitable conversation that followed. *I'm sorry, Bron. I'm sorry, Bron.* I'd nod and reach out my hand and comfort them because they needed that, particularly when they'd open with a statement of regret.

"Parents shouldn't bury their children," she added.

"No," I answered, the word catching in my mouth and forcing my teeth to chew the letters.

We were under one of the beautiful eucalyptus trees that marched beside the footpath and the lorikeets chatted about the nectar. I wondered if Olivia's social group at the country club sounded the same.

"At least she's not in pain, anymore. She's in a better place." Olivia slowly nodded, as she ticked off another sentence on the template of what to say to someone whose forever person had died.

"Olivia, I know you're grievi—" Janine's voice pushed forward and I imagined my sister in person did as well, but I didn't know because I sank, squatting on my heels.

"... but Kate's not in a better place, Olivia." Janine's words fell down the string line of her tin can telephone and wobbled in my ears. And tears, that had arrived without herald, pooled on top of my kneecaps. Tears, not for Kate, not yet, but tears for the arrows of anger and spears of sorrow, which flew over my head because, right then, I needed to breathe.

"...Kate's place is with Bron, but she's not." *That's right, J, she's not. She's not.* I swayed on my heels.

"...I reckon she'd be pretty annoyed at that situation." *Yes, she would, J. She would.* I wrapped my arms around my shins.

"...I imagine that you'd like to go in, Olivia, and speak to someone or pray. I don't know if you're a religious person, but that might be helpful."

Jack's feet, clad in sneakers bearing logos and stripes and more embroidery than actual shoe, appeared in front of my gaze.

"Aunty Bron, there's a bench seat on the grass behind the tree. I reckon Mum's got things covered here. Do you wanna sit down for a while?"

I looked up and clutched at his hand.

"Yes," I said, agreeing with all the logic and sense of his suggestion. "Yes."

I caught Rick's nod at his son, and my family remained static while my teenaged nephew led me across an ocean of green to an island of brown.

We sat.

And stared at the grass.

"Just to let you know, 'cause I don't think I've ever said. Having three awesome aunts is the best."

I felt his deep breath.

"Two aunts," I said quietly.

"Three aunts," he corrected just as quietly.

And my bones disappeared so I leant against his solid frame. Three aunts.

"I'm sorry." Somehow his statement of regret felt different, like it wasn't a regret at all. He was sorry that there was a space in our lives.

"It's not your fault."

More silence that felt heavy enough to hold, but light enough that it might contemplate drifting away.

"I'm still sorry."

My lips gave no indication that my teeth were chewing at their skin. "Me too."

His chest hiccuped with sadness. "It sucks."

We sat.

"I'm not great company. I don't have many words," I said apologetically.

"That's okay. I don't have many words either. Mum says words are a collection of letters that can't connect until coffee."

I barked a single laugh. "That's something Kate would have said."

We continued our communal staring at the grass, which was happy to be itself and the shrubs which were masquerading as trees.

Silence.

Many people discover, after they've sunk to the bottom, how still grief is. There are large moments of silence in grief. Sitting, almost folded in half, on a bench seat that sat proudly on manicured lawns seemed to me an ideal spot for grief and silence, because when you have silence you can breathe, and settle, and think, and change, then return all the way to the beginning so the air can crush your lungs.

I MADE ROOM FOR OTHER PEOPLE'S GRIEF. ALL OF US jostling into the too-full carriage of a train that wouldn't go anywhere. I consoled people each minute of each hour. Kate would have done the same. Probably better than me because she didn't use sandpaper to soften her words.

But I wasn't Kate.

People arrived with food. So much food. Who was going to eat it all? I certainly wasn't. But the thought was there. I knew that people needed to bolster the one who lived, and respect the one who didn't. Sometimes a casserole met both needs.

But all those people with their casseroles and platters of sandwiches and frozen pasta were elsewhere right then. Elsewhere from where I was; sitting on the side of our bed, settling into the little dip that my arse created. I ran my fingertips over the undulations in the quilt cover; each patchwork square a geometric wonder.

I'd kidnapped the bowl of cranes, cradling it under one arm as if I was a prop forward in an international rugby match, heading towards the try line. Except the try line was our bedroom with the patchwork quilt and the mattress that dipped and the armchair that fitted in the corner.

I stared into the kaleidoscope of lines and corners and colours and hope and peace and healing during challenging times. And love.

And love.

And love.

Kate hadn't realised but I'd labelled each crane, each gift, with the meaning she'd given it. I picked one out and flipped it over. There, in the tiniest writing, even smaller than hers, was peace.

I placed the crane on top of the pile, and pinched the wing of the final crane, the blue not-quite crane. The edges cut at my heart, the lines lifting skin, and I wanted to hurl it towards the door.

But I didn't.

"You'd get cranky at me," I whispered, and ran my fingertips across the bowl's burnished exterior. "No, you wouldn't. You'd want me to keep it, and live its potential, and..." I stared at the wall. "I will, sweetheart. Eventually."

Properly demonstrative tears refused to fall. Perhaps they were still in line at emotional immigration, and I wondered what that looked like to other people. The lack of big tears.

I rubbed at the bowl again. Aladdin's lamp. My muscles tightened.

"Hi," I whispered. Whispering was important if I wanted the silence to stay. My teeth clenched.

"Ah, fuck." My lungs pulled air; a tiny inhalation. "Shit. Swearing. Sorry," I whispered. "I'm sorry, sweetheart. I love you. I'm so sorry."

The little nose tickle, the hot breath, and the immigration agent who handed back their passports, declared their arrival.

The tears—properly demonstrative tears—fell so quickly that they were skates on ice, and my fingers rushed to cup my jaw and wipe the pools that formed in my palms across the tops of my thighs. My breathing couldn't match their speed, and eventually gave up, simply escaping in sobs that staccatoed in threes, then stopped, and then again, one, two, three.

As I leaned the bowl against the pillow, because the birds were in the rain, there was a soft knock at the door.

"Can we come in, Aunty Bron?" I turned at the voice and looked vacantly at JJ and Siobhan, standing as if they were ready to retreat even though they wanted to step forward.

"I don't know," I said in confusion.

"Oh." JJ nodded. "Right. Of course. We'll be out there," she waved in the general direction of the kitchen, "if you need us."

I hummed, accidentally sucking salty tears between my lips. "Thank you. That means everything, JJ." I swiped at my face, and beckoned. "Sorry. Come in."

Siobhan, who hadn't said a word, which was a noteworthy moment for the McIntyre annals, chose to sit in the armchair, and JJ sat next to me, smoothing out the mattress dip.

Silence

"I'm going to swear, okay? Just giving you a heads up," JJ said, the sharpest edge to her voice.

I nodded. "Okay."

"Fucking fucking fuckity fuck," she spat, her eyes filling with tears.

I turned and held her gaze. That collection of words pretty much summed it up, so I pulled her into an embrace that matched the intensity and our faces looked over each other's shoulder. "Good swear," I said, somewhat in admiration.

"Yeah." She breathed deeply and withdrew. "It's in my DNA."

I huffed a laugh, because of course JJ would find dry humour in the humidity of grief.

My tears returned, quietly sneaking up and meandering down my skin.

"It's so fucking unfair." Siobhan's eyes glistened as she added to the perfect profanity.

"She was my person, Shiv."

"I know. Anyone could see that."

"Oh God." My voice broke and JJ held my trembling hand. "The space that Kate filled. What do I fill it with now?"

Siobhan pinned me with her gaze. "Kate. You keep it filled with Kate."

"Wasn't long enough." I knew Siobhan would understand the not-even-half sentence.

Siobhan laced her fingers together against her chest and turned her knuckles white. "No. But you were each other's person every day for five years. You were each other's person even when you were on that stupid, amazing, sensible break."

I stared at her intently. "We were supposed to be the forever pair. The HEA."

She shrugged empathetically. "Life isn't always a happily ever after, hon."

I hissed wetly through my teeth. "What a stupid saying. Happily ever after. So stupid." I went to clench my fists then realised that I had one hand wrapped around JJ's. I got the feeling that she would have understood.

"No, it's not."

Siobhan hadn't broken eye contact, like if she looked away, I'd disappear.

"No, it's not," I agreed.

"They could call it a happily forever," JJ suggested.

"That would be an HF," I replied vacantly.

"Shit. That wouldn't work. Then it'd be a holy fuck," Siobhan stated blandly, and I wanted to laugh like I always did when Siobhan's wit sliced through conversation. But I couldn't, even though she'd tried so hard.

My face crumpled. "Shiv..."

We stood at the same time and Siobhan helped me fall to my knees where I burrowed into her chest, sobs wracking my body, as she whispered that she knew.

❦

LATER, AFTER EVERYONE HAD RELUCTANTLY DEPARTED, after I'd thanked people for their kind words, after Janine insisted that she was sleeping on the couch, after Mum stated that the bed in the spare room looked comfortable and she'd be trying it out for the night, I sat in the armchair and cradled my bowl of cranes.

I contemplated the half-finished origami, and tried to envision finishing it. But I couldn't. It would remain incomplete, overflowing with potential and possibility because it occurred to me that I did get a forever.

I got Kate's forever.

Kate gave me her forever and she gave me her now.

The End

About the Author

KJ writes stories because her imagination takes the wheel. Permanently anxious and overly fond of cats, KJ lives in Bendigo, Australia. She is married, and a mum, and has been told that she's funny. That last one is debatable.

A request

I sincerely hope you enjoyed reading *The Forever and The Now*. If you did, I would greatly appreciate a review on your favourite book website. Maybe a tweet. Or even a recommendation in your favourite Facebook sapphic fiction group. Reviews and recommendations are crucial for any author, and even just a line or two can make a huge difference. Thanks!

Printed in Great Britain
by Amazon